THE MARS OF MALCONTENTS

KATE MACLEOD

CONTENTS

CHAPTER ONE

FEVERISH FLEEING

For the first time in her life, Valentina del Toro was completely alone. No cousins clamoring around her demanding food and attention, no brother wrapped around her leg impeding her movements as she went about her chores, no crowds of fellow shoppers jostling her elbows as she traded a pocketful of eggs for a small sack of lentils. All around her, all the way to the distant horizon in an immense circle around her, there was no one but her.

For the first time in her life, Valentina del Toro was outside the science station that had been her birthplace, outside the polar tunnels that had been her home since she was five, out in the dim Martian sunlight she had only rarely glimpsed through the station windows; the last glimpse was nearly a decade ago. The world around her dazzled, the dull glow from the ice under her feet broken up by glittering snaky patterns as the wind played with the loose drifts of snow that dusted the glacier tops. The orange sky above her was impossibly far away. The caverns in the mine under the ice cap were colossal, containing a small city whose lights never reached the rock above, but only now did Valentina realize how small they really were, how big her world really was. And she was still seeing only a small part of it.

The realization should have filled her with awe, wonder, some sort of happy feeling, but she had no happy feelings left. And if she didn't keep her feet moving, the other feelings were going to catch up with her.

She bounded over the snowy wastes of the Martian ice cap, the sound of her own labored breathing reverberating inside her helmet, only occasionally glancing up at the southerly sun to keep track of the time. She knew she was near the magic moment, the point where if she went any further, she would not be able to make it back home before darkness fell. She had been jogging for nearly four hours in the heavy space suit, two tanks of air and another smaller one of water weighing her down. She had thought a life filled with the labors of running a farm had left her prepared for any challenge. It was humbling how quickly she'd discovered she was wrong about that.

Only four hours down, as much again to go before she could stop. Tomorrow it would be ten hours. She wouldn't have the late start that she'd had today; she could pace herself at a brisk walk. But still, ten hours on the march tomorrow, and the day after that, and the day after that. She had no idea how many days it would take her just to get off the ice cap, let alone reach the equatorial cities. The ache in her joints, the weakness in her muscles that she kept pushing past by force of will, the off smell of her own sweat inside her suit all reminded her that until this morning she had been too sick to get out of bed. The last two weeks were nothing more than a few brief moments of wakefulness lost in a sea of fever dreams.

But there was no turning back. Valentina ducked her head, bounding harder. She left the magic moment behind without even slowing down. She had woken from her long illness to find her brother Arturo gone, whisked away to the equator in a corporate rocket. What choice did she have but to go after him, however she could? And the only way she could was on foot in a sort-of-stolen pressure suit.

The vernal equinox was still a few weeks off and the days were short. That had aggravated her when she'd first set out—all the hours she could be traveling lost to waiting out the night—but now she just hoped she could build up her stamina to match the days as they grew longer.

Sometime later, when the possibility of turning back was long gone,

Valentina drew up briefly and took a short sip from the water tube near her mouth. Something in the suit was giving it a metallic tang, not unpleasant. Her feet were cold. Even with the running, her feet were cold. The suit's diagnostics had all checked out OK, but clearly at least one of the systems was not quite up to spec. The indicator on her arm told her the internal temperature of her suit was 20 degrees Celsius, but her toes achingly disagreed.

Valentina took another careful sip, tapping the screen with the gloved finger of her other hand. The indicator didn't change. It calmly persisted in lying to her. She glanced at the others. The bar for water had gone down a bit. She had filled the bottle herself and reckoned what it said she'd consumed was pretty close to the mark. So that one was working properly. The air indicators were down as well, but she had no idea how to gauge their accuracy. She knew the tanks had been full when she'd locked them into the suit, but she'd never been outside before; she had no clue how much she should expect to have used up, especially jogging as she was.

She turned at the waist, to the left and then to the right. The locater went from full green to yellow, full green to yellow. She turned all the way around and it bounced down to orange, then to full green again. She was getting signals from the science station as well as the first checkpoint; that seemed to be working. So only the heating system was wonky, and even that was marginal—not a total failure.

Yet.

Valentina pushed that thought aside, resuming her rhythmic bounding over the glacier. If she was always running in the suit, her toes wouldn't have a chance to freeze. She hadn't planned on sleeping in the suit, anyway.

Still, she couldn't help remembering don Abuelo's old friend Pedro, the rover driver. She had called him tío, and he had always had presents for her and her cousins in his many pockets, some little trinket from one of the other stations on his route. She and all her younger cousins used to run down to Hanako Willis's machine shop to see him when he climbed out of his rover. He was always the first one out, leaving his more taciturn partner in the cab while he leapt out to greet Valentina and the others.

Until the day his partner had come out first, turning to help Pedro stumble out after. She had gotten the story later, how Pedro had gone out for only a moment in his faulty suit to get his rover engine restarted. Frostbite had blackened his face and hands, the less affected parts gone whitish-gray. She hadn't known what was wrong with him at the time, only that something terrible had happened to him and he seemed to be dead.

Then he'd opened his mouth to gasp and Valentina's first thought hadn't been "he's alive" but "he's a ghoul." She'd pressed a fist to her mouth to hold back her scream, but her younger cousins had shrieked and ran. He'd lived, thanks to his partner getting him to a medico straightaway, but he'd lost several fingers, the tips of his ears, and part of his nose. When he recovered, he went back on his route, but the cousins never again clamored to see him. The ghoulishness hadn't gone away; it lurked still in his shambling walk and in the twisted scar tissue of his nose and ears.

Valentina took a deeper breath to clear her mind. The image of the frostbitten face left her, but the chattering *hurry-hurry-hurry* voice kept on. It was timing the syllables to her steps.

The sun seemed frozen, unmoving in the sky, and Valentina's bounds grew shorter, her pace slower. Finally, the lancinating pain under her ribs made it too hard to breathe, and she had to slow to a walk. She tried to rub the pain away, but from inside the suit, she barely felt the glove pressing from the outside. She pressed harder, trying to get her thumb to massage in just the right spot to ease the stabbing, but it was useless.

Valentina laughed, although that hurt, too. Her first thought upon taking don Abuelo's suit and sneaking out of the airlock had been that finally, after a lifetime in the caverns deep under the glacier, she was going outside—out into the world.

Then she had stepped out of the airlock and realized that the ice under her booted feet felt the same as the tunnel floors, and while she could catch snowflakes on her gloved palm, she couldn't feel them there. She hadn't gone outside at all, not really. She'd just shifted location to a very small station that traveled with her. Looking out her helmet was pretty much the same as looking out the science station windows when she was a young girl. Only in the science station she could scratch her nose.

But her laugh now was for the irony. She had lamented not being able to go outside, but now Mars was working its way inside. Her toes were very clear on this point. She didn't mind their complaining. She was going to worry when it stopped.

The laughter faded, leaving her dizzy, reminding her once more that just that morning she had been in her sickbed. She knew she wasn't exactly well now; her suit indicator told her that her body temperature was still elevated, and her joints ached in a way that had nothing to do with exercise fatigue. She was crazy to be doing this, and to be doing it now. But it couldn't wait. So much time had already been lost. He was so far away. There was no other way for her to follow but on foot.

She kept up a shambling walk, occasionally speeding back up to a bound to get the blood flowing. The sun had unfrozen and was moving down to the horizon faster than her locator was gaining bars. The checkpoint was directly ahead of her, but she had no idea how far. A more sophisticated suit system would tell her, but don Abuelo's suit had once been his own abuelo's suit and bordered on the outdated.

The wind picked up as the sun turned orangey-red. She couldn't feel it, but it spun the loose snow cover in hypnotic eddies over the hard-packed ice. The only way to avoid its soporific spell was to gaze straight ahead into the sun until she saw spots.

Then the sun went below the horizon. Valentina drew to another halt. She had about another half hour of workable light to get to her destination. Maybe less; the sky behind her was already a deep purple, Phobos running toward that darkness as if fleeing the fading sun. Valentina tapped the indicator. She was doing all right for air, her tanks still about a quarter full. She felt around the top of her helmet and found the switch for the headlamp, but when she flipped it, nothing happened. She rapped the light, but there was not even a flicker.

She looked down at her hands and arms, turning them over, but she had no second built-in light. That was the problem with impetuous decisions to grab a space suit and run: one had no time to pack properly.

A memory intruded—herself that morning, although it felt like a lifetime ago already. Forcing herself onto her feet, dressing in what was closest and slipping away before Hanako came back. She couldn't take the compassionate look her mother's oldest friend had given her, the way she squeezed Valentina's hand and told her it was okay to cry. Hanako with her rough mechanic's hands and burly arms to match, Hanako with her close-cut hair and almost mannish laugh; Hanako should never be saying such things.

If she started crying, she would never, ever stop. She had to get away before she broke down. And now, kilometers away in her space suit, she really couldn't risk breaking down into tears. Valentina took a deeper breath and refocused her thoughts on her current, very specific, rational and not emotional situation.

A flashlight was probably only the first of a long line of things she was going to wish she had brought with her. Not that she could imagine trying to carry a heavy pack on top of the weight of the suit. All the pockets were full to bulging; it would have to be enough.

Valentina started moving again, this time in a loping rhythm that was faster than her walk, if not as ground-eating as bounding over the ice would have been. Her eyes scanned the horizon, searching for signs of the checkpoint, but there was no place for it to be hiding on the flat plain of ice. Further south there were fissures in the ice and places where the rock jutted up over the glacier, but this close to the pole Mars was pretty featureless. She should be able to see the checkpoint— unless it was embedded in ice.

Valentina swallowed hard, but didn't slow her pace. That was a real danger. The way station was built on top of the ice and had mecha- nisms that kept it up there, hydraulic legs on wide feet that could be lifted up and stepped forward onto the new surface. But they weren't automated. They needed people to come by often enough to run them before the station got icebound. Valentina knew more about travelers than most, having spent so much of her time in Hanako Willis's machine shop, but she had met few people who had walked to the polar station. Sometimes the rover drivers used the checkpoints, but mostly they didn't; they packed enough supplies in the rover cabs to get them the whole way off the ice cap.

Valentina glanced at the indicator. Still green. If she had overshot a buried way station, she would know; the indicator would be showing the green behind her.

She kept up her slow jog as the sky before her darkened from purple to starry black. The ice reflected the starlight somewhat, but the only time in her life she had been in deeper darkness was the day their power generator had failed. Her mother had been out helping one of her sisters bring four sick children to the medico, and it had taken Valentina an eternity to find the door out of their cavern, back into the light.

She remembered the feel of Arturo's hand in hers as she'd groped along the walls. He had been five or six at the time. Her heart had been hammering in her chest as the door kept not being where she thought it should be. Arturo had been perfectly calm, occasionally squeezing her hand but never asking why she couldn't find the way out. He had trusted her completely. And it had taken three times as long as it should have, but in the end she hadn't let him down.

Something beeped in her helmet and Valentina slid to a stop, looking at the panel on her arm. The top green bar of her locater was flashing. Valentina looked around, then raised her arm and tried to use the light from the instrument panel to see. She turned slowly around, eyes straining against the dark. The sky was black, and the ground was white, but there was no sharp contrast between; everything blurred together and refused to come into focus.

Then she saw it, behind her and to her left. She had nearly walked right past it. It was smaller than she expected, windowless and feature-less in the dark. It wasn't icebound; in fact, it had been jacked up on columns nearly half a meter higher than the ice. Valentina opened the door and climbed into the airlock, noticing a light fixture over the door. She tapped the exposed bulb, but it was as dead as her head lamp.

Valentina pushed the airlock shut behind her. There was no control panel, only an unmarked lever. She pulled down on the lever and the door in front of her slowly rose. No contained atmosphere? Valentina looked at her panel. She had air left, but not much. And the coldness in her toes had spread halfway up her calves. This was bad.

Valentina climbed under when the door was halfway up, then

pushed it back down behind her before looking around. There was frost glistening on every surface: a bad sign on account of cold, but a good one because glistening meant light. Valentina turned and saw a dull greenish glow coming from a bar-shaped light over the airlock door. Then she found another source: a panel in the wall nearby. She stepped up to it, looking over all the indicators. This wasn't even as advanced as don Abuelo's suit; these were knobs and dials with lights to show what was on or off. Valentina sounded out the words as she moved from knob to knob. The heat was on but set to freezing—warmer than outside, but not remotely comfortable. Valentina cranked it to 18 degrees. The air recycler was on, if not doing much, no one having been around lately to offset its balance by breathing. She found switches for more lights and turned them all on, bathing the room in a harsh yellowish glow.

There were bunks built into the walls, a bathroom with two show-ers, and a stove. Valentina cracked the seal on her helmet and lifted it off.

The air was cold and dry, sucking the moisture out of her lungs and making each breath an ache. She leaned closer to one of the vents and felt a warm rush of air on her face. The heat was definitely working, and once the frost melted off of everything, the air wouldn't be so dry. She waited until the temperature indicator said 10 degrees before peeling off the rest of the heavy suit, shaking out her layers of clothing: thin T-shirt currently clinging to her sweaty skin, heavy long-sleeved T-shirt, flannel shirt, fisherman's sweater with roll collar, knit stock-ings, long underwear, and two skirts.

She had left her boots behind, as they wouldn't fit inside the suit. She hoped she wouldn't regret that later.

Valentina detached the air cells from the back of the suit and snapped them into the way station's air system to refill them. Then she headed for the bathroom. The water she washed her hands with was temptingly warm, but she opted not to try out the shower. The air wasn't warm enough yet to air-dry, and she had no towels.

She refilled her water bottle but didn't snap it back into the suit, just drank from the opening as she looked around the room. The frost had faded from the walls, and now she could see that they were covered in writing.

A sudden growl from her stomach distracted her, and she went back to her suit, opening the cargo pocket on the belly and taking out an energy bar. There were twenty in there, but she didn't dare have more than one a day. Perhaps further down the line she would meet other travelers willing to share food, but in case she didn't, she had to be very careful with her rationing. She had been impetuous, but she wasn't stupid. The things she'd learned hanging about Hanako's machine shop listening were going to be crucial in the next few days.

Valentina chewed on the bar, too hungry to mind its likeness to wood pulp, and walked along the wall, reading what notes she could make out. There were dates and short messages. Some were personal exchanges, inside jokes she didn't understand, but most were general comments about travel conditions, way stations in need of repairs, obstacles to avoid. She found the end of the stream of dates and read backward. The last message was dated six months ago, but that wasn't surprising. Winter was no time for traveling on foot over the ice cap.

Valentina went back to her suit and scrounged through the cargo pocket. No pen, but she found the small envelope with the last three pills inside it. She had forgotten about those. Hanako's son Kiyoshi had given them to her after she'd woken up, but he hadn't said anything to her about them. To the best of her memory, that boy had never spoken a word to her. Still, if they were like the drugs she had bought for Ma— the ones that hadn't saved her—then she was supposed to keep taking them until they were all gone. She put one in her mouth and washed it down with a drink from her water bottle, then put the rest back in the pocket. She hoped it would kick in soon. Now that she had stopped moving, the ache in her joints was pushing close to unbearable and she knew she was getting feverish again.

If she got bad sick again, too sick to get up like she'd been for the last two weeks, too out of it to even realize her brother was gone… if she got that sick here, alone…

Valentina pressed fisted hands to her temples and forced her thoughts back to more useful places. Playing the what-if game was not going to help her now. Assess the situation, figure out what you have to work with, solve the problems one at a time. That was what her mother had always taught her. Running a large household with no funds had made them both very good at those steps.

She examined the inside of the suit, halfheartedly hoping the problem with the heating system was obvious and easy to fix, but she couldn't see anything amiss. The wiring nestled between the two layers was all intact, nothing broken or frayed.

Not having anything else to do, Valentina curled up on one of the bunks, tucking her stockinged feet into her skirts, and sleepily regarded the wall. She wished she had something to write with. She wanted to leave a message for the next northbound traveler to bring to Hanako Willis. She owed her an apology for taking the suit. It had once been don Abuelo's, but her mother had sold it to Hanako years ago and it wasn't Valentina's to take. She wasn't sure if she would ever be back to return it. And then there were the protein bars, in no way hers and not something she could ever return even if she did go back.

She reached into her skirt pocket and found the note she had stuffed there. She didn't read it, just held it crumpled in her hands as the weariness of the day washed over her. She already knew the shape of every carefully rendered letter by heart. It was a brief note, the most her little brother could manage. It had been left on the little table next to her medicine, next to the other, thicker letter with a corporate logo on the seal she had never broken.

Tina, it will be OK—Arturo.

"Yes, it will," Valentina said. "It will be OK because I'm coming to get you. I have to walk the whole distance you flew over, but I'm coming. I'm coming, Arturo."

CHAPTER TWO

FELLOW TRAVELERS

Her heart was pounding and she could not draw a breath, giving the pounding a desperate, dying quality. She went from hidey-hole to secret space, searching for any coin she might have overlooked before, no matter how worthless, but there was none. The tea tin was empty; the millet sack had very little millet left in it, let alone the little pouch of coins Ma had once secreted there. Still, she searched the same places again and again fruitlessly, and her heart pounded, hard but empty.

She turned to tell Arturo that there was nothing left, no way to buy the medicine that Ma needed to live, but Arturo wasn't there.

Valentina jerked awake with a gasp. Her heart really was beating hard, and she gasped again, fearful that the station had run out of air, that she was dying, starving for oxygen, but the long breaths filled her lungs and her heart calmed down. Just a dream. Well, a memory twisted into dream, but she wasn't dying. Not at the moment.

A flash of memory filled her mind: her mother, thin and pale, barely able to sit up with Valentina's arm around her to take a small sip of the tea that never really made her any better. She was nearly weightless in Valentina's arms. Valentina had picked up toddlers with more heft.

She blinked back tears before they started to spill. Arturo was gone. And it was morning, time to move on.

Valentina suited up and went outside, the sun still some time away from rising, just a pink glow low on the horizon. She headed south as the first rays spread over the icy expanse to her right. She kept to more of a loping rhythm, hoping to maintain it for more than half the day. Exhaustion from the day before made her limbs feel heavy, but urgency still drove her.

She stopped briefly at lunchtime to eat the half an energy bar she'd put into the helmet's snack holder that morning and take some longer sips of water. The logy feeling in her arms and legs was making her feel sleepy, almost to the point of napping there in her suit, her back to a drift of ice and snow. The dazzling brightness making it hard to keep her eyes open didn't help. She didn't dare rest long for fear she really would fall asleep and lose the day and the oxygen napping when she needed to be moving.

The afternoon seemed twice as long as the morning, her feet alternating between numbing cold and blistery soreness depending on how fast she tried moving. Her water bottle was nearly gone despite her careful rationing of sips, and her stomach was an angry fist of hunger. The smell of her own sweat inside the suit still had too much of a sick fever-sweat quality to it, not a healthy exercise sweat. It made it hard to ignore the ever-present ache in her joints and behind her eyes.

This time she reached the checkpoint while the sun was still a red glow low on the horizon. It helped that the light over the door was on, glowing starlike over the snowy expanse. She climbed inside the airlock and shut the door behind her, but when she pushed down on the lever to raise the inner door, it refused to move.

She looked around but could see no locking mechanism, no obstruction. The light had been on outside; did that mean there was someone inside, locking her out? But why would the station have locks? They were supposed to be open to all travelers. There were enough bunks to handle a dozen people at a time, more if they were friendly.

Valentina glanced at her diminishing air levels, then pushed on the lever again. Nothing. Not knowing what else to try, she rapped on the door. Through her helmet, she had no idea how loud it was. She was about to try knocking again, harder, when the door started to rise. Valentina waited for the door to stop moving before stepping inside.

There were two men inside the station. The one standing at the instrument panel, turning the knob to shut the door behind her, was a few years older than she was, tall and skinny in long underwear and a jumpsuit left off above the waist, rolled down and tied by the sleeves like a belt. His hair was shaved on the back and sides, maybe half an inch of Afro left on top. A small gold hoop glinted from one ear as he turned to smile a greeting at her.

His companion only gave her half a glance and a scowl, occupied as he was with something on the stove. He was older. Valentina wouldn't want to guess how much older. He had the look of someone going through life the hard way, accumulating scars and skin damage at a rate that made his actual age a mystery. Valentina recognized the cauliflower patterns of frostbite damage to his ears and nose, and he was missing some fingers at the first or second knuckle. Wisps of oily gray hair were plastered over his pale, blotchy scalp.

She wished she could turn around and keep walking, but that wasn't an option. Instead, she unsealed her helmet and set it on the shelf next to their two suits. She resisted the urge to scratch at her sweat-streaked hair.

"Hello," she said carefully in English, the lingua franca in Hanako's shop if not common to most of the north pole. "Heading north?"

"Yah," the younger man said, putting out a hand for her to shake. She quickly slipped her arms out of her suit to take his hand.

"Valentina del Toro," she said.

"I'm Pete. That's Stu."

"Hey," said Stu, looking her over again as she stepped out of her suit and shook out her skirts. "You new to this, kid?"

"This?" Valentina repeated.

"You don't look like a merchant."

"They usually travel in groups," Pete added.

"I'm not a merchant. I'm just going south."

"Looking for work? Because there isn't any," Stu said.

"That's why we're heading north," Pete said.

"No, I'm going to see my brother."

"All alone?" Stu asked.

"Yeah," Valentina said. "It just worked out that way."

Stu made a humph sound and turned back to the stove.

"What are you cooking?" Valentina asked. There were two pots, and both were boiling like mad.

"We're not sharing," Stu said, poking the contents of one with a spoon.

"Now, Stu," Pete said.

"I'm not looking for a handout. It's just, it smells like beans, but if you keep cooking them like that, they're going to be hard as rocks."

"That's beans à la Stu," Pete said. "Comes with a side of crunchy rice."

"I don't doubt," Valentina said, watching the steam billowing from the other pot.

"I know what I'm doing," Stu said.

"I don't think you do," Pete said. "Maybe you did once, but you worked at the mining company for how many years?"

Stu mumbled an answer Valentina didn't catch. "Replaced by a damn kid," he added.

"I think you got used to eating at the canteen. I'm not criticizing. I never learned to cook in the first place. I'm just saying. Let her take a look at what you're doing. If she cooks it up better, maybe we share a little."

"A little," Stu conceded. "Not a third. She don't earn no third just for stirring what I paid for with blood, sweat, and tears."

"You never shed no tears," Pete said, giving Valentina a wink.

Valentina stepped up to the stove, taking the spoon Stu held out for her. She immediately turned the heat down to a lower setting. Then she poked at both pots with the spoon. The water was nearly gone, but nothing was sticking yet; he had indeed been a diligent stirrer. It looked like he'd just started; he hadn't had time to ruin anything yet.

"I need some water," Valentina said. "And lids, if you have them."

"What good's a lid? Aside from not seeing what you're cooking," Stu said as Pete handed her a water bottle.

"You need to contain the steam when you're cooking beans and rice both, but especially the rice," Valentina said. "Unless you like it crunchy."

Stu looked like he wanted to say that he did, but instead just grumbled, "No lids."

"OK, how about a plate that fits over the top?" Valentina asked. In the last few months, when she and Arturo had to start selling things, she had gotten quite skilled at improvising for absent equipment. Pete dug into a backpack and held out two stainless steel plates. Valentina added water to both pots, then inverted the plates over them.

"You should have started the beans first. They take longer to cook," Valentina said.

"Canned beans are quicker," Pete said with a pointed look to Stu. Clearly, he was bringing up an old argument.

"Dry beans are lighter," Stu said. "As much bitching as you've been doing about the weight of the sled, I'd think you'd be on my side on that by now." They must have pulled the sled around the back of the station; Valentina hadn't seen it. Of course, she'd been pretty focused on the light over the door.

"You've been walking far?" Valentina asked.

"We come from Alba Patera, although we had a ride across Vastitas Borealis; we've only been walking since we got on the ice cap," Pete said. "Haven't found any work yet."

"You're almost at the end of the line," Valentina said. "Nothing north of here but the polar station."

"Any work there?" Pete asked.

"Maybe, I don't really know," she admitted. She thought about mentioning the troubles, the latest flare-up of street wars between the various gangs. But such things were usually short-lived. It had probably run its course while she was too sick to get out of bed and a new gang was in charge now. The fighting was getting more frequent now that don Abuelo wasn't there to smooth things over, but she mostly kept out of it. Or she had, until the day her brother had been too near one of the fights and had been taken prisoner by a group of Nortes who mistook him for a Poltec.

She remembered standing in the middle of the brewery that was the Norte's base of operations, standing in front of their don and demanding her brother's return. He had looked to be past thirty, his bare arms a crisscross of knife scars. A particularly brutal one marred his neck from the clavicle to the missing lobe of his ear. But the scars were all old, faded to a grayish white against his brown skin. He hadn't been a part of the fighting himself in quite some time. The man and woman on either side of him had been younger, mid-twenties maybe. They were not as impressively scarred as their don, but judging by the reddish welts the man had been sporting and the bandage the woman had wrapped around her midriff under her Norte sash, they were working on it.

The don was probably dead now. Perhaps the man or woman she had seen was in charge now. Perhaps the Nortes were no more. She wasn't sure how she felt about that.

Pete and Stu were watching her face closely, and she cast her mind about for something to say. "You both have experience mining. That gives you a better chance than most, I can say that for sure."

"I was only working for the mine a few months," Pete said. "Stu is the one with the skills."

"How is the way south of here?" Valentina asked, adjusting the heat under the rice to the lowest setting, just enough to keep it warm until the beans caught up.

"You're the first person we've met since we got on the ice cap," Pete said.

"It's early in the season for anything but rovers," Valentina explained. "And rovers don't use the way stations."

"There are a few behind us that weren't operational," Pete said. "One was half buried in the ice and we couldn't get in the door. Another looked fine, but the generator wouldn't run. No power, no air."

"Sounds dangerous," Valentina said.

"People mark the walls on the stations on either side, so you know when they're coming. Stow extra supplies in your suit and prepare to march double time."

"Start before dawn, stop after dark," Stu added. "You got a locater?"

"In my suit," Valentina said.

"Otherwise you might as well turn back now," Stu said.

"I don't like walking in the dark," Pete said. "It's too big outside. I swear there are things out there, walking with us."

"There's nothing out there," Stu snorted.

"I never saw anything, but I felt it all the same. Someone or something walking with us, like it was part of our little group. Never anything there when I'd look around, though. It stayed out of the light."

"Crazy talk," Stu said, and Pete just shrugged.

They lapsed into a friendly silence as Valentina cooked the beans. Stu took some piece of equipment out of his pack and sat down with it on one of the bunks, taking off the back panel to poke at its innards with the air of someone taking up a familiar, nearly endless task. Like Valentina's mother with her knitting.

At last the beans were soft enough and Valentina turned the makeshift pot lids back into plates. She divided the food up between the two plates and handed one each to the men. Stu made a grunt that didn't sound much like a thanks, but Pete smiled at her.

"You got a fork?" he asked, and Valentina shook her head. "Then here, take my spoon. I'll share mine with you."

"Thanks," Valentina said, too hungry to do the polite refusal thing. "I haven't had black beans in ages."

"You don't get beans on the north pole?"

"Sure, but the last shipment we got from Earth was nothing but red beans and these little Japanese beans called adzuki. They're tasty enough, especially if you have some ginger on hand, but I love black beans myself."

"These are pretty bland," Pete said. "Someone forgot to pack salt."

"I heard that," Stu said around a mouthful of food.

"Salt is good, but I like them with fresh salsa made with really hot chilies."

"How do you get fresh salsa?"

"I have a garden. Or had," she corrected. "Grow lights and heaters in a cave under the ice, but you'd be surprised how much plants can grow."

"I bet you make a tidy profit, selling fresh food," Pete said.

"A bit, but it costs a lot to keep it all going. One thing breaks and it's all over."

"Sounds like us," Pete said. "We were living pretty good until out of nowhere a bunch of us were fired. No job, no place to live, no place to go. Everything changes in an instant." He held the plate closer to Valentina, encouraging her to take more. Stu was nearly done with his share, shoveling forkful after forkful into his mouth at a methodical rate.

"Hopefully, your luck changes at the north pole," Valentina said.

"It's a shame you won't be there," Pete said. "It would be nice to already have a friend. Or maybe I can convince you to come back with us?" he said with a wink that did funny things to her stomach that had nothing to do with finally having more than two mouthfuls of protein bar to fill it.

"I really can't," she said, taking another forkful of beans and rice when he once more gestured to her with his plate. "I have to find my brother."

"Oh, I thought it was just a visit," Pete said, moving his fork over the plate, collecting a little mound of sticky rice and plunging it into the sauciest pool of beans.

"No, he's been kidnapped."

"Sounds serious," Pete said. "Does the pole have no sense of community? No one would help you get him back?"

"He was taken by my father," Valentina admitted. "But they don't even know each other. My father left before Arturo was born. It's like being taken by a stranger; Arturo must be so alone and scared now in a strange place, with no one looking out for him. But no one else sees it that way. Like sharing blood means something that sharing a home doesn't. But I know he needs me. I have to get to him."

Pete offered her the plate again, but she waved it away. After days of so little food, she wasn't sure her stomach could handle so much at once. She took a sip of water from the open mouth of her suit bottle.

The last time she had seen Arturo before the confused half memory/half dream of her time in her sickbed had been after she had gone to the don to beg for his release. The don had laughed at her demands, mocked her for calling on the name of her grandfather, don Abuelo, to enlist his cooperation. Once that name had meant everything all over the north pole, was respected by even the smallest and most fringe of the street gangs. Now, just a few years after his death, his lifetime of work was a joke to those he had worked hardest for. Valentina had been shoved back out on the street empty-handed, showered with threats of what would happen if she dared to return, then left to cry hot tears among the heaps of garbage behind the brewery until Arturo himself found her. Arturo, who had talked his own way out of his captivity and had gone in search of her.

He had to help her home. The heat of the tears had not been from her frustrated anger but from the beginnings of the illness that would prevent her from protecting her own brother when he needed her most. She still wasn't exactly sure how long she had lain too ill to move or even wake up for more than a few slow blinks of dry, hot eyes that wouldn't focus on the world around her. She had fallen to her knees the moment she had entered the nearly empty cavern that was their home and Arturo had guided her crawling steps to her own bedroll. He had tucked the blankets around her as her eyes started to close and murmured a few words of comfort.

Then he had wailed, long and loud, and she had heard him but had been unable to respond, had slipped away into warm, dark unconsciousness despite fighting with every bit of her will to stay awake, to open her eyes, to sit up and put her own arms around her brother as he called for their mother again and again and again.

Valentina supposed that had been the moment, right there, when her mother had gone. Just before she herself had fallen ill. They had both abandoned Arturo at once. And he was still alone, alone among strangers.

She had to hurry. He needed her. She had to get to him, bring him home. The two of them together could figure out what that meant: home without mother.

Valentina bit her lip until the flash of pain drove the visions from her head, then got to her feet with a forced smile to help with the after-meal cleanup.

CHAPTER THREE

A BROKEN NIGHT

PETE HAD TAKEN THE DISHES INTO THE BATHROOM TO WASH THEM IN ONE of the sinks. Valentina followed with the pots and set them in the sink next to his. She let the water run as hot as it would go, scraping the burnt remains of Stu's attempt at cooking from the bottom with the edge of a spoon.

"You know, I'm bringing my brother back to the north pole once I find him," she said. "Perhaps we'll see each other then, if you're still there."

The corner of his mouth pulled up a bit as he looked over at her. The top of her head was just even with his shoulder, and the way he looked down, warm brown eyes through thick lashes that were almost too pretty, made her stomach jump again. "I look forward to it."

He finished up and carried the dishes back out to air-dry before getting repacked with the rest of their supplies. The pots took longer to clean, and when she was done, she cleaned herself up as much as she could, unbraiding and finger-combing her long hair, then braiding it back again. Perhaps at the next station she could shower.

She went to her suit and refilled the air and water bottles, taking a moment before reattaching the water to take another of the pills. Then she curled up on one of the bunks. Her body ached and longed for rest, but her mind was anxious and fought sleep.

She wasn't sure how long she was lying there, drifting between wakefulness and sleep, or how long the murmur of whispers was humming just under the sound of the air cyclers, but a frustrated noise from Pete brought her fully awake.

"We don't have to do that," he hissed.

"We have no reason not to," Stu hissed back. "She look to you like someone who has people?"

"She said she has a brother."

"What brother would let her wander around alone?"

"With no food," Pete added. They were whispering more quietly now, and Valentina strained to make out the words. "She has nothing to take."

"Everything is worth something," Stu said. "That suit of hers—"

"Is ancient."

"Did you see her stockings? She's not so destitute as she'd have you believe."

Valentina fought the urge to tuck her feet under her skirts. She had forgotten about the stockings. She had woken from her long illness wearing them and had never gotten around to switching them for a pair of her own hand-knit stockings. Her father had no doubt left them for her. The delicate, even yarn of shimmering gray, the fancy cable pattern running up the sides screamed factory-made, and that meant life inside a corporate dome.

"Look at the rest of her clothes, though. She probably stole those stockings," Pete said. "Or she was rich once, but her luck changed, like ours."

"Either way, they're still worth something. And I want to know what she has in her pockets."

"But we don't have to kill her," Pete said, and his tone said this was the crux of the argument that had wakened her.

"It would be easier if we did," Stu grumbled. "And we have no reason not to."

"Look, I'll go sit on her and you go through her pockets."

"And then what?"

"We let her go," Pete said. "What's she going to do?"

"If she makes trouble, I will kill her," Stu said.

"She won't."

Valentina didn't know what to do. There was nowhere to run; they were between her and her suit, and even if they weren't, it would take her several minutes to dress and get out of the station. She was trapped.

She watched Pete's shadow coming toward her. She remembered how kind he had been, sharing his food with her. She remembered the warmth in his brown eyes as he'd talked with her. She supposed he thought he was being kind now as well, sitting on her to keep Stu from killing her, but Valentina set the bar for kindness a little higher than that.

Pete stopped his tiptoe advance when she sat up.

"Don't fight," Pete said. "He's serious."

"Why?" Valentina asked.

"We've run out of nearly everything, no more money and no sign of jobs. We've been walking pretty much in circles for months now."

"I'm sure you'll find jobs at the polar station. You're miners."

"I wish I could make Stu feel that sure," Pete said.

"You grab her or I'm going to bash her brains in," Stu growled and Pete yanked her off the bunk, wrapping his arms around her.

"Sorry," he said, his lips brushing her ear as he whispered. "I have to do this. I'm just trying to keep you safe."

"I don't have anything worth anything," Valentina insisted. She squirmed, but the arms around her were the arms of a youth who had spent his days hauling ore around, who currently spent his days pulling a sled across the ice. She had only been out of bed after contracting Martian fever for two days, and she had spent them pushing herself to the limits of her stamina. She had nothing left to fight him with.

"What's this?" Stu asked, looking at the last pill in its paper envelope.

"Antibiotic," Valentina said. "I've been sick."

"Energy bars," Stu said, digging through the rest of her pocket. "Nasty stuff; I don't think we're that desperate."

"I told you she didn't have anything," Pete said.

"Nothing in the pockets of the suit, maybe," Stu said, throwing the suit to the ground in disgust. "But there are the stockings. Maybe more she's hiding on her person."

"I don't have anything," Valentina said, struggling against Pete's grip. "My mother just died of Martian fever. She was sick for a long time; I had to sell everything we owned to pay for the medicine that didn't even save her. I don't have anything."

"You have nice machine-made stockings, and proper antibiotics."

"My father"—she choked out the word; it felt strange saying it out loud—"left me those."

"Is that all he left you?"

"Yes, I swear."

Stu seemed to think this over and a flutter of hope wakened in Valentina's heart, but then he shook his head and stepped toward her, his eyes going hard. "You're wearing lots of layers. Lots of pockets in those layers."

Pete's arms tightened around her while Stu pawed through her clothing. He peeled the stockings off her legs, turning them inside out as if she might have hidden something within. Then he shoved his hands under her sweater to feel all over her shirt.

"If I had anything, I would have given it to you already," Valentina said, fighting tears.

"He's nearly done," Pete said, his arms squeezing in what she was sure he meant to be a comforting hug, but only made her feel more trapped.

"A-ha," Stu said, his hands emerging from her underskirt with the crinkle of squashed paper.

"That's nothing," Valentina said. "Just a note from my brother. It's not worth anything except to me."

Stu glanced at it and let it drop to the floor, but he still had something in his hand.

The other letter, the one written on thicker, smoother cream-colored paper, sealed with a corporate logo. Stu gave it a shake, frowned, then sliced open the seal with one dirty fingernail.

Valentina looked away. She knew it was irrational, this urge to have nothing to do with the words on that paper. And yet she had stuffed it in her pocket with her brother's note. She hadn't questioned it in the moment, had forgotten since that it was even there. But she had never tossed it aside.

Stu didn't read it either, just unfolded the top, bottom, and sides to reveal the shining coins within.

Valentina froze, the glint of metal in the station lights hypnotizing her. Stu let them drop from the edge of the paper into his other palm, one soft plop against his flesh and then nine more clinks of coin on coin. She didn't know what it was worth in a corporate domed city, but here at the north pole it was a fortune. She could have paid Hanako for the suit rather than stealing it. For that matter, she could have bought a better one. She could have stocked up on supplies rather than subsisting on fractions of energy bars.

She could have paid for a ride on an outgoing rover.

"Little liar," Stu said, closing his fingers over the money. "You said you had nothing."

"I didn't know," Valentina said, pressing back against Pete as Stu took half a step closer.

"She didn't, Stu," Pete said. "Look at her face. She had no idea."

"She knows now," Stu said, still stepping closer. "It's too much to just walk away from, isn't it, little girl?"

"What can I do about it?" Valentina said. "Just let me go. I just want to go. I don't even want that money." But her voice cracked at that half-truth.

"Come on, Stu," Pete said. "Let's not be monsters here. I'm hungry, just like you are. But we can eat like kings now. Set up a business of our own. That's seed money there, we both know it. We'll just keep it and let her go. Keep a clean conscience."

Valentina bit back a nervous laugh. Apparently, thievery wouldn't bother Pete's conscience. She supposed she should just be grateful that murder would. Stu dropped the coins from his left palm into his right one by one, then shoved them into the pocket of his jumpsuit. Valentina's lips had just parted to take a deep breath of relief when his now empty hand whipped out at her.

Then she was spinning away as Pete shoved her away from him

and she stumbled back onto the bunk, banging a shoulder on the metal frame. She pushed herself back up and turned to find Pete wrestling Stu into the bathroom. Pete was young and tall, but Stu was all muscle and knew how to use his lack of height to advantage. Valentina jumped off the bed, coming around to Pete's other side to help push Stu into the bathroom. Pete slammed the door, then turned and braced his back against it.

"It doesn't lock from here," he said. "I can only hold him for a minute. Run, now."

Valentina picked up her brother's note from the bunk and stuffed it into her pocket. She didn't see her stockings; Stu must still have them. She hurried into her jumpsuit as Stu's pounding and cursing grew louder from behind the trembling door.

"He'll want to chase you," Pete said. "If you hurry and get out of sight, it will be easier to convince him not to bother. Get far enough away that he can't see you from the door. You're heading south anyway, out of our way."

Stu bellowed and threw himself against the door hard enough to nearly open it. Pete grunted and pushed it shut again. Valentina could see he was tiring.

"I'm sorry. I tried to talk him out of this, but he's feeling a lot more desperate than I am. Maybe because he's used to being settled, not this nomad life. I didn't have a steady gig long enough to get used to it. You know, I really do like you," he added, but this time, the crinkling of his eyes did nothing to her stomach.

"Does he… do this a lot?" Valentina asked. She couldn't bring herself to ask if he killed people for their money.

"Times are hard," Pete said after a long moment of wrestling with the words. "He has a temper."

"Maybe you should find a different companion," Valentina said, then fastened up her suit, pulling the helmet down over her head and sealing it. Pete risked a brief raise of a hand in farewell, but Valentina didn't return the gesture.

Her heart was pounding even before she started running, bounding over the ice. It was dark, and she had no light. The ice was smooth, mostly, but occasionally there were deep fissures, blown over with snow, all but invisible until you were right on top of them. They had startled her in the daylight; the thought of them terrified her in the dark. That and Pete's story about the thing watching from the dark. But mostly she was afraid of Stu. If he caught up with her and killed her and pushed her body into a crevasse, no one would ever know what had become of her. Arturo would never know. He would think she had abandoned him to his fate.

Valentina ran as fast as she dared, head down to stare at the blackness beneath her. Phobos overhead was her only company, and he wouldn't even light her way.

The station had disappeared over the horizon behind her before she remembered the letter, left discarded on the station floor after Stu had all the coins in his hand. She would never know now what it said or what the money had been for.

CHAPTER FOUR

STRAYING FROM THE PATH

IT TOOK TWO DAYS OF HARD RUNNING TO BURN OFF THE NERVOUS paranoia, two days spent constantly looking back to be sure she wasn't followed. She didn't meet any other travelers, but she couldn't quite get comfortable in the way stations at night and slept little and badly.

The third night she was too tired to be scared anymore and slept until nearly midmorning. She still ran that day, but this time she was looking ahead to the coming way station and the setting sun and not behind.

The way station was as uninhabited as all the others had been, but in the bathroom she found a pile of rubbish left behind, perhaps by Stu and Pete or perhaps by someone else entirely. There were bean cans, quite empty, and wrappers for hard rye bread squares. There was also a map.

Valentina sat on a bunk, chewing her evening's half of an energy bar and studying the map. It showed the length of the way station line, from the north pole station all the way to the end of the ice cap. The route followed the arcing contour of Chasma Boreale, although it was several kilometers away from the canyon itself. It wasn't a very detailed map, and she doubted it was even to scale, but it would let her count how far along the line she was, and that was something.

She sounded out the words carefully, but they were mostly unknown to her. They sounded like proper names, names from all sort of cultures back on Earth, and she guessed the way stations had each been named for some early Martian explorer. She read them all twice, but del Toro wasn't mentioned—a serious oversight in her view. Yes, he had been a scientist and not technically an explorer, but the road to the north pole had been blazed by him and his companions. His ability to solve problems with little resources and less time had saved his team on more than one occasion. The way stations stood where he had once placed supply caches for his team's return journey at the end of the season.

Then she remembered she had heard all those stories from her father. It was possible they weren't even true. Her memories of life inside the science station before Arturo was born were fuzzy. Her father could have lied about the plaque commemorating the first research team that had put Antonio del Toro's name at the very top, so crucial he had been to the mission's success.

Valentina touched the memory of those stories in her mind, like she used to probe the gap of a missing tooth with her tongue when she was little, gently but persistently, waiting for the sting of exposed nerve. She decided even if they were all lies, they were still good stories. She would remember her ancestor as a scientist/hero, whether it was true or not. It's not like she'd ever meet him, anyway; he had died long before the plague on Earth had driven don Abuelo's family from México to Mars.

She should have told the stories to Arturo. She always intended to, but there was never the time. She had only ever told him her favorite, how Antonio del Toro had gotten all the team's equipment over a deep canyon before the storm had blown up that would have killed them all. It was part logic problem, part soap opera (the mission leader's wife had a bit of a thing for Antonio, or so her father always insisted), part Arctic adventure story. But Arturo had been quite young at the time; perhaps he didn't even remember it now.

The next two days passed at a more relaxed pace. Valentina was getting into the groove of bounding every day for ten or more hours. The constant hunger was harder to get used to, but she daren't eat any more than a bar a day. Even that was going to run out before she got to the end of the line, she knew that for sure now that she could count the stations on her map.

Then came the night Valentina had been dreading ever since she'd spoken to Stu and Pete about the way stations. There, written on the wall, was the message that the next station was out of service: some mysterious problem with the generator none of the other travelers had been able to solve.

She had known these words were coming, Stu and Pete had told her, but the moment they went from hypothetical to real had been a crushing one. She had harbored a secret hope that by the time she got here, someone would have fixed the problem. But the next station was down. She would have to hustle, leave before dawn and reach her destination after dark, moving as quickly as she could.

And somehow find a way to do it without using up all her oxygen.

Valentina took an extra day to gear herself up physically and emotionally for the next leg of the journey. At first she enjoyed lying about, resting her weary body until nearly lunchtime. But lunch had still been half an energy bar and all the water she could drink—not very satisfying. The night with Stu and Pete came back to her in her nightmares sometimes, but more often she dreamed of the black beans.

After lunch, she had turned up the heat and showered and washed all her clothes. Now she had nothing to do but wait for them to be dry enough to get dressed again, at which point there'd be nothing to do but wait for dinner: the other half of the energy bar.

Valentina brushed her hair back from her face. She wanted it a little drier before redoing the braid. She couldn't stand it when it was just down and floating everywhere, buoyed by the static electricity in the dry air and always in the way.

She wondered about the station further on ahead, the one buried in ice. Sooner or later someone would come out who could fix that. Would they get to it before she did? She wasn't sure how far down the line it was.

Valentina studied her map. She peered at the place she had X'd the night before, the station she was in now. She looked at the next station, the broken one, and then the station beyond that, her goal for tomorrow.

They weren't in a straight line. Not even close; they made a tight V shape.

The map didn't show, but there must be some obstacle in the way, some fissure in the glacier or perhaps even the first of the canyons, some reason for that V-shaped detour. Would it prove impassable?

She frowned and pushed her hair back again. If the obstacle was halfway between this station and her goal, she could walk out there and see, and if it really was impossible to cut across, she would have time enough to get back to this station without running out of daylight or air. She'd lose a day, but only if she had to turn back.

If it was more than halfway, things would get iffy. But not any iffier than trying to run to the broken station and beyond to the third station, surely.

The stations were set at a distance so that her locater always had a strong signal, but off-road she would be far from the place she had left and the place she was going. The signal would be weak. Her locater might get confused on where to point. She might get disoriented, lost.

She woke up hours before dawn, still not certain what she would do. She headed toward the broken way station but at an angle, not cutting directly across but veering one way. Dawn was a relief; Pete's mysterious follower sometimes made itself felt, but mostly she had visions of falling down narrow crevasses in the ice, never to be found again. Far scarier than hypothetical ghosts.

The midmorning sun blazing off the snow and ice emboldened her, and she turned, heading directly toward whatever lurked in the white spaces of the map. Best to just get it over with.

She ran as much as she could, but that wasn't as much as she'd hoped. She might be gaining stamina with all the walking and jogging every day, but her minimalist diet was also starting to make itself felt. She pushed herself until black dots started to eat her vision, then she would rest for a moment, checking the bars on her locater and trying to guess where she was. To her left was the broken station, but further ahead she was getting the barest flicker of the lowest bar. The next working station or just an anomaly? She wished she had a GPS.

Midday came and went with no obstacle reached. The signal ahead was getting stronger, and she was more and more confident that it was truly the station, but that didn't comfort her much. What if the obstacle really was impassable? If she didn't reach it soon, it would be too late to turn back. She looked at her oxygen levels. They were just over half full, but she was already exhausted from pushing her pace so hard all morning. It would take her longer to go back than it had to get here. Walking used less oxygen than running, but was it enough to compensate for the longer travel time?

Valentina took another sip of water and pressed on. There was nothing else to do.

It was late in the afternoon before she realized she was talking out loud, her voice breathless but loud inside her helmet. She wasn't talking to herself exactly, but as she was talking to Arturo—who wasn't there—she didn't think that made her any less crazy. She had been remembering her father's stories again, regretting not passing them on to her little brother, then considering how she would have worded them, testing to see if she still knew all the little details. Somehow, that had led to babbling away.

Valentina had spent her entire life with people always close around her. Don Abuelo's home had been enormous by north pole standards, a walled-off room with a tiny but separate kitchen and a deep natural cavern that he had carved out chasing a mineral seam. But the cavern had become the farm when the mine had dried up, and the living space had been a chaos of four daughters and their assorted progeny. Valentina's mother had helped her sisters raise their children and found jobs and homes for nearly all of them, a few just disappearing the way people did on Mars, swept up in circumstances that didn't allow them the opportunity to keep in touch. Perhaps one or two were simply dead.

In the end, it had just been Valentina, Arturo, and their mother, and their home had felt huge again, but they were always in each other's company. There was work to be done that required more than one pair of hands, and the work never ended. Moments alone were rare treasures.

Valentina sensed she wasn't coping well with her sudden gluttony of solitude. But she kept telling herself the stories because the day was too long, and the words kept the fear at bay.

The sun was setting when she saw the station ahead of her, the light over the door glowing like a guiding star. The ice field seemed to run unbroken between it and her, but she slowed her steps, certain there must be something. The sun was at eye level again, blinding her when she looked up, so she kept her eyes on her feet and moved in careful steps.

The ice in front of her ended in a jagged edge, and Valentina stopped just short of that, worried about fragile ledges that could crumble. When there was no sign of breaking, she crept a little closer, looking down into the chasm.

The sun was too low to shine down into the fissure. She could see a few meters of ice, then the rocky walls of the narrow canyon, but she had no clue how deep it was. Not that it mattered; the walls were too steep to climb.

Valentina took a sip of water and studied the far side. Was it too wide to jump across? She didn't like the look of the far side. The ice and snow had been swept by the wind into an artful overhang, like an upside-down frozen wave, delicately beautiful. She rather doubted it would take her weight.

Valentina looked to the left and right. It was so close to being doable, but she wasn't sure she could make it. Was there a place where the walls drew closer together, leaving a smaller gap she could more confidently jump?

She should have pushed harder, reached this place sooner when she had more light left for the search. Now she was going to have to risk the first likely point and hope for the best.

"I have to tell you, I don't like my odds, Arturo," she said as she followed the canyon to the left. "If I had a tent pole like our ancestor, I'd pole-vault over like he did, but alas, I have none."

Perhaps this was the very chasm that had stymied his team. It had the same taunting characteristics of being almost doable, the far side being just out of reach to all but the craziest risk-takers. She didn't have a storm blowing up behind her, at least.

Then she glanced at her air gauge. No, no storm for her. Her ticking clock was more like the last few grains falling through an hourglass. She looked up, surprised at how far to the right the starlike station light had gone. Then she looked back down just in time to see the bottom bar of her air gauge turn from dark orange to flashing red.

She was going to have to jump, now.

The last sliver of sun dipped below the horizon, its reddish glow remaining, but Valentina could look ahead without being blinded now. The canyon was a long, straight split in the rock, its walls never growing closer or further apart. Valentina kicked at the lip of the glacier until it splintered, then pried up a largish piece, ignoring the smaller chunks of ice that danced off the cliff edge. She stood her piece up a step away from the edge, a jagged white tombstone with the dying sunset behind it.

Then she turned and walked into the darkness several paces, her heart already hammering. Worse, she was certain she could feel the low oxygen already. Perhaps it was just fatigue, or nerves, but perhaps it was the lack of air making her vision blur and swim and then snap back to clarity. Was her brain getting foggy as well?

Valentina turned and sprinted back to the canyon, not pausing first to psych herself up or even take a deep breath. Her feet slipped and rubbed in the oversized boots, and the tanks on her back, empty as they were, suddenly felt twice as heavy as they pounded against her with each step.

She reached the marker sooner than she was really prepared for but again just flung herself into the motion, not letting her mind squeak out a thought. She had a lot of experience jumping high; chickens on Mars can get themselves aloft, and her chickens in particular had loved to play keep-away among the stalactites hanging from the ceiling of don Abuelo's cavern. She had never tried to jump long, though. She compensated as best she could, pushing hard with her last running step, launching out rather than up. The helmet made it impossible to look down as she sailed over the canyon, although she was certain she would see nothing but darkness with the sun gone from the sky. Instead, she looked straight ahead at the wave of delicate whorls of frozen ice rushing to meet her.

She stretched out her hands, which at first seemed silly as the edge of the cliff caught her right in the stomach. Then the ice and snow began to give way beneath her. Her out-flung arms and legs were distributing her weight as much as possible, but the tanks on her back were the heaviest part of her and the sculpted ice beneath them crumpled. Something jabbed her knee hard, but she didn't really feel it, scrambling as she was to move forward on her belly, afraid that trying to get a foothold would just send the entire sheet of ice tumbling into the canyon.

Her breath in her helmet was so loud. She couldn't hear the ice breaking, just her own breath coming in gasps and cries.

There was a moment when she was certain the sheet of ice she was trying to cross was already tumbling down the ravine, that she would reach the edge and touch only air. Then she was on solid, nonmoving ice. She rolled well away from the crumbling edge and lay still, her faceplate pressed to the snowy ground, and sobbed in relief.

Her knee throbbed once, hard, and then she felt the pain. Something sticky was running down her stocking; it could only be blood. She had gotten used to her feet being numb with cold all day, but it felt colder now. Painfully cold.

Valentina crawled a little farther forward, then stopped again, too tired to get to her feet. That was always an awkward exercise in a space suit; she should rest a bit first and then try it.

She knew her overwhelming sleepiness was a bad sign, but she was just too tired to care.

Her knee gave another throb of pain, then settled into a dull ache, as if it, too, were too tired to care.

She realized she had done it; she had crossed the obstacle she had been calling impassable. Was she really going to just lie here and die out of laziness?

Valentina pushed herself up off the ice, but her first attempt at getting to her feet roused her knee, which retaliated with such a savage cry of pain that she fell back to the ground and lay inert for another minute she didn't have.

She pushed herself up on her arms again, found the light of the station, and crawled on two hands and one knee dragging the other behind her.

The sky was full dark by the time she reached the step, black clouds at the edges of her vision devouring the stars and even the station light itself. She pulled herself into the airlock, waking her knee to pain once more. She had to get up on her good knee to work the inside door, but only enough to slide through on her belly. She shut it behind her, unclasped her helmet, and collapsed to the icy floor of the station.

CHAPTER FIVE

BREAK IN THE LINE

THE ICE WAS HARDER TO CHIP AWAY THE DEEPER SHE DUG, BUT VALENTINA had nothing else to do, so she kept hammering away at it, the muscles in her arm growing hot and tight. When she couldn't summon the strength for one more swing, she switched arms, leaning on her shaky, spent arm and pounding at the ice with the fresh one. Fragments exploded up into the air, sparkling in the sunlight. The days were getting longer and longer, but it didn't do her any good. She was stuck.

Something metallic glinted up at her and she changed tools, setting aside the long metal bar she used for the heavy blows and picking up the screwdriver she used for more delicate work. It looked like just another empty food can, and she already had a mountain of those, but there was always the hope that she'd find one with food still inside.

The can was frozen in place, bottom side up. The label was gone, but the bottom was stamped PINEAPPLE CHUNKS and Valentina's mouth watered just at the sight of the letters. She had never had pineapple before, but she'd smelled it in the marketplace. The kebab cart sometimes had some, and Mama Rosa's restaurant had a bread pudding she added chunks of dried pineapple to when she could get it. Valentina remembered the smell, the golden glow of the fruit pieces when Mama Rosa would scoop the pudding out of her slow cooker and heap it into a bowl before chasing Valentina and the other gawking urchins away.

She bet it was like eating sunshine.

The sun had not quite started to set when she finally pulled the can from the ice, but when she found it empty just like all the others, she tossed it aside and went back inside the way station, too dejected to do any more work that day.

Valentina cycled through the airlock and stepped inside the warm station, unsealing her helmet and putting it on the shelf before carefully unpeeling the suit. The patch at the knee was holding this time, but she was still extra gentle with it. Her suit had two layers, and the ice had torn away the tougher outer layer and broken the circuitry that ran between the two layers, but it had left the inner layer untouched. Her suit was still airtight, and the circuitry running down to the feet of her suit hadn't been functioning properly anyway, but it wouldn't take much to tear the exposed inner layer, and while the surface of Mars wasn't the vacuum of space, that would still be very bad. If she was more than a few minutes from shelter, it would likely kill her.

She wore one of her T-shirts wrapped around her knee over the hole in her suit to protect the bare patch and keep out the cold, but that was never going to be more than a temporary measure. She was very afraid of falling again.

Valentina plugged her air tanks into the refiller, then examined the control panel. She'd experimented and learned all the functions in the six days since she'd reached this station, the one she could not pass. The solar panels on the roof provided the power, stored in cells that lined the station walls when the station was not in use. Oxygen was extracted from the water ice around the station by an electrolysis unit hidden in the wall. There was also a reservoir of fuel for rovers, buried out of the way under the station itself, although the space designed to hold tons was two-thirds empty now.

But Valentina had found the most use for the motion detectors. Set at maximum like she had them now, they'd detect the smallest movement from the walls of the station out to the horizon in all directions. Of course, sometimes a gust of wind blowing up the snowy topcoat was enough to set them off, but they had already warned her once of approaching people in time for her to get into her suit and hide under the station before they arrived. If the two men had wondered why the station was running with full atmo and heat, she had no idea. She had spent an uncomfortable night in her suit, too afraid of the lack of heat to her legs to let herself sleep, but the newcomers had moved on at first light, long before her air situation would have forced her inside.

She wondered now if hiding had been the right choice. She was down to four and a half energy bars, and then there would be nothing but water until she starved. She knew from her childhood days hanging around Hanako Willis's machine shop that even men who looked tough and scary were usually not looking to rob her. But she also figured that if there was such a thing as good luck, she'd probably used hers up not getting killed by Stu, and she didn't want to risk her chances now that she had nothing of value to trade for her life.

She had had all these thoughts before, all night long, while the men had slept inside the station. She had even, in the darkest, coldest hour of the night, considered robbing them herself. They had extra air canisters in the sled they'd left parked outside the door. She was sure they were the right size to fit even her outdated suit. But in the end, she'd taken nothing. Without a partner to switch out the tanks on her back, carrying extras wouldn't make a bit of difference.

She had barely made it past one downed station, and it had cost her the integrity of her suit and she suspected one of the ligaments of her knee. She could never make it past two.

Had both stations been icebound when Stu and Pete had passed here, or had that happened after? She couldn't figure out a reason why they'd lie, or rather half-lie, and in the end she wasn't sure what difference it would have made if they'd told her the truth. Would she have gone back if she'd known? Given up on finding her brother and returned to the north pole minus even the money her father had left for her?

She didn't know what she would have done. All she knew was that the day she had reached this station, still limping from her wrenched knee, and seen the notes on the wall about the two downed stations, she had just sat on the floor, too stunned to even cry. She had neither food enough for a return journey nor courage enough to try jumping that canyon again.

She should not have hidden from those two travelers. She had nothing left to steal, and what would it have mattered if they had killed her? She was going to starve soon enough, anyhow.

Can't go forward, can't go back.

Valentina gave herself a hard shake. The days were getting longer, which meant more travelers on the road. Someone would come. Now that she wasn't walking every day, she had cut her rations down to half a bar a day; perhaps she should reduce that by half again. She just needed to hold on. To wait.

Valentina put her digging tools in the corner. She hadn't found much of value in the ice anyway, just what she'd repurposed into those tools and a large stash of empty cans. Better to conserve her energy, to wait.

Valentina looked at the quarter of an energy bar she had left herself from that morning's meal and thought about starting her new rationing scheme right then, but her stomach made a mute growl that sounded more like a whimper and she decided to wait until morning.

Never had eating a quarter of an energy bar felt so much like indulging in a holiday feast.

Valentina sat on one of the bunks, leaning back against the wall and closing her eyes. It was far too early for sleeping, but she dozed off anyway, then jerked awake at the shrill sound of the proximity alarm.

Valentina jumped to her feet, desperately wishing there was a window or some way to see outside. She waited for a moment, in case it would turn out to once more be just a gust of wind carrying snow over the glacier, but when the alarm didn't stop she switched it off herself.

It had been just what she'd been hoping for. So why was it making her stomach knot in fear?

Valentina got back into her suit, air and water fully stocked and everything but her digging tools already packed in the pockets. She slipped the screwdriver into her thigh pocket, but kept the metal bar in her hand. A weapon might be handy, assuming that anyone looking for trouble didn't have a better weapon themselves.

Valentina went out the airlock and jogged a few steps away from the station. It took her a minute to spot the approaching vehicle because she didn't expect to find it coming out of the north.

It wasn't travelers with a sled this time; it was a rover. Valentina took a few steps back then, as if that movement had created its own momentum, and ran further around the corner of the building. There was a dune of icy snow, not large but enough for her to crouch behind. In the last dying rays from the sun, she should be able to hide there. She would have to approach these people. She knew that. She just wanted to watch them a bit first.

But clearly, whoever was in the rover had already seen her; rather than stopping at the station door, it kept rolling on toward where she lay crouched in the snow. Valentina waited, desperately hoping she was wrong, that there was some other reason the rover was heading neither to this station nor the next but completely off the line to the east where she was hiding.

She could feel the glacier under her hands and knees tremble as the large machine crawled toward her on its oversized snow tires. It had a spotlight set in the front of its cab, a controllable one that was sweeping the snow, searching. Then it landed on her, its silvery glow hitting her like fire, driving her to her feet. She ran as fast as she could in the bulky suit, her not-yet-healed knee protesting.

Now there was no question about it: the rover was pursuing her. Had Stu and Pete somehow gotten hold of one and come back for her? That made no sense, but neither did any other explanation her panicked brain came up with.

Something in her knee snapped. It was a strange feeling, like it wasn't really a part of her, some inorganic component that just happened to be inside her flesh at that moment, breaking in two. There was a rush of heat, as if everything in her knee was rushing to the scene to gawk.

Then there was pain. Oh yes, that was very much a part of her.

Valentina stumbled, and the rover slowed to a halt. With a fierce cry Valentina drove herself on, loping on two hands and one foot like a deranged beast. She didn't dare turn back. Her mind flashed through all sorts of scenarios for what was going on behind her: the rover resuming pursuit, the rover door opening to discharge a horde of men in space suits, their faceplates too opaque to show if they were human or not. Somehow Pete's unseen presence got caught up in it, sometimes a spectator, sometimes a monstrous participant as the visions ended in a dozen gory deaths for Valentina.

Then hands were on her and she really did scream, raising the metal bar that she had held on to throughout her crazed flight. She brought it down with all the strength days of fighting the ice had given her, aiming for the faceplate.

The faceplate that was not opaque. Startled eyes stared back out at her.

She had swung the metal bar as hard as she could, but she must have hesitated when those eyes met hers, left just enough of a window for the intended victim to raise an arm of his own, directing her blow one way while smoothly dodging the other. The bar impacted on the ice, leaving an impressive crack.

Valentina stared at the bar embedded in the ice, horrified by what she had almost done. Then she looked back up at those eyes. They had been familiar.

It took a moment to place the face, seeing only the eyes and top of the nose, but when she did, she flung her arms around him, hugging him tight and sobbing. Her mic wasn't on, so he couldn't hear her, which was good because once she let the tears take her, there was no stopping them. Her memories of her days in bed, too sick to move, were a jumble, but those eyes were chief among them, always there while another voice expressed condolences for the loss of her mother, encouraged her that she would be well soon.

Told her that her brother was gone.

"Kiyoshi," she said over and over. "Kiyoshi Willis."

Then, when she had herself under control again, she sat back, nudged her radio on with her chin, and looked him straight in the eye.

"Kiyoshi Willis," she said. "What the hell?"

CHAPTER SIX

ONWARD OR BACKWARD

KYOSHI DIDN'T ANSWER HER, JUST PUSHED HER OUT TO ARM'S LENGTH TO look her over. He noticed the hole in the knee of her suit right away and his eyes grew even graver.

"Get in the rover," he said over the radio. "I have to fill the air tanks, but that will just take a minute. Once I'm inside, I can run life support and we can get out of our suits."

"Kiyoshi, I'm not going back," Valentina said.

"I know."

"And the next two stations are down. I've been stuck here."

"The rover can make it," he said, then walked away. Since everything she owned was already in the pockets of her suit, Valentina climbed inside the rover and pulled the door closed behind her. She was standing in a space behind the two seats that was only as wide as the door she had just shut. There were cabinets and drawers on the back wall, but the space was so narrow she'd have to step to one side to open anything. There was an even narrower door down the middle of the cabinets that she thought would be a closet but turned out to be the chemical toilet.

There was more equipment stored between the two seats and Valentina had to hold on to a handhold on the roof to make the wide step from the back of the cabin to the passenger seat. She settled into the seat to wait, but curiosity overwhelmed her and she started looking around again, opening the cabinet in front of her knees to see neat stacks of noodles and silvery packages of freeze-dried food. She leaned over to gawk at the controllers on the driver's side of the rover. The panels were a mishmash of colors and designs, all neatly arranged together as if they were a tight group of eccentric friends.

She had never really paid much attention to Kiyoshi when she'd visited Hanako, especially lately, when she'd been so busy and her visits had been short and always with an urgent purpose, but when she thought about it, she could picture him always in the background, quietly working away at some hulking machine at the back of the shop.

It must have been this rover, she decided, built from bits salvaged from several junked rovers. Having spent her life around such jury-rigged equipment, Valentina admired the flair Kiyoshi had brought to his personal project. She'd never seen something made of so many different parts that felt so much like a cohesive whole rather than a patch-up job.

The door behind her opened and Kiyoshi swung into the cabin much more gracefully than she had. He sealed the door, then pushed some buttons on a panel just over Valentina's right shoulder.

"It doesn't take long to get air," Kiyoshi said. "But the heat is slow."

"I don't mind the cold," Valentina said.

Kiyoshi climbed into the driver's seat. He looked over all the panels and leaned forward to peer out the window before starting up the engine. The rover lurched before settling into a plodding roll over the ice.

"We're going south?" she asked. He had said he understood that she didn't want to go home, but he hadn't said where he was going in his new ride. Just past the two downed stations was all she would hope for, she decided.

He nodded, but didn't offer any more information. She'd heard more words from him in the last five minutes than she had in the sixteen years before. He had a nice voice, a low rumble that was warm and comforting. "Hungry?" he asked.

"Like you wouldn't believe."

He opened the cabinet at her knees and pulled out a pack of noodles and one of the envelopes of freeze-dried food. He climbed into the back of the cabin, then reappeared with a pot of water that he set on what turned out to be a little cooker nestled between the two seats. His helmet was off, and after turning the cooker on, he pulled a knit cap out of his pocket and snugged it down over his close-cut hair.

"You can take off your helmet now," Kiyoshi said. Valentina unsealed the helmet and lifted it off her head, the cold air biting her cheeks. Kiyoshi took her helmet to stow in one of the cabinets and Valentina adjusted the braid wrapped around her head, making sure what little warmth it provided was over the tips of her ears.

Kiyoshi climbed back into his own seat before turning to offer her a square of dried goat meat. It must have been the first good look he'd gotten of her because something passed over his face, some startle of reaction that had elements of horror and pity, before he quickly looked away.

Valentina chewed the strip of goat jerky and watched as he added udon noodles to the pot simmering over the mini cooker. The meat was tough and her stomach, which had been sullenly quiet for days, protested loudly at the taste of food it hadn't started digesting yet. Kiyoshi stirred the noodles with a chopstick, glanced briefly out the front window and at the screen mounted in the middle of the dash- board, then crawled over the cooker between the seats to the back of the rover cab.

Valentina managed to work off a chunk of meat and swallowed it. Just a little peppery, but so good. She chewed some more, leaning forward to examine the screen Kiyoshi kept glancing at. The rover had some sort of sonar, and images were coming in waves off the terrain ahead. The rover was on autopilot, rolling forward at a steady pace toward the next beacon.

Kiyoshi crawled back into his seat, leaning over the cooker to dump the contents of a freeze-dried pack of mushrooms and seaweed into the broth. His eyes made another sweep out the window and at the screen before stopping on her, giving her that same pitying look as when she'd taken off her helmet.

Valentina took the jerky out of her mouth to ask, "Do I really look that bad?"

Kiyoshi blushed and shook his head, his attention back on the soup.

Valentina regarded him as she got back to work on the meat. She had always known Kiyoshi, but not well. Yes, he had always just been there, part of the background of her life she'd never given any particular attention to. They were sort of related, she remembered. His father Jeff Willis had been a rover driver who had settled down and married one of don Abuelo's sisters, and the two had started the machine shop together. But she had died trying to deliver their only child, and the baby had gone with her. Don Abuelo had insisted that Jeff stay at the north pole, that he was still part of the family. Valentina was fuzzy on the hows and whys of the next part of the story, but one way or another, three years later, Hanako had turned up. She had been a childhood friend of Jeff Willis's and was now a childless widow herself. Kiyoshi came along some time after, and then his father had died in one of the flu outbreaks. But Hanako and Kiyoshi had stayed on at the north pole running the machine shop.

So he was family, but not by blood; they were connected by don Abuelo's high regard for them. Plenty of her blood relatives had wandered away over the years, and her grandfather hadn't minded letting them drift away from the clan. But the Willises he had always been fond of. They were good people, as he often said.

"I'm sorry I took the suit. I know it's your mother's now," Valentina said. "Plus, I've pretty much ruined it. I'll find a way to pay her back."

Kiyoshi looked at the frayed edges of the hole at her knee peeking out from either side of where the T-shirt was tied, but said nothing.

"I guess you're not here for the suit anyway, since we're going south," Valentina said, then swallowed another piece of jerky. "Thanks for the ride, by the way. I couldn't go forward and didn't have enough food to walk back to the pole. I'm not sure what I would have done."

Kiyoshi turned off the cooker and handed her the entire pan with the chopsticks.

"Aren't you eating?" she asked, but he just shook his head. Valentina leaned over the soup, breathing in the aroma and basking in the touch of steam on her chilly face. The freeze-dried seaweed packet must have had powdered miso mixed in with it; there was no mistaking that smell. She poked the chopsticks in and pulled up a too-large mouthful of noodles.

He was giving her that look again.

"I've been hungry," she said around the mouthful of food. "So why are you here?" she finally asked. "It's not a coincidence. You wouldn't have come this far out just to test-drive your rover."

Kiyoshi looked out the window, then at the screen, but not at her. She almost thought he wasn't going to answer at all when, eventually, he did speak. "We didn't know where you'd gone. We knew the suit was gone, of course, but you had still been sick. We never considered that you just walked away. Mother was sure you'd hitched a ride on a rover and if she put the word out far enough, we'd find someone who knew something. We waited.

"Then these men came from the south looking for work. They had coins, corporate coins. We don't get many of those, and they were newly minted, just like the ones your father had left for you."

"I'm sorry I made you guys worry. I wanted to leave a message for you on the station wall, but I had nothing to write with."

"The men insisted you had paid them for a spare sled and some food, but Mother didn't believe them. For all we knew, they had killed you. At the very least, they had robbed you."

He looked up at her then, and this time it was Valentina looking out the window. "Robbed me," she said at last. "Yeah, that sucked." She didn't want to tell that story, didn't want to remember how afraid she had been.

"Did you really intend to walk the entire way to the equator?"

"No. I was sure I'd catch a ride somewhere. I think I had fever brain; I wasn't really thinking things through. My father turns up out of nowhere and just takes my brother while I'm too sick to know, let alone stop him? He left us before Arturo was even born; that was his choice. Now that Ma is gone, he can't just come back and take my brother away from me. That's kidnapping. He gave up being our father when he left. He can't change his mind now."

Kiyoshi didn't answer, just kept checking his monitors and the window. Apparently, he wasn't too trusting of the rover's autopilot.

Valentina couldn't stand the silence. "You're probably thinking about the note Arturo left me. I think he was just trying to be brave. That note could mean lots of things. And the money my father left for me—I didn't want it. I didn't even know it was there until I was robbed, but since then I haven't been too sad that Stu and Pete took it because it felt wrong even having it. Like he was paying me for my brother. Arturo was worth more than a few coins. I mean, yeah, it would have been enough to buy back all the animals and equipment I had to sell after Ma got sick—I could have had my farm again—but why would I even do that? What would any of it even mean after he's taken my brother away? I have no family left, not really. So what's the point?"

"So you're going to take your brother back?"

"Take?" Valentina repeated with a frown. "You sound like you don't think he would want to come home with me."

"You're going all this way just so you can talk to him?"

"Yes. But he's my brother, of course he's going to want to leave with me. I'm not taking anything."

Kiyoshi raised his hands, a gesture she took as an apology for his word choice. Valentina slurped down the last of the soup and turned her attention back to the jerky.

CHAPTER SEVEN

THE LAST STATION

THEY PASSED THE TWO DOWNED STATIONS IN THE NIGHT, REACHING THE operative one just after sunrise.

"I have to evacuate the air before I can open the door," Kiyoshi said after bringing the rover to a stop. "You'll have to suit up."

"I can come out and help with the maintenance," Valentina said as she retied the T-shirt around her aching knee. Kiyoshi frowned but nodded and climbed into the back to take their suits out of the storage cabinet.

Valentina felt more rested than she had since leaving home, and this despite waking up several times during the night. Always, Kiyoshi was awake beside her, watching the motion detector monitors, looking out the window. At one point, she almost told him about Pete's watcher that lurked in the dark, but was too sleepy to speak out loud.

Kiyoshi watched her seal then test her helmet, only pushing the button next to the door after she'd given him a thumbs-up. The panel light went from green to red; if the air rushing out of the cabin made any sound, she didn't hear it through her helmet. The clang of the door opening she could hear, although just a soft, muffled sound that was incongruous with the effort Kiyoshi made throwing the bolt back and hoisting the door up into the air.

Valentina hopped out after Kiyoshi, limping after him to the back of the rover. While he opened what appeared to be a storage box and began pulling out long hoses with capped-off ends, Valentina went to the side of the station and popped open the panel just to the left of the door. She suspected all the stations had these, although she hadn't noticed them herself until being stranded at the last station had left her so much extra time to poke around. Kiyoshi pulled over the hoses and popped open the caps one by one, jabbing each into its appropriate slot before going on to the next.

Valentina watched the indicator on the panel light up as air and then water began to flow through the hose, but when he plugged the third hose in, nothing happened.

"Is that for fuel?" she asked, peering at the panel.

"Yes. Some of the stations have a little left in their tanks, but most are dry." He recapped the hose and tossed it back into the storage box.

"Do we have enough?"

"We have more than half a tank, and I have a spare tank for emergencies. It's enough."

Ironically, this line of way stations had been a much busier road back when Mars had only a tenth of the population it had now. The polar region had been for scientific endeavors, and this had been a supply line funded by various groups back on Earth. They had worried about every conceivable problem and had built a system with redundancies on top of redundancies. After the plague on Earth and the exodus of refugees to all livable habitats in the Solar System, the people on Mars had stayed close to wherever they ended up calling home. When the first rovers finally ventured out after the plague had run its course, they found stations overstocked with fuel. What had been enough to keep the supply line running for a year was going to last their current more modest needs for decades.

Of course, that had been decades ago. Now the stores were nearly gone. Valentina knew that in the corporate domes everything was powered by electricity, so only remote regions like the north pole still used fossil fuel. But still... "I'm surprised no one has ever tried to take over a way station and sell its fuel and water and air."

"Some have," Kiyoshi said, detaching his hoses and quickly capping the ends. "The merchants don't stand for it. They're more organized than you might think."

Valentina was tempted to go inside and take a look at the wall, but in the rover a downed station or even two wasn't so dire, so being forewarned wasn't really necessarily. Once they were back underway and had restored enough air to remove their helmets, she did take out her map and X the two stations they'd passed in the night, as well as the one that was disappearing behind them now.

"We're almost at the end of the line," Valentina said, tracing the route with her fingertip. "Just two more stations." *Then what?* she wondered.

The rover cabin warmed up more during the daytime than it had at night, the dim polar sun making itself felt through the large windscreen. Valentina untied the shirt from her knee and then shimmied out of her suit.

"Let me take a look at that," Kiyoshi said, climbing into the back and taking the suit from her. "Keep an eye on where we're going. The rover drives around obstacles that jut up, but it doesn't see the fissures in the ice itself."

"We're on the trail; isn't it safe?"

"It should be, but I like to be sure."

Valentina climbed over to the driver's seat and looked over the monitors, figuring out what each did so she knew what to watch. She could get used to this; it was so much easier than bounding over the ice.

Kiyoshi opened and closed drawers, then settled to the floor with her suit draped over his crossed legs. He had taken off his own suit and rolled up the sleeves of his red flannel shirt. She could see shiny spots on his hands, little ones on his knuckles and one larger area on the back of his left hand, scars from burns and cuts accumulated over years of sticking his hands into hot and sometimes still running machines.

Valentina made another sweep of the monitors, but there was nothing to see but ice. She put her foot up on the dashboard and slowly rolled down her stocking, then pulled up the leg of her thermal underwear. Her knee was looking better, the blackish-purple bruising slowly fading to a greenish yellow, but she was more worried by what she couldn't see. That snapping feeling: something inside had torn apart, and she wasn't sure it was mending. The bones weren't broken. She had groped it enough to know that all felt normal, but something definitely wasn't right.

Kiyoshi glanced up from his work and looked at her poking at her knee.

"Do you want to wrap that?"

"Will it help?" Valentina asked. He shrugged, but opened another drawer and handed her a long strip of stretchy, flesh-colored cloth. She looked at it, then at her knee. "How do I do this? Over my clothes?"

"I think under."

Valentina wrapped her knee as tightly as she could, tying the ends snugly. The underwear wouldn't go over it, so she left it pushed up just over the bandage. The stocking stretched over it, just barely.

"I hope all this sitting around helps it heal," Valentina said, looking over the monitors again.

Kiyoshi turned her suit around on his lap. He had a shiny patch that he was carefully attaching to the suit with an adhesive. He kept picking the suit up to make sure the material still moved without catching at the patch so it wouldn't just tear again.

"Is that going to hold?" Valentina asked.

"This adhesive is just to hold the patch in place until I have it where I want it. Then I heat-seal it. That will hold."

Valentina watched him work, his hands hypnotic in their tiny motions. The patch looked nicer than the suit it was repairing. Kiyoshi wasn't the most talkative of companions, but Valentina found she didn't mind. Just having someone else nearby was enough. She still ached for her brother—her constant companion from the moment of his birth until just days ago—but at least she wasn't alone anymore.

They passed the next station before noon without stopping. Valentina stayed at the controls while Kiyoshi made an immense lunch of ramen with seaweed, jerky, and reconstituted eggs stirred in. The bowl he handed her was so large she felt her stomach would burst, and when she was done eating, she curled back up in the passenger seat and fell into a nap so deep it was like a coma.

When she awoke, the sun was low in the sky to her right and directly ahead was the starry shine of the station light. The station itself was sitting box-like on the ice, but around it were other dome-shaped structures that appeared to be made of ice.

"Igloos?" Valentina said, rubbing the sleep from her eyes.

"Readibuilt domes, like they have all over the plains of Mars," Kiyoshi said. "They just cover the outside with ice for extra protection. And aesthetics, I think."

"It does look cool," Valentina said.

Kiyoshi pulled the rover up to the station and turned off the engine. While they suited up, they could see people emerging from the domes and walking toward them.

"They're friendly, right?" Valentina asked, hating how nervous people made her. That never used to be true.

"Yes, it's a village. There is an airstrip here. It's kind of like a port back on Earth, a place where all travelers pass through and exchange cargo. My aunt lives here," Kiyoshi said.

"I didn't know you had an aunt," Valentina said.

"My mother's sister. I've never met her. She hasn't seen my mom since they were in their teens, but they exchange messages. This is where I was heading, to put the word out in a bigger way that we were looking for you." He gave her a hesitant little smile. "Not necessary now."

They put on their helmets and unsealed the rover cabin, hopping down onto the ice. The sun was nearly gone, but the station light glinted off every surface.

"Hey, strangers," the nearest local said with a gruff friendliness. Valentina wished she could see if his eyes matched his tone, but the face screen of his helmet was tinted. That was probably handy during the dazzlingly bright days, but it totally obscured his face now that it was getting dark. "Anything to trade?" he asked. The question wasn't surprising, since they had approached speaking Spanish, the language of traders.

"Not this time," Kiyoshi said. "I'm looking for Suki Kanayurak."

"What do you want with Suki?"

"She's my aunt. I have some gifts from my mother, her sister Hanako."

"Kiyoshi?"

"Yes."

"I'm John Kanayurak. Suki's my wife. I guess that makes me your uncle."

"Pleased to meet you," Kiyoshi said, putting out a hand. They clasped forearms and John gave him a friendly slap on the shoulder.

"Come on, this dome is ours," John said. Kiyoshi turned back to the rover and unlatched one of the cargo boxes, then followed his uncle across the ice to the furthest dome. Valentina trailed along behind. The other people disappeared back into their domes.

John led them down the steps to where the airlock was nestled deep in the glacial ice. The door swung out on hinges, and once they were crowded inside, he sealed it behind them by turning a large wheel set in the middle of the door. Totally mechanical, and yet once it was closed, air began to fill the tiny space. Someone was watching.

"Who's your friend?" John asked as they waited for the atmosphere to normalize.

"Valentina del Toro," Valentina said. "I'm sort of related to Kiyoshi too."

"You both came down from the north pole? Kind of early in the season for that trip. You got real lucky with the weather."

"It's kind of an emergency for me," Valentina said.

The inner door swung open, and a woman poked her head around to see them. She was short, just like Hanako, but slender where her sister was stout. Her smile of welcome brightened several degrees when they took their helmets off and she seemed to recognize Kiyoshi, even though they had never met. She rushed forward to hug him, but the rush of Japanese was lost on Valentina. She knew a few phrases, but that was all. John caught her eye and winked; she didn't think he followed it either.

At last, Suki's excitement settled back into a warm happiness and she turned her attention to Valentina.

"You are one of don Abuelo's grandchildren?" she guessed. "You have the look."

"Yes, he was my mother's father," she said. "I didn't know there was a look."

"Don Abuelo looked like an Aztec mural come to life," Suki said. "You can always tell his progeny. They have the same fierce nobility in their features."

"I didn't know my grandfather was so famous," Valentina said.

"King of the north pole," John said. "Are you kids hungry?"

Before Valentina could answer, her stomach spoke first with a loud growl.

"That's a definite yes," Suki said. "Please, make yourselves at home. John will help you with your suits."

Valentina looked around while struggling out of her suit. The entire inside of the dome was one large room, the space above filled with racks for storing crates and sacks up out of the way. The round floor was broken into four quadrants, one for cooking where Suki was pulling things from a microwave and setting them on the table so close behind her she didn't even need to take a step to reach it. The next quadrant was sunk further into the ground, a seating area shaped like a pie wedge with a triangular table in the center covered with computer tablets, some sort of electronic device in the midst of repair, and a pile of yarn topped with the beginnings of a sweater on a long circular needle. Next to that was a bed with a storage chest at the foot and tall lockers to either side, and finally was the space where they stood hooking their air tanks up to the refiller in the wall. The only rooms not in the circle of the dome were the airlock, and the similarly sized bathroom just next to it.

It was cozy. It felt like a home.

Suki beckoned them over to the table and proceeded to stuff them with pasta in red sauce, pasta in green sauce, and pasta in rich white sauce.

"What is in this?" Valentina asked as she sampled each. It was amazing, but completely unlike anything she'd had before.

"I have a friend with a farming dome in the plains and she makes the sauces out of her produce," Suki said. "The recipes change depending on what she's growing. I like to guess, but I never know for sure. Except for the white sauce, that's cheese and cream."

"Cheese and cream?" Valentina repeated. Cheese she'd had, having once kept a goat. It hadn't tasted anything like this. And cream…

"She has two cows," Suki said.

"Wow," Valentina said. "I didn't think there were any cows on Mars."

"Not many," Suki said. "They require a lot of feeding."

"This is the most fantastic thing I've ever eaten," Valentina said, and Suki smiled.

When the food was gone, Kiyoshi opened the cargo box he'd brought along and presented Suki with his mother's gifts: small items like carved figurines that didn't look like much to Valentina but must have been of personal significance to Suki, to judge by how she cooed over them. She went back to speaking Japanese. Valentina blinked sleepily.

"Let me get you a blanket," John said. "You can bed down in the sitting nook."

The cushioned benches were wide and comfortable after the last night of sleeping sitting up in the rover. She rolled into the thick blanket, pulling it like a hood over her head to block out the light from the kitchen, and was nearly asleep when the chatter in Japanese died out.

"What are your plans?" John asked and Valentina pricked up, curious to know the answer to that herself.

"Valentina has to get to her brother in one of the corporate domes in Valles Marineris," Kiyoshi said.

"That's a long journey," John said in a neutral voice.

"She walked most of the way here, before I caught up with her. I think she'd walk the whole way if she had to."

"Well, I'm guessing that if you wanted to go by shuttle, you'd've taken that out of the north pole in the first place," John said. "The airships don't come this far north until much later in the spring. The weather is just too iffy."

"Can my rover make it?" Kiyoshi asked.

"There is a road that leads off the glacier, but it doesn't see much traffic. I'm not sure if it's still navigable; no one has come up it in the last few years. The ice kept cracking and sliding off, every year leaving a narrower road, so we stopped using it. Who knows what condition it's in now?"

"I think we'll have to at least try it," Kiyoshi said.

"You're doing this because she's family?"

Kiyoshi made a sound that wasn't any answer at all. Perhaps there was a gesture which conveyed more meaning, but whatever the reason, John didn't push the point.

"You're a good boy," Suki said.

"Her mother just died a few weeks ago. She was sick right after, bad sick. That's why her father came from one of the equatorial cities, to bring her medicine. He was going to stay until she was well, but they needed him back in the city. I told him about her brother Arturo getting mixed up with the dons and he decided to take the boy back with him. Valentina woke up to find him gone. Hence all this."

"Her brother is in one of the gangs?" Suki asked. "Your mother barely mentions such things, but I know her. She's worried about what's happening at the north pole. Things have been getting bad since don Abuelo died, haven't they?"

"Yeah," Kiyoshi said. "Fights in the streets, stuff that used to be kept discreet happening out in the open. Before Valentina got sick, there was a big gang war. They were in the marketplace, up and down all the caverns, fighting each other with knives and projectiles. Arturo was too close to one of the fights. I don't think he was involved, but he has cousins in the Poltec Cartel and he might have been talking with one of them when the fight went down. I never got the whole story from him. But he disappeared, and Valentina heard about the fight and that the Nortes had taken Poltecs hostage, and rumors were wild with what they were intending to do with them. Arturo might have gone with his cousins to safety with the other Poltecs, or he might have been taken by the Nortes. Valentina went to both drug lords and demanded an audience, making it clear to everyone that her brother was not a sworn member of any group. She was… fierce."

"That could have been dangerous," Suki said. "Those people take offense at the smallest things."

"She recited her lineage," Kiyoshi said. "Her father's and don Abuelo's both. Like where those two worlds intersected was something not to be touched. But I think mostly they were impressed by her fearless-ness. The don of the Nortes even tried to recruit her."

Valentina was stunned. She'd had no idea that Kiyoshi had even known about any of that, and he talked about it as if he'd been there. Except she had been the furthest thing from fearless. She had gone, assuming everyone she dealt with would be like her cousins, rabble-rousing punks she could quell with a look or at most a few well-chosen words. She hadn't expected to be standing in front of men more like her don Abuelo, not just older but radiating power. It was very hard not to do as they wished when they spoke an order. Reciting her lineage had been to give herself the courage to stand and demand to be heard for the sake of her brother.

"How old is the boy?" John asked.

"Twelve, I think."

"If they didn't know who he was before, they do now," Suki said. "Her lineage is his lineage."

"What do you mean?" Kiyoshi asked.

"Having a descendant of don Abuelo in your group is a bonus," Suki said, "but having a link to the people inside the science station—that's the real reason they tried to recruit your friend. It's for the best that her father took the boy away."

"The people in the science station closed their doors more than a decade ago," Kiyoshi said. "We know they're still in there—Valentina's father's shuttle landed on their platform and entered the caverns through the station—but they won't come out or even speak with the rest of us since don Abuelo died."

"But perhaps they would for one of their own," Suki said. "And if the gangs could get inside the station, they could control life support. They could control everything."

A silence fell over the dome, and Valentina bit her lip. She hadn't thought about why the don of the Nortes had made his offer. When she turned him down, she had said she was just a farmer, and he had let it go. She had assumed he had only been joking in the first place. Now she almost agreed with Suki that Arturo was better off far from their reach.

Almost. She was sure that even in the corporate domes, there were cartels. There were always traps for kids with too much time and not enough money. The first things they asked you to do always seemed so reasonable. She had watched cousin after cousin get lured in, then turn around and lure their younger siblings in. She wanted better for Arturo.

And she couldn't trust her father to give it to him. If he wasn't watching closely enough, anything could happen. She had looked out for Arturo so carefully, but just one time sending him on an errand to the marketplace and she had nearly lost him in that knife fight. Where was he now? How could she ever know he was safe if she couldn't see him?

Kiyoshi settled on the bench across the triangular table from her and Suki and John put out the lights and climbed into their own bed, but it was hours and hours before Valentina's mind exhausted itself and she fell into a restless sleep filled with dreams where she hunted and hunted for her brother but never found him.

CHAPTER EIGHT

OFF THE ICE CAP

Kiyoshi and Valentina were back in the rover at dawn, heading south beyond the last station. Neither had talked about where they were going; they had just said farewell to Kiyoshi's aunt and uncle, topped off the rover's tanks, and left.

The morning passed the same as any other, although Kiyoshi was, if anything, talking less than usual. Valentina felt like they were both holding their breath. Shortly after noon, they had their first hint of something different in the landscape. The snow ahead of them was occasionally dancing up into the air. The wind tended to blow it around all over the ice cap, but there was something different about this particular pattern of upthrust. Kiyoshi slowed as they drew closer and Valentina began to realize she was seeing two different layers of icy landscape, one overlapping the other.

Kiyoshi slowed to a crawl, then stopped entirely, the treads a few meters away from the edge of a vast canyon. They had reached it not head on but at a 45-degree angle, the canyon plunging deep into the ice cap to their left and behind them, but opening out onto a vast plain before them and to the right.

"We're so high," Valentina said, her voice barely a whisper. "It goes on forever."

"It's bigger than the ice cap," Kiyoshi said. "It's going to take twice as long to cross."

"Are there way stations?" Valentina asked.

"I don't think so."

"I guess that's why everyone goes by air," Valentina said. "Or maybe the other way around: there aren't any way stations because everyone goes by air. It's so huge."

"I have solar panels," Kiyoshi said. "It will keep us moving, if more slowly than burning fuel."

"Is there enough food?"

"If we're frugal."

He started the rover moving again, this time crawling along the edge, looking for a way down. Kiyoshi's rover was small compared to most since he hadn't made any space for cargo, and Valentina remembered that this line of stations had originally been for massive supply haulers heading for the north pole. There had to be a road down, if a little disused.

"There!" she cried when she saw it, needlessly, as Kiyoshi was already driving for it. It was wide and not too steep. "It must zigzag back and forth like a staircase," she guessed.

"Switchbacks," Kiyoshi said as he eased the rover along, all of his attention on the road ahead of them.

"The turns can't be too hairpin, considering the size of the haulers they would have been built for."

Kiyoshi didn't answer, just kept watching the road ahead of them. Valentina glanced at the GPS from time to time, but mostly she was absorbed by the view of the plains spread out before them. She had seen pictures of such things, of course, but having lived her life inside a network of caves, she supposed she could be forgiven for being blown away by the real thing.

The first turn was indeed wide and roomy, and Kiyoshi managed it handily. Driving on the ice cap hadn't required him to make any sharp turns, but navigating his rover out of the machine shop, through the airlock, and up the ramp to the surface would have called for tighter navigation than this. Valentina had seen more than one rover brush up against the cave walls on the way out.

Valentina watched the road they had just driven on disappear from view, becoming indistinguishable from the canyon wall towering above them as they continued to descend.

The next two turns and the long stretches of road between were uneventful, but then they reached a place where the edge of the road had crumbled away, fissures in the ice stretching further still across the roadway.

"Is it safe to cross?" Valentina asked.

"I'll get closer to the wall," Kiyoshi said. His voice was as deeply calm as ever, but Valentina saw the way his hands on the controls were clenched, the muscles in his forearms standing out. He was nervous but trying not to show it. Valentina bit her lip and vowed to do the same. They crept along, close enough to scrape clouds of ice from the wall. If the ice beneath them gave any crack or groan of protest, they couldn't hear it from inside the cabin. With them both holding their breath, the only sound at all was the soft hiss of the air vent, the hum of the heater.

Then they were past the damage, back on solid road, and they resumed breathing at once. Valentina gave a nervous laugh.

As the day wore on, they saw more signs of wear, chunks missing from the edge of the road. In a few places, the road narrowed to leave just enough space for the rover to squeak by as before, but Valentina worried about what was still to come. It would only take one spot of damaged road too narrow to pass to stop them completely.

Then the sun seemed to go out all at once. Valentina leaned forward to look past Kiyoshi. The sun was hours away from setting, but it had disappeared beyond the canyon wall, and the road ahead, deeper in the canyon, was darker still.

Kiyoshi stopped the rover and killed the engine.

"Too dangerous to try this in the dark," Valentina guessed. "What do you think caused the damage? It looks like cannonballs or something."

"Avalanches," Kiyoshi said, and Valentina fought the urge to look up at the wall looming over them.

It was a long, sleepless night filled with visions of death falling from the sky in the form of ice boulders, or more simply, the road beneath them shearing away and dropping them into the canyon.

They had stopped facing southeast, so the first rays of the sun woke them both up at dawn. Kiyoshi made rice with reconstituted freeze-dried seaweed for both of them. Valentina doubted she would ever again take the feel of warm food in her belly for granted. After they had cleaned up, Kiyoshi judged it light enough to continue the journey.

Valentina tried to guess from looking at the opposite wall of the canyon how far down they'd come the previous day, and she figured it was about a third of the way down. Considering their late start, she hoped that meant they would be well out of avalanche range before stopping for the night.

They hadn't been rolling for even an hour when they reached another damaged section of road.

"Do you think the same avalanche did all this?" Valentina asked, trying to look up the cliff wall. She couldn't make out any details. It was all just ice from here.

"Maybe," Kiyoshi said as he slowed to a crawl and hugged the wall. Valentina watched the spray of chipped ice flying off from the caterpillar tracks, the wall itself only centimeters from her face pressed to the glass of the side window. Then there was a lurch, and she grabbed her seat. Kiyoshi's hands tightened even more on the controls, but neither of them said anything. There was nothing to be said, really. Kiyoshi kept them moving and she could feel them climbing out of whatever sinkhole they'd just made in the road.

They rolled on a few meters further when the rover lurched again and this time Valentina did yelp out loud. They were sliding downhill, slowly but increasing speed. Kiyoshi gunned the engine, trying to climb out of the deepening hole before it was too late, when everything beneath them fell away. They were tumbling, the heavier back end going down faster, tipping the front end up into the sky to give the two of them a view of the road they'd already traveled and the sky beyond.

Then they hit something, hard, and bounced away, falling sideways now. Valentina clung to her seat to keep from falling into Kiyoshi.

Kiyoshi was looking out his side window at whatever was rushing up to meet them.

They impacted again, and Valentina tasted blood in her mouth. Then they were still.

"Are we still on the road?" Valentina asked as the whirl of disturbed snow and newly fragmented ice blew all around them.

"Yes," Kiyoshi said. "We fell to the next switchback."

"I bit my tongue," Valentina said, touching the tip of it to her palm and looking at the blood streaked there.

"We're facing the wrong way," Kiyoshi said, twisting in his seat.

"You mean we have to drive backwards?" Valentina said, too close to a shriek in her own ears. She took a calming breath.

"Just until the next turn. I'll back into the turn and then go forward down the next stretch of road."

"But what if there's another landslide?"

Kiyoshi looked at her, his dark eyes inscrutable. Then she knew.

"It doesn't matter, does it? We can't go back."

"The whole road went down with us," Kiyoshi said. "In a sled with a fast-enough engine, I might be able to jump the gap, but not in this rover."

"Could we cross it on foot?"

"We don't have enough tanks to carry the air to get us back to the last station. It's too far."

Valentina nodded, wiped her mouth, saw more blood on the back of her hand. Kiyoshi reached into a pocket and handed her a handkerchief. She nodded her thanks, briefly cleaning up her face before using it to staunch the flow from her tongue.

Kiyoshi adjusted his monitors, then started the rover at a crawl. He couldn't see where they were going. He had to trust the monitors. The rover lurched and whined as it rolled over the bits of road that had fallen around them. Valentina had stopped her bleeding long before they reached the end of the turn and Kiyoshi could put the rover back into a forward gear.

Valentina didn't realize she had dozed off until the rover drew to another halt, waking her. She felt terribly guilty, like she had abandoned Kiyoshi by leaving him to deal with all of it without her being there, even for moral support. The sun was nearly at the edge of the canyon, about to disappear from view even earlier now that they were so far down into the chasm. But they were nearly at the bottom, she realized as she looked around. Maybe two or three more switchbacks...

Then she realized why he had stopped. There was no road before them. It had been sheared away and didn't resume for another five rover lengths.

She looked at Kiyoshi, who was looking out his side window.

"Can't jump it?" she said, but he didn't bother to answer.

"It's not so steep," he said at last. "Or not as steep. I think we can make it."

Valentina didn't say anything. She had never been so sure in her life that a plan wasn't going to work, but what good would it do to say so? There was no other plan. They couldn't go back, couldn't get out and walk. They could possibly try waiting for a rescue; someone passing overhead just might see them trapped here.

But probably not. They were very near the bottom and Valentina was sure no ship aiming to land at the last way station would fly so low. In any case, she didn't think she could stand waiting.

"Let's go then," Valentina said, trying to sound bold and confident. "I'd like to be well away from these walls before dinner."

"Can't argue with that," Kiyoshi said, and there was a twitch to his mouth that might almost have been a grin. Then he gunned the engine, backing them up a few lengths to a more likely appearing area. "Fasten your restraint. I don't want you biting your tongue again," he said, fishing a five-point harness out from under his seat and locking it into buckles built into the seat. Valentina leaned forward and dug under her seat until she found her own harness. She snapped all the buckles, then pulled the belts tight. It was as if the rover itself were hugging her. It was almost comforting.

Then Kiyoshi started the rover rolling over the edge, and that feeling of comfort fled. She clung to her restraints as the front end tipped down, giving them far too good of a view of the valley below, and willed herself not to scream. The heavier back end seemed to hover behind them for a long instant, torn between pitching forward and tumbling them end over end down the slope and settling down behind them to keep them level. It opted for the latter with a hearty crash.

The treads didn't have much luck finding traction, and they slid more than drove down the slope, the back end of the rover sliding first to the left and then to the right. Kiyoshi's hands on the controls were jerked around, but he kept his grip, guiding them down the slope that grew gentler as they approached the bottom. He didn't even bother trying to direct them onto the next switchback when they reached it, just kept barreling down the side of the canyon, picking up speed as they went.

By the time they reached the bottom and sped away across the flat plain of Vastitas Borealis, Valentina was whooping aloud, thrusting a fist into the air and slapping Kiyoshi on the shoulder.

Nothing ahead of them could possibly be as hairy as that. It would all be flat and boring from here.

She told herself that, but she didn't quite believe it.

CHAPTER NINE

BREAKDOWN

Flat and boring indeed. No longer having hidden glacial fissures to worry about, Kiyoshi had been charging along at full speed. They took turns watching the monitors through the night, but nothing showed up that had to be dealt with. And by midmorning the next day, they were beyond the reach of snow and ice. It was still deathly cold outside, but the surface was just sand and rock. Featureless sand and rock.

By the third day Valentina was heartily sick of it, something she would never have thought possible when she lived underground and dreamed of someday seeing the surface beyond a glimpse of ice outside the science station windows of her childhood. But sicker still was the feeling she got when she consulted the GPS and realized just how little of the plain they'd crossed in three days, and how much was left to go.

Then the fuel ran out. Kiyoshi had gone outside to set up the solar panels and Valentina had gone out too, just because once she was suited up there was no reason not to. They had to wait most of a day to store up enough charge to start moving, and once they did get going, it was at only half the speed they had been doing. And they could no longer keep going at night.

Valentina had never had this much time with nothing to do in her life. She had always had younger cousins to watch, farm chores to do, kitchen chores that never ended. It hadn't gotten any easier when her cousins had grown and left home, either. Every day after don Abuelo died was a day when her mother hadn't known where the next meal would come from. She had taken any job she could find, but while she was gone, Valentina did her mother's chores as well as her own. There had never been time enough to get it all done.

And now here she was, doing nothing at all.

Valentina didn't think Kiyoshi had spent an idle moment in his life either, but there was a subtle difference. While she and her mother had always been given work and struggled and failed to find the time, Kiyoshi seemed more used to the idea that time was something you were given and then found a use for. He had little projects he pulled out of the cabinets and fiddled with when Valentina was watching the monitors, but none of them were things that Valentina understood or could help with. She knew nothing about machines or electronics. When Kiyoshi was watching the monitors, she had nothing to do but sit, and it was driving her crazy.

She wasn't sure how she had started doing it, but somewhere along the way she found herself telling Kiyoshi all the stories she'd never told Arturo, the stories her father had told her of the del Toro line but also don Abuelo's stories. The two sets of stories covered the two ways of life prevalent on the north pole, and the more she thought about it, the more she saw how they really reflected each other. Events that happened in her father's stories had affected events in don Abuelo's stories and vice versa, but she had never realized it before.

She started telling the stories again, teasing out the interconnections. Then again, streamlining things, tweaking little turns of phrase until she was more pleased with the results. If she was driving Kiyoshi crazy with her babbling, he never said a word.

By the map in the GPS they were about halfway across the Vastitas Borealis when Valentina noticed they were moving more slowly than before, and the engine noise had a grinding quality she didn't remember noticing before. She looked at Kiyoshi and realized that he had been aware of this for some time. She hadn't been paying attention at the time, but every quiet look or extra glance at a monitor, every morning check of the solar panels before they rolled out became suddenly significant to her.

"Kiyoshi," she said, and he looked at her.

"I think it's the dust. Snow and ice, no problem, but this grit is getting into things. I'd have to take it all apart to be sure."

"It's slowing us down?"

"Measurably," Kiyoshi said with a deep frown.

"Will we make it to civilization first?"

"I don't know," he admitted. "My GPS points out landmarks but not settlements. This far south, I don't know where people even are."

"The corporate cities are along Valles Marineris," Valentina said. "But there are people all over Tharsis."

"If they are far enough north in Tharsis, then maybe," Kiyoshi said, but he looked grim.

Now that she had noticed the slowness, it was almost as if the rover gave up the effort of trying to hide its growing sickness. By the third day it was crawling along at a speed Valentina could beat bounding in her space suit, if only she could carry enough air with her to keep it up. Kiyoshi's rover had a radio distress beacon, and he turned it on. It sent out its signals day and night, but they never saw a hint of another person.

By the sixth day, they were barely moving along at all. Kiyoshi was busy in the cabin with schematic drawings spread everywhere, trying to suss out what was causing the problem. Valentina had combed out her filthy hair, thinking longingly of that last shower and wishing she had savored it more, and was rebraiding it when a blur of movement caught the corner of her eye.

"Did you see that?" she cried, leaning forward to peer out the window toward the left of the rover.

Kiyoshi's head appeared between the two seats and he frowned. "It looks like it's going to storm."

Valentina noticed the darkening skies and realized he was right, but she ignored that fact, jabbing her finger in the direction she had seen it. "There was something in the sky. Big."

"The wind is picking up. It could have just been debris blowing before the storm."

"I don't think so. I didn't get a good look at it, but its motion was so… deliberate."

Kiyoshi frowned in thought. "It doesn't hurt to turn the rover that way and see if there's anything there," he said at last, and Valentina hopped into the driver's seat to do just that. She eased the rover to the left, but although the sand and rock here were the same as anywhere, the motor added a whine to its rattle, and the rattle grew louder as if to drown the whine out.

"That doesn't sound good," Valentina said, looking back over her shoulder. Kiyoshi was still, listening, but there was alarm in his eyes.

"We'd better suit up," he said.

"You have to go out for repairs?" Valentina asked as she took the suit he handed her.

"No, I don't think this is fixable. The life support just stopped. The air isn't flowing through the vent."

"But suit up? How can we walk?" Valentina asked, or started to. The rover lurched, limped a few more meters forward, then lurched again. This time, it stopped. "Kiyoshi?"

"I don't know what's wrong. But no answer is going to come to me in the next few minutes if it didn't come to me in the last few days of worrying about it. We have to walk."

Valentina dressed, then climbed into the back of the cabin. Kiyoshi took two packs out of a cabinet and filled them with the rest of the food from the storage box.

"With both tanks full on my suit I can walk for a day, but no more," Valentina said, taking the pack he handed her.

"I'm sure that's my range as well," Kiyoshi said.

"We haven't seen any signs of habitation since we left the ice cap," she went on. "What are we going to find?"

Kiyoshi looked at the helmet in his hands, then reached out, clasping the nape of her neck and touching his forehead to hers. He didn't say a word, and his eyes were scrunched tight, but she knew what he was thinking. Walking on was their only hope, but it would likely only buy them another day and a lonely death somewhere out in the storm. Valentina reached up and squeezed his wrist. It was so strange that they had known each other all their lives and yet hadn't really, not until the last few days. But just standing like that, foreheads touching, quieted her rising panic even if just for that moment.

They stepped away from each other and put on their helmets.

"Do you have a rope?" Valentina asked suddenly as Kiyoshi was about to open the hatch.

"Rope?"

"The storm is blowing in. I don't want us to lose each other."

"Right." Kiyoshi opened a few drawers, then pulled out a long coil of nylon rope, thin but strong. He gave one end to Valentina and tied the other around his own waist. When she had finished her knot, he opened the door and Mars blew in, filling the cabin with a whirlwind of dirt in the blink of an eye.

Kiyoshi hopped out, and Valentina followed.

"Does your suit have a GPS?" Valentina asked.

Kiyoshi held up his arm, and she saw the small screen on the inside of his forearm. "Where did you see whatever you saw?" he asked.

"The rover's nose was pointing at it just as it died," Valentina said. Kiyoshi looked at the rover, then tapped on his GPS.

"This way, then. Let's find what you saw."

Valentina trudged along behind him, the wind pushing at her first from one direction, then from the other. Her knee was only mildly aching, but the strong yet erratic wind was making her nervous that she would stumble, twist it, reinjure it. If she couldn't walk…

It was impossible to see more than a few meters in the storm. Even Kiyoshi, who was close enough for her to reach up and brush her fingertips down his back, was a blurry image half lost in the background of blowing sand. It was like the ground was opening up beneath her, flying around her and up into the sky, at any moment about to crash back down and bury her. Snow had never been this sinister.

One hour's walk became two, and the storm continued unabated. Valentina wasn't sure if she had been imagining whatever she had seen or if it had been much, much larger than she had thought. She had only gotten a glimpse, something long and reflective, already obscured in the beginnings of the storm. It hadn't been remotely like the shuttles that occasionally visited the polar station—not like the shuttle her father had left on back when she was young, nor like the one he'd taken her brother away in. The shape was all wrong, and if it had been so far away when she had seen it, it must be huge.

Or they'd already walked past it. In the storm, there was no way to be sure.

Another hour or two passed. The gusts of wind were as exhausting and unpredictable as ever, but the dust-filled skies were getting darker. Kiyoshi stopped and turned to her.

"Do you need a break?" he asked.

"No, I'm fine," she said.

"Your limp is getting worse," he said. She wondered how he'd noticed, walking ahead of her as he had been. But then again, her eyes were often on her own feet, concentrating on keeping them moving. He could have been looking back at her without her noticing.

"I don't want to stop," she insisted. "I'm down to half my oxygen. I don't want to waste any of it resting. Either we get somewhere safe and I can rest then or we don't, in which case my knee hardly matters."

Kiyoshi gave a nod and continued leading the way. Valentina went back to focusing on each step. It wasn't long before she couldn't even see her feet anymore. Kiyoshi had a headlamp, for all the good it did him, lighting up a globe of sand blowing around his helmet. But although it wasn't exactly lighting his way, Valentina bet it was comforting all the same. She felt lost and alone in the dark, able to see his light but not be in it.

She stopped looking up at his light, which was the point when she fell behind.

CHAPTER TEN

HAZEL

"Val... ina... val... ntina... Valentina... VALENTINA!"

Valentina didn't see the point of opening her eyes; the world was the same inscrutable blackness with or without her eyelids in the way, so what did it matter? Then her eyelids shone red, and she realized Kiyoshi was looking right at her, his headlamp shining through her faceplate.

"What?" she snapped grumpily, pushing him away so he'd stop blinding her. She was seeing spots now, which at least was more interesting than total blackness.

"Get up!" Kiyoshi commanded, and Valentina saw she was lying on the ground, arm tucked under her helmet like a child going to sleep. She sat up and looked at her air gauge. It was flashing red at her.

"I'm out," she said. The inside of her helmet felt stifling. She wanted to go back to sleep. The spots exploding in her field of vision seemed to take on a different character. Instead of bright memories of Kiyoshi's headlamp, they were dark clouds of ink swelling to consume all the space before her, growing as they reached out to each other, tendrils joining to become one, then growing more, reaching out to others...

"I found something, Valentina," Kiyoshi said, helping her to her feet. "Just a little bit further, OK?"

"Not OK," Valentina mumbled through thick, numb lips, but she let him drag her along on feet that had stopped feeling the cold quite some time ago. She hadn't noticed.

"This way, Valentina," Kiyoshi said. He stopped and pounded on something. Valentina struggled to lift her head, to see what was in his globe of light. It was some sort of wall, the same color as the dust blowing around them. There was a metal door with a top like an arch but no knob, wheel, or panel to open it. Kiyoshi pounded again and Valentina let her head drop back. Too much work to hold it up with the heavy helmet.

Then she was falling forward, and she thought she had stumbled, but Kiyoshi's arms were still around her. He was pulling her inside the now open door, into a little space with a bench on each side and another identical door opposite. An airlock. Kiyoshi helped her sit on one of the benches before turning to pull the door shut behind them. A light in the ceiling came on and Valentina reached up, her fingers numb and stupid but able to find the catch to unseal her helmet on the third try. Kiyoshi's hands rushed towards her as if to stop her, but she brushed them away, throwing her helmet to the ground and letting her head rest on the cold metal wall behind her. There was little air in the room, but there was none left in her suit.

She passed out for a moment or two, coming to again at the sound of Kiyoshi calling her name. Valentina, he kept saying, but only her father had ever actually called her that. Her brother, all her cousins, even her mother always just said "Tina," but she had always preferred her full name.

"I'm OK," she said. It would have sounded more convincing if her tongue hadn't been so thick in her mouth, her eyes so unwilling to open and look at him. Her hand found his shaking her shoulder and gave it a squeeze. "I think your suit has a little more of an air supply than mine," she said.

"I think you have a slow leak somewhere," he said, examining the patch on her knee. "I don't see any place the seam didn't hold."

Valentina grabbed his wrist and turned it over to look at his indicator panels. "You were on red too, if just. It's a very slow leak if there is one. You did good," she said, then closed her eyes again.

After a few more moments, the inside door opened, and a man stood in the doorway looking them over. He was tall and burly, with wide shoulders and his feet planted far apart. He had blond hair that reached past his shoulders and was kept back from his face in a pair of short braids that were tied off in a mass of beads and feathers. His clothes were a chaotic jumble of Chinese canvas shoes, blue jeans, a long Indian kurta, and a sweater-vest of bright colors in an intricate abstract pattern.

"Sorry for the long time to answer, but no one ever knocks at this door. Where the heck did you come from?" he asked. He was speaking English, the common tongue of traders. She had spent enough time in Hanako's place talking with travelers to pick up some of that language, but Kiyoshi, having grown up in the shop, spoke it even better than she.

"The north pole," Kiyoshi answered. "My rover broke down north of here and we had to walk."

"You walked?" The man grabbed Kiyoshi's wrist and looked at the panel for his GPS. "You have our beacon frequency?"

"No," Kiyoshi said.

"It's not likely you did. That's a closely held secret among my clan. But it's even less likely you just found us. There's nothing else out here for thousands of kilometers."

"Valentina saw something in the sky just as the storm was starting. We had nowhere else to go, so we followed that."

The man laughed. "Didn't know what it was, did you?" he guessed.

"No," Valentina admitted. "I thought I must have imagined it. I mean, it seemed so big when I saw it and it took so long to walk here it would have to be immense if it were real."

"Well, it has to be large or it would never get off the ground," the man said. "Perhaps I'll show you later, if I find that I like you." He winked.

"OK," Valentina said with a glance at Kiyoshi.

"My name is Owen Aelita. You've stumbled upon the compound for the entire Aelita clan. Have you heard of us?"

"No," they said together.

"Well, there was a chance that you might, but being polars, probably not. We supply all the outliers in the northern plains."

"Outliers?" Kiyoshi repeated, but this one Valentina knew.

"Families that live alone, outside of the mining communities and corporate domes."

"Just so," said Owen. "With a portable dome and some basic air- and water-producing equipment, anyone can be his or her own master out here where no one cares to be boss."

"We're just passing through, actually," Kiyoshi said. "We're looking for Valentina's brother, who is south at one of the corporate domes."

"And you'd be Valentina?" Owen said to her.

"Valentina del Toro," she said, putting out a hand.

"As in Antonio del Toro? I think we have his name on a wall around here somewhere," Owen said, to her surprise, then turned to Kiyoshi.

"Kiyoshi Willis," he said.

"Pleased to meet you. Now, I don't want you to think us unfriendly. We can see you're in a bad way and storms are our common foe. You're welcome to join us for the evening meal and stay the night, but in the morning when the storm's blown past, you'll have to be moving along. There are a lot of us here to feed and things are tight this early in the spring. I'm sure you understand."

"Of course," Valentina said, but her stomach sank. Thousands of kilometers from anything else, he had said. It seemed they had only pushed back the inevitable by another day.

"You can leave those suits in the locker room here. No one will touch them," Owen said. "There are showers in the back. Help yourself. Food may be precious, but our processors extract water like nobody's business. When you're ready, just step out here and someone will bring you to dinner."

He left them alone, standing somewhat bewildered between two rows of lockers and benches.

"What do we do now?" Valentina said.

"Shower and eat," Kiyoshi said, helping her out of her bulky suit. She felt weak as a newborn animal and collapsed down onto the bench, as if the suit itself had been holding her up.

"And tomorrow?" she persisted.

"They must know that pushing us back out the door on foot is a death sentence. It would make no sense to feed us now if that was all they intended to do."

"But he said—"

"I'm sure what happens next depends on what they think of us after the meal. At minimum, we should be polite, gracious guests. But also look for any opportunity to provide them with something they need."

"We don't have anything."

"We have a rover we can't move, but they might have a use for. Other than that, just our skills."

Valentina tugged at her lip. "You can fix stuff and build stuff. I can just barely read; that's it."

Kiyoshi put his suit in the locker next to the one he'd put Valentina's in, then pulled off his sweater and the first of his shirts. "Just keep it in mind and watch for opportunities. I'm going to shower first."

Valentina nodded, doubtful she could even stand up yet. But when she shut her eyes, she found she wasn't sleepy, or at least not sleepy enough to overcome her rapidly working mind. She sat back up and rolled off her stockings to look at her feet.

The warmth of the room had made her toes hot and itchy, which meant they weren't dead, but they didn't look good. She had bright red patches, grayish patches, and even a disgusting shade of yellow, and the nails were looking like they'd prefer to drop off on their own. She wiggled each in turn and they responded reluctantly. The backs of her heels were looking blistered as well, although whether those were from cold or rubbing in the ill-fitting boots, she couldn't say. Probably both. Too many days sitting in the rover had really softened her up.

Kiyoshi came out of the shower with a bulky, colorless, homespun towel wrapped around his hips and brought his clothes to the sink to wash them as well. Valentina went into the shower. It was a large space; she counted twelve showerheads equally spaced around all four walls. She went to the corner farthest from the door, stopping just short of the puddle from Kiyoshi's shower, and took off her layers of clothes, leaving them in a neatly folded pile before stepping under the showerhead and turning on the deliciously hot water.

There was a jar of soap on a ledge between her shower space and the next, and Valentina dug her hand in, releasing the scent of honey and just a hint of lavender. Valentina washed her hair three times before it felt properly clean, then wrapped herself up in one of the towels of rough homespun cotton, gathered up her clothes, and padded out of the shower.

Kiyoshi was wearing his spare set of clothes, loose-fitting drawstring pants of a deep navy blue with a long-sleeve white T-shirt and a dark green flannel shirt. He had washed his other things, and they were hanging, draped over open locker doors, to dry.

"I'll wait out here," Kiyoshi said and ducked outside so she could dress.

Valentina had no other clothes, but if the rest of the compound was as warm as the locker room, she could get by on just one skirt and shirt and wash the rest. At least it was something.

Finally, Valentina stepped out of the locker room. Kiyoshi was nearby but didn't notice her approaching, engrossed as he was in whatever the blond girl in front of him was saying. The girl was short and thin, but with her arms moving constantly as she talked and her hair standing out from her head in two thick braided ponytails like fuzzy antennae, she seemed to take up more than her share of space. She was dressed even more chaotically than Owen, if such was possible. Bright pink stretch pants hung loosely on her bony legs, possibly hand-me-downs from a larger person, on top of that a skirt of different but matching calico patterns sewn together in irregular patches. She had at least three scarves tied around her waist, one wide and trimmed with decorative coins, the others thinner and more belt-like save for their long tasseled ends. The coins weren't the only thing on her making noise as she gestured and talked: she wore several chunky necklaces and her arms were covered with bangles of metal, plastic, and wood that rattled together when her hands moved, which was constantly. Her feet, like Valentina's, were bare and incredibly dirty, bright pink toenails still gleaming through the brown dust.

She was gabbing away about food, what dishes were going to be served, and who made them, constantly circling back to her own mastery of flatbread and how he had to be sure to try all four varieties she had prepared. Kiyoshi nodded, not bothering to try to get a word in himself, and flinched ever so slightly every time the girl touched his arm while she talked, which was a lot.

"Hello," Valentina said when it became clear neither was going to notice her.

"Hey!" the girl said. "Ain't you cold?"

"I've been colder," Valentina said, wrapping her arms around herself. Realizing that her gesture could be construed as being cold when she'd just implied she wasn't rather than simply trying to hide herself from view, she forced her arms back down to her sides.

"If you say so. Hungry?"

Valentina nodded. She could smell food cooking—meat and bread, for sure, and spicy things as well.

"Your timing couldn't be better to just drop in," the girl went on as she led them both down a hallway that sloped down. "We don't usually have clan-wide feasts, but with all the balloons in, it's a bit of a party."

"Balloons?" Valentina repeated. Had that been what she had seen?

"Geez, don't you even know who you dropped in on? We're the Aelitas. Everyone knows we're the balloon clan."

"This is Hazel," Kiyoshi said, as the girl seemed unlikely to introduce herself again. "Hazel, this is Valentina."

Hazel looked at Valentina long enough to give her a slight uplift to her chin that Valentina guessed meant hello. Then her attention was back to Kiyoshi. "What's a polar dweller doing walking across the plains, anyway?"

"We're heading south to find Valentina's brother," he said. "My rover broke down just north of here."

"You drove a rover all the way here from the north pole? I don't think I've seen that done before," Hazel said. "Air travel, that's the way to go."

"We didn't have that option," Kiyoshi said. There was a sudden burst of discordant music, like several musicians tuning up at once by playing snatches of different songs, and a squeal of children at play.

"Come on," Hazel said, breaking into a run. Kiyoshi and Valentina traded a glance, and he reached out to give her hand a quick squeeze. She smiled back; they could do this. They would figure out a way to make these people like them enough to help them.

CHAPTER ELEVEN

FLATBREAD AND FAMILY

Valentina noticed again how dirty Hazel's feet were—as she ran, the bottoms flashing at them were almost black—just as she realized why. The hallway ended in a doorway and beyond it was the same rocky soil they had been rolling over for days. But they weren't outside; the air was breathable and there was no sign of the storm. They were under a dome, a massive dome that contained an entire village of people.

They were emerging from a sort of gatehouse set in the wall that ran around everything in a great circle. Opposite them was a similar but larger gatehouse, like the wall and the building behind them built from large blocks of rock the same color as the ground. Scattered all around the space between were less sturdy-looking structures, only brightly colored canvas draped over aluminum frames like festive tents.

Valentina had been in bigger places—the marketplace back home was a bit larger, the cavern roof vaulting higher than the top of the dome here—but every part of the caverns, caves, and tunnels of her polar home had been filled with people. By comparison, the clan compound was nearly empty. It wasn't like the vast emptiness she had been traveling through for the past few weeks; that had been like passing through an alien space not meant for humans. This felt warm and inviting, just not the tight, close warmth she was used to. It was fantastic.

Hazel was running across luxuriously open space, past a gaggle of children involved in some sort of game that involved balls, disks that stacked like round pyramids, and hoops laid in the dust. The tents divided the space under the dome into an outer ring and an inner circle. Behind the tents she could see corrals filled with goats looking her way, a few chicken runs, and even a family of fat white geese. On the other side, she could catch glimpses of gardens. The tents all opened up into the central space, and before each was either a fire pit or the dome shape of a clay oven. All were smoking away, the air filled with the smell of fat dripping from goat meat onto hot coils, bread baking on the walls of the ovens until golden brown. Valentina's stomach growled, embarrassingly loudly.

Hazel stopped where the adults were laying large woven blankets on the ground and covering them with dish after dish of food. Valentina tried to make a head count and guessed there were maybe fifty people living here. Fifty people in a space that back home would hold several hundred, a thousand if they packed into the gatehouses as well. Which they would; on the north pole, no one wasted space. Her farm in the back of don Abuelo's mine was a carefully guarded secret up until the end. Valentina imagined several families were living there now, happy for the change from squatting in one of the hallways, an arbitrary line chalked on the ground defining their home.

She could see the appeal of being an outlier. You lived without the support system of a community, but in return for an investment in a little equipment, you could become a king of your own nearly infinite space. Perhaps she and Arturo could try it. Oh, to have a farm on the surface...

"Come on!" Hazel cried, dancing back to them in a happy jingle and taking Kiyoshi by the hand. Valentina trailed along behind, trying not to laugh at the look of alarm he shot her. "You must meet the others."

This was followed by a flurry of names that blew past Valentina's tired mind. Everyone was blond, most were taller than Hazel, and all wore clothes that reflected the same mishmash of cultures. Valentina nodded and tried to keep smiling, but the long walk that had nearly ended in a slow hypoxic death was catching up with her. She sat down on the edge of one of the blankets and let it all whirl around her. The band started playing music like nothing she had ever heard, rousing numbers that had people up and dancing, then slower numbers that had them all singing songs of joy or sorrow. Most weren't in English; she wasn't sure what language it was.

"Aren't you hungry?" someone asked her. She jumped, realizing she had been dozing off right there on the blanket, then looked up to see a woman of about forty tucking her long broomstick skirt around her legs as she settled down beside Val and put a large tin plate in front of her that was really more of a tray.

"Very," Valentina admitted. "I'm sorry, I know I was just told your name—"

"I'm Adelle. I'm Hazel's sister-in-law," she said with a smile.

"That's right. You're married to the oldest of the five brothers," Valentina remembered. Hazel was the youngest and the only girl. Everyone else was either a wife or child of one of the brothers or a relative the wife had brought with her when she'd come to live under the dome.

"Is there anything you don't eat?" Adelle asked.

"No, I'm an omnivore all the way," Valentina said. Adelle laughed and reached for the nearest bowl. Every time she set something down, another bowl would appear in her hands, passed by some other member of the family, and in no time the tray was overflowing with bread, kebabs, rice, and vegetables.

"Do you grow all this yourself?" Valentina asked, looking around the space under the dome.

"We have a few gardens between the tents and the dome wall, but mostly we're traders. The outliers grow the food."

"It's fantastic," Valentina said, sampling first one spiced dish, then another. Across the wide blanket, Kiyoshi was sitting with Hazel at his side. She had loaded up his plate but was also trying to put food directly in his already full mouth, anxious for him to try everything at once.

"This is the last of our stored food. We always make a feast of it, and we'll be eating the leftovers for days, but once it's gone, we're on freeze-dried rations until the first harvest."

"Thank you for sharing it with us," Valentina said.

"You look like you could use it," Adelle said, reaching over to tuck a stray hair that had escaped from Valentina's braid behind her ear.

"I was worse off before Kiyoshi found me," Valentina said. She knew from the mirror in the locker room that although she no longer had the skeletal look of having lived off half a ration bar a day, her cheeks were still hollow.

"He seems like a good boy," Adelle said, watching Hazel confronting him with a piece of flatbread in each hand, as if demanding which he thought was the best.

"He's sort of a cousin," Valentina said, but Adelle was no longer listening, absorbed instead by the sight of Valentina's bare foot just peeping out from under her skirt. She flipped the skirt out of the way, drawing the foot out onto her own lap to examine it. "My suit's not so good," Valentina said.

"Does it hurt?" Adelle asked, gently probing each gray patch.

"Some. Mostly it itches."

"I have something for this," Adelle said. "Wait here, I'll fetch it."

Valentina tucked her feet back under her, covering them more securely with her skirt. She tore off another piece of bread and used it to scoop up more of the thick lentil paste. She put it in her mouth, savoring the warming quality of the spices—was that ginger?—and saw Kiyoshi sending desperate looks her way. Valentina picked up her plate and carried it around the blanket to sit next to him.

"Isn't it fabulous?" she asked.

"Very good," Kiyoshi said.

"The Aelitas know how to live it up," Hazel said. "More fruit?"

"No, really, I couldn't," Kiyoshi said, but she piled it on his tray, anyway.

"It looks like the storm is clearing," Hazel said, looking up at the dome. Valentina tipped her head back, but it all seemed the same blackness as before. Adelle appeared at her side with something cupped in one hand and an unlabeled tube in the other.

"Take this, for the pain," she said, putting two tablets in Valentina's hand. "It's an anti-inflammatory. It should help with the itching as well."

"What's going on?" Hazel asked.

"My feet got a little nipped," Valentina said. Adelle squirted some cream from the tube on one hand, then held out the other. Valentina reluctantly slipped one foot out from under her skirt.

"Why didn't you say anything?" Kiyoshi asked.

"It's not bad. I'll still have all my toes, I'm sure," Valentina said. "It's just the suit. Even before I tore the knee, it didn't heat down to the feet on either side. I had a nice pair of knit stockings but those were stolen. Without them, the suit really rubs my feet."

Adelle rubbed the cream into Valentina's skin. "I'm going to let you have this tube," she said as she worked. "If you get blisters later, they might rupture, and there is a danger of infection. This has antibiotic in it, be sure to use it."

"Thank you," Valentina said.

"How did you even walk here on those feet?" Hazel asked, almost accusingly. "Adelle, we can't make them walk again." Adelle's lips drew into a tight line, but she said nothing. "Well, I'm going to talk with my father. This is crazy."

Hazel was up and gone before Adelle could call her back. "That girl is so headstrong," she said, mostly to herself. She squeezed more cream into her hand and gestured for Valentina's other foot.

"Can you walk?" Kiyoshi asked, his voice very low.

"I can do whatever I have to do," Valentina said. "If I arrive at my brother's side with bloody stumps for feet, I'll still just be happy to have reached him."

"You're looking for your brother?" Adelle asked, readily jumping on the change of topic.

"Yes, he's in one of the corporate domes off the Valles Marineris," Valentina said.

"That's a long way from the north pole," Adelle said.

"He was taken by shuttle," Valentina said. "My way is considerably slower."

"And you're going with her?" Adelle asked Kiyoshi. "But then I guess he's your cousin."

Kiyoshi's eyebrows shot up at that. He had to think it through. "Yes, I guess he is. Kind of."

"And when you find him, you're taking him back to the north pole?"

"No, I don't know. I don't think so. There is no one left for us there," Valentina said. In truth, her plans had all ended with finding Arturo.

"I have no plans to go back," Kiyoshi said, and it was Valentina's turn to be surprised. "I was going to use my rover to start a transport business, but that's broken down now. Perhaps I'll come back this way and set up my own outlier farm."

"It's a hard life, but rewarding," Adelle said. "What about you? Will you and your brother stick with your cousin?"

Valentina looked down at her scarred feet. She felt almost ashamed for not thinking about what would happen next. She was going to owe Kiyoshi a lot for helping her, more than she likely could ever repay.

"This is nonsense!" Hazel raged as she returned to them.

"You can't be surprised," Adelle said calmly. "We discussed it before we ever opened the door."

"But it's different now," Hazel said with an almost comedic pout.

"Four babies were born last year. Things are tighter than you're used to," Adelle said.

"But we can't just—" Hazel threw her hands up in the air as if that said everything, then dropped down onto the blanket next to Kiyoshi and buried her chin in her hands in a deep brood.

"We understand," Valentina said to Adelle. "You've been more than kind to us already."

"We're not going to push you out into the desert with nothing," she answered. "My husband will give you what supplies we can spare and enough air tanks to take you to the next stop. And definitely a new pair of socks for Valentina."

"What's the next stop?" Kiyoshi asked.

"We'll draw up a map for you. No place on the plains is easy to find if you don't know what you're looking for, but we'll show you where the outlier farms are and radio ahead to let everyone know you're coming. Anyone who can't afford to be charitable on their own we'll promise to reimburse. It'll be slow going and only take you to the edge of Tharsis, but it's all we can do."

"The settlements on Tharsis are closer together, aren't they? The mining towns and then the corporate domes—"

"Yes, once you get to Tharsis, everything will be easier, I'm sure."

"But it's not all we could do," Hazel said, but she fell silent at a hard look from her sister-in-law.

"It's more than we expected," Kiyoshi said. "You have our thanks. And please, my rover broke down only a day's walk from here. You're welcome to retrieve it and do what you will with it as payment. I'm not sure how the sand got into the engine, but I imagine you all have more experience with that than a polar mechanic like me."

"We'll bring it in and see what we can do," Adelle said. "If you ever come back this way, stop in and see us. Perhaps we can make a deal and it will be yours again."

Kiyoshi gave a smile with such relief in it that Valentina realized just how much he had loved that machine he'd poured so many hours into.

The others were gathering up the remaining food, snapping covers onto the bowls, and carrying everything into the larger guardhouse. Kiyoshi and Valentina got up to do their share, bringing several bowls each into a room just inside the building that had an open trapdoor in the floor with stairs leading down into a cold cellar. Valentina put her food on the shelf one of the other women directed her to, then turned and ran back up the steps, the metal burning with cold under her feet. It was almost worth it, that little trip back into the Martian cold, just to feel how divine the heated space under the dome was.

Standing outside the gatehouse, outside the ring of tents, Valentina saw a part of the wall that looked different from the rest; the stone was a smooth, reflective gray rather than sandy brown. She walked over to it, Kiyoshi trailing behind her. It was some sort of memorial marker; the wall looked like it had been built over and around it, as if the memorial had been here first. There was writing on the surface, and Valentina ran her fingers over the letters chipped from the stone.

"What does it say?" Kiyoshi asked.

"It's a memorial for the explorers who started their expeditions from this place long ago. I think this was one of the first landing sites, because these expeditions are going all over. This one went south to Mons Olympus. And here's the one that went to the north pole. There he is: Antonio del Toro."

"So your ancestor does have his name on a wall here," Kiyoshi said, touching the letters himself. Then they heard Hazel's voice calling for them and they turned away from the wall, heading back to the center of the dome.

Back out in the open space, the large flood lights were now out, everything lit but the strings of multicolored lights that adorned the tents, connecting one to the next in a great circle. Adelle found them both and led them into one of the tents. Valentina had expected to find one large space inside, but it was divided with more sheets of canvas forming separate rooms and even little hallways between.

"You can sleep here for the night," she said, pulling back a curtain from a doorway. The room beyond was larger than the cabin of Kiyoshi's rover, an elaborately worked carpet on the floor, blankets neatly folded on top of bolsters set in one corner. "Someone will wake you for breakfast in the morning. It's a long hike to the next farm and you'll want an early start."

"Thank you again—for everything," Valentina said. Adelle smiled and nodded, then let the curtain drop.

Kiyoshi handed her a blanket and a bolster and they bedded down, the sounds of other people doing the same thing all around them muffled somewhat by the canvas walls.

CHAPTER TWELVE

ONWARD BY BALLOON

Valentina was asleep almost at once. But it felt like she was awake again just as quickly. Someone's hand was firmly squeezing her shoulder. She opened her eyes to find Hazel kneeling between her and Kiyoshi, and while she was touching Valentina to wake her, the rest of her attention was on Kiyoshi, who was sitting up. Hazel put a finger to her lips and slipped back out of the room.

Valentina and Kiyoshi exchanged a glance, then crept after her. She was already outside, crossing the dusty open space to the gatehouse they had come in from just a few hours before. Hazel only stopped and turned to them when she reached the locker room.

"What do you say we get out of here now?" Hazel asked, crossing her arms and tipping her head, her ponytails swinging.

"Now?" Valentina asked, but Kiyoshi asked perhaps the more important question: "We?"

"The storm has cleared. We can take a balloon," she said to Valentina, then turned to Kiyoshi and gave him a teasing punch on the arm. "And of course *we,* silly. You two can't pilot a balloon."

"But you can?"

"Of course I can. I've been doing it since I was wee."

Valentina and Kiyoshi looked at each other. It was an amazing offer, so much better than time-consuming and feet-killing walking. And yet sneaking away from the others, leaving hours before dawn…

"Won't you get in trouble?" Kiyoshi asked.

"It's my balloon," Hazel said. "At least, it was supposed to be mine. It was always going to be mine. Then my dad went and made my nephew the captain. My nephew! Totally passed me by. I was promised my own balloon to captain when I turned eighteen, and now thanks to Whedon there's no way I'll get one. Balloons are hard to come by, and he just gets to take the last of the family's? No way."

"How old is your nephew?" Valentina asked, trying to puzzle out this story, which had come out at full volume and double speed.

"OK, he's twenty, and I'm still fifteen. So yes, technically, whatever. But it was supposed to be mine in three years, and now it won't be. So I'm taking it. With or without you, I'm taking it. Do you want a ride or not?"

"It's hard to say no," Kiyoshi said. Judging by Hazel's brilliant grin, she was extracting some other meaning from that phrase than Valentina was. Then she threw her arms around him and hugged him tight.

Valentina didn't say anything. She supposed she would have a similarly convoluted justification for taking don Abuelo's suit if she ever tried speaking one out loud.

"Great!" Hazel said as she let Kiyoshi go. "This is going to be awesome. You guys suit up and go out the airlock. I have to go through the other door, but I'll come around and meet you. Oh, and…" She fished in the pocket of her skirt and struggled to extract a pair of knit socks—a project to finish off a pile of yarn left over from other things, to judge by the erratic collection of a dozen colors. She pushed them into Valentina's hands and then she was gone, running silently back up the hall.

"And we're sure this isn't a trap?" Valentina said, yawning widely.

"Why would she trick us? What reason would she have?"

"You're right," Valentina said, gathering up her now dry clothing and pulling it on. She moved the antibiotic cream from her skirt pocket to the cargo pocket of her suit. "Her motivation is pretty clear."

Kiyoshi didn't answer. Clearly, he wasn't enjoying the attention at all.

Valentina pulled on the socks. They were not as smooth as the machine-knit pair she had lost and they only reached her knees, but they were a warm comfort and their thickness helped keep her feet from sliding around inside the boots of her suit.

The air tanks had been removed from their suits, but Valentina and Kiyoshi quickly found them loaded in a charger just outside the airlock door. When they were both suited up, they cycled through the airlock and stepped outside.

Dawn was too far away for even the beginnings of the sun to show, but the stars seemed brighter, more jewel-like, as if the sandstorm had buffed them clean and restored their luster. The ground was covered in a pattern of eddies, giving it a certain random beauty. Valentina yawned again.

Kiyoshi touched her arm, and she turned to see a short figure in an aqua-blue suit bounding toward them. Valentina wondered how she had gotten her giant twists of hair into that helmet—the helmet that was painted all over with an intricate arabesque of green ivy and dark pink flower buds. Hazel waved them to follow her further along the wall. The ground sloped downhill, then stopped at the edge of a ravine. Hazel dropped out of sight, but it was only after Kiyoshi followed that Valentina saw the staircase: narrow, steep steps that would take some real bounding to ascend.

The bottom of the staircase was a narrow ravine that twisted around a large chunk of harder rock before joining a larger canyon, a canyon that was filled with balloons tethered to the ground with hundreds of ropes.

"This one's mine," Hazel said over the radio, bounding to the one on the end. They all looked the same: massive half-inflated bags of air. It was only as they drew closer that Valentina noticed the gondola sitting on the ground beneath each. They were each about twice the size of Kiyoshi's rover but were dwarfed by comparison to the balloons they were attached to.

"Help me undo the ropes first," Hazel said, running from picket to picket and releasing the hooks that held the ropes to the loops. Kiyoshi and Valentina did the same, working together but in the opposite direction to Hazel. When they met again on the far side, the balloon was free, although being mostly deflated in a now windless night, it didn't do more than stir a bit.

"OK, inside the gondola," Hazel directed. The gondola was tapered front and back like an old Earth sailing ship, with a lower front deck they could jump over. The deck was the first third of the space; the middle third was a glass-walled box that held bins for equipment but clearly mostly functioned as an airlock. Once Hazel had shut the door behind them and pressurized the space, they moved into the last third of the gondola, the pilot's cabin.

"I'm filling the balloon now," Hazel said in an official-sounding voice. "It will take a few minutes before we're underway."

"And if we're caught?" Valentina asked.

"No one knows we're out here," Hazel said, pulling off her helmet and stowing it on a shelf. "Even if they do come out, they'll hardly be surprised that I'm taking my own balloon. And I can always say I kidnapped the two of you and forced you to come with me for company."

"But no one would believe that," Valentina said.

"I can be very convincing," Hazel said and gave Kiyoshi a wink. Valentina only just contained her sigh of exasperation. She hoped the three of them wouldn't be traveling together long. Then she retroactively felt bad for all the babbling she had done back in the rover. Had she annoyed Kiyoshi this much? Had he been silently wishing she'd just stop talking? She looked up at him after they'd taken off their helmets, but could read nothing from his expression.

"You have enough supplies?" Kiyoshi asked, putting his and then Valentina's helmets on the shelf next to Hazel's.

"Sure, should last the three of us for a month, and we could circle the globe in a month. Probably. I've never tried. Well, it'll be enough for where we're going for sure."

"What's down here?" Valentina asked, scuffing the toe of her boot over a trapdoor in the floor.

"That's for cargo," Hazel said. "Runs under the whole gondola, even the deck, although it gets tight at that section. Empty now. I think it was tea last trip."

Valentina opened the door to peek inside. The fragrant aroma of dried leaves wafted up at her. "Yes, definitely tea. I haven't had tea since forever."

"You should've asked last night. I don't have any packed now," Hazel said grumpily.

"She's not complaining," Kiyoshi said. "We're both very grateful to you."

"It's nothing," Hazel said. "I was fixing on leaving, anyway. Now I have some company."

The floor began to shift under them. Valentina dropped the trapdoor in favor of holding on to the doorframe behind her.

"Here we go," Hazel said, turning to the pilot controls. "I'll be gunning the engines as soon as we're out of the canyon. We can keep gaining altitude as we go. You guys can watch from the middle compartment if you want."

The third compartment had small round windows on the three back walls, but nothing like the view the glassed-in compartment could offer. Kiyoshi went out first, and Valentina reluctantly followed.

They were already several meters off the ground, but the canyon was deep, deep enough to hide the enormous balloons. They rose slowly into the air, only occasionally jostling back and forth when something decided to settle.

"Does it always move this much?" Valentina asked.

"Are you kidding me? We're going straight up in a dead calm. This is nothing!" Hazel called from behind them.

"I don't think I'm going to like this in the wind," Valentina said, already feeling green.

The canyon walls slowly passed by in front of them. As they reached the top, they could see that they were facing east, the sun directly in front of them a mere sliver over the horizon.

"Good morning!" Hazel said, whether to the two of them or to the sun, Valentina wasn't sure. Then, as promised, she gunned the engine, and they were flying over the landscape, the rocks and sand a dizzying blur below them.

"You should lie down," Kiyoshi said, and Valentina couldn't argue. He helped her into the back and Valentina felt like she was dozing off already, Hazel's shrill voice a mere drone in her ears as she gesticulated at a section of wall that folded down into bunks. Valentina clambered out of her pressure suit for what she hoped would be the last time in a great long while, then curled up on the bare bunk, her hot and itchy toes briefly objecting to the continued presence of her socks before she was asleep entirely.

CHAPTER THIRTEEN

FLYING SOUTH

VALENTINA DREAMED SHE WAS A BABY SLEEPING IN A CRADLE TIED TO A tree, like in the old rhyme. Only in her dream, a fox kept creeping up to her cradle to push it hard and send it swinging head to foot as well as side to side, and it was not comforting at all. She woke with a start, half afraid that she had been wailing aloud. The cabin was dark except for a panel light that outlined Hazel's ponytails in a bright green halo.

"Where are we?" Valentina asked, sitting up. There was a bunk directly over her, so she had to slide to the edge of her bed before she could sit up entirely, and that only by leaning forward.

"Pretty much where we were when you conked out yesterday," Hazel said. "Mars is big."

"Yesterday?" Valentina repeated. If it had been dawn, but it was dark now… "Do you mean this morning?"

"Nope, yesterday," Hazel said. She was talking softly, something Valentina wouldn't have guessed was even possible. Valentina peeked around the edge of the bunk and saw Kiyoshi fast asleep above her. "You've been out of it for like thirty-six hours, Val," Hazel went on. "The latrine is inside that cabinet there; I bet you need it."

Valentina did indeed need it. When she emerged again, Hazel was still at the controls, but a thermos of hot water was waiting for her next to two steaming stuffed flatbreads on a plate.

"You made this?" Valentina asked, biting into the fried bread. The filling was onions, potatoes, and peas, with perhaps more red pepper than Valentina would have put in. It went right to her nose, opened her sinuses wide, and definitely rid her of the last of her sleepiness.

"For the party," Hazel said. "I packed my own leftovers for our use; I thought that was fair."

"Can I ask you a question?" Valentina asked around her second mouthful of bread.

"Sure," Hazel said with exaggerated caution.

"Your family was going to send us walking to the next farm. I know there's no reason for them to put themselves out for us, but I'm curious if there was another reason they didn't offer to take us on the next balloon journey to wherever."

"There's a couple of things, really," Hazel said. "First off, most of what we service is north and west of where you were heading. We do buy supplies from the corporate cities, of course, but not this time of year. It would be months before anyone would be going your way. So offering you a ride would have just taken you to a place even further out of your way."

"But you didn't offer, just assumed."

"That's because secondly, none of the balloons will be launching for weeks. That was the reason for the party, everyone back home at the same time. It only happens once a year. Storm season."

"But we're flying," Valentina said.

"Did you want to walk?"

"Having just walked through a storm, I know I don't want to try flying through one," Valentina said.

"No, we won't," Hazel assured her. "I'll land and deflate the balloon. We'll batten down the hatches, as they say. Once the storm has passed, we'll be up and flying again, through calm weather just like this."

As if to punctuate her remark, the gondola made a soft pitch to the left, then swung back. Valentina waited for the floor to settle before resuming her meal. If this tossing about didn't bother Hazel, it wasn't going to bother her.

"You don't need to worry," Hazel went on. "I've flown through storms before, but I'm not going to do it with you two non-pilots on board. I'll know when a storm is coming in plenty of time for us to tuck away and wait it out. The Aelitas don't fly in the stormy season because it's an inefficient nuisance, not because it's too risky."

"I trust you," Valentina said, and wished she totally meant it.

"So," Hazel said several minutes later, with forced casualness. "Kiyoshi is like your cousin?"

"Cousin by marriage, not by blood," Valentina said. "My grandfather, don Abuelo, felt that blood was important, but sharing a common family vision was more important. Kiyoshi and his mother were part of our family in ways that most of our blood relatives just weren't."

"So he's an honorary del Toro?" Hazel asked. "Like the guy on the plaque?"

"No, don Abuelo was my mother's father. My father's family, the del Toros, are corporate dwellers. I don't know what that means out here, but on the north pole it means they don't mix with the rest of us more than they can help it."

"I think that's the same all over," Hazel said. "They have a special port for us. They will trade with us, take our money, even have a special pleasure hotel as part of the port for guys that want to give up even more of their money, but they never let any of us inside the actual city. Like we have raging cooties or something. It's quite rude."

"Oh," Valentina said. Her voice sounded small and far away in her own ears, and she felt like the bottom of the gondola had just dropped out beneath her and she was falling, falling, falling. It had never occurred to her that the entire corporate city would be like the science station on the north pole, closed off to all outsiders. Her brother would be somewhere inside, inaccessible to her. Would her father's name be enough to get her inside? But she had no way to prove who she was. And she would very much prefer to find a way in without involving her father. She folded her arms and tucked her chin close to her chest, getting into problem-solving mode. "We're going to have trouble getting in."

"Trouble? I'd say it will be impossible, but I can see you're the sort that doesn't consider that a real obstacle. No one gets inside the dome except them, and they never come out."

"But you meet in the port?"

"Yeah. I'm not sure how that's going to help you reach your brother, but I guess it's going to be where you'll have to start."

"How long will it take to get there?"

"Depends on the prevailing winds. Days, probably a week or two."

"And you'll help us at the port? Be a guide, or maybe more like an interpreter?"

"They speak English, but interpreter of customs might be the title I'd pick," Hazel said. "Yeah, I'm with you all the way. Maybe after you find your brother, you can recommend me to people inside the dome as a reliable transporter of people and cargo. Got to start building my own rep now that I'm out of the family."

"You don't think they'd take you back?" Valentina asked, shocked. "I mean, I know this was supposed to be your nephew's balloon, and you're taking it is a big deal, but your family seemed so nice."

"They are nice," Hazel said. "But when my father told me the balloon wasn't going to be mine, he was very, very clear what the consequences would be if I did what, let's be honest, we both knew I was going to do. I can't go back."

"I'm sorry," Valentina said. She knew what it was to have a large family always close around her and then to lose that. Hazel must not realize yet what she had just given up.

"I'm not," Hazel said with a toss of her pigtails. "I've been happier away from the dome flying in the balloons since the first trip I took with my father when I was wee. This is my life. All of that was just waiting for my life to begin."

"What about your family? Won't they worry about you?"

Hazel shrugged. Valentina studied her face closely, but if her casual attitude was a put-on to conceal genuine feelings, she saw no sign of it. Hazel glanced over at her and rolled her eyes at the look on Valentina's face. "You're going to tell me there's nothing more important than family."

"I guess I don't have to."

"Don't judge me, Val," Hazel said. "Staring at me like I'm crazy. Look, your little mission to walk across all of Mars to get a brother who, frankly, doesn't sound like he was kidnapped and is probably quite content where he is sounds absolutely nuts to me, but here I am helping you to do it. Because it's not my business to tell you how to feel about your family."

"You don't know anything about my brother," Valentina said.

"I only know what Kiyoshi told me," Hazel allowed. "But I trust his impressions." She glanced over her shoulder at Kiyoshi curled up with his back to them on the top bunk. There was a look of deep fondness in her eyes that rubbed Valentina the wrong way.

"You just met him yesterday," Valentina pointed out.

"You're still missing a day in your counting," Hazel said, clasping her hands behind her to stretch out her back. "We talked the entire day yesterday while you snored away."

"Kiyoshi talked," Valentina said, deadpan. "The entire day."

Hazel shrugged but in no way admitted she had done the bulk of the talking. "He's really cool. He knows just what he wants out of life and has a plan to get it. We're a lot alike that way."

Valentina bit at her lip. She had no plans beyond getting her brother back. She had never made any plans for a future. There had always been too much that needed to be done in the present to think about what might happen next. Beyond some vague wishes to have her farm and animals back, she didn't even have a dream.

"But then, being his cousin, I'm sure you know all about his plans, right?" Hazel said.

Valentina shot her a sharp look and Hazel's face was all benign innocence that was clearly false. She was deliberately needling Valentina for no apparent reason, and she was succeeding too well for Valentina's tastes. She felt her hands starting to curl into fists. She hadn't been this angry since she had confronted the don to demand her brother's release.

She took a deep, calming breath. What difference did it make to her if Hazel and Kiyoshi were bosom buddies now? They were both just part of the means to get her to her brother, right? Valentina put her hand in the pocket of her skirt and felt the crinkle of her brother's note there. She was getting closer, every day a little closer. She had to stay focused on that. Nothing else really mattered.

"Yes, he's my cousin, but until he rolled up in his rover when I was stuck on the ice cap, I don't think he'd ever spoken two words to me. Clearly you know him better than I." She didn't add, "After just a day."

Hazel smiled, turning her attention back to her piloting. "Don't worry too much about getting inside the city, Val," she said. "Between the three of us, we'll come up with something. There has to be a way, and we'll find it. No worries. Your happy reunion with your brother is Kiyoshi's and my first priority."

"Thanks," Valentina said and forced a smile. She knew she was meant to ask what their second and maybe third priorities were—clearly it had been discussed extensively while she slept—but she just couldn't give Hazel the satisfaction.

CHAPTER FOURTEEN

A BLINDING WIND

Despite Hazel's obvious enthusiasm for it, Valentina did not enjoy travel by balloon. She never got used to the bucking and swaying of the gondola, the blur of motion when she tried to focus on the ground. Travel by rover had been cramped, but it was still better than this.

But balloons were faster. Kiyoshi had brought up a map on the balloon's GPS and found enough places that Valentina and he were familiar with that they could gauge their progress with more than Hazel's assurances of "we're making good time," so she knew it was true. When her motion sickness was at its worst, she focused on how much less time it was taking to get to her brother than when she had set out from the north pole on foot. It helped.

There hadn't been any more storms. Hazel agreed when Valentina asked if this was unusual, and as time wore on, she almost seemed worried about it, grabbing one of her ponytails and twisting it even more crazily as she gazed at the atmospheric readings.

They were about two weeks out from Hazel's home when it all changed.

Valentina had been on the middle deck, sitting cross-legged on the floor and watching the sand blow across the foredeck outside. The wind had been gusting, and watching the sand dance took her mind off her stomach. It would pile into one corner, form long, serpentine dunes, then all at once blow away entirely. Then the process would repeat, always collecting first in the same corner.

She had known Kiyoshi and Hazel were talking in the compartment behind her, but she had been tuning them out. The two of them fell into conversation at every opportunity, and although Valentina longed for the quiet companionship of the rover journey, she had to admit to herself that Kiyoshi did not appear annoyed anymore by Hazel's constant chatter, or by the hand that frequently reached out to clasp his arm as she made some particularly strong point that apparently needed physical contact to really sink in. Far from looking annoyed, he listened intently and gave a short laugh when she made a joke. His hands were always busy tinkering on this or that part of the gondola, but more than half his attention was always on whatever Hazel was saying. Valentina was seldom included in more than a perfunctory way in whatever Hazel was going on about and Valentina had stopped bothering to listen, preferring to mull over the problem of getting into the city. A particularly tricky problem to solve since she had nearly no information about any of it.

But then the phrase "it's like a wall behind us" jumped out at her.

"What's going on?" she asked, sitting up. Kiyoshi had his face in the back porthole, looking left and right. Hazel's hands were on the controls but her eyes were on the screen showing her the topography of the ground around the balloon.

"We need to get farther ahead," Hazel said, increasing the speed. "There's nothing here but open plains; we might lose the balloon."

Valentina fought the rise and fall of the floor to push Kiyoshi aside and look out the window for herself.

It was indeed a wall, a wall of sand blotting out the sky. It was like a tidal wave of dark.

"We can't outrun that!" Valentina said.

"We don't have to outrun it. We just have to get to that ridge up ahead. There will be shelter there."

"You said if there was a storm, we wouldn't try to fly through it. You said we'd land."

"I am landing, just not here. Up there. I know what I'm doing!" Hazel growled.

Then the cabin filled with a brilliant light, followed a split second later by a rolling boom. The thin atmosphere of Mars didn't carry sound well, but this one had been close enough to reach them, echoing through the space like the gondola was a sound box.

Kiyoshi looked at Hazel, his fear in check but present all the same. Hazel glanced up from the controls to make brief eye contact. "If we land here, we're dead," Hazel said to him. "The storm will shred the balloon out in the open, and there is nowhere to walk to. I have to get us to shelter first, or it doesn't matter if we land or crash."

"How can we help?" Kiyoshi asked. He had one hand resting lightly on the doorframe, his legs adjusting to the movement of the floor as if he too had grown up flying around in balloons.

"Just suit up, be ready," Hazel said.

Kiyoshi and Valentina didn't need to be told twice. They helped each other into their bulky suits, setting their helmets over their heads but not locking them into place just yet, conserving their bottled air until they really needed it. Valentina went through the cupboards, packing the rest of the food into a sack in case they did crash, survive, and have to head out on foot. While she was doing that, Kiyoshi helped Hazel get into her own suit, never taking more than one hand off the controls and never for more than the briefest of moments.

Lightning flashed again, farther away, then closer. One bolt lit up the sky in front of them, forking and reforking until six or eight different prongs were touching the ground, whatever damage they did lost in the blowing sand.

"I'm losing visual," Hazel said tightly. She glanced again and again at the monitor to her left. It too was flickering on and off, losing signal in the deepening sandstorm.

"Did you pick out a target?" Kiyoshi asked, peering at the monitor himself.

"That one," Hazel said, touching the screen briefly. "There is a dip in the ground there, some largish boulders for cover, and a boxy thing I'm curious to look at."

"Boxy? How boxy? Man-made?" Valentina asked. She couldn't pick out what Hazel was seeing either out the window or on the dying monitor.

"Maybe. But no one lives out here. No one who would build something that size, anyway."

"Maybe it's old." Kiyoshi said. "Pre-plague."

"I admit I'm curious," Hazel said, even as a gust of wind grabbed the gondola and pulled it hard, trying to take it away from the balloon. Valentina held the edges of the bunk, trying to keep from tumbling across the floor that was now at a nearly 60-degree angle.

"How much longer to reach it?" Kiyoshi asked.

"I'm gunning the engine," Hazel said. "Hold on!" Kiyoshi wedged himself in the doorway and Valentina held onto the edge of the bunk with both hands as the sudden acceleration perpendicular to the sloped floor set her already empty stomach roiling. "We're going in low and tight," Hazel went on as if that meant something to the other two. The drop in altitude was clear enough; the other Valentina suspected referred to how fast they were going with the engine still on full, now with the added element of being at the level of the rock formations which were currently hidden behind veils of blowing sand.

"Is that it?" Kiyoshi asked, then flinched as lightning struck the ground in front of them. Valentina could swear she felt her hair stand on end when they flew through where the lightning had been a split second before.

"It's going to have to be close enough," Hazel said through gritted teeth. "The balloon is still deflating, faster than it should be for the valve I opened. Something damaged it."

The bottom of the gondola struck the surface of Mars and then rebounded, striking the bottom of the balloon that was busy collapsing around them. Then it fell again, this time bouncing two or three times before settling into a skid powered by the engine, still thrusting them forward with all speed.

"Look out!" Kiyoshi called, but Hazel was already switching off the engine. With the balloon a wreck around them, there was nothing else she could do, no way to turn to avoid the rock wall rushing up to meet them. Kiyoshi yelled something else, but Valentina didn't hear it. She had locked down her helmet, wrapping her arms around the sack of food and water bottles as if it were a nightmare-warding teddy bear.

The balloon enveloping the gondola slowed them down, but not enough. They met the side of the rock formation with a loud crunch that reminded Valentina strongly of a beverage can being crushed flat before being thrown into the recycler. Her eyes were shut tight, but her imagination was going with the image of a metal accordion closing in around her.

Then everything was still, and she opened her eyes.

"Leak," Hazel said, her voice becoming clearer as she sealed her own helmet. "Dammit, crashed my ship. This wasn't part of the plan."

"We can't stay here," Kiyoshi said. "We can't fix this. We need to get walking and find shelter."

Valentina pushed herself to her feet, hoping her knees weren't visibly shaking. The last walk had nearly killed her. But she still had the rope in her cargo pocket. She unrolled it, tying one end around her waist before handing it to Kiyoshi. He tied the middle around himself and handed the last end to Hazel. They were all within arm's reach of each other; if they had to run, it would be awkward.

"We should find that boxy structure first," Valentina said. "Maybe it's something we can get inside of."

"Better than an aimless wander," Hazel said with clearly false humor. "Kiyoshi, did you get a sense of where it was in relation to here?"

"Yes. I'll lead," Kiyoshi said.

The windows of the airlock room were cracked, and the door to the foredeck was jammed. Kiyoshi had to put his shoulder against it to get it to open and let the three of them out. Then they had to fight their way out from under the balloon itself. There were meters and meters of balloon fabric to crawl under, but it was better than the blowing sand that waited for them on the other side.

Kiyoshi forged ahead through the swirling brown darkness, Valentina and Hazel close behind them on the ends of their tethers. He walked slowly, taking small, careful steps as if being very sure of his direction. It was easy to get disoriented with the wind constantly changing direction, pushing on them first from one side, then the other, sweeping away their footprints as soon as they stepped out of them. Valentina kept expecting them to stumble back on the balloon, it felt so much to her that they were going in a circle, but they never did.

They didn't find the boxy structure, either. Kiyoshi kept walking, occasionally looking at the GPS on his wrist, which was barely getting a signal through the storm, and only intermittent and brief glimpses. Hazel walked close to his elbow, trying to help guess what the flash of an image had been and where they were in relation to it. Valentina fell farther and farther behind, head down as she trudged at the very end of her tether. Her feet were practically shrieking at the first touches of cold, particularly the open sores where her blisters had not yet healed over even with the cream. The socks helped, the thick bulky knit at least stopping the boots from rubbing on her heels even if they were defenseless against the extreme cold.

The tireder she got, the more pronounced her limp became. She wondered if there would be anything left of her to finally reach her brother, or if what was left was going to be worth anything. To cross the globe just to become a burden to him had not been the plan.

"Valentina, how are you doing?" Kiyoshi asked, and she realized they had stopped walking. She lifted her head to give him a nod, but he grabbed her wrist, looking at her gauges. "You're still bleeding oxygen," he said. He sounded angry with himself. He had spent the first few days in the gondola going over every inch of her suit and repairing even the smallest of faults with Hazel's patch kit.

"Are we almost there?" Valentina asked, barely glancing at the red glow of the last of her oxygen dropping out of the gauge.

"Yes!" Hazel suddenly yelled, tugging on the line. "The wind dropped for a second and I know I saw it! Follow me."

Kiyoshi helped Valentina along, although she didn't exactly need it. Valentina suspected he just wanted to be watching her in case she fell or collapsed like last time.

"I'm touching the wall!" Hazel said, and then Kiyoshi and Valentina were too. Hazel led the way slowly along the wall and around the first corner. Valentina's feet had stopped complaining, but she was too sleepy to care. She would have liked to lie down and rest a bit, but she didn't want to upset Kiyoshi, so she kept going, one foot after the other. She did close her eyes, though. There was nothing to see but brown wind and brown wall, anyway.

They turned two more corners and still no way in. Dark starbursts were starting to form before Valentina's closed eyes and she let herself sag against Kiyoshi.

"Where's the door? We have to get her inside!" he shouted to Hazel.

"It should be somewhere along here," Hazel said, sounding disappointed.

"Listen, get behind me and take out my tank," Kiyoshi said. "Put it in Valentina's suit."

"But—"

"I'll have enough left in my suit to find this door without having to carry her. If there's no door, it doesn't matter."

"OK," Hazel said and got behind the two of them. She made quick work of it, and Valentina snapped awake with frightening rapidity. She hated that feeling, of having just been willing to lie down and die.

"Let's hurry," she said through gritted teeth. Kiyoshi, wisely, was saving his breath.

They turned yet another corner and followed the wall nearly to the end before Hazel at last called that she had found something.

"Nearly where we started from," Valentina said. "We should have gone to the left in the first place."

"Well, duh," Hazel said, spinning the wheel that raised the door. "It's obvious now, isn't it?" When the door was halfway up, she ducked under it and Valentina followed. Kiyoshi stumbled and hit his helmet on the bottom of the door with what Valentina was sure was a loud clang echoing on the inside. Valentina closed the door while Hazel examined the inner door.

"It looks functional," Hazel said. "The panel is lit up, anyway."

"We're sealed on this end," Valentina said and heard herself gasping. She looked at her wrist: out of air again. Kiyoshi was bent over, hands on his knees. "Try it."

Hazel pushed a button, then looked around. "I can't tell if anything is happening."

Valentina couldn't either. She unfastened her helmet and lifted it off. At first she felt like she was drowning, gasping and gasping, but finally her lungs got at least a little of what they wanted. She gave a thumbs-up, still struggling for air. Hazel looked uncertain, but when Kiyoshi fell to his knees, she released his helmet for him and he too gasped deeply.

"I have air left in mine," Hazel said. "I think I'll leave my helmet on for a bit. Let you two fight over what there is out there."

Valentina sat down on the floor next to Kiyoshi and shut her eyes, trying to slow the anxious hammering of her heart. His low breathing beside her was comforting as her harsh gasping gave way to a more even rhythm.

"How is it?" Hazel asked after several minutes.

"It's thin," Kiyoshi said. "If the whole building is like this, we're going to have to be careful. We're going to get winded very, very easily."

"So, nix the workouts," Hazel said, finally unfastening her own helmet. "I think this opens the door."

The button on the panel did nothing. Kiyoshi made three attempts to get back on his feet, then started turning the wheel to open the door. He got it about a third of the way up and sat back down to rest.

"Are you getting the black starbursts?" Valentina asked, and he nodded, eyes closed.

"I'm going to see what's in there," Hazel said, getting down on her hands and knees to crawl under the door.

Valentina and Kiyoshi traded a tired look before crawling after her.

CHAPTER FIFTEEN

IN THE ABANDONED STATION

Valentina hadn't realized how loud the storm was inside the airlock until she stood up on the other side of the door. She could still hear the sandy wind scouring the outer door, but it was a soft murmur that grew softer as she stepped further into the room beyond.

Hazel and Kiyoshi turned on the flashlights built into their suit gloves, but Valentina was left in the dark. She made out details of the room as the other two passed their lights over everything around them.

"It looks like there was a riot in here," she said, switching her attention from Hazel's fast-darting light to Kiyoshi's more methodical sweeps. The room was large, taking up the entire space of the structure they had just walked around. Large parts of it were completely empty, although deep scratches and gouges marred the perfection of the polished concrete floor. Kiyoshi's light soon found out the cause of this: a jumbled pile of shelving, crushed and bent and thrown into a heap. It could almost be the start of a bonfire, were the shelves not all made of metal.

"I wonder what happened," Valentina said, staying close to Kiyoshi's elbow. Hazel wandered further in, her light trying to take everything in at once.

"This must have been some sort of supply station," Kiyoshi guessed. "Maybe even a store."

"It's so big," Valentina said.

"I think this back here was a restaurant," Hazel yelled from across the space, her voice echoing in a way that sent a chill up the back of Valentina's neck.

"Everything of value is gone, that's for sure," Kiyoshi said. "Probably a long time ago."

"I think you're right," Valentina said, hugging her arms around herself. It was warmer inside than outside in the storm, but it still wasn't exactly comfortable. "It feels like an old place."

"What's that smell?" Kiyoshi asked, looking around.

"Smell?"

"Like, mousy?" he said, and once he put a name on it, Valentina could smell it too.

"It smells a bit like the guinea pig hutch we had back home," Valentina said. "Although maybe a little wilder, if you know what I mean."

"I smell it too," Hazel said as she walked up to them, still looking all around. "It reminds me of..." She stopped herself with a shiver that sent her pigtails swinging.

"Of what?" Kiyoshi asked.

"It's a terrible story," Hazel said, and for once she didn't seem to be joking. "I was like six at the time, so I don't remember all the details. It was the beginning of the season and I was with my father on the trade route, going from farm to farm and buying and selling. Well, along the way we reached a farm owned by a man my father had known since they were kids, so when no one answered our hail, Dad got worried. We had to break inside the airlock and—"

Something loud clanged behind her and she looked back over her shoulder, completely calm, although Valentina's heart was racing.

"I was touching one of the piles," Hazel said. "Must have disrupted the delicate balance."

They waited a few more minutes, but when nothing else stirred, Valentina said, "Go on. You broke into the airlock."

"It smelled like this in there. I mean, it was way stronger there.

Made my eyes water. Something had happened to the family—maybe they got sick, or sometimes people living in tight quarters for so long just get the crazies. Whatever the reason, the people had all died. And the rats had taken over."

"It was full of rats?" Valentina said, trying to block out the image of rats feasting on people.

"Not anymore," Hazel said. "By the time we got there, the rat population had boomed and busted. There were skeletons every-where, bones stripped of all flesh, rat and human both. But there were only a few rats left alive. They were big and mean, and very hungry."

Kiyoshi looked around again. Valentina's ears strained to hear anything besides the three of them breathing and the barely audible rage of the storm. She didn't think she heard anything skittering, but she kind of felt like something was crawling all over her.

"Let's not get jumpy over nothing," Kiyoshi said. "Maybe the same thing happened here, but look at the dust on the floor. No tracks. If the rats ruled when men fell, the rats fell in their turn long ago."

"What do we do now?" Valentina asked. "Wait out the storm and try to repair the balloon?"

"I'm not sure that's even fixable," Hazel said. "If the balloon itself wasn't damaged too badly, we could fly out in a non-airtight gondola wearing our suits, but we won't get far."

"That might still be our best plan," Kiyoshi said. He glanced at Valentina, who was still hugging herself against the cold.

"I think we should look around here first," Valentina said. "Give it a more thorough search. Maybe there's a communications station or something we could use to call for help. Maybe the rats ate all the food but left a rover."

"I doubt we'll be that lucky," Hazel said.

"We won't know until we look," Kiyoshi said.

"I don't have a light," Valentina said, holding up her bare wrists.

"Stick with me, then," Kiyoshi said. Hazel seemed on the verge of objecting but shrugged and pointed to the direction she would take first.

"Something must still be functional," Kiyoshi said as he and

Valentina made their way along the outside wall starting from the airlock. "We can breathe the air, thin as it is, and there is some heat."

"It's like the way stations when I would go inside them," Valentina said. "Even if they had full power, all the systems were dialed down to conserve resources. I would have to go to the main panel and turn up the heat and oxygen. This is like the same, left at the bare minimum by whoever was the last traveler out."

"He may have overdone the conserving of resources," Kiyoshi said as the main panel came into view. The metal bar used to smash it to unusable pieces was still embedded in the display screen. "There'll be no fixing that."

"There must be another if we keep looking," Valentina said. Kiyoshi looked at her intently and Valentina realized with painful slowness that her teeth were chattering.

"Your suit," he said. Valentina looked at her indicator panels, but they weren't lit up. Kiyoshi grabbed her by the shoulders to turn her around and look at the back panels she couldn't see.

"Can you fix it?" she asked, hoping not only that the answer would be yes, but that it wouldn't require her to take it off first.

"No, there's nothing I can do. Your power cell is dead," he said.

"I thought those things were good for decades," Valentina said, shivering even harder now that she knew she wasn't getting any more heat, ever.

"The suit is decades old," Kiyoshi said.

Hazel walked up to them, apparently having caught the end of the conversation.

"Flying without an airtight gondola is off the table," Kiyoshi said as Valentina clenched her jaw to stop the chattering that was too loud in the echoing space.

Hazel nodded, then dug into the front pouch of her own suit. She came up with a cap knit from a bulky, irregularly spun yarn, just as inexpertly dyed an orange that faded to yellow in places and intensified nearly to red in others. She pulled it over Valentina's head, tucking her braids in. The hat was snug and ended at her eyebrows with flaps that covered her ears. Hazel spun the tasseled ends through her hands, tying the flaps tight under Valentina's chin.

"Thanks," Valentina said.

"I made it myself," Hazel said.

"When you were little?"

"No," Hazel said, completely unembarrassed, "on my last flight out, just before I met you guys. That's why it was still in my suit."

"Oh," Valentina said, knowing that the cold air wasn't going to explain all the redness of her cheeks.

"I know how to make a conventional hat," Hazel said. "I was experimenting with some new techniques."

"Lots of new techniques," Kiyoshi added, and Valentina laughed out loud. It was what she was thinking, but the last thing she had expected him to say.

Hazel grinned, taking no offense. "So," she said when the laughter had died down. "This place looks like a store. What's up with that?"

"Maybe it was a supply station," Valentina said.

"Yeah, but why here? There's nothing out here."

"It's old," Valentina said. "Maybe something used to be out here."

"No," Kiyoshi said. "We would have seen structures when we flew in."

"My theory is that this place was built because they were planning to expand out this way."

"Who's they?" Valentina asked, but Kiyoshi understood better.

"You think this is pre–Earth plague?" he said, looking around. "From the original settlement mission?"

"It's very boxy."

Valentina frowned, but then she understood what Hazel was saying. Before the Earth plague, building on Mars had been funded by Earth organizations, governments and private corporations both. They had specific design specifications for everything they built. But after the plague hit and the governments and corporations collapsed, the Martian survivors had built whatever they could with whatever was handy. They wouldn't have gone to such effort to square off edges when the constant sandstorms made round structures easier to build and maintain.

"They were never this far north, though," Valentina said. "Except for the polar stations, everyone was clustered around the equator."

"They were going to expand," Hazel said. "This place was like an outreach of the infrastructure, encouraging others to expand."

"That makes no sense," Valentina said. "If the corporations had wanted a community here, they would have just built one."

"No, I know what Hazel is talking about," Kiyoshi said. "Right at the end there, just before the plague hit, Mars had been opening up to smaller ventures. The corporations were building infrastructure to supply the people coming, like homesteaders."

"I've not heard that," Valentina said.

"It's in the data files," Kiyoshi said. "My mother had a tablet that was linked to the polar station mainframe."

"Really?" Valentina was genuinely surprised. It was as if the mechanic had been hiding a vast underground cavern filled with books and no one had ever known. She was also jealous; she could read a little, which was a rare skill in the world she had grown up in. Now it sounded like Kiyoshi could read a lot, and did. And she had never known.

"I don't know about data files, just trader talk," Hazel said. "But as I've heard it, their plans for expansion were a bit mistimed. They would have been ready for waves of immigration in another ten years or so, but not when the exodus came of people fleeing the plague on Earth. The refugees overwhelmed everything just before it was properly ready."

"So this place was raided by refugees from Earth way back when?" Valentina said.

"That's my theory," Hazel said, but Kiyoshi was nodding along.

"So what's that mean for us?" Valentina asked.

Hazel and Kiyoshi shared a long look, almost as if they were communicating telepathically.

"Guys?"

"Just a trade station out here makes no sense," Kiyoshi said.

"But there wasn't room topside for an airstrip or landing pad," Hazel said. "They wouldn't have put this so far into the rocky terrain if they were using the open plain for transport."

"And there would be more buildings anyway," Kiyoshi said.

"Barracks, comm tower, whatnot," Hazel went on.

"So how was it connected to the rest of Martian civilization?" Kiyoshi asked.

"Where is the lifeline?" Hazel added, but she was grinning now.

"Nowhere, unless the stories are true," Kiyoshi said.

"You guys are driving me nuts," Valentina said, hopping from foot to foot to keep them from dozing off in the growing cold. "What stories are we talking about now?"

"The Underground," Kiyoshi said, but Hazel was already racing away, running along the wall, her fingers skimming over the smooth surface.

"No," Valentina said. "Not this far north. The Underground only ran up and down the Valles Marineris."

"If they were looking to expand, they'd build the branch line first, then the supply station," Hazel said. "We are at the outskirts of the mountains; it's not inconceivable for a lava tube to extend this far. Especially if they had the equipment to tunnel out the narrower spaces, which they would have."

"So hold on," Valentina said, pushing back the hat that was slipping down over her eyes. "You're telling me that maybe, possibly, we just found one end of an environmentally sealed tunnel system that will let us just walk up to the basement door of any of the corporate domes?"

"It's going to be a long walk," Kiyoshi said. "But, yes."

CHAPTER SIXTEEN

IN THE TUNNEL

Kiyoshi lit the way with his wrist light, and Valentina stayed close to his side. There was more debris on this end of the building, more puzzling stories hinted at in the swirling patterns of the dust on the floor. She snuggled down into the collar of her suit, grateful for the hat even though her feet were the ones really feeling the pain.

"The smell is stronger," Kiyoshi said with distaste, but Valentina perked up.

"The air is warmer too," she said.

"Are you sure?"

"Can't you feel it? There's a breeze. Well, maybe more like a draft, but there's definitely air moving, and it feels warmer."

She ignored the look he was giving her, like he thought she was going into hypothermic delirium or something. She knew she was right.

Ahead of them a light appeared on the floor, then bounced up to waist level before Hazel appeared.

"There's a staircase!" she said, turning and rushing away from them again.

"Staircase going down," Valentina mused. Perhaps the two of them were right after all.

The staircase was wide, built to accommodate a lot of people, with rails dividing the space into four columns. On either side of the staircase were ramps, each wide enough to fit a small rover, also sloping down. Valentina could see the light from Hazel's suit dimly shining up at them. It was a long way down. That also argued for the lava tube theory; anything entirely man-made would have been tunneled at a more convenient depth.

As they neared the bottom, she could make out in more detail what Hazel was shining her light on. The opening to whatever lay beyond was massive, spanning the entire width from ramp to ramp and arching high above them. But it was entirely filled with debris.

"This was a bit of work," Hazel said, grinning at them as they approached. "Not an easy doorway to barricade. Look, there are at least four rovers in there, down at the bottom."

"Functional?" Valentina asked.

"Who knows? We'd never get them back out to check," Hazel said. "Not with twenty meters of junk on top of them, and who knows how deep."

"This is no good," Kiyoshi said, playing his own light over the twisted mess of vehicles, shelving, crates, and flat-out garbage.

"Why did they build it?" Valentina asked.

"Well, it's a barricade," Hazel said.

"Yeah, I get that. But to keep out what?" Valentina asked. "And which side are we on?"

"It's been so long it probably doesn't matter," Kiyoshi said, but he didn't sound convinced.

Valentina crept closer to examine one of the rovers—no easy task by the dim light of Hazel's and Kiyoshi's otherwise directed flashlights. The rovers had probably been derelicts before they were put to this use, but she could feel deep dents, punctured doors and smashed windscreens. Even if the motors could still operate, they were useless on the surface without an operative suit.

"I think there's a tunnel through," Kiyoshi called, and Valentina gingerly picked her way over to his side. He was at the far end of the barricade at the bottom of one of the ramps. He dropped down to one knee to shine his light through what could be called a crawl space if one was feeling particularly generous.

"Does it go through?" Hazel asked.

"Maybe," Kiyoshi said, angling his light this way and that. "It's hard to say; this barricade is quite deep."

"I'll go first, if you like," Hazel said.

"No, I'll go. You stay with Valentina, be her light," he said. He stood up, putting his helmet back on his head but not sealing it.

"If the wall collapses, that's not going to help you much," Valentina said.

"The wall has been here for generations. It's not going anywhere now," Kiyoshi said, his voice muffled through the helmet. "I just don't want to hit my head on anything while I'm crawling through the slag. It looks like it's going to be tight in places, and there are lots of things poking into the space."

"Be careful," Valentina said.

He nodded, then disappeared through the hole.

It felt colder when he was gone, and darker. Valentina put her own helmet on, just to have something to do. Hazel bounced on her toes, clearly longing to explore more but not wanting to abandon Valentina after Kiyoshi's admonition. Her hair bounced with her body, tails swinging when she turned her head.

"It's cold," she said. Valentina didn't answer.

"OK, I'm through," Kiyoshi said, his voice coming over the radio in Valentina's helmet.

"What do you see?" she asked.

"Come through next and you'll see for yourself," he said. "I'll shine my light down this end so you can see what you're aiming for. But the tunnels make a few turns around bigger objects. You might not always be able to see me."

"I'll be OK," Valentina said, although she wasn't looking forward to this at all.

"You were right about the draft," he said. "It's quite warm on this end."

Valentina didn't answer. He was only saying it to give her a reason to crawl through meters of darkness. He knew she was scared and was extending a kindness. She should say something, but she just couldn't get the words out.

"I'll shine my light from this end too," Hazel said, having put her own helmet on when she realized the other two were talking to each other over the radio. "It might not do you much good coming from behind you, but I guess it's something."

Valentina nodded, then got down on her hands and knees. Her feet were already numb, but now her hands felt the shock of the cold floor, even through her gloves. It felt cold enough to freeze flesh at the touch, like some magical creature from a fairy tale. She had an image of herself, frozen solid like a statue, buried for all time under a mountain of junk deep inside the Martian crust. Yep, she could totally spin a fairy tale out of that.

Biting down on her lip to stop the scream that would have trouble getting past her chattering teeth anyway, Valentina started the long crawl.

Valentina wasn't claustrophobic, not after growing up in the tunnels below the polar station. The thought of all the different elements that made up the barricade piled on top of her was a bit disconcerting; it was fairly easy to imagine it all tumbling down and crushing her beneath tons of twisted metal. But it had stood here for decades and was unlikely to move now.

No, it was the darkness that bothered her—or, more specifically, the constant feeling that something in the dark was about to strike her. This fear was constantly fueled by the things in the dark she did bump into; handles of motorbikes, sharp edges of shelving, corners of containers all intruded on the tunnel she was crawling through, and with no light, she couldn't see any of them before they rang against her helmet.

She crawled along as slowly as she dared, running her hands along the sides to sense when the tunnel twisted around larger pieces of debris. She was reminded again of that day when the lights when out, trapping her and Arturo in the dark of her grandfather's hidden cavern. The memory was strangely comforting now. She remembered the way Arturo's hand had felt in hers, warm and trusting, giving little squeezes of encouragement as she led them along the irregular walls in search of the door. She imagined Arturo with her now, quietly confident that she would succeed.

Valentina had to turn on her side to get around what felt too large to even be a rover—perhaps a train car if Kiyoshi's theory was correct—then finally saw the dim glimmer of Kiyoshi's light in front of her. She was at the last stretch of tunnel. She increased her speed as much as she could on hands and knees in the bulky suit and at last emerged out from under the mountain of junk. Kiyoshi helped her to her feet, and she pulled her stifling helmet off to take big lungfuls of air.

"It is warmer here," she said. Her breath still fogged in the air, but it remained a glistening, wet mist until it dissipated, not instantly freezing into crystals in a thick mass like before.

"This place is enormous!" Hazel said, scrambling to her feet to point her light around the space. She had been right behind Valentina the entire time and Valentina hadn't even realized she was there.

"Look, there are three tracks," Kiyoshi said, shining his light over the rails for Valentina's benefit.

"Coming, going, and waiting?" Valentina guessed. "But I thought this was the end of the line. This tunnel goes both ways."

"There might be more stations like this one, waiting for homesteaders," Kiyoshi said. Hazel had already jumped down off the platform and was hopping over the rails.

"Which way do we go?" Valentina asked. Their wrist lights did so little to illuminate the cavern it was hard to get a picture of anything.

"My GPS can point us south," Kiyoshi said. "Plus, there's a wall map on the other side of the barricade."

Hazel's light bounced merrily below them and to their left as they walked past the towering barricade to the other side of the archway. The map wasn't a touch screen but an elaborate, stylized painting. There was no reference to any geographical markers on the surface of Mars, just a series of different-colored lines traveling in ovals and circles and rounded-off rectangles.

"Where are we?" Valentina wondered.

"Here, at the star. See how the lines here are drawn in crosshatches? I think that means they weren't finished constructing them yet."

"I think this is like my map of the way stations: not to scale," Valentina said.

"I agree. But look—these stations here are in a line, closer together, with more lines running between them. That has to be Valles Marineris."

"That would make sense," Valentina said. "So we're at the star, but which way are we facing?"

Kiyoshi lifted his arm to show her his GPS screen. "We're going that way, to the right."

"It's going to be a long walk," Valentina said.

"If we don't find more food or some source of water, there will be trouble," Kiyoshi added.

"Your and Hazel's suits have recycling systems?"

"Sure, but if we each give a third of what we have to you, we're all going to be walking thirsty. We should try to find more water."

Valentina nodded, not wanting to add that in order for her to be included in their water recycling system, she'd have to put one of their suits on just to pee in it. She doubted she could fit in Hazel's; the girl was nearly a foot shorter than her.

"Nothing here, really," Hazel said, bounding back up onto the platform. "There used to be machines that sold food, but they're all smashed now. Maybe there will be more up ahead."

"It would be really old food," Kiyoshi said. "All of this was abandoned decades ago."

"If they put enough preservative in it, it would scarcely matter," Hazel said. "I've eaten stuff from before the exodus before."

"You have?" Valentina said.

"Sure. People find stashes from time to time and it all disperses through the trade routes. I've had potato chips and cookies and even chocolate. The chocolate one tasted a little funny, but the others were OK."

"I wouldn't get our hopes up," Kiyoshi said. "We should plan to make what we have last as long as possible."

"Which way?" Hazel asked. Kiyoshi pointed, and they all hopped down off the platform, heading south.

"I was right," Kiyoshi said as they reached the far wall of the station and the three tracks became two. His light could just reach the walls of the tunnel on either side of the tracks. The walls of the station had been smooth and flat, but here the walls were irregular, like a tunnel dug out by a worm. Above them were occasional outcroppings that had come too low and had been sheared off, their round contours suddenly becoming sharp and flat.

"So this is what a lava tube looks like?" Valentina said.

Hazel, who had been walking in the front, suddenly pulled up short. "Do you hear that?" she whispered.

The three stood perfectly still, holding their breaths as they strained to hear. Valentina thought she could hear a drip, like water, but it was so close to being inaudible that she wasn't sure if she was hearing it or just imagining it.

Then another sound came, louder and closer, and she knew Hazel hadn't been hearing the sound of dripping. Something was scuttling, a whisper of sound that stopped as suddenly as it had started.

"We're not alone," Hazel said.

"Rats?" Valentina guessed.

"If they ate all that food decades ago, there can't be many left now," Kiyoshi said. "We dealt with rats all the time back home, nothing to worry about."

"It's just—that barricade," Valentina said. "Which side of it are we on? What happened to the people it was supposed to protect?"

"Perhaps they didn't need it anymore, so they dug that crawl space and left," Kiyoshi said.

"Perhaps the threat was on both sides and they were trapped," Hazel said. "If they had barricaded themselves into the station when they ran out of food, they would have had no choice but to break out of their own defenses and take their chances getting back to the cities."

"Maybe that's true," Kiyoshi said. "But it was all a long time ago. What could live that long in these tunnels with no food?"

Valentina didn't say anything. There was just too much they didn't know about this place.

In the end, there was nothing they could do but walk on, each walking as softly as they could, always listening.

CHAPTER SEVENTEEN

A SLEEPLESS NIGHT

THE THIRD TIME VALENTINA TRIPPED OVER HER OWN FEET, KIYOSHI insisted they stop for a rest.

"I should just ditch this suit," Valentina grumbled. "It's broken and too big for me. I'd be better off just walking in my own clothes."

"You don't have any shoes," Kiyoshi said. "Mine are too big and Hazel's are too small. We might get to a place where walking in your stocking feet would be dangerous."

"What about the lights?" Hazel said.

"Lights?" Valentina repeated.

"Are we planning on running them all day and night? Won't they wear out?"

"You're not running any of your environmental systems, just the light, and Kiyoshi has his GPS. That can't be taxing your power cells too much."

"The bulbs might go," Hazel said. "Yours were out even before your suit died."

"My suit was really old," Valentina said. "Plus, do you really want to sit here in the dark?"

"Beats trying to walk out of here in the dark," Hazel said.

"The lights should be fine," Kiyoshi said. "The bulbs are highly unlikely to burn out."

"If you're sure," Hazel said. The three of them settled down between the rail and the wall and tried to get comfortable. Although the stone was warmer than in the station above, it was still none too comfortable for sleeping on.

Valentina couldn't sleep. She hugged her arms around herself, snuggling down into the itchy warmth of Hazel's hat, and tried not to squirm around too much lest she wake the others. Kiyoshi and Hazel had turned their helmet lights on and set them near the tracks, aiming one in each direction. Valentina's eyes would only close for a second or two before she had to open them again to look up and down the tracks as far as the light would reach.

Valentina felt like she was awake for hours listening to the slow breathing of the others, but she must have drifted off herself for a minute or two because the scuttling sound roused her awake. She sat up straight, looking both ways. Hazel and Kiyoshi were awake as well. The three exchanged looks as they listened. Hazel pointed back the way they came, but Valentina shook her head and pointed further ahead. Kiyoshi frowned for a moment, then pointed both ways.

The scuttling stopped, which was horrible. When they could hear it, they could try to guess how far away the creature was, but when it moved in silence, it could be anywhere.

They waited for a quarter of an hour, but no more sounds came. Valentina couldn't even find the dripping sound she had heard before, just the sound of air moving through the tunnel that was almost certainly her imagination.

"We should sleep in watches," Kiyoshi said. "I'll watch first. You two sleep. I'll wake one of you up in two hours to take over."

"Me," Hazel said. "I'm used to sleeping in shifts when I crew the balloons." She laid back down, curled up like a cat, and dropped off to sleep instantly.

Valentina sat with her back against the wall, but sleep was nowhere near her. She found herself watching Kiyoshi as he alternated looking up and down the tunnel, sitting cross-legged in his bulky suit with his back to her.

"Can I ask you a question?"

"Sure," he said, looking back the way they'd come.

"I heard you telling your aunt and uncle how I went to the cartel dons to keep Arturo out of their grudge match. How did you know about that?"

"Everyone knew about that."

Valentina mulled that over. It was likely true; it would be the sort of story that everyone would want to retell. Still. "You talked about it like you were there."

Kiyoshi sat still for a minute, then gave her the briefest of glances before turning his attention up the tunnel.

Valentina couldn't parse out what that look had meant. Then she remembered the moment when she had been fleeing the room, head down, just trying to get back out into the lanes, the Martian flu already spinning in her head. She had bumped into something tall and broad on the way to the door. She remembered a hand on her shoulder, steadying her, but she had kept on charging out of the factory.

"You were there," she said, suddenly sure.

"I was sent to bring you home, to tell you about your ma," he said without looking at her. "I didn't know Arturo was missing until I heard you say so to the don."

"You tried to catch me at the door," Valentina said. "I didn't realize it was you."

"You were upset," he said.

"Also sick already, although I didn't know it," she said.

Kiyoshi kept looking up and down the tunnel, and Valentina was settling into a warm drowsiness when he spoke again. "Can I ask you a question?"

"Yeah," she said, half asleep already.

"Why do you keep telling people I'm your cousin?"

"Don Abuelo always told me you and your mother were family, not by blood, but by stronger bonds. I've always believed that was true. No one has done more for my ma and Arturo and me than your mother and you. The sisters she gave up everything to help raise were never any help, that's for sure."

He didn't answer, but his back seemed straighter than before, his body too rigidly upright, he too studiously not looking at her. She sat up, pushing the hat back from her eyes. "You don't think we're family?" she asked, unable to keep the hurt from her voice.

"It's not that," he said, starting to turn toward her but stopping before she could get a look at his face. She stopped too, sitting very still and straining to hear. Hazel, asleep as she was, sensed the change in their demeanors and opened her eyes as well. None of them spoke.

Kiyoshi reached out a hand to pick up his helmet, rising onto a knee into a low crouch. The path of the light swooped to one side as he moved the helmet, reflecting off dozens of pairs of eyes that had been lurking just outside of its beam.

"Get up!" Kiyoshi yelled, but Hazel was already somersaulting to her own helmet, landing on her feet with the helmet on in a blur of motion. Black bodies the size of dogs were swarming all over her, clawing their way up her suit. Her shriek was cut off when she sealed her helmet.

Valentina backed against the wall, but there was nothing to climb and nowhere to hide. They were rats, she could tell by the whiplike tails, narrow heads with bulbous black eyes and teeth that flashed whitely in the light. No longer able to hide in the darkness, they swarmed, climbing over each other in a writhing mass of oily black fur to reach the three of them pressed against the wall. Hazel kept pulling them off her legs and flinging them into the darkness, but two more took their place.

Then Valentina felt a hard pinch, like her ankle was in a vise, and kicked hard, sending another one spinning down the tunnel. They were the size of terriers, and their teeth didn't penetrate the pressure suits, but their jaws clamped down hard, and they were tenacious.

"We've got to get out of here," Kiyoshi said, swinging his helmet through the mass like a bludgeon.

"To where?" Valentina asked, kicking and spinning as fast as she could. She found her own helmet in the mass of snarling bodies and scooped it up, swinging it like Kiyoshi was doing with his.

"Further up the tunnel," he said. "There were other stations on the map. Perhaps they were blockaded like the first. Or we might find something besides helmets that will function as a weapon."

Hazel, with her helmet sealed, couldn't possibly hear them, but she saw they were talking and must have intuited about what, because after flinging another pair of rats down the tunnel she took off at a run toward the next station. Kiyoshi pushed Valentina to follow her, staying close behind her with his helmet constantly swinging.

Valentina stumbled in her too-big boots, scrambling desperately to stay on her feet. If she fell, they would be all over her. They would get to her face, claw at her skin and eyes...

Valentina stopped swinging her own helmet and put it on. She couldn't seal her suit like Hazel, but she felt like it was better for protection than just the orange hat.

Hazel was getting further and further ahead of her, the light from her helmet and wrists more and more obscured by the waves of rats trailing behind her. Valentina tried to push herself to run faster, but black explosions were obscuring her vision. Which one of them had said it, that the air here was too thin for workouts? She bit back the sudden urge to laugh and put all her focus into not passing out.

Which took attention away from not stumbling, she realized as she crashed down to her knees. Kiyoshi caught her elbow and hauled her back up, giving her a little push to get her moving forward again. She saw his helmet was now sealed as well; she was alone in the thin air, alone in the choking musty stench of the rats' bodies. Somewhere was the sharp tang of blood, and Valentina guessed somewhere in the darkness some of the rats had decided to settle for a meal of other rats.

A light blazed full in her face, driving her out of a daze she hadn't realized she had been in. Hazel was standing still, facing her but waving her arm to get her attention. She saw a mass of crushed vehicles, shelving, and miscellaneous trash. They had reached the next station, and it had been blockaded. Hazel's light fixed on a gap high in the wall and Valentina climbed to it. A hand stopped her just before she crawled inside, Kiyoshi shaking his head at her. He shone a light down the tunnel but no eyes reflected back at him, although the rats were scrambling up behind them, so they clearly had no trouble climbing. Kiyoshi went into the tunnel first, shining his light and proceeding at a slow, careful pace. Hazel pushed Valentina to follow but lingered outside the opening herself, kicking and throwing rats that attempted to follow. Valentina stayed just inside the tunnel, reaching out to help when she could, looking back over her shoulder to try to make out how Kiyoshi was progressing.

The barricade was much thinner than the last had been, no thicker than the length of a rover, but the other end of the opening was blocked. Valentina saw Kiyoshi kick and push at something, then turn so his lights were shining back her way, bracing his back against the obstacle and pushing with his arms and legs against the sides of the tunnel. Then there was a crash and his lights disappeared. Valentina started after him, but clearly not fast enough for Hazel, who kept pushing on her from behind to hurry her along. Didn't she realize Valentina was doing this blind?

She tried to remember how far along Kiyoshi had been, just the length of a rover, but the light from Hazel's helmet behind her illuminated nothing. Valentina's hand went down on nothing and she tried to pull back, but Hazel picked that moment to give her another hurrying shove and she tumbled forward, her helmet singing out as she hit something protruding from the wall. She landed on something soft enough to probably be Kiyoshi, but before she could get up Hazel was landing on top of her, knocking the little bit of air she had out of her.

Hazel and Kiyoshi scrambled up, working together to move the obstacle Kiyoshi had pushed out back up to block the tunnel. Valentina straightened her askew helmet, stumbling back out of the way. She was certain they were communicating over their comms; their teamwork was too good to be doing it by mime. She was better off not trying to help, especially as the blow to her head hadn't done the exploding black fireworks any favors. After a few moments of nothing rushing out of the darkness at her, Valentina took off the useless helmet and gasped at the thin air, desperately trying to extract more oxygen from it before she passed out.

Also, she was thirsty. The voice in the back of her head wanted her to be aware of that even as she fought for breath.

Kiyoshi and Hazel climbed back down the barricade, their work done. Hazel started a slow circuit around the space, searching every corner with her lights for anything dangerous or potentially useful. Kiyoshi took off his helmet and bent over Valentina.

"… mfine," she said. "… will be…"

"We shouldn't have tried running," Kiyoshi said.

Valentina managed a scoff, but no words. It wasn't like they'd had any choice. She could still hear the rats, clawing at the outside of the barricade, looking for a way in.

"It's well blocked," he assured her after following her gaze. "We barely got in ourselves. They aren't strong enough."

Valentina nodded, her breath coming easier now that her heart was slowing its too-rapid pulse.

Hazel came back to stand over them, taking off her own helmet. "There are control panels here like the other station, but they're also smashed. There is a manual airlock that looks functional, for all the good that does us."

Valentina looked over her suit. The only hole was the one in the knee she'd had before, but even seeing it intact didn't stop the crawling feeling of her skin, and she stood up and started taking it off.

"What are you doing? You need that," Hazel said.

"I know, I just have to see."

"I wish we could make a fire," Hazel said, setting her helmet down. "Everything feels safer when there's a fire, you know?"

"We don't have many open flames on the north pole," Kiyoshi said. "Fuel is too precious."

"You can trust me. Fires are just the thing for warding off pestilent beasts," Hazel said.

Valentina stepped out of her suit and peeled off her stockings. The place where she had felt the viselike bite was already black. She had other bruises on her arms and legs, but none were so bad as that one. She opened the pouch on the front of her suit and retrieved the cream for her feet, as long as she had her stockings off.

"No day or night down here," Hazel said. "There's never really going to be a safer time to travel."

Kiyoshi was examining the barricade. There was a small four-wheeled rover near the bottom that looked to be in pretty good shape. He cleared off enough other debris to peek at the engine, but didn't say anything to the other two. Valentina guessed that even if it was repairable, they had no way of digging it out without becoming rat dinner, so it was a moot point.

"We can make clubs out of some of this," Hazel said. "Smaller things will make good projectiles. We're going to want to keep our helmets on."

"I don't have much air left," Kiyoshi said.

"Nor I. I was thinking head protection."

"He's worrying about the thin air," Valentina said. "Too thin for running. Maybe too thin for intense rat fighting. If one of us should faint—"

"I can paint my own grim pictures, thank you very much," Hazel said.

"You said there was an airlock," Valentina said.

"Even if I took all of Kiyoshi's air as well as mine, I wouldn't have enough to get back to my wreck of a balloon, let alone repair it and fly out for help. If that's what you were thinking."

Valentina put her cream away and put her stockings and suit back on. The smell inside the suit was nearly as bad as the rat smell.

"Let's try getting some rest again," Kiyoshi said. "Then we make what weapons we can and try our luck with the rats. Our only chance is to get further towards civilization, find other people with better resources."

"We certainly can't go back or stay here," Hazel agreed, then once again curled up like a cat and dropped off to sleep with startling speed.

"I'll watch," Kiyoshi said. "Just in case."

Valentina nodded and snugged the hat down over her ears, hugging her helmet to her chest. She tried not to think that if not for her, the other two wouldn't even be in this mess.

Arturo had never felt farther away.

CHAPTER EIGHTEEN

WALKING THE LINE

After they had each taken a turn at watch and two turns at sleeping badly, they shared a few sips of water. They were all in silent agreement not to try for another set of watches; none of them was going to get any more sleep.

Hazel and Valentina went to the far end of the room and managed the difficult business of Valentina getting into Hazel's much smaller suit just enough to use the waste recycling system. The tunnels were long, and they seemed likely to walk for days. There must be water somewhere, given the rats, but they didn't want to bet too heavily on finding it. By the time they got back to their campsite, Kiyoshi had laid out a little breakfast from the food they had brought with them from the crashed balloon, mostly hard tack and tubes of various nut pastes guaranteed to make them thirst again in a hurry.

They ate slowly without really speaking to each other, too weary from their nightmare-plagued attempts at sleep for talk. Each had spent part of their watch constructing weapons, mostly long pieces of shelving that would serve as clubs or blunt spears, but Hazel had collected a sack of heavy, round things.

"For throwing?" Valentina asked.

"No, something better," Hazel said, pulling a long strip of cloth out of her suit pocket. "I made a sling."

"I think those are harder to use than you might think," Valentina said.

Hazel stuffed the last of her ration bar in her mouth and stood up, putting a knob from a gear shaft into her sling and spinning it around a few times before letting go of one end, sending her missile neatly through a rover window.

"You could have just said you've done it before," Valentina said while Hazel ran to retrieve the knob. "They've been quiet out there since I was on watch; I hope you didn't just bring them all back."

"Quiet doesn't mean gone," Kiyoshi said. "But I agree. It might be better if we were sneakier."

"Sorry," Hazel said, "I couldn't resist."

"Do you want to wait a bit to see if they swarm again, or sneak out now?" Valentina asked.

"Now," Kiyoshi said after a moment's consideration.

"Yes, now," Hazel agreed.

Valentina nodded; that had been her feeling as well. She slipped her makeshift club through a tool loop on her suit and hefted her spear, or perhaps it was a staff; she guessed she'd know which when she was pressed to use it. Hazel had her bag of missiles slung across her body, sling in one hand. The club she held in the other was a shelf support that ended in a crosspiece, giving it just the hint of a hacking surface like a crude, blunt ax. Kiyoshi had two clubs, larger than Hazel's and Valentina's, one fashioned from a support leg for some heavy piece of equipment and the other part of a robotic arm. He also had a tire iron tucked into a loop at the back of his suit, but it was the clubs that got Valentina's attention.

"Those are outdoor things," she said.

"There is a lot of wrecked exploration and science equipment at the far end of the barricade," Kiyoshi said.

"They went outside from here more than from the other station," she guessed. "There might still be something out there."

"Wouldn't do us any good," Hazel said. "We don't have enough air left for exploring."

"There must be an air charging unit by the airlock; that's standard," Valentina said.

"Broken," Hazel said.

"But Kiyoshi might be able to fix it," Valentina persisted.

"It has a chair embedded in it," Hazel said. "It's just like the other station: it was all sabotaged or destroyed beyond repair."

"Why?" Valentina said, to the universe at large, really; she knew the other two couldn't do more than guess.

"I know, given enough time, you could fix anything," Hazel said to Kiyoshi, gazing up at him as she spun the empty sling in her hand. He didn't answer, just stepped closer to where Valentina waited nearer the barricade.

"Ready?" Kiyoshi asked.

"As ever," Valentina said.

They climbed back up to the top of the barricade and Kiyoshi pulled down the satellite dish that was blockading the tunnel. He quickly peered inside, using the lights on his wrists to thoroughly search the narrow space and what could be seen beyond.

"I think they've gone," he said. "You two go through first. I want to re-block this end in case we, or anyone else, ever need this space again."

Hazel plunged through first and Valentina followed, staying as close to the other girl's light as she could.

"All clear," Hazel said after a long moment, looking around from the other end of the tunnel. She climbed out and Valentina followed, clutching her spear/staff tightly and trying to look everywhere at once, the dark pressing in around them. When Kiyoshi crawled out, they dropped to the ground and continued down the tunnel at a brisk walk, Hazel and Kiyoshi constantly shining their lights around them. The little bit of ground or wall they illuminated only made the rest of the dark tunnel feel that much more immense.

They were reluctant to talk, especially here, where the echoes carried so far. They occasionally stopped at the hand sign one or another of them gave, each thinking they heard something that stopped when they stopped walking. Occasionally Valentina could hear the far-off trickle of water, but it never grew loud enough for the others to hear it too, and she worried that her thirst was making her hallucinate sounds.

They kept walking for hours, not even stopping for lunch but eating a little more nut paste directly from the foil packets as they walked.

Valentina thought of the station map they had looked at on the first day. She guessed it wasn't to scale, only an indication of the order of the stations and not how far apart they truly were. Certainly the station they were heading for next was farther away than the last had been from the first.

Valentina kept her head down, focusing on moving one foot after the other. Kiyoshi stayed a half step behind her while Hazel matched his stride, giving her steps an extra bounce to make up for her shorter legs.

As lunch fell more and more hours into the past and dinner became a more pressing thought, the exhaustion from the long walk added to the weariness left over from the sleepless night. Her spear/staff became a walking stick, the only thing keeping her on her feet. She felt herself walking more and more slowly, tripping more often and feeling each time like the trip had woken her from a walking doze.

"We need to get to the next station," Kiyoshi said to her after catching her from yet another fall.

"I know," Valentina said, but Hazel put up a hand to hush them both.

This time, they all heard it. The skittering was back.

"Run?" Hazel hissed.

"No," Kiyoshi said firmly. "If any of us faint out here—"

"Walk faster then?" Hazel persisted desperately.

They walked on, faster than before, but the skittering grew louder. The rats weren't going to try to sneak up on them this time.

"Look up ahead!" Hazel cried.

Valentina, who had been walking with her head down, focusing on not stumbling, stopped and looked up, fearing the sight of the rats closing in around them. What she saw was possibly worse. The tunnel before them narrowed down to a slender tube.

"This can't be right," Kiyoshi said.

"I don't know. It looks big enough for a train to squeeze through. Barely," Hazel said. "It only looks small because the rest is so big."

Valentina looked around, frustrated once more by the lights the other two flashed about, never where she was trying to look. But she got brief glimpses of the rails converging. Only one train at a time would have passed through this bottleneck.

"There's still plenty of room," she said.

"Assuming it's not full of rats," Hazel said. "If I were a rat, that would be where I'd lay my ratty ambush."

"Are they that intelligent?" Kiyoshi asked, but none of them wanted to answer.

"The station must be just on the other side," Valentina said. "That would be the logical place, right? Where one train or another would have to wait its turn?"

"We can't really debate it," Hazel said. "They are getting louder behind us. Can't you hear it?"

"I'm tempted to run again," Valentina said.

"No," Kiyoshi said firmly. "You can't fall down again. They are too close—they'd be all over you before I could get you back up."

Hazel took one of her missiles out of her bag and used her sling to hurl it down the tunnel. They could hear it clank on the metal rail and skitter along the rocky floor, but nothing else.

"Let's go," she said, and the others followed.

It should have been comforting, being in a place where their lights could reach every corner. But they couldn't reach every corner at once, and the tunnel just kept going on and on.

"Move faster," Kiyoshi said suddenly, his hand pressing on Valentina's back. "Fast as you can."

"Why?" Valentina looked back to ask, but the word died on her lips; the tunnel walls behind him were a writhing mass of oily black hair and red eyes, a mass that was swirling and whirling up the tunnel towards them, about to crash over them like a wave of biting, clawing hunger.

Hazel's sling whirred, and a rock the size of a fist sang through the air but disappeared into that swarm without a sound. It must have hit something soft—not wall—but there was no cry of pain, only the endless skittering of nails on rock.

Despite Kiyoshi's warning, Valentina did run then, her staff held tight across her chest. The tunnel took a bend and she couldn't see beyond it. The others with their lights too far behind her, but she was certain the station would be there; it had to be.

She rounded the bend, and the darkness in front of her growled, a low warning sound. Valentina stopped running, her too-big boots tripping her up again. She thrust her staff into the ground to catch her balance, but still went down hard on her good knee. The darkness growled again, more insistently. The lights behind her weren't getting any closer. She didn't want to look away from the growling darkness but she risked just a short glance, enough to show her Hazel walking towards her but facing the other way, sending missile after missile into the swarm of rats. Kiyoshi was even further away, rats forming a cautious circle around him. He was keeping them at bay with his twin clubs, but they slinked around him, just out of reach, waiting for an opening.

Valentina pushed herself back onto her feet, holding her staff out more spear-like now, but her eyes could pick nothing out of the darkness before her. It sounded big, that growling thing. But was it a really big rat or something else entirely?

She backed away slowly. Whatever it was, the three of them would have to face it together. She should not have run on ahead; now the rats had them separated. Keeping her spearpoint trained on the darkness, she turned to make a more sideways retreat. Hazel's bag of missiles was empty, and she tucked her sling into her belt, pulling her club free as she ran to help Kiyoshi, taking her light even further from Valentina.

"Wait!" Valentina called, her voice lost in the skittering of the rats. But the thing in the tunnel heard her, its low growl building into a shriek that brought a horrible loose feeling to her insides, as if all of her internal organs were surrendering and preparing to melt out of her. She had a brief sense of the other rats finally using their own voices, joining in that terrible shrieking, but then the darkness reached out and caught her, teeth sinking into her calf, piercing the suit and then her own flesh, and she shrieked louder than any of them.

The teeth in her leg yanked, and she went down hard, jaw meeting rock floor in a hard snap that nearly took out the tip of her tongue. The world was suddenly filled with dancing lights even as it tipped first one way then the other.

Valentina scrambled madly, getting her staff under her and trying desperately to get back up, but the teeth still in her leg yanked again and she crashed back down to the ground; this time she was dragged along the floor, dragged back into the darkness. She dropped her spear, hands grasping for any purchase, but the lava tube was too smooth, the bits that did jut out too small to cling to.

She heard Kiyoshi yelling her name and lifted her head to find him, but the exploding stars were brighter than the suit lights. The teeth let her go, the feel of them sliding out of her calf nearly as painful as the entry had been, but this time she didn't even whimper. She had to move fast. She got her hands beneath her and tried once more to get up.

Then the weight of the thing was on her back, heavier than a person. Its hot breath was on her neck, saliva dripping down into her hair. She laced her fingers around the back of her head, trying to protect what she could. The rat thing leaned close, hissing near her ear; she could almost swear it was enjoying her fear. Valentina turned her face to one side, still not able to see more than red eyes in darkness but now able to let loose a string of curses at her attacker. She might not be able to get out from under its weight, might not be able to save herself from dying far from home, far from her brother, torn apart by mutated rats, but she didn't have to meet her fate quietly.

The rat narrowed its eyes, almost as if it understood her Spanish curses. Then it leaned closer, close enough that she really could see its teeth. She kept her head twisted to the side to look back over her shoulder at her approaching death. She would not cover her face and cower in fear. The rat thing's hissing built into a roar, the teeth opening so wide her entire head could fit inside. Valentina yelled back, trying to sound fierce, but her fear made her voice tremble.

The teeth came down, and despite her strongest intentions, Valentina blinked.

CHAPTER NINETEEN

GRENDEL AND THE WARRIOR-POETS

In the speed of that eye-blink, something big hurled itself at the monster on Valentina's back and the two rolled off into the darkness together. The roar it made as it charged the rat thing had sounded human. She barely had time to register that when she realized the cave was full of human sounds, the sounds of weapons and grunts of effort or pain, but most of all, the sounds of battle cries.

"Revolution!" one shouted.

"Revolution!" several others echoed, although a few were more properly shouting, "Revolución!" Valentina crawled back to where her spear had fallen, then thrust it into the ground to hoist herself up. Her leg was on fire, but she didn't let it give way beneath her. The exploding stars faded, but the scene they had been hiding didn't make much sense, anyway.

The tunnel was filled with what appeared to be young warriors, all about her age, mostly boys but a few girls as well. They were laughing and battle-crying as they drove back the rats with clubs and axes and even a few swords. The rats hissed and spat but were retreating.

Valentina turned to look for whatever had just been on her. The tunnel was no longer lost to darkness; these young warriors had brought immense portable lights with them, the sort used to mark temporary landing sights on the surface. They were incredibly bright and lit up the entire space like midday out in the sun. But the monster that had been about to bite off her head was nowhere to be seen.

The rats fled, and the warriors cheered, but Valentina ignored them, still searching the tunnel. A hand touched her shoulder, and she turned to look at Hazel.

"What happened?" Hazel asked.

Valentina opened her mouth, then closed it again. It had only been a few moments since she had run on ahead, and yet it was already a long story.

"Kiyoshi?" she asked instead.

"Here," he said, limping toward them.

"You're bit?" she asked, but he shook his head.

"Another massive bruise, I'm sure, but my suit held up."

"Valentina!" Hazel cried, and Valentina looked down at the blood oozing from her own leg.

One of the young warriors ran up to them, a thin young man with brown skin and an excess of tightly curled back hair. "Where's Hero?"

"Hero?"

"You had Grendel on your back and he went after it."

"Grendel?" Valentina echoed again.

"Grendel!" another of the warriors boomed. This one was as broad as he was tall, his hair a shaggy strawberry-blond mane just barely tamed by a few well-placed braids. "Grendel is my mortal enemy."

"Grendel was about to bite her head clean off, or I'm sure Hero would have let you take it," the first one said.

"Who is Hero? Who are you?" Valentina asked.

"Grendel took a bite out of you," the tall one noticed. "We should get to the station and take care of that. Here, I'll carry you."

"I can walk," Valentina said, gripping her staff.

"It's not far," the dark-haired one said, and they started walking, the lights mounted on wagons rolling along with them.

At least she had been right about the station; it was just behind the bend where the tunnel once more widened to immense proportions and the one set of tracks became two. To her surprise, the tracks were not empty; there were six vehicles that looked like no more than open platforms on electromagnets lined up on the two tracks.

"Sit on that bench there," the blond one said, pointing up the stairs to the station. This station had the same hastily built blockade as the others, but here the benches had been left at regular intervals up and down the platform. Valentina limped up the stairs and slumped gratefully on the nearest bench. The tall warrior knelt before her to take her leg in his hands and examine the wound.

"We can take care of it ourselves," Kiyoshi said.

"Maybe, but I've got experience with this," the warrior said. Valentina flinched as he pulled out a knife, but before she could protest he was slicing through her suit leg, cutting both layers and all the circuitry between and tossing everything below the knee into a corner.

"Kavi, I need the grog," he said.

"No, it's not necessary," Valentina said.

"Grendel bites are nasty things," he said as the thin one with the dark curly hair handed him a stainless steel thermos. He took a drink, then offered it to her. She shook her head, and he shrugged, then dumped the rest of the contents over her wound.

Her scream echoed impressively through the cavern.

"I have antibiotics!" she said through gritted teeth.

"Why didn't you say so before? I could have saved the grog."

Valentina just shut her eyes, waiting for the burning in her leg to subside.

"You've seen bites like this before?" Kiyoshi asked.

"Sure, more times than I can count," he said. "Grendel is my mortal foe. Someday his head will hang on my trophy wall. Provided Stephen Hero doesn't hijack my destiny first."

"Here he comes," Kavi said.

The warriors were straggling back, working in pairs to pull the heavy lights, but between them jogged a lanky youth with bright red hair.

"Any wounded?" he asked as he skipped up the stairs.

"Just her, and she was hurt when we got there," the tall one said. "You went after Grendel."

"I was only driving it back. You know I would never take your kill," Hero said.

"I think you mean *never could*."

"Who are you people?" Hazel demanded.

"I'm Stephen Hero. The tall fellow here is Skald, and that is Kavi."

"Those sound like made-up names," Hazel said, narrowing her eyes.

"That's because they are, my clever friend," Hero said. He had his hands in his pockets and kept rolling his weight from the heels to toes of his sneakered feet. "We are warrior-poets, and being a warrior-poet means choosing your own perfect name."

"You're all warrior-poets?" Hazel asked.

"We're all revolutionaries, but the three of us are also warrior-poets. A few of the others aspire to join our ranks, but their craft still needs a little work. We can recite for you later when we celebrate this victory over our ratty foes."

"But I shall have no new verses for my epic poem of my ongoing fight with the monster Grendel, because Hero stepped in," Skald said.

"Don't be sore. He had her on the ground. I couldn't wait for you," Hero said.

"Thank you," Valentina said, touching the back of her head. She could feel where the creature's spittle was drying on her braids.

"My pleasure," he said with a sly smile, as if, when he said it, it wasn't just a polite cliché, as if real pleasure had been involved. She didn't know what to make of that and was grateful when Hazel drew his attention back to her.

"So you fight the rats in these tunnels and then write poems about it?"

"That rat fighting is just a sideline, really," Hero said with a dismissive wave. "As revolutionaries, our main goal is to overthrow the outdated corporate structures that are still ruling the cities of Mars and restore power to the people."

"The twelve of you?" Hazel asked.

"There are nearly a hundred of us, actually, and our numbers grow every day. But if you've read Earth history, you know it only took twenty men to overthrow Cuba."

"If you say so," Hazel said, her skepticism unabated.

"We should get inside the station," Kavi said. "The scout patrol found another food stash, and the others are anxious for the feasting to begin."

"Can you walk?" Hero asked Valentina. She nodded, gritting her teeth as she leaned on her staff to get up off the bench.

"We should dress that wound," Kiyoshi said.

"We will once we're inside," Hero said. "The rats mostly avoid us, but Grendel makes them bold. Better to blockade the doors when he's around."

This station, like the others, was walled off from the tunnel with a mountain of wrecked equipment and shelving, but the tunnel through it was large enough for them to comfortably walk through and each end had a door that could be secured with a heavy bar.

"You come here a lot?" Hazel asked as they followed Hero through the tunnel. The other warriors were setting up a camp, but he led them to some low stools arranged around an oil stove with a bright open flame dancing on top of it.

"We work our way up and down the line," he said. "As revolutionaries, it's best if we stay mobile. We don't usually go north of here, though. Rat territory. Where did you come from?"

"My balloon crashed outside of the northernmost station," Hazel said. "I'm Hazel Aelita. You've heard of the Aelita traders?"

"Sorry, no," he said. "Balloon, that sounds cool. Are you two traders as well?"

"No," Valentina said. "I'm Valentina del Toro, and this is Kiyoshi Willis. We're from the north pole. I'm heading south looking for my brother. He's in one of the corporate cities."

"Which one?"

"Valles Marineris V."

"My hometown," Hero said. "How old is your brother?"

"Twelve. Our father works for the corporation."

"Of course. Del Toro. I thought your name sounded familiar."

Valentina tried to gauge what he was thinking, but his manner was too deadpan. Before she could find words to probe, he turned to Kiyoshi. "And what's your destination?"

"I go where she goes," he said.

Valentina felt her face flush. While she couldn't dispute the words given how far they had traveled together, something in his tone was almost possessive. She wasn't sure she liked it. But Hero didn't seem to find anything unusual, just shrugged. "Fair enough. You guys hungry?"

"We have some food," Kiyoshi said, but Hero waved him off.

"Some variety of field rations, I'm sure. Hold on to it until you're starving. That's the best time for that sort of joyless food. You're welcome to join in our rat feast. Rat might not sound tasty, but we have a crate full of sauces that make it quite palatable. Plus, apparently, our scouts found some fresh goodies. We are revolutionaries. We share everything equally."

"If we eat your food, are we joining your cause?" Hazel asked.

"You think we'd trap you like the faeries from my grandmother's motherland, is that it? Our hospitality has no strings attached," Hero said. "Except perhaps one. After the feasting, we tell stories. If you've come here all the way from the north pole, that is an epic tale we'd all be dying to hear. Not that we ever get tired of telling each other our own epic tales over and over."

"I'm not much of a storyteller," Kiyoshi said.

"I came in pretty near the end," Hazel added.

"And you?" Hero asked, looking at Valentina.

"Sure, I can tell the tale," Valentina said. She remembered how her father told stories when she was young. She could take a shot at mimicking his technique.

"I'm going to dress that wound now," Kiyoshi said.

"Hold on," Hero said, then caught someone's attention with a waving gesture. They nodded and ran to the other side of the camp, digging into a mountain of crates before returning with a white first-aid box. "Sterile dressings are better. Also, we have aspirin in here that is just a little past date, probably safe. It helps with the pain."

Valentina nodded gratefully and swallowed two of the bitter pills with a swig from another stainless steel thermos. She had been fearing it was more grog, but this one was water, slightly metallic-tasting but so good.

"The suit is definitely not reparable now," she said as Kiyoshi examined her wound.

"You lost the hat as well," Hazel said, and Valentina reached up and felt nothing but her own braids.

"I must have lost it when the Grendel thing tackled me," she said. "I'm sorry."

"I'm just worried you'll get cold," Hazel said.

"Not even a worry," Hero said. "Sit close to the stove; I'll be right back."

Kiyoshi watched him go. Valentina dug the antibiotic cream out of her suit pocket and he took it from her before she could wrestle the cap off. He squeezed what was left of the tube into his hand and divided it equally among the tooth marks on both sides of her calf.

"That's already getting red," Hazel said. "Maybe we should ask if they have some oral antibiotics, just to be on the safe side."

"I think if they had any he would have offered it already," Valentina said, gritting her teeth as Kiyoshi's fingers found a particularly tender spot.

"They are very hospitable," Kiyoshi said in a low whisper.

"If you're thinking perhaps too hospitable, I'm with you," Hazel said.

"He comes from the same city Arturo is in now. He might be able to help," Valentina said.

"In return for what? Joining his revolution?" Hazel asked.

"I need to get to Arturo," Valentina said.

"At any cost?" Hazel asked. Valentina didn't answer. Kiyoshi looked up at her as he wrapped the linen around her leg, not speaking either.

She hadn't introduced him to Hero as her cousin. Had he noticed?

"I don't have another hat, but I have a little pouch," Hazel said, digging through her suit pocket. "If you're ditching your suit, you're going to need something to carry all your stuff. It's not strong enough for sling missiles, but it should handle dry rations and whatnot." She pulled out a knit pouch of bright magenta on a long cord with a row of fringe along the bottom. It was small, but probably large enough for what little Valentina still carried with her.

"Thanks," Valentina said, emptying out her pockets as Kiyoshi tied off the ends of the bandage. When he was finished, she put a hand on his shoulder to hoist herself up and the other two helped her step out of the tattered remains of don Abuelo's suit.

"I had hoped to be able to return that to your mother," Valentina said with regret.

"She never expected to see it again," Kiyoshi said. "It was just a useless antique you managed to wring a little more use out of. Don't worry about it."

Valentina smiled—perhaps not the widest of smiles—but was too tired and sore to manage more effusive thanks.

Hero returned with an armful of clothes. "Here," he said, handing her a thick wool sweater. "One of mine my mother knit for me, alas, too small for me now. It will keep you warm; it's like wearing a blanket."

"I can't take a gift from your mother—"

"Don't be silly. It's too small to do me any good, and we revolutionaries try not to form sentimental attachments to objects. We share what we have and take care of each other. This is going to keep you warmer than that old suit. Besides, the maroon clashes horribly with my hair. Don't know what she was thinking. Here," he said, pulling it over her head and helping her find the sleeves. It was a thick cable knit with a tall roll collar that reached her earlobes. It fell nearly to her knees, and she had to push back the sleeves to uncover her hands. "Yes, that color looks much better on you."

"Thanks," Valentina said. "I'm warmer already." She also felt incredibly tiny, although among the people of the north pole she was of average height. Kiyoshi had towered over everyone back home, but among the revolutionaries, he was average. Hero was a bit taller; Skald was a proper giant.

"I've got more stuff here," Hero said, turning back to the pile of clothes he had dumped on his stool. "Stockings, leggings, pants, and a skirt—pick what you like. Also..." He turned back to her and displayed a pair of ankle boots with a flourish. "I'm guessing these will fit. Certainly better than that clunky suit, which I'm guessing wasn't even yours."

"No, it was my grandfather's," Valentina said, peeling off the remains of the stockings Hazel's family had given her, now torn and stiff with dried blood, and pulling on a pair of black leggings under her skirts, then a pair of thick knit stockings, and then the boots. "Perfect."

"You won't need all the layers when we get inside the Valles Marineris cities."

"Are you all heading that way?" she asked.

"The same way you are, in fact. Valles Marineris V is first on our agenda. My former home. Long overdue visit."

The warm feeling of relief that spilled over Valentina was only cooled a bit by the look Hazel and Kiyoshi exchanged. She knew they were suspicious, but she didn't care. Anything that got her closer to her brother was a good thing.

A cheer filled the room and Valentina turned to see four warriors coming through the tunnel, carrying skinned rats on skewers. They paraded them around the room, then brought them to the immense oil stove. There was room enough across the surface to set six rats at a time, slowly turning on spits over the flickering flame. The smell soon filled the room, but the warriors didn't wait for the meat to be ready to start the feasting. A large canvas sack was dragged to where Hero was sitting and he got up from his stool to open the sack and peer inside.

"Oh, well done!" he declared to the two warriors who had brought it to them—the scouts who had found this stash, Valentina guessed. "We haven't had a score like this in ages!" Then he started handing out the contents of the sack: packets of crackers with square blocks of bright orange cheese, plastic pouches of dried fruit, and bags of nuts, more kinds of nuts than Valentina had names for.

"Give a little bit of everything to our guests," Hero commanded everyone, and then Kiyoshi, Hazel, and Valentina were inundated with people handing them crackers spread with cheese, handfuls of fruit carefully selected to contain one of each kind, and all sorts of nuts.

"I bet you've never had anything like this before," Hero said.

"I have," Hazel said. "My family are traders, like I said."

"Probably not so much at once, though," Hero said, but Hazel just shrugged.

"I think it's fantastic," Valentina said.

"We don't eat like this every night," he admitted. "Most nights it's porridge or beans or rice, whatever we can find. But every so often we find something really good some plague survivor stashed away and forgot about. Here, try this."

Valentina held out her hand, but he shook his head.

"Close your eyes and open your mouth. It's a surprise."

Valentina hesitated, but all the other food had been so good she had to try whatever he clearly thought topped it all. She closed her eyes, and he put a square of something on her tongue. She closed her mouth and the smooth sweetness melted over her tongue, filling her mouth with a rich goodness she had no name for. She only opened her eyes when the last bit had melted away and slid effortlessly down her throat.

"That," Hero said with another sly grin, "was chocolate."

The first batch of rat meat was passed around the group, everyone tearing off hunks and passing the skewers to the next person. A second batch was already roasting, so no one need worry about not getting enough. Each rat had been brushed with a different sauce as it roasted over the flame, some sweet, some sour, some spicy hot, all good. More thermoses of grog were passed around, but Valentina stuck with the water. The whiff of grog she had gotten when Skald poured it over her leg had burned her nose hairs; she was sure one sip would be enough to send her right to bed, and she still had a story to tell.

Many of the warriors were already telling theirs. For a fight that had lasted no more than a few minutes, the stories took much longer to tell, each moment rendered in loving detail, every gesture or thought given full discourse. The others cheered and yawped at the highlights and there was much backslapping and fists pumped into the air.

By the third batch of rat meat, some of the others were calling for Skald's tale. Although he made a grumpy show of not having a new verse to relate, he inevitably conceded to tell once more the epic of Skald versus Grendel. It was a long poem with a driving rhythm, and it was clear the warriors knew it well, punctuating certain verses with cries of "Skald, warrior true!" or "Grendel, curse of the deep!" Valentina had never heard poetry before, but she knew stories, and while she doubted many of the details were true, it was a rousing tale.

"Hero, tell us about your fight with Grendel!" someone called when Skald was done.

"No, no," he begged off. "I didn't really fight Grendel today, just added another moment of building tension to Skald's tale."

"Go on, build the tension, then," Skald said, but Hero waved his request away. "No, let Kavi tell one."

The room fell silent as Kavi stood before the dancing flames and recited a long passage in a language Valentina had never heard before. The words twisted and swooped in a rhythm he controlled with a nonchalant ease. She didn't understand a word of it, but Valentina felt like by listening to it she could understand what poetry was meant to be. When he finished, the room erupted into thunderous applause. Kavi bowed and sat back down on his camp stool. Valentina leaned behind Hero to catch his sleeve and he looked at her questioningly.

"What language was that?"

"Bengali, my mother tongue."

"Can you tell me the poem in English?"

"I could try, but it would lose all that made it a poem."

"Do all the revolutionaries speak Bengali?"

"Not a one of them. I reckon there are only ten people on all of Mars who could understand my poetry. But it's not the same in any other language. My heart speaks Bengali always."

"The life of a poet," Hero said. "It often feels like spilling out your heart to the unlistening void. But Kavi lives to the extremes. His warrior style is equally obscure."

Kavi shrugged and went back to eating.

"No poetry from you?" Valentina asked.

"Not tonight. Tonight, you tell us the tale of your journey here."

One of the others overheard Hero's remark and shouted for her tale, and others took up the cry. Valentina leveraged herself up on her staff, shooing away Kiyoshi's attempt to get her to stay seated. Her calf throbbed, but the burning had faded. She reckoned it looked worse than it was.

Her audience fell silent, and she was aware of every pair of eyes on her, waiting for her to begin. But the journey wasn't the important part, really. She had to get them all to understand how crucial it was that she get to her brother. They were young and more than a little wild, but they didn't have the dangerous recklessness of the polar cartel kids. She could make them feel as she felt if she chose her words carefully enough.

So she started her tale before the beginning of her journey. She started with the day her brother had gone missing. She started with her face-off with the don.

CHAPTER TWENTY

AMONG THE REVOLUTIONARIES

THE RICH SMELL OF COFFEE DRAGGED VALENTINA AWAKE. SHE KNEW THE smell from the marketplace back home but had never tasted it; in the days when she could have afforded it, she had been too young to want to try any. She opened her eyes to find Stephen Hero bent over her camp bed, a steaming mug in his hands.

"Good morning," he said. "We're going to be moving out soon. You're coming with us?"

"Yes, of course," Valentina said, sitting up and rubbing the sleep from her eyes. Everything from the night before after telling her long tale was a blur; she only vaguely remembered being led by someone to the far end of the room and given a blanket to roll up in. The air was cooler this far from the oil stove, but the mug Hero pressed into her hands warmed her. She leaned her face into the steam and filled her lungs with its aroma.

"Some of the boys are making a pot of porridge with what's left of the fruit and nuts, should be pretty tasty. Then it's a long day's ride; we want to be at the end of the red line before we stop. How's your leg?"

"It doesn't feel too bad, but I should probably change the dressing." She flexed her foot. It felt like there were hot knots in her calf muscle, but it wasn't nearly as bad to walk on as her other leg had been when she'd wrenched her knee jumping the crevasse.

"The first-aid kit is still by the stove. Do you want some help?"

"No, I've got it. Thanks."

He nodded and left, moving through the groups of young revolutionaries, stopping now and again to speak with one or another of them. One of the guards from the doorway came bounding up to him, catching his elbow to speak a word in his ear, then they both went bounding back to the door the other guards were opening to let just one person slip inside. It was a kid younger even than Arturo, his dark head neatly shaven and bare despite the cold. He was waifishly thin, but he spoke to Hero with an intensity she could feel even though she was too far away to hear his words. Hero nodded and listened, his face grave. Then he glanced up, saw her watching him, and gave her a quick smile, pointing with his chin toward the campfire. She nodded and got to her feet, taking another long sniff of the coffee before trying a sip.

Valentina grimaced. The smell was divine, but the taste was bitter. Still, she could feel the caffeine jolt, like lifting a gauzy veil from before her eyes, a veil she hadn't even realized was there. She took another, bigger sip, grimaced again, then brought the mug with her as she went to where they had been sitting the night before next to the stove. The two young boys stirring the porridge gave her a friendly nod as she settled on one of the camp stools and set her mug down to peel back layers of leggings and socks and unwind the dressing.

Despite the hot, knotted feeling where the teeth had pierced her flesh, the wound looked clean. She dug through the kit and found alcohol swabs, but no antibiotic cream. She cleaned the surface of the wound with the alcohol, sucking in her breath when she wiped over the open sores, then wrapped the area in fresh linen. When she was done, one of the boys handed her a bowl of porridge. That, at least, was every bit as good as it smelled.

"I liked your story last night," the younger of the two boys said. "Did you really jump a chasm of ice?"

"It's all true," Valentina said. "As real as that Grendel thing that took a bite out of me yesterday."

"You've seen like half of Mars!"

"Not quite, but more than I ever expected to."

"I've never been out of these tunnels," he said glumly. "I'd love to see the surface just once."

"Weren't you born in one of the cities?" she asked.

"No, my family was kicked out before I was born."

"Where are they now?" she asked, looking around the room. She spotted Kiyoshi and Hazel talking together near the camp beds.

"All dead and gone. I run with the band now; it's better than being alone."

Valentina frowned as she watched her two friends talking. They seemed so intent, standing close and glancing around as if fearful of being overheard. Then she remembered the boy talking to her and turned to him with a small smile.

"I didn't see the surface myself until this whole adventure began. I'm sure you'll get there someday."

"I want to fly in a balloon like your friend. Do you think she'd let me?"

"You'd have to ask her," Valentina said. "Although her balloon was wrecked when we crashed. I'm not sure how she'll get her hands on another one."

Kiyoshi glanced her way and saw her watching them. Valentina quickly dropped her eyes, finding her now cold coffee sitting on the ground next to her stool and downing the contents in a few long swallows.

"You want some more?" the boy asked.

"No, I'm good," Valentina said. As the packing up was completed, more and more revolutionaries came to the stove for their share of the porridge. Valentina picked up her staff and backed out of the way.

"Hey," Hazel said by way of greeting as she and Kiyoshi walked up to Valentina.

"Hey," Valentina answered. "Did you two eat?"

"We're good," Hazel said vaguely, standing with crossed arms as she watched the others eating hurriedly and passing the bowl back to be refilled and given to another.

"Are you guys angry?" Valentina said, not sure what else their sullen demeanors could mean. "I hope you don't think I misrepresented you in my story. I mean, I could fix it if I got something wrong, or you could tell your own stories. These guys really like stories."

"Yes, they do," Hazel said, but she let the rest of what Valentina had said pass without comment. Valentina looked to Kiyoshi but he wouldn't meet her eyes.

"Ready to ride?" Hero asked as he suddenly appeared at Valentina's elbow.

"I think so," she said. She wanted to ask him about the boy he had been talking to but sensed it wasn't the time.

"I ride on the front car," he went on, "or rather the first car in the convoy, behind the scout car. Would you like to come with me?"

"Sure," Valentina said. She looked to her two scowling friends, but the invitation for them to join her and Hero died on her lips. She couldn't understand how they could be so rude after being treated with such hospitality, but she couldn't ask them about it now. She turned to Hero instead. "Let's go."

The two doors were unbarred and set aside, and a pair of scouts slipped out first, weapons at the ready. When they whistled the all clear, another pair of revolutionaries followed, each pulling one of the massive airstrip lights on the back of a wagon. Then Hero put a hand on her back and the two of them passed through the long doorway to the train tunnel.

The two lights in front of them lit every corner of the space, more and more brightly as other lights came through the doorway to join them and be dispersed among the six train cars. The bigger camping equipment was left inside the station, but the bedding and food stores were packed into crates and carried out onto the train.

"Did you build these?" Valentina asked. They didn't look remotely like the trains she had seen in pictures.

"No, they were for the maintenance crews originally; we found them in a separate storage area and carried them onto the tracks. They aren't as fast as the full-sized trains, but they suit us just fine."

"Won't we fall off?" Valentina asked as he helped her onto the platform. She knew they were floating on magnets, but it didn't feel like floating; it felt completely solid. But the rail that ran around the sides of the car only came up to her ankles.

"We won't be going all that fast. Just sit in the middle and you'll be fine."

Valentina settled herself with her staff across her lap, her back to a crate full of sleeping bags. She turned to look back over her shoulder and saw Kiyoshi and Hazel climbing onto another train car, sitting together but not looking her way. For some reason, she had been afraid they would turn and walk the other way, but that way led back to the rats. They clearly weren't comfortable among the revolutionaries, but even crazy armed-to-the-teeth young people with a love for violent stories were less frightening than those mutated rodents.

Hero sat down beside her and flipped open a floor panel she hadn't even noticed. The train car parallel to them zipped forward, its light disappearing in the long tunnel ahead. Then Hero turned a knob, and they started after it, albeit much more slowly. Slow being a relative thing; Valentina watched the ground zipping past them and judged they were moving along three times as fast as Kiyoshi's rover had managed at top speed. She tried to imagine how it would feel to be flying along on that scout train but couldn't imagine it. There was nothing to hold on to but the crate behind her, which was no more secure than she was.

"I liked your story," Hero said.

"So you said last night. A couple of times. But thanks."

"You think I'm not serious. I don't just mean what you did was fantastic, because it was. I'm saying you tell it really well. I think you might be a warrior-poet yourself."

"I don't think either title really applies."

"Maybe not yet, but I don't know that it does for any of us. Not really." He leaned in closer, speaking in a conspiratorial whisper. "It's more of an aspiration. We aspire to be warriors and poets."

"I still don't think that fits me."

"I'll admit you work in prose and not verse, but it's a sort of poetry."

"That's not what I meant."

"Oh, it's 'warrior' you don't like."

"I just said I don't think it applies, not that I don't like it," Valentina said.

"But it's true. You don't like that word."

Valentina sighed. "Where I grew up, there was a lot of fighting. Don Abuelo, my grandfather, kept it to a minimum, always negotiating between the different cartels, finding ways to keep everyone happy. He didn't always succeed, but the fights that did break out were small, short, and infrequent. Ever since he died, no one has been willing to fill his shoes, and the violence has gotten out of control."

"But you fight against it, in your own way."

"I stood up to a don once, for the sake of my brother, and that brother was taken away so soon afterward I don't know if even that was effective," she admitted.

"You stood up to him once, but by your same logic, you left the north pole before it might have been necessary for you to do so again. See, I think if you had stayed, and the need arose, you would have done it again. Furthermore, you'd learn something each time. The dons would listen to you like they listened to your grandfather."

Valentina scoffed. "They listened to don Abuelo because, before he came to Mars, his father had been the head of a cartel in México. He had a name that others feared."

"Don Abuelo? Doesn't that just mean like 'lord grandfather'?"

"That's not the feared name. That's the loved name. I won't speak the other," Valentina said. "But I'd be a fool to think I could take his place."

"It sounded from your story like the north pole might be lost to years of cartels fighting cartels now."

"Maybe. The one good thing about my brother being kidnapped is that it took him away from there. When I get my brother back, we're not going back home, that's for sure. We don't even have a home there anymore."

"He's not necessarily better off where he is," Hero said.

"There are cartels in the city?"

"No, the danger in the cities is not from so honest a source."

"So honest? Cartels are gangsters, you know."

"I know, but you know what to expect with a gangster and how to engage his self-interest, right? The evil in the city is more insidious. It has no recognizable face to fight; it's everywhere. It's in all the people."

"I don't understand."

"The people are being brainwashed to act against their own self-interest. Look at my band of revolutionaries; every one of us was thrown away by the cities, left to die on the surface or in these tunnels. Why? Because the cities are overpopulated and banishing criminals is easier for the people to accept than family size laws? If I say it that way, it sounds obvious the answer is yes, but then I'd make you dig further. Talk to my compatriots about their so-called crimes. We were labeled as criminals because they wanted to be rid of us. We broke no laws, at least no important ones. It was because we don't fit in with their narrow definitions—we think and do for ourselves. That's why we are the ones who have to set the others free. They don't even see the danger."

Valentina rubbed at her head. It was a lot of vague rhetoric, but he seemed so sincere.

"But as I was saying, as a warrior-poet, which you are, you need a name."

"I have a name."

"No, every warrior-poet takes a second name. A nom de plume, if you will."

"Nom de guerre," Valentina mumbled, but he laughed.

"Yes, that too. So what shall we call you?"

"Honestly, I have no idea. Where does your name come from?"

"Ireland," he said proudly. "My grandmother's motherland. It's the name of a fictional character, someone whose life story was never quite finished. He started out well, being clever and different from all the others. Then when he had totally formed who he was, like the idealized version of himself but, you know, one that existed in the real world, he headed out away from his homeland to find his destiny. And nothing more was ever written. Except my own scribblings, maybe. I like to imagine what he did next. Although I don't think I'll really a grasp of it until my own story moves past that point."

"I don't really know any writers or characters," Valentina admitted.

"The stories I learned were all family stories, and I already have those names."

"And you're too young to be a dona Abuela, that's for sure," Hero said. "Skald's name is just the Norse word for the reciter of poetry. And Kavi is the same in Sanskrit. How would you say something like storyteller in Spanish?"

"Cuentista," Valentina said. "Or maybe cronista is more what you're looking for. Like a chronicler."

"Yes. Cronista del Norte. That suits you," Hero said.

Valentina laughed. "If you say so."

CHAPTER TWENTY-ONE

CONNECTIONS AND DISCONNECTIONS

THE DAY PASSED QUICKLY. VALENTINA SCARCELY NOTICED THE GENTLE throbbing of her wounded calf, occupied as she was with describing every element of life under the polar ice cap. Hero listened intently, always with another question at the ready when she had finished answering the last one.

"You don't have a residual corporate structure, but it's not so different on the pole as it is in the equatorial cities," Hero said. "There is an uncrossable line dividing the people who have the power and the people who do all the work."

"Actually, the cartel power structures are quite fluid," Valentina said.

"Not them, the scientists who sit inside the station proper and never come out. Or more properly, the descendants of scientists, like the rest of you are the descendants of the refugees. Am I right?"

"It's not uncrossable, though. My father was descended from the scientists and my mother from the refugees."

"But I'm guessing you're pretty unique, Cronista," Hero persisted.

"Yes," she admitted.

"And your parents split up ages ago."

"Yes. And the station doors shut a few years ago. They don't come out and we don't go in. I don't know what changed, why they did that. It's a relatively new thing."

Valentina saw the light of the scout car ahead of them. She had caught occasional glimpses of it before when the rails ran in a straight line for long enough, but now it was growing brighter; they were catching up to it. Or rather, it was slowing to match their speed, running parallel to them on the other track. The boy from that morning was one of the riders and he was beckoning to Hero.

"Who is that kid?" Valentina asked, but Hero ignored the question.

"Man the controls," he said, getting to his feet.

"What? How?"

"Well, since I just need you to keep it steady, that means don't touch anything." He laughed dryly. "It'll be fine. I'll be right back."

Then he leapt from their train car to the other, completely oblivious to the ground racing beneath him. The scouts on the other car had their hands out to catch him if he needed it, but he landed neatly on one toe, bringing the other foot up beside it to stand casually, like he did this sort of thing all the time.

Valentina looked at the controls, but the labels were not in Spanish or English. She supposed pushing the stick forward made it go faster, and pulling it back would slow down or stop, but the two dials beside it were a complete mystery. She kept her hands in her lap.

Then Hero landed back on their train car with a soft thump and sat beside her once more, acting for all the word like their conversation had never been interrupted.

"Things are starting to build to a breaking point all over Mars," he said. "Population pressures. Too many descendants of refugees are beginning to notice that we outnumber the people manning the controls and hoarding the best of everything for themselves. We might not even have to move into every city for the revolution to happen. We might just motivate a lot of people, people who are already feeling the same way we do, to do something about it."

Valentina watched the scout car race off ahead of them again. "Did they have news of trouble up ahead?" she asked.

"No, everything is progressing smoothly. A bit quicker than I had expected, actually, but that's not a bad thing."

"What's moving quicker?"

"The revolution," he said with that infectious grin. "Like I said, we are about to show the way. Soon the rest of Mars will follow. We will all have equal access to everything, equal say in how our resources get dispersed."

Valentina nodded, but she doubted the cartels would ever set their differences aside to join forces against the science station that controlled most of the air, water, heat, and power at the north pole.

The train cars didn't stop for lunch; Hero merely opened a container of cold, leftover rat meat and some crackers and they ate as they talked. Without her suit chronometer, Valentina had no way to gauge the time, but it felt like it was deep into the night before she saw the light of the scout car once more in front of them. Valentina thought it was coming back their way, but then she realized it was stationary and they were running up to it. Hero slowed them down gradually until they coasted to a gentle halt next to the scout car. Two of the scouts were already unloading the light from their vehicle and bringing it up the steps to another blockaded station.

Hero helped Valentina down to the ground and called one of the scouts back to help him unload the crates. The other train cars were pulling up behind them on both tracks, with many shouted greetings as people were once more close enough to talk to someone besides their travel partner. One of the cars came in too fast and bumped the car in front of it with a shriek of metal and many jeers and catcalls.

Valentina stayed where she was beside the front car, leaning on her staff, until Kiyoshi and Hazel walked up the line to her.

"We're making good time, I reckon," Valentina said to them. "This is so much nicer than walking through the dark."

"They say the rats don't really come down this way, so we're probably safer too," Hazel said. "I guess if these folks can deliver us right to your brother's doorstep, there's no reason not to travel with them."

"No, no reason," Valentina agreed, but there was something strange in the way Hazel had said it. "Is there?"

"I'm not sure these are the nicest of people," Hazel said, leaning closer and pitching her voice low. "I get the sense that intruders into their space are usually treated much like the rats."

"Why would you think that? They've been nothing but kind to us so far."

"We weren't in their territory when they found us," Kiyoshi said.

"But they stuck their necks out for us, anyway."

"You don't think they just like to fight rats?" Hazel asked.

"Obviously they do. But then they fed us, gave me a bunch of warm clothes; I'm so grateful not to be marching in that suit anymore, tripping over my own feet. And they're taking me to my brother."

"You've only really been talking to Hero," Hazel said. "He's a good talker."

"And?"

"We've been chatting with some of the others. Some of the things they have to say are a bit disturbing."

"Like what?" She looked from Kiyoshi to Hazel and back again, but they both seemed reluctant to offer a response.

In the end Kiyoshi just repeated, "They're not nice people."

"If they're nice to us and get us where we're going, I guess that's good enough for me."

"Yes, but why are they nice to us?" Hazel asked. "What do they want from us?"

"I would guess they'd like to recruit us to their revolution, only no one has been trying to sell me on that. Have they been trying to win you over?" Valentina asked.

"No," Kiyoshi said.

"So what then?"

Kiyoshi waved his hand in a vague gesture, but Hazel leaned closer in. "He's coming back over. Just keep your eyes open, please, Valentina?"

Hero strolled up to them, hands in his pockets, nodding a greeting at Kiyoshi and Hazel. "You guys doing OK? Anything you need?" he asked.

"We're good," Hazel said.

"We should get inside so they can seal the doors for the night. The teams we were scheduled to meet up with beat us here, so we're just waiting on you."

"Sorry we held you up," Valentina said, but Hero waved it off. She took a step that was more of a limp than she expected. She took a few more and her muscles started to loosen.

"How's your leg?" Kiyoshi asked Valentina.

"It's not bad. I'm just a little stiff from sitting all day. It's actually my other knee that still twinges a bit when I walk. I don't think that injury ever healed properly."

"When you find your father, he can probably get that fixed for you with the miracles of corporate medicine," Hazel said.

Valentina stopped dead just outside the door and clutched her staff tightly. A little voice in the back of her mind was whispering to her that she was just tired and cranky, but the big voice in the rest of her mind was angry that her quest would be so grossly misunderstood, that anyone could think her motive was one of such self-interest. "I'm not looking for my father," Valentina said coldly.

"Yeah, I know," Hazel said, startled by her reaction. "But he's going to be there when you find your brother, right?"

Valentina sighed and rubbed at her head, letting the little voice have its say. "Sorry I snapped. It's just—I hadn't thought I'd be seeing my father. But you're probably right, I'll have to. And he will try to sway me with his riches. Again. Like my love for my brother could be sold for a price."

"We can get to your brother without dealing with your father," Hero said, waving them into the tunnel through the blockade. "No worries, Cronista."

Valentina saw Kiyoshi and Hazel trade a glance, and Hazel mouthed, "Cronista?" but Valentina ignored them.

"You're going to help me that far?" she asked Hero. "I only expected help getting to the city."

"I told you, I know that place like the back of my hand. I know all the secret ways."

"And you'll help me?"

"I have some revolutionary business that is going to take me back inside the city. No reason not to take you along."

Valentina turned to smile back at him as they emerged through the other end of the tunnel, but out of the corner of her eye she saw the hard look Hazel was shooting her way. Was she foolish to trust him so much? But then he smiled back, gave her shoulder a friendly punch, and moved on to talk to the nearest group of revolutionaries, who greeted him warmly. She didn't feel foolish. He seemed absolutely sincere, not like he was hiding anything. He was confident, but not overly so.

Valentina blinked at the sudden thought that entered her head, but she couldn't argue the truth of it; he reminded her of don Abuelo.

That night with twice as many revolutionaries gathered around the fire the storytelling was twice as raucous, the choruses of Skald's epic rang twice as loud, and Valentina got to tell her story again, finessing some parts she thought she could tell better than she had the night before. She also told some other stories, her father's old tales of her ancestors and their exploits. The food was not as extensive, more dried foodstuffs like beans, lentils, and rice with rat leftovers and no choco-late, but the companionship made even the meager fare into a high feast.

Valentina sat beside Hero and was introduced to every one of the revolutionaries who had been waiting at the rendezvous point and who wanted to say a few words to Hero. Skald and Kavi were also busy hearing reports from the other groups and, where needed, giving a few words of guidance with what to do with the supplies the groups had brought back. Valentina kept looking across the flames from the oil stove to where Hazel and Kiyoshi sat. They ate everything offered to them and talked with the people sitting near them, but it was like they sat inside an invisible bubble, never quite letting themselves be part of what was going on around them. She frowned, not sure what to make of this. She was listening and observing, just like they asked, but everything she heard sounded perfectly benign. The groups reporting in had found abandoned stashes of food or clothing or other supplies. A few reported brief encounters with what they described as security details from the cities, but only one reported a fight and that had ended with the revolutionaries retreating. It was nothing at all like the bravado among the cartels. She couldn't understand what Hazel was worried about. But then she had grown up among traders; perhaps this felt like something else to someone not used to real violence.

So why did Kiyoshi agree with her?

In the morning, they divided themselves among the train cars again. The groups they had met up with had been traveling on foot, so there were twice as many people climbing onto the six cars, but Hero made sure that only Valentina rode his car with him, artfully deflecting anyone who approached to one of the other cars.

When they were once again up to speed, she turned to him. "So yesterday I told you all about the north pole. Now it's your turn to tell me about life in the equatorial cities."

"It's surprisingly alike in a lot of ways. Under a dome rather than in mining caves, but a lot alike."

"But you have no cartels. Doesn't the corporation provide everything you need? Although I guess you said they hoard it."

"They're providers in the sense that they decide what it is you need to be given. You eat what they give you, wear what they provide for you, live where they tell you to."

"Is that bad?"

"Not if you're higher up the corporate ladder. But for bottom-dwellers like my mother and me, things aren't so nice. There's over-crowding, that's true all over Mars. All over the Solar System, really. Places designed for small populations took in way too many refugees after the plague and now we're all stuck together in teeny tiny places, at the mercy of whoever controls the livable environments.

"My father died when I was five, so I don't really remember him. My mother works in a kitchen. She has arthritis and sometimes it gets so bad she can't really work. Rather than give her more meds, which are expensive, they dock her for the hours she can't work because her hands are gnarled into talons that are no good for chopping onions. We live in the hallway of an apartment complex; the people who live in the actual apartments have to walk through our 'house' to get to theirs. They aren't much better off—the apartments are tiny pods and we all share a bathroom at the end of the hall—but at least they have some privacy. When she was having a particularly bad spell, our food chits would get docked as well. No meat, no dairy, just the blandest of porridges and dals and all the farmed algae you want. But no one ever wants much of that; farmed algae is nasty. Always tastes like the vats they grow it in, no matter how they try to flavor it."

"Your mother is still there?" Valentina asked.

"So far as I know; I can't really communicate with her. When I was twelve, I started cutting school to do odd jobs for some shady people who worked in the black market. I got paid in proper money, which is a rare thing, and used that money to buy food that was better than the swill the cafeterias would serve us. But mostly I used it to buy medicines for my mom. The drugs the corporate doctor told her she needed are hard to find; I couldn't get them often, but when I did, it was amazing to see how much she changed. Her hands would unclench. She could work more, but it wasn't just that. Without that constant pain, her personality was totally different, like how she had been when I was little. The pain makes her withdrawn, tired. Without it, she sings and laughs and tells stories. I love seeing her that way. But then the drugs run out and the pain comes back. When I couldn't find the real drugs, I tried some folk remedies. All the folk remedies, really. They're never worth a spit."

"I know," Valentina said, remembering the endless cups of herbal tea that had done nothing to stop her own mother's decline.

"I kept that up for two years or so, but I was arrested while doing deliveries for my boss—illicit chocolate, of all things. It was a first offense, but they threw in the truancy as well, and somehow that totaled up to someone who didn't deserve the glories of corporate life. If I had meant to be a good citizen, I would have been dozing through endless mindless lessons, only designed to make me a good worker drone, not hustling to provide what my mother needed but couldn't get. They didn't offer me a second chance, not that I would have taken it. Well, I might have. They pushed me out the airlock without even letting my mother say goodbye. The last time I saw her was before she went to work the day I was arrested."

"They pushed you out an airlock? That's a death sentence! How did you survive that?"

"They push a lot of people out the airlock. Always the same one. There's a little shack village just on the other side, bits of garbage welded airtight and kept livable by the remains of the environmental systems of the refugee ship that is its heart. I was only outside for a minute. Less than that. Two of them with suits came out and brought me inside. The terraforming has a long way to go, but it's not like it was when humans first came to Mars. The pressure is low, both my eardrums blew out, and it was cold, wicked cold. But I was inside their village before I ran out of air in my lungs."

"That's horrible," Valentina said.

"We've had some close brushes with death, you and I, yeah?" he said with a dry laugh. "I lived in the village for a bit. There are a lot of throwaways living there. The corporation pushes a kid or two out every week and those stern separatists save them all, give them work to do inside their community or help them move on to some other place if they have a place to go. The original occupiers of that downed ship had voluntarily left the corporation long ago. They didn't like the lifestyle inside. But they didn't like me preaching revolution to the other throwaways, either. So as soon as I'd earned enough doing odd jobs to get my own suit and oxygen, I walked on to the next dome and the trash village that had sprung up at its doorstep, and I preached some more. Then I met a kid who knew about this metro line. There are ways in from all the cities as well as from the surface. Once we had a place to go, we left the villages and gathered here. I still send people to preach the revolution in the villages; new kids are thrown out of the cities every day, but it's getting to be time for the next step."

"Revolution," Valentina said. "That means war."

"Not necessarily," Hero said. "I would prefer to avoid violence if at all possible. But we have to be prepared. War may be the only way to justice."

CHAPTER TWENTY-TWO

VIOLENCE AND PARTINGS

THE SOUND OF SHOUTING UP AHEAD PUT VALENTINA ON EDGE, BUT HERO only grinned, and she realized the shouts were celebratory and not angry.

"The red line. This is where we stop for the night," he told her. "Sounds like one of the other patrols found something good."

"More food?"

"Maybe. Or maybe some weapons. That's what we're truly hunting for. Can't really storm a city with clubs and handmade blades."

Valentina didn't answer. The shouting and laughing still sounded aggressive to her. Then they drew nearer, and she saw the scout train stopped on the other track, the two warriors that had been riding on it laughing and backslapping another group of young revolutionaries. The new group was four boys and two girls, all red-cheeked and sweaty, as if they had just been running. Or fighting; a few were cleaning their weapons with cloths or the legs of their own pants.

"Hero!" one cried as Hero stopped their train car next to the other. The new group swarmed forward to circle their leader as he leapt down. Valentina climbed down after but stayed near the car, clutching her staff anxiously. She didn't like the look of these new guys. Their eyes were too wild.

"So, Taub, what did you find?" Hero asked. "Food?"

"Better: fuel," Taub said. Valentina guessed he was the leader of this smaller group. He certainly had the tallest hair. She wondered what he had plastered it with to get it to stand straight up in spikes like that.

"Oh, very nice," Hero said, inspecting the canisters they brought out to show him. "This will last us for months."

"It's scarce on the open market," Skald said, examining the canisters, unscrewing the tops to first look inside and then take a tentative sniff. "This is the real thing. We can trade it for weapons—it's worth enough to get us guns, I know it is."

"Viva la revolución," Taub said smugly. A few others echoed the sentiment, but Valentina was distracted by a figure making its way toward them from down the red line. It appeared to be a man, but he was barely walking upright, leaning against the wall of the tunnel so that he was lost to shadows.

"Please, stop," the man said as he drew nearer.

"This guy again? Gil, you told me he was out cold," Taub said.

"He was out cold," Gil said. The man pushed away from the wall and stumbled towards them. In the light, they could see his face was half covered in blood.

"I need that fuel. I can't let you take it."

"Let us?" Taub laughed.

"It belongs to the corporation, it's not mine," the man went on.

"Why is the corporation moving fuel through the metro lines?" Hero asked, frowning.

"It was a gift from our governor to the governor of our sister city."

"Was he alone?" Hero asked Taub.

"There were two younger guys. They fought harder than this one. They won't be a problem now," Taub said, and Hero nodded.

Valentina's stomach went hot and sour. They fought harder, so they had been killed? What else could he have meant?

"A secret gift, then, or you would have had a regiment of security going with you, am I right?" Hero said, but the man didn't answer, just pressed the corner of his shirt to the bleeding gash in his head. "Hey, I understand. I used to do your job. I was never trusted with anything as valuable as fuel, but I know how the market of secret gifts and favors operates."

"Then you know if I return without it, I'm as good as dead," he said.

"You're halfway there now," Taub said, but he stopped laughing at a sharp little shake of Hero's head.

"You take on all the risk, but none of the reward. And you do it because you have to, am I right?" Hero said. "It's a failed system. You might not have heard of us, but we're revolutionaries. We need this fuel to fund our movement. We plan to overthrow the governing structures in all the cities one by one. We'll replace them with something where everyone has equal opportunities. No rich officials trading favors and gifts, no poor bastards with no better options than to do risky illegal work for a pittance. It's going to be a better life for all of us. If you'll really be a dead man if you return, you might as well just stay and be one of us."

The man shot a look of deep loathing at Taub and Gil. "No, thanks."

"What do you have to go home to?" Hero asked.

"Wife. Two girls."

"They won't let you see them," Hero said. "When I was caught, I had a quick hearing with a predetermined outcome and then it was out the airlock for me. For all of us; we all share an origin story here. Why go home when I promise you they won't even let you say goodbye? They might never even tell your wife where you've gone."

"I'll take my chances."

"They'll dock your family's accounts," Hero persisted. "They'll have some way of dressing it up on the books, but your family will end up being charged for the value of the fuel one way or another. I'm guessing that's more than you have. Probably more than you and your wife could ever earn. But you'll still be shoved out an airlock. It'll be your wife, alone with your two daughters, who'll be stuck with that unpayable debt."

"I have absolutely no reason to believe a punk kid like you," the man said, spitting blood in disgust.

"Yeah, but you do believe, don't you? You already know it's all true. You've seen it happen to other guys. Am I right?"

The man didn't answer, just spit again. Hero reached out a hand, but the man sneered and turned away, stumbling back the way he'd come.

"He knows we're down here," Taub said.

"Leave him be. He's not going home," Hero said. "And if he does, he won't tell anyone about us."

"He might," Skald said.

Hero sighed and rubbed the back of his neck tiredly. "Maybe it's time they knew we were down here. We should be sending recruiters into the cities, anyway."

"That's going to make our sneak attack a lot less sneaky," Skald said.

"Let's argue later; I'm starving," Hero said. This was met with cheers, and the shadows around them jumped and swooped as the lights were taken from the train cars and carried up the station steps and through the barricade.

Valentina stayed at the end of the red line, watching the shadow of the man fade into the black. She didn't know how he was even walking; his head had had skull fragments showing amongst the constant oozing of blood. Even if he had stayed, she doubted the contents of the first-aid kit would be enough to save him. But the thought of him dying alone in the dark was too terrible to dwell on.

"Cronista, are you OK?" Hero asked. It was nearly completely dark, only one light still outside the barricade, the revolutionary beside it watching Hero approach her. He had noticed her absence and come back for her. "Is your leg bothering you?"

"My leg?" she repeated stupidly; such a thing had been far from her thoughts. "I'm fine. That man—"

"I know," Hero said with a sigh. "I don't like it either."

"Your group killed three people today. None of them were the top of the power structure. The ones you say are your enemy. They were people doing the best they can. People like us."

"I hate it too, but the fact is, we need what they were guarding, and they weren't just going to give it to us. But don't you see? That's how the system is so insidious. We can't even fight our real enemy. They make sure we have to get past layers and layers of our own people first. And those layers of people are trapped in the system, trapped by family bonds like that fellow, trapped by the certainty in their minds that there is no life outside the corporate system. Most of them don't know there are people down here, or that there even is a 'down here.' They don't know about the villages right outside their airlocks. In their minds, all that's outside the airlocks is death, and they would do anything to avoid death, make any compromise even if it's not to their advantage, not remotely to their advantage. The system has to be changed, and the truth of it is, those won't be the last of our kind that get caught in the crossfire. You just have to remember who the real enemy is. That's where your hate should go."

"I don't hate anybody," Valentina said. "I'm just..." She didn't finish her thought. "Sad" was too small a word for what she was feeling.

"I know," Hero said, putting his arms around her to give her a quick hug. "I promise I feel the same. I know just what it is, the whole world making you want to weep. It's hard to channel that feeling of helplessness into a drive for change, but we have to. We're revolutionaries. Come on, they'll be closing the doors."

Valentina followed him into the station, surprised to find the number of people bustling around the camp stove was again twice that of the night before. Taub's group wasn't the only one meeting up with them at the red line; the others had already gone into the station to start preparations for the evening's feasting.

The smell of roasting chicken went a long way toward lifting Valentina's spirits. She was ashamed of how much that was true. Then someone handed her a flatbread stuffed with garlic and onions and brightly colored spices that set her mouth on fire, traveling up her nose to dispel the fog of a long day's travel from her brain. She was suddenly awake, hearing and seeing everything: the laughter and singing as the revolutionaries worked together to prepare more food, share out grog and water, arrange bedding for later. They all worked together seamlessly, joyfully. Hero was once again moving through them, talking to each as if they were all old friends, slapping shoulders before moving on to the next group.

Valentina looked around and found Hazel and Kiyoshi standing together near the barricade, far enough from the gateway that the pair of guards chatting there didn't really notice them. Valentina took another bite of her flatbread and walked over to them.

"You guys aren't really mixing with the group," she said.

"No," Kiyoshi said.

Hazel grabbed Valentina's hand to examine the flatbread.

"Do you want the rest of mine?" Valentina asked.

"No, I'm thinking I'd better show these revolutionaries how flatbread is properly made," Hazel said.

"I don't know. This tastes pretty good," Valentina said. "A little spicier than yours, maybe…" But Hazel was already gone, her pigtails bouncing as madly as ever as she marched up to the stove.

"Do you want it?" Valentina asked, but Kiyoshi shook his head. Valentina took another bite. The spices were so warming she felt like she was suddenly hyperaware. Like colors were brighter.

"I would ask if you've been observing like Hazel and I asked, but I don't see how you could miss the man who just wandered off to bleed to death alone in the dark."

Valentina swallowed the last of her flatbread, but it sank like a heavy weight in her stomach.

"I saw him. I didn't like it either."

"These kids are up to no good," Kiyoshi said.

"No, that's not true," Valentina said. "I've been talking with Hero about what life is like in the cities. It's worse than the north pole in a lot of ways. Things are tight back home, but at least we have freedom there. I can see why they want to change things. And with the people in charge of the corporations controlling all the resources, I can see how revolution is the only way to achieve meaningful change."

"No matter what the cost?"

"I didn't say that," Valentina said. "We've only been with them two days, and we haven't even seen the cities yet. I don't know what's true. But I believe Hero is sincere. I'm willing to hear him out."

"If it gets you closer to your brother?"

"I didn't say that either."

"These kids robbed a man of goods he could never repay, and they killed him in the process. What more is there to hear out?"

"I don't know. Maybe you just don't know what it's like. You were always safe with your mother in the machine shop making a tidy living. I watched my cousins disappear into the cartels one after another. Maybe I'm more used to violence. Maybe I feel the injustice more."

"You're not used to it," Kiyoshi said. "I saw your face while you were watching that man limp away. But then Hero went back for you and talked you around to his point of view. I can't imagine what he could say that would make what they did to that man OK."

"I told you what he said. I guess he says it better."

"He's changing you."

"Don't be stupid."

"He's changed your name."

"It's a nickname. That's just a friendly gesture."

"Cronista, the chronicler. You like that nickname?"

"I prefer it to Hazel calling me Val." She glowered for a minute, but took a deep breath and tried again. "I'm not different. I'm the same me. I just want my brother back and to have a quiet life to ourselves out of the hubbub, just us and some animals. I'm not joining the revolution. I can't believe you'd think that of me."

"Hazel and I have been hearing a lot of fragments of conversations, things being said and quickly dropped when they realize we outsiders are listening. They are planning something big. A major attack."

"Hero said he'd prefer not to use violence," Valentina said.

"Prefer, but still be willing if deemed necessary, right?" he said, and she didn't answer. "He's not the one in charge, you know. He, Skald, and Kavi seem to have equal roles, but Skald and Kavi are in lockstep on everything while he's been spending all his time with you."

"Even if Skald and Kavi were planning something big and violent, do you really think this bunch could pull it off? There are more here than there were fighting the rats, but nowhere near enough to frighten anyone in the domed cities. Not with spears and swords. You must have misunderstood, or maybe some of them are playing games with you because you seem so skittish. I should talk to Hero—"

"Hazel and I are leaving," Kiyoshi said suddenly.

"Leaving? Where?"

"Back the way we came. We're going to see if we can repair Hazel's balloon. She wants to start her own trading post at that first station."

"OK," Valentina said. "I get why Hazel wants that. But I thought you were coming with me to get Arturo."

"Your new friends seem better equipped to help you."

"I thought we were doing this together," Valentina said.

Kiyoshi said nothing, but he didn't need to. Valentina was suddenly aware of how seldom they'd been together since meeting up with the revolutionaries. That was mostly because Kiyoshi and Hazel had withdrawn to themselves, not even trying to be more than coolly polite. But maybe she should have been looking out for them more.

"I can't go with you," Valentina said at last. "I have to get to my brother."

"I know. I wasn't asking."

Valentina nodded, but her stomach had plummeted at his words. He wasn't asking her to come with him. Wasn't asking. "We're so close now. He's just a few days away. And we've come so far."

"Valentina," Kiyoshi said, putting a hand on her arm. "Have you prepared yourself for the possibility that your brother is happy where he is?"

"If he had left willingly, he would have at least waited until I woke up to say goodbye. He wouldn't have disappeared like that," Valentina said.

"The shuttle was going back with or without them; they couldn't stay. He left you a note," Kiyoshi said.

"Yes, I have it." Her eyes were hot and itchy, but she wasn't going to cry. It wasn't true about her brother; she knew him better than anybody and he wouldn't have abandoned her like that. And she certainly wasn't crying about being abandoned now by Kiyoshi, who clearly never thought of himself as her family at all.

"I think you do need to find him," Kiyoshi said. "You need to talk to him and understand things, I get that. But please, don't set your heart on him coming away with you. I saw him with your father while you were ill. I'm sure he was sad to leave you, but he wasn't dragged away."

"I don't believe you," Valentina said, blinking hard.

"I know," Kiyoshi said with a sigh and took his hand off her arm. "I wasn't going to say anything. I know you don't want to hear it. I was just going to be there when you realized it was true. But now I won't be there."

"I'm not going to fall apart," Valentina said.

"You have had exactly one thing to hold on to since your mother died, and you're about to lose that."

"You don't know me so well as you think."

"I know you."

"Before you showed up in your rover to get me past the downed stations, I don't think you'd said three words to me, ever. Certainly not all in a row."

"I was quiet, but I was there. I was there when you used to tag along with Don Abuelo, visiting all the cartels and honest businesses and keeping the north pole running smoothly. I was there when he died and left your mother and brother and all your cousins with nothing to live on. I was there when your cousins started to disappear, reinventing themselves with gangster nicknames or simply dying in street fights. I was there when your mother got sick and all you could do for her was give her cup after cup of herbal tea and hope it would be enough. But it wasn't. I was there when you sold everything to buy her medicine, too late. I was there when you fell sick, and I was there when you were well again and took off after your brother when you should have been recuperating. You never noticed me, but I always noticed you. I know your generosity and courage, the sense of honor that don Abuelo instilled in you. I know how hard you worked to provide for your brother and cousins, and how you sacrificed and economized. I know how you put your own grief aside to keep fighting to hold your family together.

"But if this, this revolution, this taking up of arms for glory and the poetry of it all—if this is really something you believe in, then I guess you're right. I don't know you at all."

Valentina was stunned. She also realized it was true. He had always been there, too quiet for her to notice. And there had to be a reason he had come after her. He had left everything behind, his entire world, his own mother. But what did that matter now? Now he was leaving her.

"Hey, Kiyoshi. Did you get something to eat?" Hero asked as he stepped up to Valentina's side and casually threw an arm over her shoulders. Valentina felt a flash of anger and wanted to shrug that arm away; his gesture was more for Kiyoshi's benefit than hers, she was sure. But she didn't. She just kept staring at a point on the floor and blinking back hot, angry tears.

"No, thank you. Hazel and I are going to head back the way we came."

"Really? I'm sorry to hear that. Not much up that way."

"We're going to try to repair her balloon, perhaps a few of the vehicles that make up the blockade. She wants to start a trading business of her own."

"Interesting," Hero said. "I admit it sounds like a long-shot venture to me, but if you manage to make a go of it, that would be tremendous. We tunnel dwellers can always use more connections to marketplaces. I tell you what—when we finish up in Valles Marineris V, I will send some parties north with weapons. We should have plenty of resources then; we can help you clear the rats out and establish a proper trade route through the tunnels."

"That sounds mutually beneficial," Kiyoshi said neutrally.

Valentina was still staring at the ground when Hazel bounded up. "Ready to go?" she asked. Valentina looked up then, straight into Kiyoshi's eyes.

She wouldn't beg him to stay. At first this made her feel sad, but then she summoned up her anger and drew her spine up straighter, never dropping her gaze. He was the one who looked away.

"Yes, I'm ready," he said.

"You have enough supplies?" Hero asked.

"We'll manage," Kiyoshi said.

"Good luck to you then."

Kiyoshi nodded, but he didn't look Valentina's way again. Hazel gave her a quick hug, whispering in her ear, "Watch them. Listen. And be safe."

They started to walk away, but Kiyoshi spun back to also pull

Valentina into a tight hug. "I will always be your family," he whispered in her ear.

He pulled away from her, still not looking at her, and went back to Hazel's side.

And then they were gone.

CHAPTER TWENTY-THREE

UNDER VALLES MARINERIS V

IN THE MORNING, WHEN THEY LOADED UP ON THE TRAIN CARS, IT WAS NO longer possible for Hero and Valentina to ride alone. That suited her fine; since Kiyoshi and Hazel had left the night before, she knew she had been withdrawn, lost in her own head, and that he felt shut out. She hadn't joined in the storytelling, just sat by herself, perhaps casting too many glances toward the door. Hero had tried to tempt her with extra helpings of food, but in the end she had just wrapped herself up in one of the camp blankets and feigned sleep until at some point deep in the night, long after the others had at last wandered to bed themselves, it became a real, if fitful, slumber.

The others who joined them on their train car were all in one group, following the lead of a girl with dark skin and a crewcut Valentina had noticed talking with Hero the night before. Her shape was hard to make out under the oversized military coat she wore, every pocket bulging, but she had taken it off to sleep in a bunk near Valentina's and under it she was all lean, hard muscle, like she worked in the mines. She settled herself next to Valentina on the train car and the others packed in around them.

"Cronista, right?" she said to Valentina.

"Yes. I'm sorry. I don't think I caught your name."

"Nandi," she said and put out her hand to give Valentina a firm but warm handshake. "These are my commandos, the Alis."

"Alis?"

"From Muhammad Ali, a boxer back on Earth. He said he floated like a butterfly and stung like a bee. That's us. We can sneak inside anywhere and get back out, never been caught."

"She's not exaggerating," Hero said as he sat on the other side of Nandi to start up the train car. "The Alis are all kinds of awesome."

"We're not warrior-poets, but we do our best," she said with a teasing wink.

"You guys known each other long?"

"Nandi is my oldest friend," Hero said. "Her dad is the one who caught me when I was pushed out the airlock and the two of them nursed me back to health."

"Then he converted me to his revolution," Nandi added.

"I found my revolution thanks to you," Hero said. "I wasn't reading the right stuff at all."

"You guys have probably read more books than even exist in the polar caves," Valentina said.

"Corporate schools will do that for you," Nandi said. "They have all the books, even if they prefer you'd read only a select few. I only lived in the city until I was ten. I didn't get as much schooling as Hero here, but I got enough of a start to carry on myself once my dad found an old reader on the derelict. I'm not sure who originally owned it, but the thing was full of biographies and autobiographies of famous people."

"It's where I learned about Che Guevara and Cuba," Hero added. "Definitely didn't pick that up in the corporate school."

"Or James Joyce either. You found that on your own," Nandi said.

"James Joyce?"

"The writer whose work I took my name from," Hero explained. "Well, as much as the schools would like to only churn out graduates ready to work as drones—aimless pursuits like poetry and literature are not encouraged—once you teach a kid to read, their further education is really out of your hands."

"If they're sufficiently motivated," Nandi added, and Hero nodded.

"I can only read a little," Valentina admitted. "My brother

always wanted me to teach him, but there was just never any time. My ma started getting sick all the time just when he was old enough, and the two of us had to take up the slack. I suppose he's learning now. I bet he picks it up quick; he's a smart kid."

"Given who your dad is, I'm sure he's got a whole squad of tutors getting him caught up with the other kids his age," Hero said.

"Wait, who's her dad?"

"Enrique del Toro."

Valentina nearly jumped with surprise at the sound of the name. But then when she had introduced herself he had seemed to recognize it, and given how long ago Hero had left the city, it wouldn't be Arturo that he had heard of before.

Nandi gave a low whistle.

"I don't understand," Valentina said.

"Your dad is the head of security branch in Valles Marineris V. Basically, he controls an army."

"He's the one pushing kids out of airlocks?" Valentina asked.

"That's complicated," Hero said. "Lots of different departments work together to make that happen, spread the blame around."

"But security branch is the one monitoring everyone for suspicious activities and determining who gets arrested," Nandi said.

"They have to meet quotas sent down from above," Hero said.

"Why are you defending him, Hero?" Nandi asked.

"I'm not," Hero said. "Well, maybe a little. I just don't think anyone should hate their own father."

"I hated him long before knowing any of this," Valentina said. "He left my mother alone in the polar caves while he flew south to take this appalling job, and our lives ran steadily downhill after that. He didn't turn up again until she was dead and gone, and then only to snatch my brother away while I was too weak to stop him, too sick to even know it was happening."

"You know, your dad is pretty high on our enemies list," Nandi said.

"Sounds like he deserves it," Valentina said, but the words left a strange taste in her mouth. Perhaps it was the irony that his storytelling skills were a part of what had bonded her with the revolutionaries in the first place.

"He's a department head. He's definitely going to have to go," Nandi said. "All the department heads have to be taken out so the people see that we're serious about change."

"Then what?" Valentina asked.

"Then the people take over," Nandi said.

"That sounds pretty vague," Valentina said.

"We have allies on the inside," Hero said. "People who are more talk than action, but that has a place too. Once the smoke clears, they'll stand with us with all the support they've been organizing on the inside."

"It's not really important now," Nandi said with a dismissive wave. "Taking over the city as quickly as we can is what we're focused on now. We're few in number compared to security branch, but controlling the marketplace and hitting a few key buildings in the center of the city should give us the advantage we need."

"We'll talk strategy later, after we recon," Hero said, and Nandi nodded, although the intent look in her eyes told Valentina that she was still going over it in her head.

"So what you're talking about isn't some long-term goal. You have something planned," Valentina said.

"Yes, we do," he admitted. "I didn't want to tell you because you weren't really involved, but since your brother is inside the dome, I guess you kind of are."

"You knew that since we met, though," she said.

"Well, I had to make sure you were cool before I started talking about my plans to overthrow the corporate structure in my hometown."

"You've been talking about that since we met, too. But not that a specific thing is about to happen."

"It's all right if you want to tell her," Nandi said to Hero, then turned to Valentina. "We've been working on the details for a very long time, practically since we met. We wouldn't be moving now if we weren't absolutely sure it was the right time."

"Maximum effect with minimum casualties," Hero said. "That's what the 'right time' gives us. Your brother will be perfectly safe."

"But other people are going to be hurt."

"As few as possible, I swear."

Nandi nodded absently in agreement, lost once more in her own thoughts. Valentina was less than reassured.

Kiyoshi had been right, at least partly, but Valentina still felt in her gut that he was overreacting. Hero's grief over the wounded man on the red line had been so real; she believed him when he said he was trying to harm as few others as possible.

True to Hero's word, Valentina started to feel almost too warm as they drew nearer to the cities. Some of it was residual heat from the cities, but mostly it was just because they were closer to the still-active volcanoes, the ones forming lava tubes like the one they were traveling through. She peeled off a layer of knit stockings and put them in the fringed magenta bag Hazel had given her, but she was reluctant to take off Hero's sweater. When she buried her nose inside the roll collar, she could smell him under the wool smell, and it was nice.

They stopped much earlier in the day than before because they had reached the end of their journey: the metro station built under Valles Marineris V, the one that was supposed to service the people of that city, although almost none of them even knew it was there. The revolutionaries set up camp once more. Hero was called away the very minute he stepped down from the train, and Nandi and her Alis jumped off the far side of the car to disappear into the darkness further down the tracks. Valentina was left standing awkwardly alone on the train platform.

Somewhere far to the north, Kiyoshi and Hazel were walking through the same tunnel, lit only by the lights on their suit. It would be days before they even got back to the rats. How would they ever fight their way back through that swarm? Why hadn't she tried to talk them out of it?

She suspected Kiyoshi was right. There was no real plan beyond the violent overthrow. The bit about the allies on the inside had been so vague. Who were they? More teenagers? What would they do once they were in charge? There was no one here older than twenty-two, no one who looked like they had any experience running anything. She probably had more experience than any of them, having spent years managing a family farm, but she knew that didn't even compare to running a city.

It was almost like they didn't expect to win.

Valentina wrapped her arms around herself, although the cold she felt was in her own heart. She should not be here, getting mixed up with things like this.

But somewhere in the city just over her head was her brother. So close she could almost sense him. He must be so pleased about finally learning to read.

"Cronista," Hero called, and she snapped out of her reverie. He beckoned her over, and she went up the steps to where he stood with a group all wearing the same red flaming skull symbol on their upper arms.

"Check out this veg," he said to her, and the flaming skulls held out crates filled with small potatoes and green tomatoes and long, thick carrots.

"The carrots are good, but why did you pick the others so early?" she asked.

"What you mean?" the boy with the tomato crate asked.

"You pick them when they're red, not green," Valentina said.

"I pick 'em when I find 'em," he said, and the three of them laughed.

"Stolen, then," Valentina said.

"Donations to the cause," the boy corrected her.

"They're still edible, though, right?" Hero asked.

"They'd be good fried, maybe," she said, "if you had breading and cooking oil." She still thought stomachaches were more likely. They were hard as rocks.

"Tell the cooks," Hero said to the threesome. "Make sure they slice everything up thin as they can. We need to share this equally among everyone."

"Sure thing," the boy said. Hero watched them go with a shake of his head.

"In the cities, only the rich can cook for themselves every day. The rest of us eat from the public cafeterias. Knowing how to handle food is one of those skills you don't learn in the corporate schools unless they're training you to work in food service, and even then you only learn the small part that is your job. Not like you and others living out here, doing the whole process on your own."

Valentina nodded and noticed she was still hugging herself. She dropped her arms, but that only made her feel more self-conscious.

"You miss your friends," he said.

"I've only known Hazel a few days, really," Valentina said.

"So you miss Kiyoshi."

"I guess, yeah."

"I get that," Hero said. "He's from your hometown. When he was traveling with you, it was like taking a bit of home with you. Without him, you're finally feeling homesick. Am I close?"

"Maybe that's part of it," she said, although inside she was thinking, *not really.*

"But you were never going back anyway, right? So this pain is just part of letting go. You'll make a new home here."

"Kiyoshi," Valentina said, feeling just how much he would hate her for saying this out loud to Hero, "is family. I've never been without family before. I don't just have a ma and a brother, you know. I have five aunts, dozens of cousins. Plus, Kiyoshi and his mother are family by marriage. Most days I have more family around me than I really even want, back home. Now I have nothing, no one. It feels… weird. Wrong." Lonely.

"You know, Nandi's father died shortly after I went out the airlock. He was trying to save another kid and the kid must have panicked, knocked something loose on his jury-rigged pressure suit. Just like that, Nandi was an orphan, and I didn't think I'd ever see my ma again. We became each other's family and have been ever since."

Valentina nodded, but she still felt torn apart. Nandi and Hero were from the same hometown; they'd had a lot of the same experiences, including nearly dying on the surface of Mars. She could see how they would form a bond. But she had none of that with anyone around her. She had had that with Kiyoshi.

"Let's get something to eat and then get as much sleep as we can.

We're going on a recon mission early tomorrow morning before the city day shift starts."

Food was shared and songs sung and stories told. Valentina even told her story again to the biggest crowd yet, and for a moment she did feel connected, a part of everyone around her.

Then she sat back down, and Hero handed her a plate of food. The potatoes and carrots had been roasted. The tomatoes had been thinly sliced and fried, and although there was no egg or breading on them, they were still tart and good. Mostly, what she noticed was that they took up half her plate. Hero's as well. She looked around, trying not to be obvious, but it didn't take much of a scan around the campfire. The warrior-poets ate more food than the others. So did the flaming skulls. The vegetables had not been divided equally. The ones who had found it had kept more for themselves and kicked up extra to their leaders. And no one seemed to notice—not the ones with extra, not even the ones who had been shorted.

Surely Hero must realize, as she did, that the amount in those crates divided over this many people should have made a much smaller portion. And yet he ate without comment.

Valentina turned her attention back to her own plate. The way everyone clamored around Hero, Skald, and Kavi at every stop, she would guess they were given extra food all the time. The first few nights had been proper feasts with more than enough for everyone, but Valentina tried to remember the last night when they had been down to lentils and rice. Had she and the warrior poets gotten extra then too? She couldn't remember, but she suspected they had.

She could ask Hero about it when they were alone. She was sure he would have some explanation that would sound reasonable, maybe even was reasonable.

In the end, it didn't really matter. In the morning, she would be going up to the city, and then she'd find her brother at last.

CHAPTER TWENTY-FOUR

RECON

Nandi woke Valentina in the morning with a brisk shake of her shoulder. Valentina got up and quietly followed her out of the camp to the edge of the platform, where the warrior-poets were waiting.

"You're not bringing the Alis?" Valentina asked.

"Not for recon," Nandi said. "They can rest up today; our mission is a night op."

"Recon means we're just looking around?" Valentina asked.

"Looking around, gathering intel," Kavi said. "We already have maps of the city, but we're looking for some specific details."

"We won't be going into the city," Hero said. "Just peeking through vents in the ductwork. We'll be in the environmental systems. Here." He handed Valentina a paper surgical mask. "Some of the places we'll be crawling through get dusty, but sneezing might draw attention."

"What do I contribute?" Valentina asked.

"Good question," Skald said under his breath.

"I wanted to show you what the plan was for tomorrow. Once we have the city in our power, finding your brother won't be a problem at all. How's your leg? Your staff is going to be cumbersome and noisy where we're going; can you manage without it?"

Valentina nodded. Her leg felt fine, but her stomach was quietly sinking. She should have realized that would be the order of things: revolution first, finding her brother second. She would rather find her brother first so the two of them could get out of the city before the revolution started, leave all of this behind like the north pole and its warring cartels. Find a quiet place to live out their lives.

Kavi led the way up the stairs at the back of the platform, up a long ramp that would have taken them all the way into the city proper if it hadn't been blocked off by a wall of concrete blocks mortared into place.

"What's on the other side?" Valentina asked, touching the wall. It was newer than the metro station, but still old. Who had done this and why? Was it something to do with the plague back on Earth, with the sudden arrival of shuttles full of refugees?

"It must just look like any other wall and not a patch job like on this side, or they would know this is down here," Nandi said.

"I think they do know, or a few of them do," Hero said. "The other side is probably a secured area, off limits to everyone, even if it does just look like a wall."

"This is our way in," Kavi said, opening a vent set high in the wall several meters short of the blockade. He secured his mask, tucked his tablet into the back of his pants, hopped, and caught the bottom edge of the vent, then pulled himself inside. Nandi followed, making the climb up look even more effortless.

"I'll boost you up," Skald said before Valentina could find her voice to express doubts of her ability to follow.

"Thanks," she said, stepping into his interlaced hands. Kavi and Nandi reached out to catch her arms and pull her inside. It was a little awkward—she would have preferred doing at least some of the work herself—but they got her inside and out of the way so Hero could climb up next. The vent was not quite tall enough for them to sit up in, but when she crawled forward, she quickly reached another large shaft, large enough so that she could nearly but not quite stand up.

"They get bigger the further in you get," Hero said as he followed her to the larger shaft. "We're going this way. Here." He put a small flashlight into her hand. He had another just like it, as did Kavi. Nandi had an even smaller one that put out a pinpoint of intense light, and

Skald had a larger boxy one with a handle on the top that lit up the entire shaft in front of them.

"When do we see the city?" Valentina asked. She knew it was unlikely that peering out of random vents in a crowded city would ever give her a glimpse of her brother, but she couldn't quell the hope.

"We're going straight to the top first, get the lay of the land and discuss some strategy. Then we're going back down to get closer looks at the security building and marketplace," he said.

They followed the shaft in a stooped-over walk that was particularly uncomfortable for Skald until they reached the bottom of a ladder. The ladder ended in an even larger shaft, more like a breezy, dusty hallway. This one wasn't level, it was tipped about 30 degrees. Kavi led the way uphill.

Valentina could tell they were getting closer to the actual environmental station when the bare hum she hadn't quite noticed grew into a roar that made talking impossible without shouting, which might draw attention. The others communicated with hand signals that Valentina could mostly guess the meaning of, although Nandi and Hero had a fluency and vocabulary the other two didn't seem to share.

It was also warmer, especially with the uphill walking. Valentina paused to peel off the maroon sweater, tying it by its sleeves around her waist.

The air was dustier as they climbed and Valentina was grateful for the mask keeping the worst of it out of her lungs. Dust balls clung to any protrusion in the ductwork, any raised bolt or bit of debris on the floor. Where one length of duct connected to the next, there was a join that made a ridge all the way around the duct, and the dust balls here formed long swathes that fluttered in the breeze. Valentina accidentally brushed one with her hand in passing; the puffy cottony-looking dust was far oilier than she would have thought. She wiped it away with revulsion, moving to walk closer to the middle of the space.

At last, their uphill duct ended in a massive space like a cathedral back on Earth, flat with ducts feeding into it at regular intervals. Kavi waved and pointed to their destination directly across the way, and they jogged to cross the open space. It was beyond breezy, the wind strong enough to be a blinding sandstorm if it were happening outside.

Valentina jogged to keep up with the others but looked both ways as she did. There were enormous fans on both sides of the room, moving the air through, directing it all to where the roar was loudest.

Then they were on the other side, another duct sloping uphill like before, but now the breeze was blowing the other way. As they walked, the roar faded behind them and it was once again possible to talk.

"Here it is," Hero said as the duct ended in another ladder. Valentina followed Nandi up into another tight crawl space that ran several meters before ending in a space that got wider and deeper, but no taller. The entire floor was grillwork that filled the space with indirect but natural light.

"I haven't seen sunlight in days," Valentina said, surprised to find she had missed it.

"Weeks for me," Nandi said. "Go ahead, you can crawl out onto it. It'll take all our weight and then some."

Valentina gingerly crawled out onto the grill. It certainly felt sturdy, although the metal parts were so thin they dug into her hands and even more painfully into her knees. She crawled far enough out to make space for the others behind her, then sat down with the thick sweater a cushion beneath her and got her first good look at a Martian city from above.

She had been picturing the north pole community but bigger; she had been picturing all wrong. While the north pole was built in a series of mining caves all centered around an immense natural cavern, the dome below her could hold hundreds of north pole communities, maybe thousands. They weren't quite at the highest point; they were off to one side but facing the center, so Valentina could see how the soaring buildings were taller where the dome was highest and tapered with the curve to disappear entirely near the rim. Every building had a rooftop garden spilling over with greenery, and many were built with terraces every dozen stories or so, the building getting narrower towards the top but with more gardens on all the terraces.

Dozens of stories. It didn't seem conceivable, but Valentina counted windows and it seemed true.

"The tallest is an apartment building called Tharsis Heights, in the center," Hero said as he crouched beside her. "Two hundred and twelve floors."

"And you lived here," Valentina said, whispering out of awe rather than a fear of being overheard. Beneath them was a nearly thousand-meter drop to the street below, where she could just make out people moving around on foot or in carts. A few of the rooftop gardens were closer and she could see people there as well: a man sitting on a bench reading a tablet, a woman carefully pruning dried leaves from the plants that grew at the very edge.

"It's a wonder, I don't deny it," Hero said. "It's like a fairyland compared to other places on Mars. But what you can't see from here is the poverty so many workers struggle with. Those buildings are enormous, but while those over there are overcrowded with people like my mother, people closer to the center have an abundance of space. Some of the top-level executives own multiple floors of those buildings, sometimes even the gardens. I wouldn't care; if they work hard, they deserve to relax in a quiet place with nice things. But my ma works hard too. Why does she have to come home to a section of hallway and roll out her futon to sleep while people step over her to get to the bathroom?"

"It seems like there should be enough space for everyone," Valentina said.

"There should be. And enough food. Enough everything. Or if there isn't, we have the resources to expand the city, to grow the community. To start manufacturing things here instead of relying on supply shuttles from Earth."

He glanced over to where Kavi and Skald were talking together, Kavi scrolling through maps on his tablet.

"We're going to swing around clockwise," Skald said, "get some more views from up high."

"I'm going to head back down," Nandi said. "My target is on the ground level, so I'm going to scope it out from there."

"Valentina and I will get closer to the marketplace," Hero said.

"Do you remember the way?" Kavi asked.

"Yeah, but I have my own map too," Hero said, digging a smaller palm-sized tablet out of his pocket. Kavi nodded and crawled back down the duct to the ladder with Skald, Nandi having already disappeared.

"Did you crawl through these spaces when you lived here?" Valentina asked.

"No, never even dreamed of it," Hero said. "I suppose I knew it was possible—you can see these vents from anywhere in the city—but it never occurred to me to try. I don't think even the criminal elements use them."

"Why not?" Valentina asked.

"There is a security system in place that will sound an alarm if the grills are opened or moved," Hero said. "We can't tamper with it from here; the controls are on the other side. That's why we're doing such careful recon. Some of our allies on the inside will disable the alarms on a few key entry points, but only a few, and once we announce our presence, there's no going back. If we don't take the city, the city will come after us."

"Through the metro tunnels no one knows are there?"

"Some do, and use them to move things between cities, like that fellow on the red line was doing. But it's a secret kept among the higher-ups. Of course, if security branch pursues us down there, it won't be a secret anymore."

"That might be a good thing. Then the tunnels won't be something only the most powerful can use."

"It would mean the arrest and probable death of every revolutionary to bring them out into the open that way," Hero said. "We were all sentenced to death once already, for inconsequential crimes. There will be no mercy if they catch us. Plus, there are many open secrets, things some people know about, but only the higher-ups can use. One more won't tip the masses into riot, even if it should."

"I understand," Valentina said, rubbing at her sore knee. All the walking up and down slopes was wearing on her.

"Let's get down to the marketplace," Hero said. "You can't see as much of the city from there, but you can see more of the people."

They put their masks back on and went back down the ladder. Once they reached the lower duct, Valentina fell into step next to Hero.

"There are cities on both sides of the canyon. Are they all connected by the metro?"

"No, only the odd-numbered ones on the north side," Hero said. "There might be a separate system that connects the southern, but I'm not sure. We've explored this one thoroughly and nothing runs that far south. I don't think they have as much volcanic activity down there, not as many lava tubes. The metro system on this side is very opportunistic of existing tunnels."

"The maps looked so straight—is that how lava tubes form? In straight lines?"

"No, that's just how you draw a metro map: only showing the order of the stations, nothing to scale. Here." He fished the tablet out of his pocket and tapped the screen a number of times before handing it to her. "This is what it actually looks like."

Valentina looked closely at the black-and-white map. The lava tubes ran in all sorts of directions. The ones that had been picked for metro lines were the longest, straightest, and widest.

"There are more tubes near the cities and as you go west," Hero said. "Clearly the other ends of the metro, like where you came in, were built because they were convenient to the best tubes."

"That's what Kiyoshi speculated," Valentina said, handing him back his tablet. "The cities were going to follow later. Only they never did."

"No more raw materials after the plague hit Earth, and no inclination after the refugees brought it here. But the time is ripe to get back on those projects. Can you imagine a united Mars? Anyone could travel anywhere, not just the rich and powerful in their shuttles. We could start massive farms in the plains of the north; every settlement could have access to the ore from the mines for building."

"You don't dream small," Valentina said.

"No, no point in that," Hero said.

"I'm not sure I understand how you're going to do all this. You'd have to know so much," Valentina said.

"Actually, no. People here already know all these things. It's just a matter of getting them together, letting them work together. Take this city, for instance. Every low-level manager knows how to run his department, even if he's not allowed to blow his nose without checking with his higher-up. Our coup is going to take out those higher-ups, get rid of the vampires at the top of the power structure, and let those managers run their own departments for everyone's benefit. We don't have to know how to run the environmental systems, grow the food, or anything because the workers here already know how to do that. We just need to get everyone working together."

Valentina could see he made a certain sense, but she greatly doubted it would be as easy as all that. "What if the managers are loyal to their employers?"

"We'll bring them around. Don't worry."

The roaring was growing too loud for them to continue talking, but Valentina didn't mind having that particular conversation interrupted. They crossed the large space between the fans and took the sloping hallway at an easy jog. The journey back seemed much quicker, but Valentina was sure it wasn't. Her stomach was telling her it was close to lunchtime, and she'd missed breakfast.

Then the smell of coffee, caramelized onions, and pineapple wafted up to her out of nowhere, and her stomach really did growl out loud.

"The marketplace," Hero said, smelling it too. "We're nearly there. We'll be looking over it, but from a much lower height this time."

They headed down a series of ever smaller ducts until finally reaching a low room with a grilled floor, much like the other one but smaller and sitting at an angle, the far end higher up. Hero put a finger to the mask over his mouth in a hushing gesture and Valentina nodded. She could hear the sound of crowds below, children laughing, merchants hawking their wares, shoppers chatting or haggling. Then they crouched at the edge of the grill and peered out at the world below.

The marketplace was four times the size of the one on the north pole and much more spaciously arrayed, with wide lanes between rows of permanent shops and larger cross streets where food carts set up to sell lunch to the passersby. Valentina pressed her face close to the grill to try to find the source of the pineapple smell and found a cart selling meat and pineapple kebabs that the owner roasted right there before his customers' eyes. Another was selling rolls and twists of bread baked to a rich golden brown. And then there was the coffee, perhaps just as bitter as what the revolutionaries had, but it still smelled divine.

Hero had his tablet back out, tracing with his fingertip on a map of the marketplace and murmuring to himself. "Scaffold goes all the way around, just like I said, one level up just under the vent. Good for sniping if we need to, controlling the space. We'll need to block the streets here, here, here, and here. Some might get out through the lanes, but we'll have enough."

"Enough what?" Valentina whispered.

"Hostages," Hero said and gave her a look like he knew what she was thinking. "It's necessary. We move them all here to the commons."

Valentina looked at the spot he was marking on his map, then back out the grill. She could see it now, a wide-open area at the other end of the marketplace where some very young children were watching a puppet show and shrieking with delight.

"There will be kids here tomorrow too," she said.

"I don't like it any better than you do," he said.

"There has to be another way. Doesn't there?"

Hero turned off his tablet and put it back in his pocket, then led the way back to the larger duct.

"Doesn't there?" she persisted when they were far enough away to talk above a whisper.

"I'm not the first revolutionary," he told her. "There have been others trying all sorts of ways. They've met very bad ends. Striking fast, getting control before they can react, removing the higher-ups before they can start wheedling and bribing their way out of any attempts at change—that's the only way."

"And you don't worry that it might just be another bad end?"

"I worry more about not trying anything at all," he said and gave her a look so hard she took half a step back. She was pushing too much, asking too many questions. Even his affable nature had its limits.

She heard footsteps approaching, heavy ones, but it was just Kavi and Skald coming up the slope from wherever they had gone on their own, further down the line.

"I want to get my brother," Valentina said.

"You will," he said, but he was almost snapping at her, impatient. Kavi and Skald stopped in front of them. "No need to wait for Nandi. She can make her own way out. Come on."

"What's going on?" Kavi asked, looking from Hero to Valentina and back again.

"I want to get my brother—"

"We know that," Skald growled.

"—now."

"No," Kavi said to Hero.

"Obviously no. Why would I say yes?"

Kavi mumbled something in Bengali.

"I want him safe," Valentina said.

"He will be safe. He'll be in school well before we start the invasion," Hero said. "By protocol, once we take the marketplace, all the schools will go into lockdown. We'll be in charge before those doors will open again. Perfectly safe."

"How can you be sure?" she persisted.

"It doesn't matter," Kavi said. He took Hero's arm to pull him to one side, but nowhere near far enough to even pretend the others couldn't overhear. "Why are you trying to reason with her? The only thing that matters is that no one who knows our plans gets into the city before the invasion."

"I wouldn't say a word to anyone," Valentina said, barely containing her anger.

"First of all, we have no reason to believe you," Skald said. "Secondly, when you get picked up by security and put to the question, you will talk. Everyone does."

"I'm sorry, Cronista," Hero said, twisting his arm out of Kavi's grip. "They're right. But I do promise you no harm will come to your brother, and this will all be over by sundown tomorrow. You'll be back with your brother by nightfall, I swear it."

Valentina nodded and Skald stepped back, no longer looming over her in that way that made her want to melt into the floor. She could only agree; she was afraid of what they would do to her if she didn't.

But Skald was right. They had no reason to believe her. If she was going to get to her brother, she was on her own. On her own, against both the revolutionaries and their corporate foes.

CHAPTER TWENTY-FIVE

FEASTING AND BRAGGING

WHEN THEY GOT BACK TO CAMP, THE TRAIN PLATFORM WAS FILLED WITH the pounding beat of music. Hero ran up ahead, yelling at the kids nearest the music player to shut it off, but Valentina staggered to a stop. It was all too familiar, the young warriors dancing together, bare limbs twining up to the sky, feet stomping with the beat.

It was just like the party she had crashed looking for her brother, all the cartel brats celebrating their victorious street fight. Only these kids were celebrating a battle they hadn't even fought yet, let alone won.

And now that she was looking with those eyes, she started noticing other details. The scars that clearly hadn't come from rat fights. The violent nature of a lot of the designs inked on their clothing or on their very skins. The casual way they were constantly punching and pushing at each other, little gestures that quickly spun out of control until others had to intervene to keep the party going. She remembered the stories, the things she had taken to be exaggerations or outright fabrications. She accepted every detail as true and looked at those kids again.

Valentina reached out a hand, found a pillar, and pressed her forehead to the cool concrete. Kiyoshi was right.

The music stopped. The silence was unbroken, even by a single protest.

"I know there's a lot of concrete between us and them, but we can't take the chance," Hero said. "Tomorrow is the day."

This was met with carefully restrained battle cries.

"You'll be divided up into teams and assigned a team leader," Kavi said, consulting his tablet. "Discipline is paramount. We are up against a much larger, much better-armed foe."

"We can do this," Hero added. "Our plan will work, but everyone must execute their role in it perfectly. Are you with me?"

The shouts now were a bit less restrained. Valentina closed her eyes, just feeling the coolness of the pillar. What was she going to do?

Kavi started reading off names and people moved to form the groups he had designated. Hero left him to it and crossed the platform to stand near Valentina.

"Nervous?" he asked, running a hand down her arm. "Worried about your brother?" When she still didn't respond, he tried again. "Missing your friends?"

"This is never going to work," Valentina said. "They don't have your discipline."

"They'll be fine," Hero said.

"Don't you see what they are? Brawlers looking for an excuse to brawl. Your plan isn't going to give them what they want. Or rather it is, if you're giving them each their own gun to make mayhem with."

"They all believe in the revolution, every one of them," Hero said.

"They believe in the fight, surely. They believe in your stories of a mythical perfect future, maybe," Valentina said. "But they don't even think about all the work that will have to go into making that future."

"That's why I like having you around," Hero said. "I need having you around. You think about these things. I know you don't want to have any part in our invasion; I'm not asking you to pick up a gun for the cause. But surely after, you can help. Organizing, keeping the city running as smoothly as possible while we transition. That's where you're going to come in."

"That's an impossible task. I don't think you're going to get the existing department heads to work with you. They're not going to want to take orders from a teenager."

"I'm twenty. Nearly."

"But you're never going to get far enough to try," Valentina went on. "Don't you see? You send this lot into the marketplace armed to take hostages, and it's going to be a bloodbath. You won't be able to control them. They have too much anger."

"It's going to be fine," he said. A hard edge was creeping into his voice.

"No, it really isn't," she whispered.

Skald called out Hero's name, and he turned and walked away from her without so much as a backwards glance.

Valentina sat apart for that mealtime, although somehow she still ended up with more beans and rice than most of the others. Whether she liked it or not, Cronista del Norte was one of the warrior-poets. The storytelling that night was all hypothetical battles, each revolutionary imagining going up against some member of the corporate establishment who had crossed them in some way and going into sometimes gruesome detail on what would happen next. Valentina set down her bowl, still half filled with beans and rice, and crept off to the back of the platform.

"Hey."

It was a soft sound, hesitant, almost apologetic. Valentina turned to watch as Hero walked up to her.

"OK, I see what you're saying," he said with a vague wave back over his shoulder. "They are getting keyed up to fight, and yes, it does sound scary. But do you know what we're going up against tomorrow? Security branch is an army. We have a few guns, but mostly spears and knives. They have tanks, tear gas, control of the environmental systems. Everyone back there knows it. And we'd be crazy not to be afraid. This bravado, it's just a way of dealing with that fear."

"There will be kids in that marketplace tomorrow," she said. "Frankly, everyone who will be at risk tomorrow is not your actual enemy. They're your own people."

"I know. But they are being used as pawns against us. We have to turn the tables on that. And the only people we intend to harm are the soldiers in security branch."

"How does one become a soldier?" Valentina asked.

"What do you mean?"

"Are they volunteers?"

"It's the same way anyone gets any kind of job. We take tests at age fourteen and finish school training for the job we have the most aptitude for and the corporation has a need for. It's supposed to be purely based on merit, but kids of high-ranking administrators tend to become the next generation of high-ranking administrators, and descendants from the original refugee ships always get worse jobs than descendants of the original corporate employees. It's officially denied, but everyone knows it's true. It's blatantly obvious."

"And the soldiers come from…?"

Hero sighed and ran a hand through his hair. "Yes, you're right. The officers are corporate stock and the foot soldiers and beat cops are refugee stock. It's just the way it is. It's what we're trying to change."

"You're going to make life better for the descendants of refugees, but in the process, you have to kill a lot of descendants of refugees."

"Because we can't get at the others."

"Why not?" Valentina persisted. "You are few, but so are they, your actual enemies. Wouldn't that be more of a fair fight?"

"If we could get them out in the open, sure. But that's never going to happen. They live on the top floors of the tallest buildings behind layers and layers of security we can't penetrate. And behind layers and layers of our own people, I've already told you. The only place where all the strata of the city mix together is the marketplace. That's why we have to get our hostages there. I promise you I've given this plan a lot of careful thought."

"I know you have. And if you had an army of yous to execute it, I wouldn't worry. But you don't. You have those kids, and they are not worthy of you."

Hero smiled and stepped closer to her. "That's kind of you to say."

"I meant everything else I said too," she said.

He caught a stray lock of her hair and tried to tuck it back into her braid. "I know. But I meant what I said too. After this is done, we're going to need you. I'm going to need you."

"But I don't want this," she said. "I just want to get my brother and go lead a quiet life. Get a farm going somewhere. I don't want to run a city."

"I know," he said, still trying to work that hair back into the braid. "But I think when called to serve, you will step up. With every bit of the drive you brought to stand before that don."

Valentina brushed Hero's hands away. "It doesn't work like that. You can't just jam things in. You have to start over from scratch." He looked puzzled, and she uncoiled her hair and unplaited the braid.

"Nice metaphor," he said.

"I wasn't making one."

"Sure you were."

Valentina started smoothing out her hair with her hands, but Hero held up a finger, ran to a pile of sacks near the camp cots, and returned with a comb. She held out her hand, but he refused to hand it over.

"I don't get the comb unless I promise to help rebuild your city?" she asked.

"Don't be silly. Turn around."

Valentina sat on the edge of the nearest cot with her back to him and he sat behind her, gently teasing the snarls out of her hair.

"I haven't had a wash in days," she said. "Not since we were on the balloon, and that was… rudimentary."

"Once we have the city, you can bathe in a tub the size of a swimming pool."

"That sounds nice—divine, actually—but I just want my brother."

"I know." His fingers separated her hair into thirds and began weaving them around each other.

"You've done this before."

"The family next to ours in the hallway was a single father with three little girls. I used to help get them ready for school."

"That was kind of you."

"People should take care of each other."

When he had finished, he tied off the end, and she left it hanging down her back. There was no reason to pin it out of the way now that her helmet-sealing days were behind her. Hero laid down on the cot and gently tugged her to lie down beside him, tucked close to him with his arm around her.

"We march upstairs in the morning. You can wait here. When it's all done, I'll send someone for you. Then we'll find your brother. And then you can decide what happens next. OK?"

"OK," Valentina said. But the arm around her didn't feel comforting. It felt confining. She tried to remember—had Hero been speaking to anyone before he left his place near the stove to come talk to her? Had perhaps Kavi and Skald sent him to placate her, to keep her near, to do anything necessary to prevent her from getting to her brother before the attack? Or was she just being paranoid?

She listened to his breath grow slower and deeper, debating with herself whether he was falling asleep or only pretending to fall asleep. Then she couldn't stand it any longer. She lifted his hand off her hip and slipped quietly off the cot. He stirred, rubbed at his face with his now free hand, then settled into a deeper sleep. Or pretended to. Valentina decided to risk it. As silently as she could, she moved further from the lights of the party around the cookstove and deeper into the shadows at the back of the platform.

She had the sudden urge to hop back down onto the tracks, to start walking north and find Kiyoshi and Hazel. But it would take her months to get to where they had started their own journey, and she had no supplies. Still, the urge surprised her. With her brother so close, she was tempted to abandon her whole quest?

But she had to admit, Kiyoshi's words had been eating at her. What would Arturo do when she found him? She couldn't imagine a life without him, her brother, who had been at her side constantly since birth. But she had been living just such a life for weeks now. The pain was not what it had been when she had first woken to find him gone. What was it like for him? Maybe he had never missed her the way she missed him.

Valentina crept further along the wall, finding the opening for the stairway up, then the bricked-off passageway, and then the vent leading to the city above all, navigating by touch in the semidarkness.

There was only one way to find out.

CHAPTER TWENTY-SIX

INTO THE CITY

She didn't exactly have a plan. She wanted to reach Arturo, but she couldn't see the steps that would get her to him. The city was huge; there was no way to find him by just sneaking about. She'd listened to enough revolutionary tales of life in the city to know teenagers weren't supposed to be out unaccompanied after sundown and that the patrol officers with nightsticks and flashlights had a strict hit-first, never-listen-to-explanations policy. If kids who had grown up in the city couldn't effectively evade capture, she stood little chance.

The only way she could see to get to Arturo was through her father. She knew where he worked. If she got to him and told him about the invasion planned for the morning, perhaps she could save some lives. He might be grateful enough to let her see her brother. She might even be able to plea for some clemency for the revolutionaries.

Valentina stopped where the tunnel was bricked off and looked up at the vent. She felt sick to her stomach; this was never going to work. She would betray Hero and likely get nothing in return. But she couldn't turn back. She had nothing else to try. The more she thought about how it would all fall apart in the end, the more paralyzed by doubt she became, so she decided to focus only on the beginning, only on one step at a time.

Step one: get into the city.

Valentina looked up at the vent and sighed.

Revised step one: get up into that vent.

She jumped, caught the edge with her fingertips, and almost immediately dropped back down to the ground. Nandi had made it all look so easy. But then, Nandi had those wiry, strong arms. Valentina wasn't a weakling, but farm work had not given her arms like those. Her legs were strong, but as she jumped again, harder, they both twinged, her knee protesting on one side and the rat-torn calf on the other. She held on longer but still couldn't get herself pulled up before her arms collapsed and she was back on the ground.

On the fifth try, she managed to jump, catch the edge of the vent, and pull herself inside before her arms gave out. She doubted she would have managed it without the adrenaline surge of anger and frustration driving her. As it was, it hadn't been the quietest of ascents. She lingered near the opening, looking back the way she'd come to see if any of the revolutionaries would come to investigate, but the tunnel remained empty. She turned and crawled deeper inside, only turning on her flashlight when she reached the larger shaft.

Step two: find the marketplace.

The shafts were a labyrinth, and she hadn't paid enough attention when she'd come through before with Kavi leading the way, but she had been watching on the walk back out. She was pretty sure she could find the marketplace again. It was the one vent she had visited that she could crawl out of. And there would be people there.

She found the vent, but not the people.

Life at the north pole went on constantly, with no way to mark days from nights. That far underground, the lights were all artificial, and no one bothered to dim them just to mark an arbitrary designation of sleeping and waking. There were times when the marketplace was filled with folks buying food and other necessities, and times when it was safer to stay inside your own space and leave the alleys to the cartels, but there was always activity in the central cavern.

So it was a bit of a shock for Valentina to discover the marketplace of Valles Marineris V completely deserted. Did the curfew now apply to everyone? She had been hoping for more background noise to cover the sounds of her prying the vent panel open. She wasn't sure how she would do it without any tools but a flashlight and her two hands. She shone the light along the edge, looking for any catch or hinge, but whatever was holding it in place was all on the outside. In the end, she had to resort to lying flat and kicking out hard with both legs. The bottom catch snapped free, and the top hung askew. She flinched, expecting a blare of alarms, but the quiet was undisturbed. It could still be a silent alarm, alerting security personnel to come and investigate. She climbed out onto the walkway overlooking the marketplace and gently set the vent back in place. It was crooked, but only slightly so. Anyone giving a cursory glance wouldn't notice anything amiss; that would have to be good enough.

She heard a murmur of voices below her and froze, her hands still on the grill she had been adjusting, listening. It was whispering, a child fussing. She crept to the edge of the walkway and looked down. It took a moment in the darkness to make out the details, but there were people below her. There were living areas tucked into spaces between shops where families had futons and storage cabinets like Hero had described in his life in the hallway. Others were sleeping with just a blanket around them on the sidewalks in front of the shops. She saw the sweep of a flashlight as a patrol officer worked his way up and down the lanes and the whispering died away as he approached. If anyone had heard her—and given the volume of the crash when the grill sprung free, they must have—no one told the patrol officer. And, apparently, no silent alarm had tipped him off. Hero had said that certain alarms would be disabled by a spy on the inside. That spy must have done it already, and of course, the marketplace would be one of those points. The patrol officer turned a corner and made his way back up the next lane. For the moment, she was safe.

Step three: get the word out.

But how? She could simply call out and that patrol officer would come to her. She had expected to be arrested the moment she stepped out of the duct, but now that it hadn't happened, she wasn't sure it was the best plan. Something about the way no one even reported the sound of her breaking in made her doubt going to him with any kind of story would be a good idea. The people here didn't trust him. From what Hero had told her, life in the corporate dome was all about what level of society you belonged to. She supposed the sorts of people who lived out in the open in the marketplace were the ones who couldn't afford the luxury of a section of apartment building hallway. And if she met up with security branch here, she would be taken for one of those people. She was already highly unlikely to be listened to, no need to compound it. She should head for the taller buildings. If she couldn't find the security building, at least when she was inevitably caught, she'd be mistaken for someone from the nicer part of the city, someone more inclined to be listened to.

The walkway was built like a large ring tipped to one side, like a disk in the last few lazy spins before falling to the ground. She followed the slope down to the main level, but hesitated before leaving the marketplace behind her. Should she find one of the people who lived here and tell them what would be happening tomorrow? They had a right to know, but would they believe her? What could they do about it if they did? In the end, she turned away, hustling down the nearest street. The risk of getting caught was too high. The people in the marketplace might be able to avoid being there in the morning, maybe, if they believed her and if they had somewhere else to go, but only security branch could stop the invasion before it happened.

Valentina looked around, picked the nearest tall building, and headed toward it as directly as she could. She was on a wide street, so wide there was a row of trees growing down the middle, their branches interlocking with those of other rows on either side of the street so that she felt like she was walking through a tunnel of greenery. There were buildings on either side, but everything was dark and quiet. The street crossed another even wider street, and she turned to follow it as it appeared to run straight to a large building full of windows, some of which were glowing with light. She tipped her head back to look up at the dome, something she hadn't been able to do when peering out through the vents.

She could see stars and one of the moons. She had lived her whole life without seeing them until a few weeks ago, but she found that just a few days back underground had been enough for her to miss them again. Wherever she and Arturo ended up, she hoped it had some sky.

Her steps slowed as she approached her destination. People were going in and out of the main door, patrol officers mostly. This had to be the place.

Valentina crouched behind a trash can and watched the front of the building, once more uncertain she was doing the best thing. Somewhere in the city around her was her brother; he was so close. If only there were a way to find him. She was afraid she would risk everything and still not get to see him. But she was more afraid of doing nothing and people getting hurt.

She had just made up her mind when she felt something tapping her shoulder. She froze, then slowly turned to look up at a patrol officer, standing over Valentina with her nightstick resting against her own shoulder.

"Stand up, then," she said.

"I need to speak to someone in charge," Valentina said as she straightened out of her crouch.

"At the moment, that's me," she said. "Put your hands behind your back."

She heard the zip of the cuffs and felt the narrow plastic bite into the flesh of her wrists. Valentina couldn't help feeling it was unnecessarily tight; she was going along quietly.

"Where's your ID?" the patrol officer asked, pulling at Valentina's sleeves. The city dwellers all had tattoos that could be scanned, but of course Valentina didn't.

"I'm not from here," Valentina said. "I'm from the north pole. And I really need to talk to someone in charge."

"That's a new one," the woman answered, but put her hand on Valentina's shoulder to direct her forward. "You'll have your moment before the judge like anybody."

The woman marched Valentina up the steps and into the doors. There was a man behind a desk, just as Valentina had imagined there'd be, but he didn't even look up as the two of them walked by. They continued on down a hall that was clean and well lit but empty, although Valentina could hear the murmur of voices behind some of the closed doors. The hall ended in a stairwell and the patrolwoman clutched her elbow as they descended, but not to restrain her, more to be ready to catch her if she stumbled while walking with her hands behind her.

They went down three levels and exited into another identical clean, cold hallway. Finally, the woman drew Valentina to a halt at one of the closed doors. She swung her wrist over a featureless pad in the wall at doorknob level, although the door itself had no knob, and the door clicked open on its own. She swung it the rest of the way open and nudged Valentina inside.

The room beyond was small and bare except for a low table set along the wall to her right. The far wall was all bars, and beyond the bars was another, more dimly lit hallway.

"Strip to your underwear," the woman said, cutting Valentina's bonds with a little knife that promptly disappeared into one of the many pockets on her uniform. Valentina started pulling off her sweater.

"I really do need to talk to someone in charge," Valentina said as she peeled off layer after layer of clothing. The woman took each item from her and carefully searched the pockets before setting it on the table.

"You'll have your moment with the judge," the woman said again.

"You know I'm not one of your citizens. I broke in here to tell you there is a threat to your city. Your security team must be warned."

"We are accustomed to dealing with such threats," the woman said. She had found Arturo's note inside the pocket of Valentina's innermost skirt. She unfolded it, glanced at it, then put it inside Hazel's fringed bag with the other things she'd found.

"I'm not sure you're taking me seriously. I want to meet someone I can give specific information to. Time is running out," Valentina said.

"Look, you seem like a good kid," the woman said, turning Valentina around by the shoulders to run her fingers over and through her hair all the way to the end of the braid, then patting her down quickly in case she was hiding anything in her underwear. "I'm sure you've heard many a fanciful tale about the easy life inside the domes. But life on Mars isn't easy anywhere, and we don't have anything to spare for vagrants. Wherever you came from, you'll just have to go back there."

"I didn't sneak in here because I wanted to stay. I wanted to warn you. A lot of people are going to be hurt in the morning, maybe even killed."

"You'll have your moment with the judge," the woman said for the third time. "Although you should know if I've heard all these stories a thousand times, he's heard them a million. Get dressed. I'll be holding on to your bag for now."

Valentina dressed quickly, hoping the judge would be more willing to listen. She had a sinking feeling he wouldn't. But if she told him everything, in as much detail as she knew, surely he would have to take her seriously.

The officer swung her wrist near the bars and the middle four rose into the ceiling, making a doorway. She pushed Valentina through ahead of her, swinging the fringed bag over one shoulder before following.

There were no doors along this hallway, just more bars dividing off small rooms with empty tables like the one they had just left. Then they turned a corner, and the hallway became a corridor between two long lines of bars, the space beyond on each side filled with prisoners. Some were adults sleeping in bunk beds, two to a room, but most were kids, some as young as Arturo, packed in ten to a room. They were surprisingly quiet. None were sleeping, and yet they made not a sound as Valentina and the patrolwoman walked past them, just watched them go by with glassy eyes too strung out to hope. They had been loosely grouped by age, it seemed, and the patrolwoman stopped at the last room of the row where six older kids were imprisoned, two sleeping on the bunks, the others standing or sitting on the floor. The woman opened the bars and Valentina stepped inside.

"Someone will be by with food in case you're hungry," the woman said. "The judge has a backlog of cases, so you might be waiting for a while."

"Can't you tell your boss what I told you?" Valentina pleaded as the bars came down between them. "I know your head of security. Enrique del Toro. And he knows me. Please, if you just go get him, he can back up everything I've told you."

"You work it hard, kid; I respect that," the woman said. "Good luck back on the outside."

"I'm not lying!" Valentina yelled, but the woman just walked back the way they'd come, Hazel's bag shining brightly against the drab gray of her uniform.

Valentina turned back around to look at the other kids in the cell with her. The two stretched out on the bunks, a girl and a boy and the oldest of the group, were looking at her but quickly shut their eyes again, preferring feigned slumber to conversation. Two boys sat together with their backs against the edge of the bunk; they looked like they might be brothers. One girl was by herself, tucked into the far corner and staring off through layer after layer of cell bars. The last girl reminded Valentina of Hazel before she even started talking. She had the same way of standing, arms and legs thrown anywhere, even with her own brand of crazy hair.

"It's the airlock for all of us, you know," the girl said.

"I know," Valentina said. "That doesn't scare me."

"Wow. I'd call you a liar, but you're totally being honest," the girl said, leaning in close to look Valentina in the eye.

"There are people outside that catch you," Valentina said, although she wasn't sure that was still true. Hero had said when he was thrown out, it had been one or two kids a week. There were more than a hundred kids packed in the cells around her. And no one was acting like this was unusual.

"So it's all a big scare tactic? Tough love?" the girl asked, flicking her matted hair out of her eyes.

"Oh no, your corporate masters are totally throwing you away," Valentina said. "It's just that there are other people out there who would rather not watch you die on their doorstep."

"But there's nothing outside the dome," the girl said. "Nothing can live out there."

"I'm not from here," Valentina said. "If you need proof that they are lying to you, I'm it. Domes are nice, but they're not the only way to live on Mars."

"It's not really proof if we have to take your word for it," one of the brothers said.

"True enough. You'll have your own proof when they push you outside," Valentina said.

"You talk funny," the girl said, leaning in again as if there were something on Valentina's face that would identify her accent.

"I'm from the north pole," she said. "Mostly we speak Spanish there. English is only used to talk with traders. I've been getting used to it since I fell in with the revolutionaries, but my polar accent is there to stay."

"Revolutionaries?" the brother repeated.

"They are attacking in the morning. That's what I've been trying to warn everyone about, but no one will listen to me."

"It does sound crazy," the girl said, flicking the hair out of her eyes once more. It fell right back where it had been.

"That's why I'm not worried about the airlock. I know that will turn out OK. But my brother lives here. If this attack happens, he might get hurt."

"All our families live here too," the brother said. "We have parents and stuff."

"I know. I'm sorry. Is there any more I can do? She said I could talk to the judge—"

"He won't listen either," the girl said.

The sound of footsteps approaching made them all fall silent again, and Valentina turned to see a man approaching with something covered on a tray. He stopped at their cell and set the tray on a little ledge built into the outside of the bars. He removed the cover and opened a small gap in the bars above the ledge.

"Take it," he instructed when Valentina hadn't moved. She reached through the gap and took the plastic bowl full of something warm, a pair of chopsticks jutting out of the top. The bars closed back down and the man left, tapping the tray absently against his thigh as he walked.

Valentina looked down at the contents of the plastic bowl. The rice looked all right, but the vegetables strewn over the top looked so over-cooked they were nearly gelatinous.

"Your arresting officer is a softy," the girl said. "But then you do look half-starved."

"Actually, I've been eating pretty well since I met up with the revo-lutionaries. Are you hungry?"

"Give it to her," the girl said, indicating the quiet girl in the corner. "She's been here the longest."

Valentina brought the bowl over to the girl. "Are you hungry?"

The girl looked over at her with red-rimmed eyes. She nodded slowly, as if suspecting a trick but unable to help herself.

"Take it, please," Valentina said, putting the bowl in her hands. "At least it's hot, and the rice doesn't look too bad."

"Thank you," the girl said in a soft whisper and took the bowl, using the chopsticks to bring a dainty bit of rice and limp vegetable to her mouth. She closed her eyes, almost humming in pleasure. Despite everything, Valentina smiled. Shyly, the girl smiled back.

A door banged open and Valentina turned to see four guards march down the corridor to one of the other cells. The bars lifted, and the ten terrified children inside were herded out and marched back down the corridor. The door banged shut again.

"They are going to see the judge?" Valentina asked.

"If by 'see' you mean 'catch a glimpse of across the room,' sure," the girl with the crazy hair said.

"But the woman who arrested me said I would get to talk to the judge," Valentina said.

"She's speaking more from theory than from practice," the girl said. "Once they drop you off here, the rest of the bureaucracy is someone else's problem."

"She might not have been lying to you," the boy said. "She just might not know."

"We're supposed to get individual trials with evidence and witnesses and everything," the girl went on. "We're promised that in the charter. But lately it's been more than the judges can keep up with, so they push us through pretty fast and to hell with what the charter promised."

"Our parents will never know what happened to us," the boy said and hugged his brother closer. "We were only late getting home from work. We were nearly there. Half a block from our apartment, that's where they arrested us."

"I was making trouble," the girl admitted. "I have *ideas*."

"They shouldn't lump us all in together," the boy said. "I'm sorry, I don't think it's fair what they're doing to you either. People should be free to speak their minds. But my brother and I were working because my father is too sick to work and food prices keep climbing."

"Too many of us, that's what they say," the girl said. "Driving the prices up, all demand and so little supply. But I think it's all a lie."

"Aren't you with the revolution already?" Valentina asked. "You sound like you could be one of their inside allies."

"I would totally do that. But alas, you're the first person I've met who didn't use the word 'revolution' in a strictly astronomical context." She spun a finger in the air to demonstrate the principle.

The door banged open again, and another cell's worth of kids was led down the corridor. No one spoke when the guards were present, and the kids being led away kept their eyes carefully on their own feet.

"No one expects to get out of this, do they?" Valentina said once the guards were gone.

"No one has ever been arrested and then seen again," the girl said. "Once the patrol stops you for any reason at all, if they don't let you go right away, you're done for."

"The only way out of the detention center is through the airlock," the boy said. "Everyone knows that."

"So what's the point of this trial?" Valentina asked.

"Bureaucracy?" the girl said with a shrug.

"If they are making a record of everything, even a secret one, there's a chance someone could find it. Someone could expose all this."

"What good would that do? Everyone already knows, and the only people who care are the ones who are powerless to change anything."

"You're never going to see your families again, and you're just going to lie there and take it?"

"Would banging on the bars and cursing and wailing help?" the girl asked. She flashed a hint of a grin, like she hoped the answer was yes just so she could try it.

The night wore on, and most of the others slept in snatches, but Valentina was too keyed up to even sit down. If all the corporation's secrets were exposed, if what everyone knew unofficially became official, would that be fuel enough for nonviolent change? Valentina was sure that what the boy referred to as the powerless ones far outnumbered the others. Surely the threat of that would be enough to make those in power open their eyes. If they banded together, let their numbers be seen, would the ultimate conclusion be obvious enough that the higher-ups would surrender without a fight? Well, she doubted a total surrender of power, but what if just enough concessions were made to make life under the dome more equitable?

But she had no idea how to do it. If the records of this phony court were being kept, she was not the one who was ever going to be able to find them. And if she could, she had no idea who to bring it to. And time was growing shorter.

The guards marched back into the room, this time stopping at the door to Valentina's cell. The two older kids sleeping on the bunks sat up quickly the moment the bars rose and lined up with the others to be led down the corridor to the open door. Two more guards stood on either side of this door, one counting off prisoners as they walked by, making marks on a tablet built into the arm of his uniform. The other yawned widely.

The hallway beyond was so bright after the semi-dark of the cells that Valentina had to shut her eyes, stumbling along with the others until they reached a darker space. She heard more bars slide shut and opened her eyes again.

They were in another cell, this one set on a platform over a large open room. The room was full of row after row of tables, but no chairs. Patrol officers were standing in clumps, talking amongst themselves. The tables ended, the last row forming a line perpendicular to the middle of their elevated cell. A few patrol officers stood here, waiting patiently with their arms folded or hands behind their back. They were facing another elevated platform to the far left of the cell where a man sat at a table made from gleaming wood, a rarity on Mars. Valentina had occasionally seen small wooden objects, figurines, or instruments, but never something so large. It glowed like it was still alive. It was one of the most beautiful things she had ever seen, but the man sitting with his elbows resting on its warm, honey-colored surface didn't even seem to notice. He looked exhausted, with the bright eyes of someone working on too much caffeine and too little sleep.

No one was looking up at the cell.

"Who's next?" the judge asked, tapping at one of three screens set into the table before him.

"Avery Smitts, your honor," a patrol officer said. The boy who had been sleeping on the bunk straightened a little.

"Charges?"

"Breaking curfew. Possible moonlighting."

"Possible?"

"He had a lot of packages on him, your honor. He said it was all shopping for his mother, but he couldn't identify the contents of any of the packages."

"Illicit goods?"

"No, just food, medicine, clothing. Some of it has been hard to find in the marketplace recently; we guess it's black market stuff."

"But you couldn't prove it," the judge said, tapping at his screen. "Not that it matters. If he was out after curfew, we only need to try him for that. I'm striking the moonlighting from the record. Defendant is guilty of curfew violations; under current security guidelines that condemns him to expulsion from our community. Next."

Valentina bit her lip as Avery just nodded, not having expected any other outcome. Valentina was even more frustrated with the extent to which this was all being played as if it were fair, striking the unproven offense off his record, and yet Avery's parents would never learn that he had been pushed out an airlock for being out on the streets after curfew. They couldn't even be here to say goodbye. If these were rules everyone was aware of, if they were being enforced fairly, then why all the secrecy?

The other cases were heard with a similar brevity. All save the girl with the wild hair, Susanna Big Moon. Her crimes were numerous, and she beamed with pride as they were read aloud. The four patrol officers that were speaking against her had two tables loaded with carefully labeled evidence, but the judge waved it away.

"It's clear this sentence has been a long time coming. I would say Ms. Big Moon has been begging for us to catch her for quite some time now. Expulsion. Next?"

"The last case is an anomaly, your honor," said a woman who was holding Valentina's bag. "She has no tracer, no mark of a tracer having

been removed, and facial and vocal recognition finds no matches in
our database."

"Who is she?" the judge asked.

"She says she's from the north pole. Since we have no record of her,
I would assume she entered the dome illegally."

"Do we even need to waste my time on this one?" the judge sighed.
"If she doesn't belong here, I don't need to see her."

"Don't you even want to hear my name?" Valentina cried. Some of
the patrol officers gaped up at her, as if surprised to find her in atten-
dance. The judge merely ignored her.

"I wasn't thinking of sentencing so much as the possible need for
interrogation, which would require your signature," the woman went
on, also ignoring Valentina's outburst. "If she got in without being
noticed, there could be a leak we need to plug."

"Yes, interrogate me!" Valentina yelled, trying to shake the bars for
good measure, but they were too sturdy to rattle. "I have so much I
want to tell you!"

"Is that really necessary for just one? I could see if a flood of them
were getting in, but just one girl worming her way in here doesn't
seem like much cause for alarm."

"But your honor—"

"Interrogation requires a lot more hoop-jumping on my part than
you seem to realize. Have a little mercy, patrol officer. My shift started
sixteen hours ago. Expulsion should cover it. Send her out with the
others. No need to document anything extra."

"Yes, your honor," the woman said, clearly not pleased.

"No, you want to interrogate me!" Valentina yelled, pounding on
the bars with her fist. How she longed for a tin cup to bang with. She
could hear the bars behind her sliding up, the others shuffling out to
meet their final fate. Valentina shimmied up the bars to hang from the
ceiling, hoping the height would let her voice carry further. "You want
to hear what I have to say! Believe me, you want to know my name! I
am Valentina Maria Guadalupe Suárez del Toro—" Her cry ended in a
scream that choked off as she fell to the cell floor, her limbs stiffening
and her teeth clamping down hard, just missing her tongue. A guard

stood over her, his face grim as he tucked his stun stick back into his belt.

"Don't make me do it again, kid," the guard said as he yanked her to her feet. "Nothing you have to say is going to change anything."

"I'm Valentina del Toro, from the north pole," she said, but her voice wouldn't rise above a rasp.

"If you say so," the guard said, pulling her along. She looked back over her shoulder, just catching a glimpse of the judge's face before she was pulled out of view. He looked puzzled. Had he heard her? Would he realize what she had been about to say next? That the head of their security force was her father?

But surely her father was one of those who knew about all this and didn't care.

CHAPTER TWENTY-SEVEN

AIRLOCKS AND CULVERTS

VALENTINA WRENCHED HER ARM OUT OF THE GUARD'S GRASP BUT DIDN'T attempt to flee. There was nowhere to run. She just preferred to stumble along under her own power. The light in the too-bright hallway was like a blade stabbing through her eyes to her brain and she caught Susanna's sleeve with one hand, shading her eyes with the other.

"The weird feeling will pass in a minute," Susanna said. "I've been stung more than once myself, so you can trust me."

"They didn't listen," Valentina said, struggling with her suddenly thick tongue. "I didn't even get to warn them. The revolution is coming."

"The revolution is always coming," Susanna said. "Yet it never seems to arrive."

"It will, in just a few hours."

"A few hours after we get pushed out an airlock. There's irony for you," Susanna said.

The guards brought them back up to the main level, but not to the front door. They followed a maze of hallways through the building to a more remote set of double doors that Valentina guessed was in the back of the building. They stopped here and two of the guards cuffed the kids once more, this time with their hands in front of them. Valentina half expected them all to be chained together, but they were not. One of the guards worked his way down the line, checking every pair of cuffs to be sure they were secure, then nodded to the guard at the front of the line, who nodded back and swiped his wrist over the pad near the door. The doors swung open, out into a dimly lit alley.

"Walk in pairs, stay together," the guard said as the kids were pushed into a double file and led out into the alley. An old man nearby was sweeping small bits of trash into a bin with a broom, but he didn't look up as the group passed.

The alley opened out onto a large boulevard, two roads with a line of towering trees between them. The branches of the trees loomed skeletally over them in the eerie glow of the streetlights. The sense of being in a protective cave was gone. Valentina wasn't sure what had changed—perhaps it was an aftereffect of the shock or the long sleepless night—but she fought the urge to cover her head. Something about the reaching delicacy of their limbs just didn't feel secure, and she didn't like the feeling of walking under them. The sharp crack of a fallen stick under her foot did nothing to reassure her.

They weren't on the boulevard for long before the guards herded them into another narrow alley between tall buildings. This one ran on as far as the eye could see, past pair after pair of towering buildings. Here or there, a window glowed with a dim light despite the hour being closer to dawn than sunset. Valentina could sense all the people crowded within, almost hear the soft breathing and snoring, despite the thick concrete and steel walls. It made her homesick. She remembered her younger days, when all her aunts and cousins still lived with her and my ma and don Abuelo. The kids had slept in a warm pile, a tangle of arms and legs, heads and feet in all orientations. She missed it.

The buildings got shorter and shorter until the alley finally ended in an open space, and Valentina gasped to see the dome so close overhead. The stars were still bright, the east not yet showing signs of dawn. The road under her feet became a spongier material, narrower than the alley, and she realized as they passed under one of the streetlights that it was a path across a lawn of grass. She had only ever seen such a thing in pictures before. It seemed to go on forever to her left and to her right, like a ring around the entire city. Then the open field began to be dotted with trees, smaller than the ones on the boulevard but with more closely woven branches. Valentina saw fruit hanging from some of them.

Then the fruit trees gave way to three long rows of vines snaking over trellises.

And beyond the vines were vegetable gardens.

Valentina felt tears pricking at her eyes. She had never seen such an expanse of food. This place should be a utopia.

The dome was getting closer overhead, the angle sharper. The path continued past rows of tomato plants and a few meager rows of corn, then ended in a pair of double doors, handleless and knobless, just like every door in the detention center.

The guards nearest the door turned to watch as the guards in back herded the kids closer together. Then, suddenly, something seemed to fall from the sky, right in the middle of all of them. Susanna gave a cry and pushed at Valentina, sending them both tumbling into the dry cornstalks. Valentina looked back over her shoulder in time to be blinded by a sudden flash of light accompanied by a loud crack and boom.

Valentina tried to get back onto her feet, but her hands were still bound together, and they were growing numb. Her eyes watered and she couldn't focus on more than the vague outline of the corn around her. She was sure it must be pandemonium behind her, but her ears were muffled, as if she were in a pressure suit with no working sound system.

An arm snaked around her, pulling her to her feet and holding her close as she was propelled forward into a run. She felt cornstalks slapping at her, then she was pulled sideways, back through tomato plants and into a vegetable patch. She whimpered out loud as she trampled over green shoots just starting out on life. Such needless destruction. She drove her feet into the ground, twisting out of the arm's grasp.

She got a sense of a voice somewhere under all that muffled grayness that had become her world, but she couldn't make out a word or even guess if the speaker were male or female. She took a few more steps, mostly to get herself off the plants, but the arm caught her again, this time spinning her around.

The face centimeters from hers, imploring, she would know anywhere, even if the dim light and her still-watering eyes made it impossible to discern the redness of the hair.

Hero pointed where he wanted to go, and she nodded, following him through the vegetable patch. He must have realized what had upset her; he was running between the green rows now and not over them. They reached the long vines on their chest-high trellis. Valentina held out her cuffed hands and Hero shook his head, holding out his own empty hands. No knife to free her with. He jumped the trellis, then reached back for her. She jumped, hitting the top of the trellis with her stomach, but he caught her and held her there long enough for her to get a leg over, then helped her balance until she could get the other leg over and hop down to the ground. He signaled her to stop with a touch of his hand and she did, watching as he peered back the way they had come, head tilted ever so slightly as he listened. The muffled quality of her hearing was gradually giving way to a persistent whine; if they were being followed, she would be no help in spotting it.

Hero tugged at her sleeve and they continued on over the next two trellises and into the fruit trees.

Her vision was spotty, her hearing useless, but her sense of smell was as acute as ever. The tang of apples became sharper when she stepped on a fallen fruit half eaten and left to rot. Then the more delicate scent of pears. The decadent aroma of lush, ripe peaches.

"Come on," Hero said, his voice just carrying through the whine in her ears. He led her away from the trees, through the field of grass, to a boxed-off patch of open Martian soil covered with strange structures, boxes and platforms and tubes, all too short to be of any use. Hero pulled her inside a tube, then stopped just short of where the tube opened out under one of the platforms. Valentina watched him listen. Just as she was beginning to catch her breath, they went on again, out from under the platform and on across the open field of grass, not toward the city but following the ring of grass around it.

Valentina was looking up at the sky through the dome where the first signs of dawn were just becoming visible over the orchard of trees when her foot slipped on the slick grass and she stumbled. She recovered her balance before she fell on her face and bound hands, but her knee protested every time she set her foot down and her run became a hobbled walk. Hero slowed his own run, looking back at her quizzically. She tried to pick up her pace, but her knee wouldn't cooperate and she nearly tumbled to the ground again.

"Rat bite?" Hero asked.

"No, it's the other one. My gorge-jumping injury," she said, stabbing at humor but not really feeling it.

"This way," he said and took her arm to help keep her upright. He guided them up to a jagged gash like a mini-canyon in the field. The path hopped over it on a delicately arched bridge, but Hero led her under that bridge and then further up to where the canyon ended in a dark culvert. There was a trickle of water at the bottom, but that was easy to avoid.

Hero stopped at a point just out of sight from anyone peering in from the opening, then pulled Valentina to sit down beside him. This time, they were still for more than a few minutes. Once she had her breath back, she suddenly felt all the exhaustion of a night spent not sleeping, ending with a mad dash through uneven terrain, punctuated somewhere near the middle with a stun stick blast she was still feeling the effects of. Her tongue had a metal tang to it. Her vision was back, but her hearing was still more high-pitched whine than useful information about the world around her.

The smell of apple on her boot was making her hungry.

"We'll stay here and rest your knee until it's safe," Hero said, slumping back to rest his head against the curve of the concrete behind them.

"When will that be?" Valentina asked, being extra careful to speak quietly despite the noise in her ears. She could barely hear herself, but judging by his flinch, she had still been too loud.

"In a few hours, when the city wakes up. We can blend with the others, then find our way back to the train platform."

"That's going to be tough," Valentina said, raising her still-bound hands. Hero looked around and found a small piece of broken concrete. He pulled her hands onto his lap and sawed away at the plastic with the sharp edge of the rock. Valentina reckoned he might just be done before it was time to go.

"You're not angry," she said.

"No one was ever going to believe you," Hero said.

"My father would have."

"You were never going to talk to your father if you could help it." He gave her a little grin that, in that moment, she found not quite as charming as usual.

"I tried, actually. I gave them his name."

"But they didn't believe that either," Hero guessed.

"I think I deployed it too late," Valentina said. Hero stopped sawing at her cuffs, putting a finger to her lips as he looked over her shoulder, back out the culvert. Valentina slowly turned to look as well. She could see the outline of a man walking along the canyon, searching. She looked the other way, past Hero. If the culvert made it all the way to some place they could escape to, she had no idea; all she could see was inky blackness. She didn't know if she moved closer to Hero or he to her, but they pressed against each other, faces tucked out of sight between them as the light from the man's flashlight danced over them.

They were at the very edge of his light's range. He swept his light over them twice, three times, and Valentina held her breath, certain he was about to charge in, to raise the alarm, or both.

Then he was gone.

Hero's face had drained of color during that long moment, but then he grinned at her, even managing a wink as he resumed sawing at the cuff around her wrists.

"No worries. We'll be back with the others soon enough."

"You think that's not a worry for me?" Valentina asked.

"No one else even knows that you're gone," Hero said.

"They sent you to keep an eye on me. Last night when I left the feast. Don't lie."

"I won't lie. They did ask me to watch you. Kavi and Skald are getting antsy for the big fight. Is that so hard to understand?"

"But you're the only one who noticed I was gone?"

"Everyone else is still sleeping. Or if they see you're gone, they see I'm gone too, so like I said, no worries."

"When did you realize I left? How did you know where I went?" Valentina asked.

"I realized you left when you sat up and walked away. I wasn't sleeping. And I wasn't sure which way you'd go, into the city or back toward your friends, so I followed you."

"But you didn't stop me?"

"I would have if you'd tried to walk back up the line. That's a long walk, and you weren't taking any supplies. But like I said, no one in the city was ever going to believe you. I grew up here. I've been through the whole long-night-at-court-followed-by-a-quick-trip-through-the-airlock experience. I know this city and how it runs. Now you do too. I figure living it was more convincing than me telling you."

"I don't want to see people get hurt."

"I know," Hero said, glancing up from his sawing to look into her eyes. "To be honest, I lost you after you left the marketplace. I thought for sure you were after your brother. It took me a while to realize which way you must have gone."

"I don't know where to find my brother. You said you didn't either."

"I know the neighborhoods he's likely to be in. Too big to search, but you seemed… driven. But I should have realized. You were worried about more than your own brother."

"It didn't do any good," Valentina said.

"It might not have helped them a bit, but it did something for you," he said, looking up at her again. Her heart beat a little faster each time he did that. His fingers, twined through her cuff, were pressed against the pulse in her wrist. Did he notice? "You know where I'm coming from now, don't you?"

"A bit," she allowed. "The others at the airlock?"

"They are smart kids; they ran in all directions when I threw that flashbang. The guards recovered quicker than I thought they would, and they might have recaptured one or two, but most of them got away like we did. They will have to hide out, their names are on record, but after the overthrow this morning, none of that will matter."

"You're much more optimistic than I am. I just have this knot of fear in my belly that won't loosen up," she said.

"I've put a lot of time and thought into this. It's going to be fine, I promise. Just think, by dinnertime you'll be with your brother again."

"A lot can happen between now and dinnertime."

"A lot will. But it won't all be bad."

The cuff gave way with a snap and he dropped the rock, taking her hands in both of his. His thumbs traced over her wrists as if inspecting them for damage, but his eyes were on hers again. Then his hands were touching her cheeks, sliding into her hair. His thumb brushed the curve of her lower lip, but she couldn't stand the soft slowness of it all anymore and buried her hands in his own red curls, pulling him down into a kiss that he met eagerly. The ringing sound rushed back in her ears, but this time it was just part of the bliss. All other thoughts fell away, such a welcome sensation after the long night of being hounded by so many fears and worries. But then he pulled away.

"Best keep our guard up," he said, tucking her closer against him but looking over her shoulder to the mouth of the culvert. "When it gets lighter, we'll sneak out. We just have to wait here a bit first."

Valentina snuggled into his shoulder, enjoying the smell of him, her fingers still tangled in his hair. He kissed her now and then, her forehead, her cheeks, teasingly on her lips, but his eyes were fixed on danger now.

"I kind of wish we could stay here forever," she said, knowing it sounded silly.

"When we run the city, we can come here as often as you like," he promised with a little grin.

She nodded, but the blissful warmth in her belly turned back to ice.

That was never going to happen. But she didn't know what *was* going to happen. Where would they be when the invasion failed?

CHAPTER TWENTY-EIGHT

THE REVOLUTION BEGINS

VALENTINA DOZED OFF AND ON, BUT EACH TIME HER EYES FLEW BACK open, Hero was still awake, still watching the opening behind her. He would rub her arm softly, almost absently, and she would drift off again only to snap back awake. It was not the time for sleep.

She had seen the first light of dawn before they had plunged into the culvert. It must be brightening out there in the park, but she couldn't tell even when she turned to look out into the grassy canyon herself.

At last Hero felt that enough time had passed, and he got to his feet, holding out a hand to help her up. Lying on cold concrete had made her muscles go stiff, but by the time they emerged from the culvert and climbed back up the grassy slope to the path, she had loosened up and felt surprisingly good for the little sleep she'd gotten. Her knee still twinged with each step and she wasn't sure she could handle another run, but walking through the city felt doable. Her ears were no longer ringing. Somewhere in the distance she could hear a little dog barking, then another deeper bark answering. She hadn't heard dogs since she'd left the north pole; such a small thing to bring a stab of homesickness.

Hero led the way to the nearest exit out of the park. Valentina walked as briskly as she could beside him, also anxious to get out of the open. There were sounds of people moving in the city ahead of them, but the park was empty at that hour and she felt very exposed.

The gate out of the park opened onto a large boulevard with trees on both sides as well as down the middle. People were walking, pushing carts or carrying large packs balanced on their shoulders.

"At this hour, it's just merchants who are up," Hero said to her as he took her arm to guide her to the nearest alley. "Mostly heading to the marketplace, although some of the food vendors have street corners out in the city. They'll have all sorts of breakfast items all ready to sell by the time the buses start running and the other workers head out to their jobs."

"It already smells so good," Valentina said as they jogged across another, larger side street to plunge back into another alley. A vendor was setting up his cart on a street corner not far from the alley. The smell of cinnamon and sausage and fry oil hit her empty stomach like the sweetest of come-ons. She had no idea what he was selling, she just knew she wanted to try it.

"Sadly, we'll have to wait until we get back to camp to eat, and it won't be this appetizing," Hero said. "But tomorrow, I promise, I'll treat you to the best the city has to offer."

Valentina didn't answer. He sounded so certain it was useless to argue with him. She remembered the anxious violence of the revolutionaries the night before. If the revolution was successful, it would still be an end won by needlessly bloody means. She didn't see the citizens around her accepting their conquerors with the open arms Hero was expecting.

"You and your brother, of course," Hero said, guessing at the reason for her silence.

"I knew you meant that," Valentina said with an attempt at a smile. She had completely failed to stop the battle by warning the city's security forces. Could she still stop it by talking Hero out of it?

"Are you worried you'll be recognized?" she asked when he guided her down another even narrower alley.

"Not really," Hero said. "I was fourteen when I was thrown out the airlock; I don't look anything like I used to. Well, the red hair would be a giveaway, but I never had a lot of friends."

"I find that hard to believe," Valentina said.

"I'm different from I used to be," Hero said. "To be honest, I'm not sure my own mother would even know me anymore. If she still lives."

"Of course she still lives," Valentina said, moved by the way his voice had threatened to crack on that last word. "You're going to see her soon, just like me and Arturo, right?"

"She was sick, the kind of sick that never quite goes away. I hope someone has been taking care of her since I left, although I can't imagine who would."

"We could find her now," Valentina said. "If she doesn't live in the same place, someone there would know where she's gone, right? You could make sure she's safe before the battle."

"No, there's no time," Hero said. "We're already delaying things by not being there."

"They won't start without you?" Valentina asked, trying not to sound too hopeful.

"They will," Hero said, pausing at the end of the alley to scan the scene before walking quickly across the street to the next alley. The buildings around them were getting taller and taller, the streets more and more crowded. Valentina looked around as they crossed the street. If no one would be able to recognize him, she supposed he was looking out for patrol officers. But it wasn't after curfew, and he insisted he was an unknown in the city these days. They would have to be looking for her.

"I didn't tell them how I got into the city," Valentina said. "There was going to be an interrogation, but the judge didn't want to do it."

"That's good news," Hero said, but offhandedly, as if he'd already known. Valentina realized he must have known or he would have asked before. But how had he known? Had he been in contact with one of his inside people before he rescued her at the airlock? She was reluctant to ask and risk his irritation again.

"Can we get back out through the marketplace without being seen?" she asked instead.

"We'll have to move fast and hope for the best," Hero said.

The alleys ended far from the marketplace, but it was late enough in the morning now for the streets to be crowded with people: adults heading off to work, children bustling off to school. Long, low buses rolled along the streets, smaller one- or two-passenger auto-rickshaws darting around them to take passengers with more cash along faster routes. Hero and Valentina walked side by side, blending in with the rest of the foot traffic. He guided her toward the marketplace with little nudges, but their surroundings were starting to look familiar to her from their earlier recon as well as her midnight journey.

The sounds of feet scuffling along and random conversations between pedestrians began to be drowned out by the more chaotic sounds of the marketplace opening for the day. Awnings were snapping open, doors and gates being swung up or out and fastened out of the way. Vendors greeted each other and the early morning shoppers alike. Valentina could smell coffee again, rich and inviting.

Hero caught her elbow and pulled her out of the flow of traffic, looking around in a quick glance before heading up the steep slope to the catwalk. Valentina followed, hands in her pockets in a desperate attempt to look casual. But no one seemed to notice them. They passed vent after vent before stopping at the one she had left closed but not fastened.

"Just a minute," Hero said, looking around one more time. His hand was on the edge of the grill, ready to raise it just enough for them both to slip under and away, when he suddenly froze. Valentina followed his gaze but saw nothing.

"Patrol?" she whispered, searching for the dark uniform among the crowd of shoppers below.

"No," Hero said. "I thought I saw my mother."

"Are you sure?" Valentina asked, touching his hand. "It's been six years. She would look different."

"No, I'm not sure," he said at last. Valentina frowned. He might have been admitting to rational logic when he said he had no way to be sure, but she sensed that his gut was not so willing to concede to any doubt.

"Did you want to find her, talk to her?"

"No, no," he said, shaking his head. He looked ashen.

"Warn her to get out of the marketplace?"

"No," he said, more firmly. "Absolutely not. Anyway, it probably wasn't even her. She worked in food service. She would be serving breakfast in a workers' cafe ten blocks north of here."

"It's been six years," Valentina said again.

"No, no, I can't go back down there. We need to hurry." He lifted the edge of the grill and she slipped inside as quickly as she could. He followed her, adjusting the loosely hanging grill behind them. Then he tugged her sleeve, urging her to follow as he broke into a run.

"You said they would start without you," Valentina said.

"It's better if I'm there," Hero said. "We still have a bit of time."

"They'll be angry with me," Valentina said, and the minute the words were out, she felt the truth of them. She remembered Skald looming over her, the dark scowl on Kavi's face. They were going to be very angry with her, indeed.

"It'll be OK," Hero insisted, turning back to catch her hand and pull her after him. "No one is going to hurt you while I'm there."

"They'll think I gave you all up," Valentina said.

"Of course they'll think that. That's what you were planning to do," he snapped. "But like I said, no one was ever going to believe you. They know that as well as I."

"I don't think they'll be as inclined as you to just let it go," she said, then dug her heels in to yank her wrist out of his grasp. "I don't feel like running toward people who intend me harm."

"Cronista," Hero said. "There are two things I can swear to you. No one will harm you while I am there, and this invasion is happening with or without me. There's no good in trying to delay me, and you are safest by my side. Now can we just go?"

"I don't want to be a part of it. I don't want to even see it."

"Then you can stay below in the camp."

"Or I could stay right here," Valentina said. "Or you could at least point me in the direction of where you suspect my brother lives."

"Cronista," Hero said, then more softly, "Valentina. I want you to stay near me, where I can see you and know that you're safe. Is that so strange?"

"It doesn't feel safe," she said, but he stepped closer to her, his hand caressing her cheek before his lips found hers again, and she realized that wasn't entirely true. He broke off the kiss to look into her eyes, and she sighed. His absolute sincerity, the way he completely committed to every word he said, every promise he made, was very, very seductive.

"They're going to be angry," she whispered.

He touched her cheek again. "Let them."

They could hear the sounds of squad commanders organizing their troops even before they made the leap down from the air vent to the station floor. Hero grasped her hand firmly and Valentina let him, not sure which of them was giving and which receiving support. Perhaps in that moment it was flowing both ways.

Nandi was the first to see them from where she sat on a crate at the bottom of the sloping hallway. "Hero's here," she called out, but the look on her face as she stood to greet them was anything but pleased. "I know you better than to think you sneaked away for a private rendezvous at this of all times."

"Yes, you do," Hero said. "Is everyone ready to roll out?"

"Everyone but you. I have something to show you. It's what they call a game changer."

"Lead the way," Hero said.

Nandi looked pointedly at Valentina and their hands clasped together but said nothing, just turned on her booted heel and led them to where Skald and Kavi were standing among stacks of crates dispersing the contents among the squad commanders. There were guns, as Valentina had expected, but also armored vests with SECURITY written on them, with visored helmets to match, and grenades. There were three distinct shapes to the grenades, but she shivered to think what that meant. It was far more firepower than she had expected them to have.

As if echoing her thoughts, Hero said, "This is a lot more than I thought you'd manage to steal. Especially the vests—that is really going to raise the confusion factor in the crowds. They'll comply with our commands much more readily."

He glanced at Valentina, and while she supposed it was true and could mean less violence as the revolutionaries herded up their hostages, she couldn't take her mind off the grenades.

"That's not even the game changer," Nandi said, slinging her rifle over her shoulder by its strap to lift the lid off a crate positioned farthest from where Skald and Kavi were working. Hero and Valentina crouched down to peer under the lid she raised only enough for them to see inside.

Valentina didn't know what she was looking at; they were just plain gray boxy objects with a few unlabeled buttons on their narrow sides. But Nandi was grinning widely and Hero gave a low whistle of appreciation.

"That does change things."

"They must have had something of their own planned to have two crates of this stacked in their active-use armory."

"You broke into the active-use armory?"

"Believe me, it's easier than breaking into deep storage."

"But they'll miss it sooner. As in probably already."

"It won't matter if we move fast," Nandi said. "These dial in to a ten-second fuse. I've already assigned half the Alis to the task, and Skald has picked the targets."

"Is ten seconds enough to get clear?" Hero asked.

"Probably, but even if it isn't, my team is willing to risk it."

"They are going to explode," Valentina guessed. Nandi and Hero both glanced at her as if for a moment they'd forgotten she was there.

"You're not on bomb duty?" Hero asked Nandi.

"I would volunteer in a heartbeat, but you wanted me to lead the hostage roundup."

"Yes, it's crucial that you're there with me," Hero said. "We want minimum bloodshed. I know you're with me on that."

"Absolutely. And Skald has chosen military targets for the bombs."

"Which targets?" Hero asked, fishing his tablet out of his pocket and bringing up the map of the city.

"Security headquarters," Skald said as he and Kavi approached. The rest of the crates were empty, the squad leaders now dividing their portions of the assorted firearms amongst their squads.

Hero nodded. "That should slow their response. What else?"

"This building here, and this one there. When they fall, they will block these two roads and isolate the marketplace," Skald said, pointing to positions on the tablet.

"What are those buildings?" Valentina asked.

"I don't know," he said, but Valentina knew without question that he was lying.

"Let me see," Hero said, tapping and zooming in on his map. "Apartment complexes. Apartment complexes, Skald?"

"Security has tanks. With those two roads blocked, they won't be able to use them against us in the marketplace. I don't need to tell you that tanks firing at our hostage takers are going to hit a lot of hostages."

"Which is why they won't do it," Hero said, and Valentina sensed they were rehashing an old argument. "I don't like bombing homes."

"It's after work hours begin," Kavi said. "The only ones inside will be—"

"The sick, the elderly. The young," Hero said pointedly.

"We're also taking out this building," Skald said, stabbing the map with one thick finger.

"The corporate headquarters," Hero said, not needing to zoom in to recognize that building. The outline was like a capital H with a circular dome in the center.

"The apartment buildings we're only going to raze a little, knock down enough of the outer wall to obstruct the street," Kavi said. "Security, we just need to block their entrances, especially to the motor pools. But this building we're collapsing to the ground."

"You would need engineering knowledge to do that properly," Hero said.

"We're saving it for last. We've already contacted our engineer on the inside and he's working the problem. After the Alis take out the other targets, they will rendezvous with the engineer for instructions, then take down the heart of the corporation."

"You're never going to gain these people's trust after that much carnage," Valentina said.

"We have to take out the corporate structure. This is so much better than demanding their heads one by one in exchange for hostages in the marketplace," Skald said.

"The people we need, the ones who actually run the departments, are not in this building," Hero told her. "They work closer to the systems they're responsible for. This just takes out the top levels, the parasites who don't work, just direct people about, enforce the system where the few have much and the many have little."

"I think it's brilliant," Nandi said. "We get them all in one blow. It's more than we could have asked for. Our enemy will be headless."

"So we're not going for bloodless anymore?" Valentina asked.

"The people in the marketplace, the people of the city—their blood is what I wanted to avoid spilling. A few might be inside that building, but only a very few."

"An acceptable few?" Valentina said.

"It's necessary to achieve our mission," Skald said.

"The mission to improve the lives of everyone under the dome?" Valentina asked. "Or the mission to provide you with the revenge you're so clearly thirsting for?"

"Cronista," Hero said, shaking his head. But it was too late. She'd already crossed Skald's line.

"Listen," Skald growled, grabbing a fistful of the front of Valentina's sweater and pulling her up into the air. She squeaked, her feet kicking helplessly far from the ground. She grasped his arm, not remotely able to break his hold but pulling herself up enough to relieve some of the pressure on her throat. Hero made a yelp of protest, but Kavi caught him in an armlock, holding him back. Skald's other hand reached up, lifting the strawberry blond locks back away from his forehead. "Do you see?"

For a long moment she only saw the rage burning in his eyes, but then she glanced up towards his fingers and saw the series of tiny burn marks lined up all along his hairline, tucked just out of view until the day his hair started thinning. Then it would look like he was wearing a crown of pinprick burns, overlapping again and again.

"What is that?" she whispered.

"That's what happens in the corporation when you don't conform to their standards. Spend your time pursuing the wrong interests."

"I thought they just pushed you out an airlock," Valentina gasped. It was getting harder to breathe.

"Not when you're six. When you're six, they still try to fix you. Fix your brain. This,"—he pointed at the path of burns—"is nothing compared to what they've destroyed in here." He made a fist and rapped on his own skull hard enough to make Valentina flinch.

"That wasn't here," Hero said, still pinned by Kavi but no longer struggling, just talking. "The head of the medical department in Valles Marineris III is clearly pathologically insane and should be made to die slowly and painfully, but that wasn't here."

Skald turned from red to purple, but then let out a whooshing breath and dropped Valentina. Her knee collapsed under her and she fell to the ground.

"They're all the same," Skald said. "And they're all going down. This mission we're going to complete today isn't my personal revenge. I promise you my revenge would be very, very different. *Will* be, when it's my hometown we're taking. I don't need some girl from the other side of Mars judging me."

"Time grows short," Nandi said. While the others were arguing, she had suited up in a security vest and helmet, visor up so they could still see her face. The pants were all wrong, but Valentina had to admit it wouldn't be hard to mistake her for an actual officer. Especially the way people inside the dome avoided making eye contact with them. Once she started shouting orders, she wouldn't even need to wave her rifle around to get compliance.

"Why can't you stick with the original plan?" Valentina asked. "You've added too many complications at the last minute. It's all going to go wrong."

"My Alis can handle it," Nandi said.

"It will be clean," Hero said. "Surgical hits. Don't worry." He twisted a little in Kavi's grip. Skald gave a nod and Kavi let him go to crouch beside Valentina, who was hugging her throbbing knee. "It will all be over soon, and then the rebuilding will start."

"They're going to be prepared for you," Valentina said.

"I told you not to worry about that; no one believed you."

"She ratted?" Skald said.

"Can you think of any conceivable reason these explosives would be in such easy reach?" Valentina said.

"Hey, it was anything but easy," Nandi said.

"They will know by now exactly what's missing," Valentina said.

"Which is why we have to move out now," Kavi said.

"Don't you see? It's a trap."

"You're just being paranoid," Hero said. He touched her knee, but when she flinched, he grasped her wrist instead.

"I've had enough of this. Tie her to a pole if you have to, but it's time for us to go," Skald growled.

"Why bother tying her? What's she going to do?" Kavi said.

"Good point. Hero, are you suiting up?"

Hero looked at her desperately.

"You know I'm right," Valentina said. "It's a trap. You're about to lead all your people into a trap. The security branch has been baiting you. How do you even have access to an engineer with the schematics necessary to bring down the corporate headquarters? That and the explosives to do it? Isn't it just hugely coincidental?"

"Hero, let's go!" Kavi said, cuffing him on the shoulder with the butt of his rifle.

"You need to be sure because you're about to lose everything," Valentina persisted.

Hero was still looking straight into her eyes. Valentina's gaze didn't waver. She was a bit surprised that the idea of revolutionaries dying horribly made her just as sad as civilians being caught in the fray, but it did. She hadn't been friendly with more than a few of them, but she had grown used to having them around. Another week on the road and she might really have made them her new family.

Hero nodded, looking away from her and up to Skald and Kavi. He opened his mouth, but before he had a chance to speak, Kavi's rifle butt connected with his head.

"Hero!" Valentina cried as he collapsed across her lap, eyes glassy and face already a smear of blood.

"Was that really necessary?" Nandi asked, a dangerous edge to her voice.

"You told me you put the revolution before Hero. You still mean that?" Kavi demanded. She nodded curtly, but the anger didn't leave her eyes. "Lead the troops out," Kavi ordered. "Now."

Valentina felt Nandi hesitating, although she kept her own eyes on Hero, looking for signs of consciousness as she held the sleeve of her sweater to his wound and softly called his name. Then Nandi in her oversized boots was marching away, and she was alone with the warrior-poets.

"I knew you'd be trouble," Kavi grumbled, catching her arms and dragging her away from Hero. Her legs slid out from under him and his head hit the concrete with a crack.

"How can you do this? He's your friend!" she cried, but she could not twist out of his grip.

"It'd be easier just to kill her," Skald said as she slid past his feet.

"You're the one who said tie her to a pole," Kavi grunted, still dragging her despite her kicking. Then the edge of a pillar of cold concrete met her back. Skald came around the other side of her to help Kavi twist her arms behind her. Her wrists just barely met around the square column, the edges digging painfully into her arms just above the elbow, the center of her back.

"Good enough," Kavi said after cinching tight the plastic cuffs he'd found in the pocket of his security vest.

"Hero," Valentina said. He looked so far away, bleeding on the floor.

"He'll be fine," Kavi said and slammed the visor of his helmet shut.

"And when we get back down, we can continue our conversation," Skald said, punching a gloved fist into the palm of his other hand. "Oh, and we'll be sure to keep an eye out for your brother."

Kavi didn't join in Skald's raucous laughter, but the blank silence as he looked at her one last time through the mirrored visor of his helmet was somehow more frightening.

CHAPTER TWENTY-NINE

SMOKE AND BLOOD

Kavi had overlapped Valentina's wrists before tightening the cuffs, so as much as she tried, she could not saw away at the plastic on the edge of the concrete column, she just scraped the hell out of her own wrists. But she couldn't stop trying to do it, anyway; there was nothing else to do but watch the blood run down Hero's gray face to splash to the ground in an inky puddle.

It was quiet, so quiet she swore she could hear a breeze whistling through the lava tube. She tilted her head, straining her ears, but if the fight had already broken out above them, she could hear not a clue of it.

"How did I get caught up in all this?" she hissed at herself as she resumed twisting her wrists and attempting to saw at the plastic. Had it all been inevitable? She had stolen her grandfather's pressure suit, went out an airlock, and started walking off the ice cap in search of her brother. Was this always going to be where it all ended? Was there ever a point at which she could have made a different choice? "I should have left with Kiyoshi and Hazel." But she never could have done that. She had come too far to change course away from finding her brother. And if it had been too far that day when Kiyoshi and Hazel turned back, it was definitely too far now.

Hero groaned faintly.

"Hero?" she called, not sure if she had imagined it.

"Ow." He was definitely blinking now, but he looked confused.

"Can you sit up?" she asked, leaning as far forward as the cuffs would let her, which wasn't very far.

"Yeah, gimme a minute." He pressed a hand to the floor and slowly pushed himself up into a low slouch that was still technically sitting up. He hung his head low over his lap, his hair hiding his face from view.

"You all right?"

"Will be," he murmured. "Skald hit me?"

"Kavi, actually."

"Wow," he said, pressing the back of his hand to the gash on his forehead, then looking at the blood that stained his fingers. "Skald, I might have expected, but Kavi? What the hell is happening?"

"They are carrying on bombing and taking hostages without you. They don't share your interest in rebuilding, do they?"

"No, no, they don't," he admitted with a sigh. He ran both his hands through his hair, and as if that gesture rejuvenated him, he sat up straighter and looked her way. He was pale, but that was a definite improvement over ash gray. "That's why I needed you so badly. I have all these plans, but no one to help execute them. Everyone thirsts for the battle, but no one wants to sing songs about what has to be done next. Nandi is with me on all of it, has been since the beginning, but she doesn't want to lead more than her little band of commandos. I thought I was close to bringing Kavi around. We would talk about reconstruction and he had some good ideas. This is all very disappointing."

"We have to stop it before people start dying. I haven't heard any bombs go off yet. I don't think we're too late."

"We have no weapons—what possible good can we do?"

"Kavi and Skald might outnumber and outgun you, but neither of them talks half as good as you do."

"You want me to go up there and talk my own troops out of their victory?"

"Honestly, I think just convincing Nandi to pull her Alis out of the equation will be enough."

Hero looked around, saw a thermos nearby, and tipped his head back to let the water run over his face. He scrubbed at his skin with the ends of his flannel shirt and shook the water from his hair before standing up.

"You're quite right," he said, sounding like his old self again—cocky but sincere. "Nandi will listen, and her Alis will follow her to the death or away from it if she asks. Let's go."

"I'm tied up here. Got a knife?"

Hero found one in one of the crates. "This is getting to be a bit of a pattern with us," he said with a grin as he walked up to her.

"Your head is still bleeding. We should bandage that before we go," she said.

"You don't think I'm more persuasive with blood running down my face?" he joked, then all the laughter went out of his voice. "Cronista, how long was I out?"

"I'm not sure. Felt like forever," Valentina said.

"Your wrists are a mess." The plastic cuff snapped away under his blade and Valentina groaned aloud with the relief that she could finally bring her arms forward.

"I didn't realize I was bleeding," she said. Under the blood, her flesh was puffy and sore; *that* she had felt.

"I think you would have chewed off one of your own hands if you'd been able to reach it," Hero said, quickly winding a bandage roll around first one wrist and then the other, tying off the ends. Valentina found an adhesive patch in the same first-aid box and pulled Hero's hair back to affix it over his wound.

"Nice lump there," she said as he flinched from even her gentlest touch.

"We can stop this together, right?" he asked.

"Of course. We're not that banged up."

"And afterward, we can plan the next step together too?"

"Hero—"

"I know you want to find your brother," he said.

"It's not that. I don't want to be a fighter. I can help you stop this fight now; I'll risk my life to do that if need be. But I won't help you plan the next battle. I can't do that."

"I know. That's not what I'm asking."

"Then what do you mean?"

"I think the way to do this is maybe something else. Fighting is part of it—I'll always believe that some circumstances just demand it and it's the only path to liberty. But I've also been thinking lately that maybe it's not the best place to start. You keep talking about how the people up there have no reason to trust us. But what if they did have a reason? What if we started with a small community and created it as a proof of concept about how we think a city should be run? And spread stories about it. Create a reality they will all want to be a part of."

"It sounds like a lot of work, and we'll have to go over a lot more specifics before I'll really have a handle on what you're thinking, but yes, absolutely that sounds like something I could do. Yes."

Hero smiled, such a look of relief on his face she had no idea how certain he had been that she would say no. He kissed her firmly, as if sealing the deal, then pulled her to her feet.

"Time to go stop this madness."

Hero and Valentina ran through the ducts towards the marketplace. They could hear voices yelling, crying, children shrieking in terrified alarm even before they reached the final stretch of duct that ended in the grill Valentina had broken open just hours before. It was no longer hanging askew; it was gone completely. Hero signaled for her to follow behind him as he crept out onto the walkway and peered over the side to the open market below.

"It's already started," Valentina whispered as she crouched beside him. "Look, there's Nandi, up on the stage." She had her rifle down at her side, pointing to the floor, but her other hand was waving instructions to her Alis and they had their rifles up, herding the people into a tighter huddle at the base of the stage.

"It's not too late," Hero said, looking up and down the empty alleys of the marketplace, counting off revolutionaries as he saw them searching for stragglers or setting up barricades. "I can still get to Nandi. The walkway over there is pretty close to the stage."

"Close, but about a dozen meters over it. How are you going to get down?" Valentina asked. Hero stroked his lip as he thought, looking over their surroundings closely.

"I can climb it."

"Shimmy down that pole? I don't think so," Valentina said.

"This is going so well," he said wonderingly.

"What's going well?"

"My plan. The invasion plan. I don't see any injured or dying. They brought all the hostages to the stage and I don't think any of them have yet fired a shot."

"Hero, didn't we come here to stop this?"

"We came to stop the bombs. My original plan was solid. Is solid. Look."

"We need to get to Nandi to stop the other Alis. And I don't see Kavi or Skald. That has me very nervous."

"You're right, I don't like that either. OK, I'm going to follow the walkway to the stage and slide down that pole."

"You want me to just stay here?"

"I think that would be best. I mean, Nandi likes you, but it would probably be better if you weren't on that stage with me. Not just now. In the future, we're always going to be a team, but—"

"Just go already," Valentina said, giving him a shove. "We've lost too much time already."

"Right," he agreed, but he still pulled her close for one last, perhaps overly long, kiss. The clang of his steps running up the walkway had faded before she opened her eyes. Hero was already a small figure bounding around the bend of the walkway, so she turned her attention back to the marketplace below.

The Alis were still controlling the hostages in the stage area, separating families from the others and moving them into the relative protection of the orchestra pit. Out in the narrow lanes between the shops the other revolutionaries were still patrolling, some manning barricades but others walking in pairs or threesomes. There seemed to be more of them than before, perhaps manning up for the inevitable response from the city's security. Up on the stage, Nandi was walking and nodding, her free hand pressed to her ear. Valentina felt a rush of alarm, realizing she must be talking with the other half of her team—the half on bomb duty.

Then a roar shook the dome, and she crouched low, hands pressed over her ears until the rumbling faded away and the walkway stopped shaking beneath her. She stood up, searching for the source. It wasn't hard to spot: a mountain of smoke and dust billowing out into the streets and curling up to collect against the top curve of the dome. She knew that building. She'd been inside it just hours before.

That had just been the bombs intended to seal off the exits from the security headquarters. What was it going to be like when the corporate headquarters collapsed? And it would have to happen soon. If the building was evacuated before the revolutionaries blew it, the whole thing would be a pointless gesture.

Valentina scanned the buildings under the dome, trying to orient herself with her memories of the map and figure out where the head-quarters was. Her hands hovered near her ears, ready to duck back under the wall. The smoke and dust from the security building blew over the marketplace, filling her lungs with the acrid smell of burnt concrete. Still, she waited for the worst to follow. After several long minutes of nothing, she dropped her hands. Had that part of the plan failed?

Then she heard something else: a rumble punctuated by metallic creaks and rattles. She crouched back down, out of sight, then peeked over the edge.

Tanks. Dozens of them. She could see them from her vantage point, but the revolutionaries manning the barricades were calling to each other in confusion. They could hear the tanks approaching, but couldn't see them. It was as if the drivers knew exactly where the barri-cades were positioned and which alleys to roll down to get as close as possible while still staying out of sight.

The tanks that were supposed to have been trapped inside the secu-rity motor pools when the bombs went off.

Valentina looked back towards the stage where Nandi was still pacing and talking into her communicator. She swept her gaze up the thin support beam until she found Hero a third of the way down, hanging at a standstill as he, too, watched the tanks move into position.

Then there was a burst of gunfire, and Valentina instinctively ducked again. Slowly, she risked another peek below. Now she knew she had been right. There were more revolutionaries patrolling the alleys than before—but they weren't all revolutionaries, as they were now shooting at each other. The revolutionaries and security forces were wearing the same uniforms, which made things confusing. But she could see some fighters in black uniforms creeping up behind the barricades to quickly dispatch the pairs waiting besides piles of grenades. Valentina knew from the warrior-poets' battle plans that these were revolutionaries manning their posts, but watching over the top of the barricade for an incoming attack, they never realized the ones with guns coming up behind them weren't on their side.

Valentina wept, but couldn't look away. The revolutionaries manning the barricades were the youngest, some only Arturo's age. And the security officers that had infiltrated the marketplace were taking them out with head shots before they could even put their hands up to surrender. Then she saw others sprawled out on the roofs of shops, carefully aiming long rifles supported by tripods. Snipers.

"Hero!" she screamed as loud as she could, the word tearing at her throat. He didn't look her way, but then he was focused on climbing down the pole as quickly as he could. Too quickly to be safe, she thought as his slide took on too much speed and he disappeared behind the curve of the clamshell that covered the stage.

A single shot rang out, somehow louder than the others. Then Nandi dropped her rifle, hand going to her neck as if she'd been stung by some angry insect. She looked up, perhaps searching for the sniper, but her eyes met Valentina's instead. Then her knees buckled under her and she fell facedown on the stage.

Valentina knew she was the one screaming, but it still sounded so far away in her own ears, lost behind the sudden roar of tank fire. Crates and wall panels from the barricades soared up into the air, drifting back down to be ground into the dust under the heavy treads as the tanks advanced. Valentina bit her own lip to stop herself from screaming, hands fisted tight, her whole body tense to the point of pain as she sought for some sign of Hero. Had he made it to the stage? In the smoke and clouds of reddish dust, she couldn't see clearly.

She heard a click behind her and froze, certain it came from a gun trained on her back, but then the air started whooshing past her, sucked into the vent behind her, bringing the smoke and dust with it. Valentina dropped to her knees—the force of the suction was growing stronger, and with the grill gone, there was nothing to keep her from tumbling down those long hallways to the massive fans. She tried crawling along the walkway, eyes squeezed tight against the debris whirling around her. She didn't realize how much she was still being pulled until her hip bashed against the canyon wall at the edge of the vent. She scrambled forward, stopping only when the wind was no longer tugging at her, and sat with her back against the wall. She opened her eyes.

She was about where she thought she'd be, halfway between the vent she had crawled out of and the next vent along the walkway. Each one was like a sideways tornado, pulling smoke and dust out of the marketplace. Other objects were mixed up in that vortex: waxed paper from the food vendors, a few birds that had drifted over from the parks, a rag doll.

Valentina dropped her head into her hands, relief making her entire body shake. She pushed loose strands of hair back from her face and noticed blood on her fingers. Something had struck her while she had been crawling away and she had been too driven to notice.

She could hear gunfire below, gunfire and screams. The wind between the two vents was intense, but not strong enough to push her, so she decided to risk another look below. She crawled to the edge of the walkway, hunkering as low as she could, and peered over the rail. The smoke was less intense, but enough of it remained to confuse her view, making images waver like a heat mirage. She saw Nandi lying on the stage, her head in someone's lap. Another twist of the smoke in the wind and she caught a glimpse of red curls. Hero was with her, and still safe.

A sharp cry more directly below her grabbed her attention, and she saw a woman with a child in her arms running back toward the stage area. Through wisps of smoke and dust Valentina saw other people she took for escaped hostages moving through the narrow lanes of the marketplace, but no matter how many times she blinked and strained her eyes, she couldn't erase the vision that their own security force was firing at them, driving them back toward the revolutionaries they were fleeing from. She saw bodies fall, crying out in pain or lying lifelessly still in the dust. What was going on?

Then there was another click, only this time when she looked up there was a gun trained on her, or rather three.

"Stand up slowly and put your hands behind you," the officer in the middle ordered.

Valentina complied, allowing herself to be cuffed for the third time in less than half a day. If they weren't as gentle with it as the first woman had been, at least they didn't twist her wrists into painful contortions first as Kavi had done.

"Why is she bandaged up like that?" one of the other officers asked the one cuffing her.

"Who knows?" the first one answered.

"Is it some sort of trick to let her escape from the cuffs? Maybe you should cinch them up tighter."

"No, the blood is legit. See?" He peeled back the bandage to show his buddy and a hiss of pain escaped Valentina's clenched teeth.

"What's up with that?" the second one persisted, coming around to look Valentina in the eye.

"It's been a long day," Valentina said. "Where are you taking me? Why are you shooting at everyone down there but cuffing me?"

The man—barely more than a boy, really—frowned and looked over the rail at the chaos below.

"We have nonlethal force orders," he said, looking over at the officer that had cuffed Valentina. He stood poker-faced, but his eyes told the younger officer that nothing was going to be discussed in front of their prisoner.

The third officer, a woman, jogged back down the walkway towards them. Valentina hadn't even realized she was gone. "All clear. She's the only one up here."

"OK, let's move out," the senior of the three said, prodding

Valentina with the butt of his gun between her shoulder blades. "Just keep walking."

"To where? If you're going to shoot me, you might as well do it here."

"We're not going to shoot you," he said, pushing her again. "Get walking. It's not exactly safe up here. I don't want to take a sniper round on your account."

"It's definitely not safe down there," Valentina said, digging her heels in. She looked back over her shoulder, hoping for another glimpse of red hair, but the swirls of smoke weren't complying.

"We're not going into the marketplace," the younger officer said. "We have a holding area set up well away from the fighting."

"Would you shut it?"

"She might not even be one of them. She might be one of ours."

"Then she was in an off-limits area. That's a violation."

"Let's just get her to the holding area. They can sort it out there," the woman said.

"You could ask me who I am; I'd be happy to tell you," Valentina offered. "I'm Valentina Maria Guadalupe Suárez del Toro. I tried to warn you all last night that this was going down, but no one would listen. I tried to prevent all this."

"Did she say del Toro?" the younger asked, but the woman talked over him.

"We've known about 'all this' for months, sister," she said.

"And you let explosives fall into their hands? Are you insane? Or are you trying to take down your own government?"

"A few booms around our headquarters are hardly something to panic about, especially once we've moved all of our equipment to other garages."

"And the corporate headquarters? How did you stop that? Did you catch the Alis?"

"The what?"

The explosions were so far in the distance they sounded like no more than a string of fireworks, but the roar of a building buckling to the ground echoed through the dome, louder than the gunfire below.

Valentina closed her eyes. She hadn't managed to stop a single thing. She only hoped with the long delay that everyone had been evacuated from that building.

The three officers around her were arguing again, but she was beyond caring. When the rifle butt pushed her again, she stumbled into a walk.

She wondered where Kiyoshi and Hazel were now. If she could, she'd trade places, put herself back in that tunnel in the dark, facing the Grendel rat blindly with no more than a staff of scrap metal in her hands. At least then she knew who her enemy was.

CHAPTER THIRTY

BROKEN

THE GUARDS BROUGHT HER DOWN OFF THE CATWALK AND SKIRTED THE marketplace to bring her to a nearby apartment building. The entire bottom floor was an open cafeteria that had been turned into a holding area. A medical center had been set up in one corner with cots and basic equipment situated near a glass door through which Valentina could see a pair of ambulances waiting outside. Only a few people were there being treated by an overly large team of medics. Her guards brought her to the other end of the cafeteria, the one near the kitchens.

"Who do we turn this one in to?" the younger of her guards asked.

"I'll take her," said a middle-aged man in an officer's uniform. "Which side?"

"We think she's one of them," her female guard said.

"But she says her name is del Toro," the younger one quickly added.

The officer leaned in to examine her face closely.

"She doesn't have an ID tattoo. I already checked," the woman said. "Just her word."

"Yes, but he said his daughter might be here," the officer said. "Do you three need to head back out?"

"Yes, we're still sweeping for strays around the perimeter."

"Very good, carry on. I'll keep an eye on this one until the chief gets here."

The three saluted, then turned and bounded back out of the room.

"You hungry?" the officer asked. He didn't wait for an answer, just took her arm and guided her up to the food counter. He poured out a mug of dark black coffee, then loaded up a plate with processed eggs, strips of unidentifiable meat, and a large, dusty biscuit. It didn't look appetizing, but her stomach growled anyway. A lot had happened since dinner the night before. He tried to hand her the food, but she shrugged, her hands still cuffed behind her.

"You tried to run?" he asked.

"No, they cuffed me right away."

"Turn around. I'll have those off in a jiff," he said, setting the plate and mug aside to fish a small knife out of a belt pouch. "We're in the center of a lot of security forces in a highly adrenalized state, so you'd be a fool to try to sneak away. If he's your father like you claim, he'll find you here faster than you could find him out there."

"I didn't tell them he was my father," Valentina said as the cuffs fell to the floor.

"You told the judge last night," the officer said. "We've been watching for you. Have a seat with the others, eat your breakfast."

Valentina took her food to a chair near the window so she could watch what was happening outside. There wasn't much to see; the road outside was cluttered with tanks and troop-carrying vehicles, and beyond those was smoke and dust. She loaded the eggs and meat into the biscuit and took a bite, chewing mechanically as she turned her attention to the other people around her. She didn't see any revolutionaries she recognized; she guessed everyone else had fled the marketplace. So they weren't all being shot. She took another bite, turning the other way in her chair to look at the medical center. She saw two boys she recognized. The young kid who had given her porridge that first morning was sitting in a chair, one eye bandaged but the rest of him unharmed. He was sitting near a cot where the other boy from that morning was stretched out, motionless, as two medics cut layers of burned clothing off his body. One of the other medics came to stand behind the boy with the eye patch, leaning down to whisper something to him as she squeezed his shoulder comfortingly. The boy didn't look at her, only at his friend.

Valentina left the last of her sandwich and all the coffee behind, walking over to the two boys. She had crossed half the room when the doors she had come in through, the doors facing away from the battle, burst open with a bang and crash of glass. Someone screamed; someone else started yelling orders. Valentina turned toward the door to see Kavi leading a group of ten revolutionaries dressed as security officers, all firing their weapons randomly around the room. Valentina threw a table over onto its side and crouched behind it, knowing its thin plastic surface wasn't going to stop anything. Her only hope was that they hadn't seen her. She hunkered down as low as she could, risking a glance to her right where the medical team was hustling patients out the back door, half of them pushing cots or wheelchairs, the other half covering their retreat with pistols they fired with much greater accuracy than Kavi's handpicked team.

She glanced the other way and saw too many bodies on the floor. The officer who had given her food was bleeding from the shoulder but still had his pistol in his hand, crouching behind the coffee machine and waiting for a lull in the fire. He met Valentina's eyes briefly, then pointed with his chin toward the back door the medics were using. She nodded, but sat motionless. There were several meters of open floor between her and the next spot of cover behind a bank of medical cabinets on wheels. She doubted she could make it.

The gunfire died down as the last of the medics disappeared out the back.

"Give chase?" someone asked.

"No, let them go," Kavi said. "You two, barricade this door. The rest of you clear this area. We might need to hunker down here for a while."

Valentina could hear boots crunching over broken glass. She fought the urge to close her eyes, glancing again at the officer, who was still waiting with his gun at the ready. Two sets of boots drew nearer to her. She looked around, but there was no other cover. She looked out the windows, but there was no sign of anyone outside. Surely the medics would send help?

Kavi must have been thinking the same thing. "Barricade that door," he ordered, and the two boots near her position jogged past her, pushing the wheeled machinery and supply cabinets against the door, blocking out the sunlight. When they had moved everything they could, they turned back, and in that moment, both of them saw Valentina with her back pressed to the table.

Too late, she wished that she had thought to play dead.

One of them raised his rifle, but before he could fire there was a loud crack from behind Valentina and his head rocked back, rifle falling from his lifeless fingers as his body crumpled to the ground. The other guard spun away, the second shot whizzing past his ear. Then he fired a long spray of bullets and Valentina squeezed her eyes shut, covering her ears with her hands, not wanting to see what remained of the officer who had just saved her life.

More orders were shouted, then silence.

She wasn't being shot.

Valentina opened her eyes to see Kavi squatting on one knee in front of her.

"My father is coming for me," she said.

He ignored her. "Where is Hero?"

"The last time I saw him, he was on the stage with Nandi. She had been hit."

"That was before the headquarters went down."

"Yes."

"Could be anywhere then," Kavi said, looking around as if anywhere included the cafeteria they were in. "Skald isn't answering either."

"What are you going to do?"

Kavi looked at her as if seeing her for the first time. "You mean with you?"

Valentina swallowed. That hadn't been what she meant, but now that he had said it, she desperately wanted to know the answer.

"I did what I came here to do. I'm giving it a few more minutes for the others to contact me, then I'll be bugging out. You," he said and pushed the barrel of a pistol against her temple. "You, I have no quarrel with."

"What?" Valentina stammered as the gun disappeared back in its holster.

"Someone ratted us out. More than that, something else entirely is going on here. It's weird. But there's no way any of it was you. It's too big to be you. You were just a distraction. Wait here. Once we're gone, you can go find your brother."

Valentina tried to murmur a thanks, but the sounds she managed to get out weren't entirely intelligible.

"Movement over here, boss," someone called, and Kavi bounded over to investigate.

Valentina stood up but wasn't sure where to go. She righted the table and one of the chairs and sat down, the exhaustion suddenly crippling her. She wished she had drunk the coffee. She thought about getting another mug but remembered that the officer had been there, using the machine for cover. She really didn't want to see what he looked like now. She kept her back to the refugees from the marketplace who had been eating with her just moments ago. Her brief glance of them earlier was going to stay with her forever—the sightless eyes imploring, the limbs at improbable angles. The blood everywhere.

Valentina dropped her head to her hands, but tears wouldn't come. That was for later, after she was out of the nightmare. For now, she was just numb.

"This side too, boss. They're definitely up to something," one of the revolutionaries was saying.

"We get out through the bottom," Kavi said, his fingers scanning and spinning through the layouts on his tablet. "In the back of the kitchens, there's a drain."

"A drain?" someone said, his voice tinged with the beginnings of panic.

Then there was another loud bang; this time it was a section of wall imploding into the room, concrete debris raining across the floor. Valentina barely registered it before the air was filled with yellowish smoke. She buried her nose and mouth in the heavy roll collar of Hero's sweater and crawled back under the table. She could hear shouts and coughing as Kavi and his team ran to the kitchens. There were a few sporadic bursts of gunfire, more shouting. The room was getting hotter and hotter, the air almost oppressive. Valentina wondered if she was inside an inferno, or if the noxious smoke had given her an instantaneous case of Martian fever. She buried her face deeper into the sweater and tried to crawl out from under the table. She wanted to find clean air, but wasn't sure where to go. All the exits were blocked, and Kavi had gone into the kitchens.

She took a few steps toward the hole that had just been blasted into the wall. Then her knee buckled, and she was back on the floor.

She fought to keep her thoughts from scattering away. It couldn't end here. She still had to find Arturo.

She crawled a little farther, but the spots in her vision swam over everything and she only vaguely, distantly, felt her head impact the ground.

CHAPTER THIRTY-ONE

AT LONG LAST, ARTURO

VALENTINA LAY STILL WITH HER EYES CLOSED, FEELING STRANGE. THE
light beyond her eyelids was bright and the space around her was
quiet, save for the soft sound of someone nearby breathing. That was
weird enough, considering when her consciousness had slipped away
she had been surrounded by gunfire and explosions, harsh bursts of
light, and the flickering heat of fires burning out of control. But it
wasn't the strangest thing.

She could swear she was only wearing a single thin garment,
sleeveless and not long enough to cover her legs, and there was only a
whisper-thin layer of sheet and baby-soft blanket over that. So how
could she be so perfectly warm?

This was definitely the oddest thing she'd ever felt. The lack of pain
in her entire body—in her wrists, her calf, her knee—was odd as well.
How long had she been out? And yet she wasn't hungry either,
although her mouth was a little dry.

At last she opened her eyes, reaching up to wipe the sticky sleep
from her lashes. She was in a room, brightly lit from two windows, one
to her right and the other behind her, between the bed she was lying
on and the other bed in the room. Her bed had a chair next to it and a

little table that held a single pitcher of fresh flowers, flowers in colors she hadn't even realized flowers could come in.

How long had she been asleep here?

The other bed also had a table and chair but, unlike hers, was surrounded with machines attached to the girl lying there, quietly breathing. Valentina sat up, then threw back the covers to put her bare feet on the pleasantly warm floor, the tile softly baking in the light from the window. She took the two steps to the other bedside, shaky from lying still too long, but definitely feeling no twinges of pain from any of her old injuries. Then she leaned closer to be sure the girl was who she thought it was.

She was paler, her skin dulled almost to gray, and she looked even thinner than she had been before, but the arms still spoke of wiry strength, and the hair had not yet begun to grow out of its close cut. It was Nandi, still alive. And Valentina might have been out for a day or two, but definitely not for weeks like last time.

Valentina looked at the screens of the machines around the bed, trying to make sense of the graphics. Nandi's neck was bandaged, and there was a tube dripping fluid in her arm, but she was breathing on her own. Valentina slipped her hand into Nandi's and gave it a squeeze.

"Hey," Nandi said before her eyes even opened.

"Oh, I didn't mean to wake you," Valentina said.

"It's OK. I was awake before. I kind of drift in and out."

"They fixed you."

"You too."

"I wasn't shot."

"Do you know where we are?"

"Hospital, and a nice one at that," Nandi said, closing her eyes as if talking were exhausting her. Her voice had a raspy quality, and the words came slowly, but she didn't stop. "Look out the window. Tell me what you see."

Valentina's eyes were dazzled by the bright sunlight, but it only took a few blinks to adjust. "We're very high up," she said, feeling a whoosh of vertigo in her belly as she tried to look down. "Wow, higher than we were in Hazel's balloon, I'd swear." She looked around at the other buildings around them, tall ones nearly touching the apex of the dome. She crossed to the other window. "I can see the corporate center from here, or what's left of it."

"This has to be a hospital reserved for the higher levels of corporate hierarchy," Nandi said slowly. "I can see why you're here, but what about me?"

"Did you see what happened to Stephen Hero?" Valentina asked, coming back to sit on the edge of Nandi's bed and taking her hand again.

"No. He was with me when I kind of faded out, but not when I faded back in."

"Maybe he's here somewhere too."

"Maybe. But I kind of hope not. Cronista, I can only think of a few reasons they'd pull me back from death's door, and I don't like any of them."

"I know," Valentina said, although she really didn't. She had no idea what Nandi feared.

"I think I might need to sleep again," Nandi said.

"I'm sorry. I didn't mean to wear you out."

"I'm just glad I'm not here alone." She was quiet after that and Valentina thought she must be sleeping, but several minutes later, a single tear slipped from the corner of her eye. Valentina kept holding her hand.

What were the two of them going to do? What could they do?

The sun kept moving, disappearing behind one of the other buildings, and Valentina felt, if not exactly cold, then at least less warm than she had been before. She looked down at her knee and her calf, hunting for signs of injury or surgery. There were faint marks on her calf, like silvery half-moons she could only see at certain angles, but her knee was unblemished. What else had they done to her? She felt different, but couldn't put her finger on it. More awake, more aware? But how could they do that? She must be imagining it.

At last, she slipped her hand out of Nandi's. She padded over to the door and gently pulled down on the handle, but it wouldn't turn. She had expected as much. Having nothing else to do, she got back in her own bed. She had no machines with puzzling graphics around her, but there was a screen built into the wall over the head of her bed. She touched it, bringing up pages and pages of text. All in English, and the words were long and unfamiliar. Still, she kept scrolling through, looking for anything that might give her a hint.

"Your diagnosis," Nandi said, still sounding half asleep. Her eyes were mere slits, but she hiked herself up a bit on one elbow. "Can you read it?"

"Not really," Valentina admitted. "I can read, a little, but these words are so long."

"Turn it my way," Nandi said, hiking herself up a little higher, "and enlarge the text."

Valentina examined the edges of the screen until she could see how to swing it out and away from the wall to face it toward Nandi. She tapped the command to make the text larger until Nandi made a little noise in her throat. Then she carefully turned Nandi's bed to face the screen more directly and arranged her pillows so she could sit up without having to support herself on her elbows.

"This is a list," Nandi said, pausing every few words for breath. "The treatment you've received. Explosion blew your eardrums. Old injuries to your knee. Nasty bite giving you septicemia."

"What's that?" Valentina asked.

"Infection. Your body might have fought it off. Eventually. On its own. But more likely, you were about to be very sick."

Valentina looked down at her calf, the teeth marks barely visible now. The bite wound had felt hard and hot, but not exactly painful, right up until she had lost consciousness. She had been tuning it out for so long it seemed strange to have it actually feel all right now, to not just have to ignore what she couldn't fix.

"They gave you all your vaccinations," Nandi said. "Everything you've missed since you were a kid. And antiparasitics."

"Why would I need that?"

"They don't trust what you've been eating," Nandi said.

"Mutant rat," Valentina said, and the corner of Nandi's mouth quirked up.

"What else can this screen tell me?" Valentina asked.

"Touch that there—that says contact information," Nandi said, pointing. Those words Valentina could sound out and she quickly found the correct tab. The top rows were for information they had on her, lots of blanks for things like identification number and school history.

Under that was information on her father. Including his home address.

"He's been here," Nandi said. "Every day at five o'clock. He brought those flowers. Said they were from Arturo."

Valentina read the numbers and words over and over, memorizing the address. Did the screen have a map feature?

"It's nearly three now," Nandi said. "You can talk to him soon. Then see your brother."

Valentina nodded, but said nothing. That wasn't how she wanted to do it. She didn't come this far, so her father could bring her the last bit of the way like some magnanimous gift. She would get to Arturo the same way she had gotten all the way to the equator, on her own two feet.

"Look out the window," Nandi said, and Valentina stepped closer to the glass. "Look straight ahead, past the tall buildings. Do you see smaller houses with lots of trees?"

Valentina pressed her forehead to the cool glass, rising up on tiptoes as if that would help. The tall buildings were clustered close together, but she found a gap, a narrow slash, but enough to see what Nandi had described. Everything was so tiny from this height, but she could just make out straight rows of houses and the green smudges of treetops planted in the same places around each house.

"Yes," she said, tracing the path back to the hospital building. It was a straight line; there was no way she could get lost.

"You have to read addresses from the end first," Nandi said, closing her eyes but still getting the words out. "Treevale: that means that neighborhood you just saw. Find that first."

"OK," Valentina said.

"The next bit is the street name, Cartesian Street. I don't know that neighborhood. You'll have to walk until you find it."

"OK," Valentina said.

"The numbers will be near the doors, even on one side of the street and odd on the other."

"Got it," Valentina said.

"You're not going to blend in there," Nandi said. "People will be watching from the windows. You might not see them, but they'll see you. You'll likely be arrested again."

"I'll take the chance," Valentina said.

"Of course you will," Nandi said with a weak smile. With a visible effort, she peeled her eyes open again. "Go to the hospital map, that button in the corner there."

Valentina tapped the button. A 3-D rendering of the entire skyscraper filled the screen, then spun and zoomed in until they were looking at a floor plan for just their level.

"Look for an unlabeled room, probably tucked away off the main hallways, with details that look like benches and lockers."

Valentina scanned the image until she found what Nandi was describing. "A locker room," she said.

"If you're lucky, you'll find one that isn't locked," Nandi said. "You can't wander Treevale in a hospital gown."

"OK, but the door is locked," Valentina pointed out.

"I'm going to create a diversion," Nandi said. "Be ready. You can slip out and find the locker room. Did you memorize the floor plan?"

"Wait, where are we?" Valentina asked, turning back to the screen.

"The red one," Nandi said, closing her eyes again and sinking back into the pillows. "Do you have it?"

Valentina traced the route with her finger, forcing her mind to translate an overhead view of what she would see when she got out of the room. "Yes," she said at last, pushing the screen back where she had found it and moving Nandi's bed back into place. "But what are you going to do?"

Nandi smiled, eyes just visible under droopy lids but shining brightly. Her hand closed around the bundle of cords connecting her to the machines around her. Valentina leaned down to plant a kiss of farewell on her friend's forehead.

"I hope we see each other again," Valentina said.

"Me too," Nandi said. "And perhaps even meet your brother." Her grip on the cords tightened and Valentina stepped back, tucking herself against the wall near the door but not so close to the door to be in the way of anyone rushing in.

Nandi managed the smallest of winks, then pulled the cords loose with more strength than Valentina would have thought she had left in her. The machines lit up and sang out, a cacophony of alarm, and sooner than Valentina expected, the door was flung open and three attendants rushed to Nandi's side. Nandi's eyes were rolling back into her head, her body twitching spasmodically, and for a second Valentina was worried that she wasn't acting, that disconnecting herself from her machines had done her real harm.

But she couldn't stay to be sure. She sidestepped along the wall and slipped into the hallway, stepping aside as more attendants raced down the hall to join the others in the room.

They didn't even give her a second look.

She looked both ways, momentarily panicking that she had forgotten the way already, but then she spotted the circular monitoring station where the hallways crossed and quickly oriented herself with the floor plan. She stayed close to the wall, shoulder sliding along it as she walked, not entirely playacting. She had been in that bed for a few days, and while she had felt amazing sitting up and talking with Nandi in the room, she felt less recovered now that she was trying to move. She was winded almost at once and her muscles started shaking like once they had at the end of a long day of bounding over the polar ice cap.

She found the locker room and allowed herself a brief rest on one of the benches, fingers clenching the molded plastic seat as her eyes swept the room, looking for any sign of an open locker. She didn't find one, but she did spot a receptacle between the showers and the lockers. Pushing herself back to her feet, she lifted the lid and found what she had been hoping for: a pile of clothing waiting to be laundered. Most of it was hospital scrubs, but a pair of jeans was balled up at the bottom. Judging by the brown stains on the thighs, someone had had an accident involving a cup of coffee. They were too big for her, but not so big that walking would be awkward. She pulled them on. She found a pair of thick socks with rubberized soles, but of course no shoes.

They were dark gray; if no one looked too closely, she might be OK. But her only shirt options were the gown she was wearing, or the brightly colored scrubs. She left the gown on, rolling it up and tucking it into the overly large jeans. From a distance, it looked like she was wearing a T-shirt. She hoped.

The fact was, her disguise wasn't going to pass more than the most cursory of glances. She was going to have to keep moving, and fast. A wave of fatigue washed over her, but she clenched her fists and forced it to pass.

Her brother was so close. She couldn't let him down.

Valentina opened her eyes and headed out of the locker room.

CHAPTER THIRTY-TWO

FACE TO FACE WITH FATHER

OUTSIDE OF THE LOCKER ROOM WAS A SMALL ELEVATOR, SEPARATE FROM the main bank near the monitoring station. She suspected it was for employees only, but when she pressed the button, the doors opened and let her inside. She pressed the button for the ground floor and spent what felt like an eternity sliding down the building.

The elevator was positioned just as remotely on the ground floor as it had been above; the hallway was empty, although she could hear the murmur of voices from behind closed doors on either side. She could see sunlight dappling the floor of a hallway on her right and turned that way, following the light out of the building and into a large arcade dominated by a fountain shooting water up into the air. Small children chased each other around the fountain under the gaze of their parents grouped on benches tucked under arching, flowering hedges. The sound of laughter gave Valentina a chill, dancing close to her memories of children screaming in the marketplace.

She hadn't come out of the same side of the building she had looked out of from above, but she could see one of the familiar skyscrapers off to her left, so she headed that way. Head down, hands in pockets mainly to keep her pants from catching under her heels, she walked as quickly as she dared around the perimeter of the arcade to the walkway that ran alongside the road. Children were everywhere, small ones chasing and playing, older ones walking in groups wearing coordinated outfits with the names of their schools stitched on them. A few gave her strange looks but none of them tried to stop her or speak to her.

She found the two skyscrapers that had formed the narrow gap she had peered through from above and then the street that ran between them. She knew there was a way to time how to cross the streets without getting hit by traffic, but she had just been following Stephen's lead before and hadn't asked him the secret. This time she waited until a group of school kids came her way and fell in close behind them until they were on the other side of the many lanes of traffic, then slowed her steps until she was far behind them. She looked back over her shoulder at the hospital building, her eyes sweeping up to the narrow spire at its apex. There was no way to tell which window she had looked out of. She bid Nandi one last mental good-bye, then turned her eyes to the walkway in front of her, walking quickly with her head down.

The buildings around her grew shorter and shorter, the traffic lessened, and more and more of the school kids walking all around her peeled away to head down side streets. There were still a few groups around her when the road became a treelined boulevard, a sign in the strip of trees down the middle of the road declaring this Treevale. There was a stylized map of the neighborhood in the corner of the sign; no street names, but it was clear that the boulevard she was walking on would traverse the heart of the district. If Cartesian ran perpendicular to the boulevard, she would cross it. If it was parallel, she wouldn't know for sure until she had walked all of Treevale.

At least the socks on her feet were comfortable. Much better than ill-fitting boots.

Something flitted through the air in front of her, startling her to a stop. A dancing leaf? No—it was burnt orange in color, but there were definitely wings. It flitted up and out of view before she could be sure what it was. Something else buzzed close to her but never emerged from the leafy canopy over her head. And all around her was a constant barrage of tweets and whistles. That had to be from birds. She was surrounded by living things, hiding in the lush green of other living things. Oh, to live in such a place as this.

The fourth street to cross the boulevard was Cartesian, and Valentina turned to her right. She saw which way the numbers were running and turned around to go the other way.

The house she was looking for was the third house from the boulevard, otherwise indistinguishable from all the others. She looked up and down the walkway, but the last group of school kids had continued down the boulevard; she was alone. She stepped through the gate into the yard.

A short path lined with stones led up the steps to the door. On either side of the path was a multilevel terrace of flowerbeds, blooms spilling over the sides in a carefully tended tangle of leaves and vines. She recognized some of the flowers from her bouquet back at the hospital. Then she heard the buzzing again, and this time she found the source: bees hovering over the blossoms, circling in to feed on the nectar before dancing away again. She had never seen a bee before, only heard don Abuelo lamenting the lack of them on the north pole. But there was no mistaking what she was seeing, or the soft buzz of their wings as they bobbed through the air. It was exactly like he had described.

She couldn't bring herself to step up to the door. She just couldn't. Instead she crept around the plants to peer in the front window. The window was open, and across the tiny house was a back door flanked on both sides with windows also thrown wide open, the scent and soft sounds of the garden carrying through the house. Chairs were arranged under one window, a work desk under the other. A dining table sat under one window looking out onto the back garden and the kitchen centered around the other.

And in the back garden, sitting on a cobblestone patio under the branches of a tree, was Arturo. He had his back to her. He was filling his hands with dried fallen leaves and throwing them up into the air to rain down on a baby, who laughed a throaty baby laugh and clapped her hands for more.

Valentina took half a step back, but the hedge behind her would not let her retreat further. The baby laughed again and Valentina felt a tight knot in her throat all but choking her.

She had imagined so many scenarios for this moment, but not a one of them had involved her brother so content, so perfectly a part of this heavenly world around him. His happy, round cheeks leaned close to the equally happy, equally round cheeks of the baby as he blew blubbery kisses against her cheek and made her laugh again.

Valentina looked down at herself, tattered and dirty, shoeless, her unbraided hair tangled in the hedge behind her. She couldn't let him see her like this.

The baby's laugh became a cough that became a fit and Arturo scooped her up into his arms, balancing her on one hip as he came in from the garden to find a cup in the kitchen and encouraged the baby to take little sips. Valentina watched him fuss over the baby, dabbing away water that had missed her mouth and babbling at her until she laughed once more.

"Arturo!" a woman called, and Valentina ducked further into the tangling hedge as the woman appeared from a part of the house out of view from the window.

"She's OK, she just coughed a bit," Arturo said, brushing a lock of hair from the baby's eyes.

"Oh, I know," the woman rushed to assure him. "I never worry about her when she's with you. No, it's about your other sister. Your father just called. She's disappeared from the hospital room."

Arturo's face darkened. "He should have let me talk to her."

"She wasn't awake yet."

"And now it's too late," he said. "I should have—" But his words were lost as he turned with the baby still on his hip and his eyes found Valentina's through the window. Both froze for the longest moment of their lives.

"Arturo," she said at last, but everything she had wanted to say was suddenly gone.

Arturo thrust the baby into the woman's arms and flung open the front door. "Tina!" he cried as he jumped into the hedge, charging into her with an enthusiasm she remembered well. He hugged her tightly, burying his face into her shoulder, and for a moment, just a moment, she didn't feel like an intruder. She felt like she belonged.

"You're so tall," Valentina said when at last the hug ended.

"Taller than you," he said, moving a hand from the top of his head to a point just above hers. "Must be all the food. Do you know how wonderful it is to eat until you're full?"

"Yes," Valentina said with a small smile. "I've had a few of those meals myself."

"Not enough; you look awful," he said.

"I've looked worse," Valentina said. "It was a long road to get here."

"Yeah," Arturo said. The woman was standing into the doorway, the baby cooing in her arms. She raised a single eyebrow at Arturo.

"Valentina, this is Beth, our stepmom. Beth, Valentina."

"This is not how I pictured us meeting," Beth said, extending a hand to Valentina and deftly pulling her out of the hedge. Arturo saw that Valentina's hair was caught and began gingerly untangling the strands.

"I had to see him," Valentina said, raising her chin.

"No one was ever going to prevent that," Beth said. "We just wanted you to be well first. How are you feeling?"

Dirty? Tired? Emotionally overwhelmed? Valentina tucked a lock of hair behind her ear. "Better."

"I'm glad," Beth said. "I'd better call your father and set his mind at ease. He's very worried about you."

Valentina said nothing, but she couldn't stop the scowl from spreading over her features. Arturo gave her a puzzled frown but Beth just mustered another smile.

"Arturo, why don't you and your sister take a walk around the block? Dinner will be ready by the time you get back," Beth said.

"Come on," Arturo said, leading the way back through the front garden to the street.

He kept looking over at her as they walked, but each time he seemed unable to find any words. He nearly spoke a few times, and Valentina sensed he wanted to talk about their father, which was the last thing she wanted to talk about. She searched her mind for any other topic.

"It's so quiet here," Valentina said. Then, "You look different."

"So do you," he said.

"Yes, but for you it's in a good way."

"I'm sorry I said you looked awful. You looked much worse the last time I saw you, at the north pole."

"Gee, thanks," Valentina said, nudging him with her shoulder. He laughed and jostled her back. Then he grew quiet.

"I was afraid you'd be mad at me. For leaving. You understood, didn't you?"

"I do now," Valentina said.

"Why didn't you use the money to get the farm running again? Why did you use it to get here?"

"Actually, I didn't use the money for anything. I probably should have. I wasn't thinking clearly there in the beginning. Then the money was stolen, just like that."

"How did you get here without the money? Did you sneak on board a shuttle?"

Valentina took a deep breath. Then she told him everything. His expression grew more and more glum as her tale unfolded.

"Then I woke up in the hospital," she finished.

"I could tell you everything I've been doing since we last saw each other, but next to your story I'm sure it would sound terribly dull. But it really wasn't." He kicked a fallen twig off the walkway, out of her path, then said almost shyly, "Growing up with all the cousins never really felt like being in a family, you know."

"We were a family," Valentina said, her voice sounding too harsh even to her own ears.

"It was a chaotic mess is what it was," Arturo said. "I know it felt different to you. I think you had a vision of things in your head of what things were like before, when don Abuelo was still alive and maybe the family had really been a family. But I don't remember those days. I barely remember don Abuelo. I just remember you and Ma worn out all the time, the cousins disappearing one by one. Chaos."

"I'm not going back there," Valentina said. "There's nothing left there. Family now is just you and me."

"No, it isn't," Arturo said. "Not anymore."

"You have a new family now," she said past the growing lump in her throat. She had known this is how it would end. The moment she had seen him playing with his new baby sister she had known.

"*We* have a new family now," he corrected her. "Dad isn't what you think he is. Beth isn't Ma, but she's nice. You two have a lot in common, you'll see when you talk to her."

"Arturo, I don't think I can stay here," Valentina said.

"Dad will work something out," Arturo said. "Ana María and I fill out the child quota, but you're practically an adult anyway. He can find a job for you, then you can stay."

"That's not what I meant," Valentina said. "It doesn't feel right."

"You just got here. Give it a chance, OK?"

"Have you been to other parts of the city? Have you seen how other people live here? It's not all treelined streets and private gardens."

"Not yet, but someday it will be," Arturo said. "I'm learning, everything I can as fast as I can. And someday I'm going to help Dad make this a better place."

"Is there nothing I can say that will make you come with me? Anywhere at all?" Valentina asked.

"Apparently just as much as there's nothing I can say to make you stay," Arturo said. "I belong here. I like being a part of a small family. I like going to school and having friends who aren't armed to the teeth, spoiling for a fight or always expecting an ambush." Then his voice dropped to barely more than a whisper. "I like being a big brother rather than a little one."

Valentina only nodded. The words hurt, but she felt the truth in them. "It looks like you're good at it," she managed.

"I learned from the best," Arturo said, nudging her with his shoulder. "But I'm done being on the receiving end, OK?"

"I get it."

"You went through a lot just to get here," he said.

"I just needed to be sure you were OK."

"I'm more than OK."

"Yes," Valentina admitted. "Yes, you are."

The smell of roast chicken met them on their way up the path to the door. Beth was just setting a bowl of potatoes and peas on the table as they came in. Arturo brought Valentina to the kitchen sink to wash their hands. She wished she could wash up more thoroughly. Standing in Beth's neat kitchen, drying her hands on a gorgeously white towel, she felt more out of place than ever; her hair was still tangled from the hedge, the socks on her feet an even darker gray and starting to wear through in places already, the coffee stains over someone else's too-big jeans.

But even cleaned up she didn't belong here. That was becoming clearer by the moment.

"Valentina."

She knew that voice. She hadn't been able to call it back to mind for years, no matter how she had tried. She had said the old stories back to herself in her mind word for word, getting just the right intonation, just the right cadence, but had never been able to bring that voice back. And yet she knew it at once, as if she had never forgotten it.

She ran her hands around and around in the towel far past the point of dryness but at last she had to hang it back up on its hook near the sink and turn around to face her father.

He looked different. His hair was shorter and filled with streaks of silver, his face lined from worry and stress where once it had been smooth, but the eyes were the same. Her heart tried to swell up and pound hard at the same time and she found no words to answer him. She couldn't say "Dad"—it didn't feel right—or "Father." She couldn't say anything.

"It's good to see you. Awake and healthy," he added. "The last time I saw you at the north pole you were so sick, too delirious to even recognize me. And then when I saw you here, after the explosion? Well, that was worse."

He spoke in fits and starts, as if working to maintain his upbeat tone. She was blinking back tears herself.

Nothing in the world was going to make her talk or even lift her head. She had found Arturo and he wasn't leaving, and she knew she wasn't staying. There was nothing more to say. Not about herself, anyway. But . . .

"What are you planning to do with Nandi?"

"Nandi?"

"Nandi, my roommate back in the hospital. One of your snipers shot her in the neck. And then you brought her there—the swankiest of hospitals, apparently—to patch her up. Why?"

He exchanged a long look with his wife, a shorter glance with Arturo, then took Valentina's elbow to guide her out to the backyard, shutting the glass door behind them. Valentina didn't like being led about, but when he brought her to the bench she gratefully took a seat. Once again she was pushing too hard to start walking about too soon after getting out of her sickbed. She brushed her hair back out of her face and waited for him to choose his words.

"Valentina, I can only imagine what's going on in your head or how you fell in with such a group—"

"You don't have to imagine, I'm quite willing to tell you," she said. "I tried to stop everything that happened."

"I know you did," he said, turning to the window that overlooked the remains of the headquarters. "It's complicated."

"I don't really care about the politics of it all," Valentina said. "I just worry about my friends."

"We need her. For . . . political reasons."

"I'd appreciate a straight answer," Valentina said. "A lot of my friends died today. Well, I guess it wasn't today. Feels like today."

"It was three days ago," her father said. He turned back from the window. "Let's put the whole story together, the three of us. Tell me your side first."

Valentina took a deep breath. Then she told her father everything she knew, everything that had happened.

"The explosives were a plant, weren't they?" Valentina asked when her tale was done.

"I think they were, but they weren't planted by us."

"Then who?"

"Like you said, it's political. The cities are taking the first steps toward an alliance that would be good for everyone on Mars. If we work together, we can expand the livable space, ease the overpopulation problems. But there are factions in every one of the cities who disagree over one issue or another. Some of those factions are quite powerful. And I fear some of them are even working together. Yes, I agree the explosives you found in the armory were planted there for you to find, but not by us. By someone who wanted the corporation in charge of Valles Marineris V to crumble but didn't want to risk exposure by doing it themselves. So they used your little band as a tool."

"Who?"

"I wish I knew. Our intelligence is lacking, and that's becoming a dangerous lack. Honestly, we're hoping that's where Nandi comes in. When she's fully recovered."

"You want to make her into a spy? For you?" Valentina choked back a humorless laugh.

"We're trying to change things," he said. "I've been trying since I got here. My end of the story is long and complicated; I wouldn't know where to begin. Honestly, it began before I even left the north pole. It's why I left. I was asked to come here specifically because I was an outsider. I and a few others have been working tirelessly to root out the corruption in this place. I can guess why you joined that revolution, but that was a gesture doomed to fail. I believe with all my heart that what we're doing, while slower and less dramatic, is what will succeed. And while I wouldn't expect your friend Nandi to accept the mission without many more details and assurances, I truly hope she will accept it. We need her. She is in a unique position. She is to us quite irreplaceable."

Valentina bit her lip. He was all but begging her to talk to Nandi for him, to convince her. She didn't want to answer that request. "And what of the others?" she asked instead.

"We have lists of the dead, wounded, and missing," he said. "I can show you." He took a small tablet out of his pocket and started navigating through endless screens. "I never wanted to leave you behind in that place, all those years ago," he said, still scrolling. "The north pole is livable inside the science station, but not in the caves. I wanted us all to move here, but your mother wouldn't come. I should have fought that harder. I kept asking; every year on our anniversary I asked again for her to come. On your birthdays I asked for you two, if not to move here, then at least to visit. She never answered."

"I didn't know about that," Valentina said.

"I know. Arturo and I have talked about it a lot."

"You left me behind twice, though," she said, as casually as she could.

"I have a wife here, now," he said. "And a daughter, just nine months old. It was a difficult delivery, and while my wife could have another child, she doesn't want to. That left us with an unused allowance for one more child, but only one. I wasn't sure how you felt about things, and I was so hoping you would wake up before I left, but the antibiotics just didn't work that fast. Arturo wanted to come, desperately. He said I didn't have to worry about you because you could take care of yourself. He said you were a wiz with farming, learned everything at your don Abuelo's knee. Lost everything when your ma got sick, but with some startup money you could have your farm back, chickens and goats and rabbits, and you could repair the hydroponic gardens in your grandfather's back cavern. He said he knew you'd be OK. And that you deserved to be out on your own, no responsibilities. That taking care of him and his cousins had kept you from doing so many things, and you deserved the chance to start doing some of them. He may have oversold it."

"I didn't want to be alone," Valentina said.

"I'm sorry. I didn't want to leave you, but I had to come back. So much was spinning out of control while I was away. I guess I let myself believe Arturo knew you better than I did, so I left you with more than enough money to get your farm running again. I didn't know what more to do."

Valentina didn't know what to say. She wasn't sure what to feel about his version of events.

He had stopped touching his tablet moments before, and she pointed to it with her chin. "Show me the names, please," she said.

He nodded, putting the tablet in her hands. "Most of the kids were born inside the domes, so they still had their corporate implants. Others were born who knows where; those are at the end of the list with photos and every detail we could piece together in case you two or someone else can identify them later."

"Corporate implants—that's going to give their birth names," Valentina said. "They didn't go by their birth names. At least, the leaders didn't. The warrior-poets."

He arched an eyebrow at that title. "We identified three ringleaders from our intelligence reports," he said. "Stephen Collins, Roar Jorgenssen, and Saradindu Bhattacharya."

"That's them," Valentina said.

"They're all on the missing list," he said.

"Escaped?"

"Or still in the rubble around the headquarters. We haven't finished the cleanup there. The building was evacuated before the explosives went off, but the ones who set the explosions didn't have time to get clear."

"The Alis," Valentina said under her breath. Her heart panged for what Nandi must be feeling, if she even knew. "Hero—I mean Stephen, um, Collins—wasn't there. He was with Nandi when she was shot. And Kavi escaped through tunnels under the building I was in. That was long after the headquarters blast. Skald, this Roar Jorgenssen, I don't know about."

"So possibly all three escaped?" Valentina's father scanned through the lists. "Not with enough fighters to try this again, I don't think. Still, we'll have to keep our ear to the ground for when they join forces again."

"I don't think that will happen," Valentina said. "Not after they knocked Hero unconscious and shackled me to a pillar."

"They have common goals. I don't think they can just walk away from each other," he said.

Valentina didn't answer. She was certain that Hero, wherever he was, was in danger. Kavi and Skald would be looking for him, but not to rejoin forces. It might be beyond even Hero's ability to talk himself out of a tight spot to convince them the failure of the grand plan wasn't because of him.

"What now?" Valentina asked.

He put his tablet back in his pocket. "Now, let's eat."

Beth and Arturo were waiting for them, and the food smelled divine. There was so much more to talk about, but it could wait until after they ate. Space had been made for Valentina between her father and the baby in her high chair, the desk chair pulled over for her to sit in. She felt just as mismatched as her chair as the others talked and ate together, sharing jokes she didn't understand, talking about people she didn't know.

She didn't have anything to contribute. Her life was so different, her stories more appropriate for the revolutionaries' epic feasts than this simple daily meal.

"The peas come from the garden, you know," Arturo said, and Valentina realized he was talking to her. "Beth grows them."

"They're very good," Valentina said.

"Arturo tells me you raised animals. Goats and chickens and rabbits, was it?"

"Yes," Valentina said. "Once upon a time."

"Do you plan to do that again? Raise more animals?"

"I don't know what my plans are," Valentina admitted. "I feel like I only just woke up."

"That's because you did," Arturo said, although what Valentina had really meant was that everything that had happened since she fell ill with the Martian fever felt like one big blur. "She can stay with us until she figures things out, right?"

Beth and their father traded a long look.

"I'm going to take Ana María upstairs for her bath and bedtime," Beth announced. "Arturo, you have the dishes?"

"Of course," Arturo said, getting up and stacking empty plates to carry them to the kitchen.

"I can't stay, can I?" Valentina said. She hadn't expected to, still didn't really want to, but the rejection still hurt.

"You can, actually, but you'd have to make your decision now," he said. "I'm sorry, I wish I could give you more time. But it's not up to me."

"What decision do I have to make?"

"You can stay as a full citizen, with all the rights and privileges attached to that, but you'd have to take the only job they're offering you."

"Not raising farm animals," Valentina guessed.

"They want you to work with Nandi."

"Be a spy? I barely know the people they'd want me spying on. The revolutionaries didn't trust me before, they certainly won't trust me now."

"I know."

"So what do you want me to do?"

Her father tried to speak, but the words failed him. He put a hand over his eyes and his shoulders slumped. He suddenly looked so old it was alarming.

"Dad?" she said. For the first time, but it felt like the right thing to say.

He pulled his hand away from his eyes, making a fist that dropped away in helpless frustration. "I don't want you to do it. It's too dangerous. But I don't want to lose you again either. I don't want to send you away."

"If it's my choice, you're not sending me away," Valentina said.

"They won't budge. They owe you a great debt, and they owe me more than I can tell you, but they won't budge."

"It sounds like we should all walk away," Valentina said.

"I can't do that. I've put in so much work; things might still work out in the long term. I can't give up."

"Arturo following in your footsteps—is that what you mean by long term?" Valentina said. "As in, you'll die before your goal is achieved?"

"Perhaps. Probably."

"Things don't change overnight," Arturo said.

"Sometimes they do," Valentina said.

"It can be done without violence," her father said. "But Arturo is right, not overnight."

"The slow way is just spreading out the violence so it's easier to ignore," Valentina said. "They're pushing kids out of airlocks, you know."

"I didn't before. I've been uncovering that since I first heard you were here. It won't be happening anymore."

"Something else will take its place," Valentina said. "It has to. Your population pressures here are too great."

"That's why we're working to unify Mars. The more we network with other livable spaces, the more options we have."

"How long before I have to make my decision?" Valentina asked.

"Just one night," her father said.

"In that case, I need to talk to Nandi again."

"I'll take you in the morning."

They joined Arturo in the kitchen to help with the last of the dishes in a companionable silence, then her father made a pot of tea and they settled into the chairs under the garden window. Some variety of night-blooming plant hung from a trellis near the window, filling the air with thick perfume so rich it made Valentina's head swim. She was going to miss being so warm and comfortable.

She wiped at her face, then again. Her hand came back wet and, like not feeling the pain from a wound until you saw it, she realized she was crying. The realization was followed by a crushing grief. Her brother, alarmed, rushed to put his arms around her, and her father came nearer to take her hand.

"She's gone," Valentina sobbed. "She's just gone."

"I know," Arturo said, patting her back awkwardly, his own tears falling on the top of her head. "I miss her too. Every day."

"She would be so proud of you, both of you," her father said. "There is so much of your grandfather in both of you. I know how much that would have meant to her."

At last her tears subsided and Arturo sat down in his own chair next to hers, still holding her hand.

The three of them sipped tea in silence, then Arturo prompted their father to tell them the story of their ancestors' journey to the north pole. One story led to another, sometimes Valentina telling it, sometimes Arturo, now that he knew them too, but the best was when her father took over, the rich familiarity of his voice warming her even more than the tea until at last they all drifted off to sleep together in the soft chairs.

The morning came all too soon. They ate a quick breakfast of toast with real cow's-milk butter, then her father went to his desk to call for a vehicle to take them back to the hospital.

"I will be seeing you again," Arturo said to his sister.

"I don't know how," Valentina said, and yet she had complete confidence he would. "I'm going to see Nandi because I have to talk to her again, but I'm not taking the spy job. I'm not as trusting as you two on the eventual good end to a long series of questionable steps."

"I know," Arturo said. "I don't want you to do it any more than Dad does. I just meant—" He stepped nearer, his voice dropping to a whisper. "I know kids who know stuff. We're not like friends or anything, but I think that's about to change."

"You mean kids with a revolutionary bent?"

"Maybe more like anarchists, I don't know," Arturo admitted. "But they know how to get in and out of the city."

"Even if you didn't get caught, how would you find me?"

"Easy, just follow the metro line all the way north," Arturo said. "That's where you're going, right? Back to Kiyoshi and Hazel?"

She hadn't thought about anything past talking to Nandi, but when she looked into his eyes, she realized he was right.

"It would be risky," Valentina said.

"Rats," Arturo said.

"And other things. But we can find a way to get messages to each other."

"Definitely."

"Arturo, keep your eyes open," Valentina said. "You might not be as safe here as you think. Especially if you start poking around."

"I know. I'll be careful. I have a little sister who needs me, you know?"

"Yes, I know."

At the hospital, Nandi was awake when Valentina stepped into the room, looking over a tablet showing a long list of names. She looked up as Valentina sat on the edge of her bed.

"You're going," Nandi said.

"The powers that be can't let me stay," she said.

"I think it has less to do with you than it does with controlling him," Nandi said, pointing with her chin to the closed door. "It's probably better for you to be gone."

"My brother won't come with me."

"I'm sorry."

"He seems good, though."

"I'll keep an eye on him for you," Nandi said. "As much as I can."

"Thank you."

"Don't go looking for him."

Valentina was puzzled for a moment. Then she realized Nandi wasn't talking about Arturo. She opened her mouth to speak, but Nandi shook her head.

"Don't tell me you weren't going to, I know better."

"I was going to head back to Kiyoshi and Hazel. If they'll have me."

"That's the best plan. I didn't get to meet them, but they seem like worthy friends."

Valentina nodded, picking at a loose thread on Nandi's blanket. "But I'm just curious, why the warning?"

"He's going to hook back up with the others and it's all going to start up again, and you don't want any part of that."

"I don't know about that. We were talking just before we parted ways, and I think he has other plans now."

"He always makes other plans," Nandi said. "But in the end he does what Kavi and Skald want. I know it seems like it flows the other way but it really doesn't."

"Maybe things would be different if I were with him."

"See, that's exactly why I'm telling you to run the other way. They only difference would be you in the middle getting ground up."

"I don't know . . ."

"Trust me. I'm his best friend. I love him to pieces, his heart is in the right place, but I know this pattern all too well."

"That's an awfully grim view. You don't think he'll ever change?"

"He will, but not because of anything you or I do. And I think it's going to take him getting ground into hamburger first. You don't want to be there for that."

"I wouldn't know where to start looking for him anyway," Valentina said.

"Clearly you decided to start by coming to me," Nandi said. Valentina flushed red; she could feel the heat washing over her cheeks to her ears. "And I know you're thinking that if you go back to Kiyoshi and Hazel, he'll always know where to find you."

"I have nowhere else to go," Valentina said.

"Just don't wait for him," Nandi said. "Maybe he'll go looking for you and maybe he won't. Don't waste your time waiting."

"If there's another revolution, what will you do? Which side will you be on?"

"I don't know," Nandi said. "I know what I'm working toward, I just don't see how to get there."

"I know the feeling."

"I'll probably wander up and down the tracks again. I'll stop in and see how you're doing," Nandi promised.

"Be safe," Valentina said, squeezing her hand.

"That's probably not doable, but I'll give it my best shot."

Valentina hugged Nandi carefully, mindful of the many wires and tubes that connected her to the machines hovering around the bed. Then she stepped back out into the hallway where her father waited with an inexplicably eager expression on his face.

"I have news," he said. "I've been trying to organize something with some of my allies in other city departments. I didn't want to say anything, it was kind of a long shot, but . . ."

Valentina didn't want to venture a guess, didn't want to break the rare happy moment by guessing too big. "What is it, Dad?"

"A have a job for you. Not in the city, but as sort of an envoy."

"Envoy? What do you mean?"

"Trust me, Valentina. You're going to like this."

CHAPTER THIRTY-THREE

TRAINS AND TRADE

VALENTINA WAS SURPRISED TO SEE A TRAIN CAR PARKED OUTSIDE THE northernmost depot as her own car glided along the tracks and slowed to a crawl before she engaged the brake. But then it made sense; being safely enclosed in a high-speed vehicle was really the only way to get past the legions of rats. Of course, the train car was clearly an amalgamation of several vehicles, some trains and some clearly not. Kiyoshi and Hazel must have thrown it together from parts from the barricades of one of the other depots. It was small; the two of them would have been quite cramped inside. Nowhere near as luxurious a journey as the one Valentina had just had, flying up the line in one afternoon in a five-car train filled with goodies.

Valentina climbed out of her ride and skipped up the steps to the barricade wall. The tunnel opening had been widened, now a long narrow gash that split the wall in two. She slipped through the canyon, having to turn sideways to squeeze past in a few places, but nothing like the last time she had gone through. The far side had been sealed off with a wall built from shelving from the ground level area, but at the bottom was a door.

Valentina could hear music playing, a steady beat of drums, two soaring guitars, and a vocal track she couldn't match up to any language she'd ever heard. Still, it was catchy. She knocked on the door, but the thickness of her gloves muffled the sound too much. She peeled one off and knocked again. The music dimmed, footsteps approached.

The door opened.

Kiyoshi looked down at her. He must have been working near a space heater; her breath was fogging the air and yet he was stripped down to an oil-streaked T-shirt. She smiled hesitantly.

"I guess you didn't hear me pull up?" she said. "You guys have been busy; I shouldn't be surprised. Speaking of surprises…" She trailed off, his blank silence muffling her attempts at friendly banter. "You're not happy to see me at all?"

The stoic look on his face finally softened, and he pulled her close into a tight hug.

"Of course I'm happy to see you," he said. She breathed in his own scent of machine oil and sweat. She had missed that.

Then he stepped back, waving her through the doorway.

"I have some things out there…" she hesitated.

"They will be all right for now," Kiyoshi said. "The rats make themselves scarce when train cars pass."

"You've been traveling a lot?"

"Hazel and I have scavenged most of the other depots on this line."

"I can see you've been busy," Valentina said, wandering over to where the space heater sat next to a large array of lights and a little music player. Kiyoshi latched the door, then followed her, wiping his face and arms on a grayish towel before pulling on another shirt and sweater.

"I hope you don't mind," he said as he switched off the heater. "We have to conserve the oil. It's just for when I'm working in narrow spots where sleeves would be a hassle."

"It's fine," Valentina said. "I like the cold."

"You must have reached your father," Kiyoshi said, touching the sleek sleeve of her coat. All of her clothes were new, made to her size, magically lightweight yet warm.

"Yes, I did."

"And how is Arturo?"

Valentina took a breath. This was the perfect opportunity for him to say, "I told you so," and yet she couldn't imagine anyone less inclined to say those words than Kiyoshi. "He's good. Very good. He's like, this tall," she said, putting her hand a sizable margin over her own head.

"Did you come back alone, or are you warming me up to spring some guests on me later?"

"No, I'm alone," Valentina said, burying the bottom of her face in the zipped-up collar of her coat. "Arturo stayed in the city. He wants to come visit someday. Nandi might wander by someday as well."

"I don't remember Nandi," Kiyoshi said.

"She showed up after you two left. She's been Stephen Hero's best friend since forever, but she has no illusions about him. You'll like her."

"And the others?" Kiyoshi said.

"Their plans didn't work out too well. Lots of kids died or were captured. Some escaped maybe. They're counted as missing. But even if they lived, I don't expect they have any reason to come this way."

"Do you want to talk about it?"

"Not really. I mean, maybe later, but with both of you, so I don't have to tell it twice. The important thing is that I've come with a train-load of supplies. I've been appointed an envoy of the city. They want to help establish trade routes to other parts of Mars, starting with every-thing connected by the old metro system."

"They're going to take over our station?" Kiyoshi frowned.

"No, you're considered a sovereign entity, totally independent. I'm the city representative, but all that really means is that I have brought enough goods to get a proper supply depot started. The cities collectively will be reclaiming the tunnels, killing the rats and getting the trains running. They would like us to be their go-between with the people living on the surface in the north, people like Hazel's family at first. The north pole is a distant goal. We'll be the connec-tion between the train line and the rovers and balloons on the surface."

"I don't know. I don't like making deals with people I haven't met."

"The stuff on the train is a no-obligation gift. I also brought a very long contract for you to read through. They told me they are willing to negotiate any changes you want to make. I assume you'll be able to wrap your head around it; I certainly can't read more than a fraction of it."

"It's not just my decision," Kiyoshi said. "Hazel and I are a team."

"Yes, of course," Valentina said, burying her face in her collar again. "So you two are, like, partners, then?" Not what she wanted to ask, just all she could get out.

"Business partners."

"Oh."

Kiyoshi picked up a tool, turning it over in his hands absently. "Frankly, if you're here to stay, it's a bit of a relief. She'll have someone else to talk to at least half the time. She is an exhausting companion."

"I'm here to stay, if you'll have me," Valentina said, hiding her smile inside her collar.

"And Stephen Hero?" Kiyoshi asked, eyes still on the tool spinning between his fingers.

"He's missing," Valentina said. "I don't think he's dead. But I don't think I'll ever see him again either." She tried to sound sure about that, not like she'd spent the entire journey gazing out the windows, stopping at every depot to hunt for signs of someone hiding out, some clue that maybe he'd passed by already. "He wouldn't go north," she said. "He has plans still, and those plans are all south of here."

Kiyoshi nodded, still twirling the tool. Valentina fought the urge to snatch it away from him.

"I've missed you," he said, barely more than a growl of sound out of his throat.

"I've missed you too," she said. "I missed you every day, but you were right to turn back. Everything that happened after you left was one big disaster. Not the least of which was finally seeing Arturo. He has a new family now, a new life. I spent a day there, eating dinner with his family. I felt so out of place."

"They're your family too," Kiyoshi said. "As much as his."

"No, not really," Valentina said. "He fits in so well. He is doing well in their schools and is totally going to follow in our father's footsteps. But I could never do it. I can't live in a community like that, with so much inequality, constantly pretending it's OK because maybe tomorrow it will be better. I'd rather be out here. I suppose I'll always be never quite warm enough, never quite have a meal that doesn't leave me still just a little bit hungry, but that's OK. At least I'll know what I'm doing and who it benefits, and that no one is really being harmed by any of it."

"That might change, if we sign that contract."

"That's why I want you to read it. To make sure that it doesn't. We have to stay who we are, right?"

Kiyoshi spun the tool out of his hand, caught it, then set it down on a workbench. "We have to talk to Hazel."

"Do you mind if I talk to her alone first?"

"Take all the time you need," Kiyoshi said. "I'll be here when you need me."

Valentina jogged up the steps to the trading area. There was a patch of darkness beyond the reach of Kiyoshi's work lights, but that soon gave way to the even more brilliant display up ahead. The entire room in all if its immensity was bathed in a cold, silver light. At the top of the steps two little structures, half huts/half tents built from shelving material and balloon silk, sat side by side with a cook stove built from vehicle parts a little distance away from their door flaps. Two stools sat beside it, a crate of neatly stacked cooking utensils and food packages between them.

Beyond the tents were the same piles of scrap from before. Valentina followed the sound of more music coming from up ahead, nearer to the airlock. Here the shelves had been pushed back up and repaired, row after row of empty shelves, but nearest the airlock a few held some potential trade items: lights and radios and other equipment scavenged from the barricades, Valentina would guess.

Hazel was digging through a crate of random objects, holding things up to the light and examining them as she sang along to the same foreign song Kiyoshi had been playing before.

"Hey," Valentina said as she stepped closer.

"Hey yourself!" Hazel said, tossing aside the object in her hand to charge up to Valentina and tackle her in a tight hug. "I knew you'd be back! I knew you wouldn't get yourself killed for those crazy kids and their cause. I told Kiyoshi you were too smart for that."

"This came up a lot?" Valentina asked.

"Constantly."

"He talked about me?"

"Him? He never talks if he can help it. But I can tell what he's think-ing, so it's like the same thing."

Valentina gave a weak smile, not wanting to contemplate what that had been like for Kiyoshi. Which was worse—that she was really able to guess what he was thinking and then would babble about it inces-santly, or that she was way off target, babbling about things he wasn't even worried about?

"You guys have been busy," she said instead.

"Tell me about it," Hazel said, rolling her eyes. "Hey, we have tea. Do you want some tea? It's Earl Grey, ever had it? So dark and smoky, you have to try it."

"Sure," Valentina said, following Hazel back to the camp stove. Hazel filled a kettle with water from a recycling unit, then set it on the stove before digging out a teapot and carefully spooning tea into the basket set inside the pot.

"My family found us. Did Kiyoshi tell you?" Hazel asked as they waited for the water to heat.

"No, he didn't mention that," Valentina said.

"They found the balloon, even though it was half buried in sand. That led them to us. I thought my dad would be madder than he was, but I guess he understood. The balloon itself was shredded; we've been using the material here for the tents and such. They took the gondola back home, though. It's still going to be my nephew's balloon, once they replace the silk."

"I'm sorry. I know that meant a lot to you," Valentina said.

"Yeah, but it's OK. I have this place now. And when the trading season starts, we're going to be on the route. Of course, we don't have much to trade yet, just scrap metal and machine parts, but that will change." She took the kettle off the stove and poured steaming water into the teapot. Valentina got just a whiff of the tea before Hazel dropped the lid back down.

"That's already changed," Valentina said. "I've come back with a trainload of trade goods. Food, fuel, clothing, tools. You name it. And it's just a start; the city wants to trade through this depot. Through you guys."

"What about you?"

"I'm here as an envoy to make the offer," Valentina said.

"Then you go back to the city?" Hazel asked.

"Not if you'll let me stay. I'd like to stay," Valentina said. Hazel poured out two mugs of tea and handed one to Valentina. Valentina unzipped her collar down to her throat and breathed in the tea's aroma. Smoky indeed.

"Kiyoshi and I have a nice arrangement," Hazel said as she blew on her tea. "He travels up and down the metro line, finding things he can either repair or scrap for parts, and I run the trade stand, or will once the season starts. I'm scarcely going to be ready in time. This is all so exciting!"

Valentina nodded, risking a small sip of her tea. It was too hot, but so much nicer than coffee.

"So I'd love to have you stay, you know that, but I'm not sure what you would do," Hazel said. "I don't want to disrupt the balance, you know?"

"I have a plan," Valentina said. "But I need to show you something first."

"OK," Hazel said. She pounded the tea in one long gulp, then waited impatiently while Valentina finished hers.

"We definitely have to trade for more of that," Valentina said as the two headed back down the stairs.

"I know, right?" Hazel said.

Kiyoshi looked up as they drew near.

"Valentina has something to show us," Hazel said.

The three of them went out the double doors, back out onto the train platform. Kiyoshi's eyes widened, but Hazel fairly squealed with delight at the sight of the train.

"What did you bring us?" she demanded.

"Remember, this first trainload is a gift. Any further shipments will depend on signing their contract and whatever deal we negotiate."

"Sure, sure," Hazel said.

Valentina opened the doors of the first three cars one by one.

"Trade goods," she said, throwing her arms wide. "Machine-made tools, fabrics, dry goods, even a few luxuries from Earth."

"Like chocolate?" Hazel said, spotting the shiny packages tucked in one corner.

"Like chocolate," Valentina agreed.

"Trade goods," Kiyoshi said. "Not for personal use."

"I know," Hazel said. "I was talking about for trade. Chocolate is a good thing to have on hand, always in high demand."

"And the other two cars?" Kiyoshi asked.

"Those are what I bring to our little community," Valentina said, opening the first door. "Hydroponic gardening equipment. Heaters, lights, seeds and whatnot. A variety of fresh vegetables, enough to feed us and our livestock, with a bit left over to trade."

"Livestock?" Hazel repeated, and Valentina grinned as she opened the final train door.

"I have in here a pair of goats, a dozen chickens, rabbits galore, and my favorite." She waved Hazel to lean in closer to peer inside a crate set near the door.

"Puppies!" Hazel cried.

"We won't be eating those, of course, but so long as rats are a potential problem, we could use extra sentries and guards."

"But they're so small."

"They get bigger, lots bigger." Valentina shared Hazel's wide grin. She had never had a dog before, either.

The three of them set to work, carrying the contents of the train inside the barricade wall. The animals came first, although they would have to stay in their crates until Valentina could build proper enclosures. There was nothing more capable of chaos than a goat on the loose. Valentina and Hazel kept up a running dialog, puzzling out where the best place for the gardens and animal enclosures would be in relation to the trade station. They would want to keep a center area clear for traffic moving through from the train platform to the airlock. Someday there could be a lot of people moving through.

Kiyoshi was content to let the two of them do all the talking, but Valentina could tell by the look in his eyes that he really was happy she was there, drawing the Hazel babble away from him.

At last Valentina brought her own things in, setting them inside a square of upended shelving that was rapidly becoming a third tent near the cookstove as Kiyoshi and Hazel stretched balloon silk over the top to make a snugger enclosed space. She had a cot and a lushly warm sleeping bag, bags filled with more clothes, and a frame filled with pictures of Arturo and the rest of the family. There were even a few of her mother from before she and her father had split up.

Kiyoshi brought a few empty crates inside and set one near the cot to function as a table, stacking others against the wall to make a shelving unit. Then he went back outside and Valentina unpacked, spreading the sleeping bag over the cot and setting the picture frame on the crate by the bed along with the school reader her father had given her, one with a program designed to help her reading skills until she was confident enough to delve into the reader's real treasures: a copy of every book brought to Mars from Earth, as well as every book ever written on Mars. Then she unpacked her clothes, setting them into the crates stacked on their sides. It was all factory-made, thin and warm in deliciously bright colors, all but the single hand-knit sweater lurking on the bottom of her bag. She took that out, held it close to her face to breathe in its scent. Then she set it carefully in the back of the bottom crate, out of sight.

She didn't want to forget Stephen Hero, but she was very aware that what she and Kiyoshi and Hazel were building together was like a dream: everything she always wanted but oh so fragile. She couldn't quite stop hoping that she would see him again someday, even knowing that his presence would likely leave everything in ruins. He wouldn't mean it to, but trouble would follow him.

Skald and Kavi would either kill him or bring him back into their fold. Neither option was good. She didn't want to get mixed up in it. She definitely didn't want to get Hazel and Kiyoshi mixed up in it.

"Val, we're eating!" Hazel called from outside, and Valentina hastily wiped at her eyes before stepping outside to join them.

Her family was waiting.

NEW SERIES: THE FORGOTTEN PLANET

Coming soon from Ratatoskr Press Books, the new YA sci-fi series THE FORGOTTEN PLANET starts with book 1: Raiding the Forgotten Derelict.

History sleeps beneath them all, but only she sees it.

Lafayette Eloi always knew her parents thought differently from others. They kept their books buried beneath her mother's house. They spoke an old language in the dead of night, whispering behind closed doors and bolted shutters. She grew up in a village where no one was related to her, and she never knew why.

Then, after her mother died, her father came to fetch her. Now she and her mother's dog assist her father in his work. The work discussed in whispers in the dark. The work that had cost Lafayette so much all her young life.

But now she learns just how much her father's work means to their entire world. Only no one knows anything about it. Only her father. And only Lafayette.

Because the work that consumed her father's entire life and her mother's too now nibbles at the fringe's of Lafayette's own life. And she cannot refuse its call.

Raiding the Forgotten Derelict, first book in the new YA sci-fu series THE FORGOTTEN PLANET, available in September 2024 from Ratatoskr Press Books.

COMPLETE SERIES: THE RITCHIE AND FITZ SCI-FI MURDER MYSTERIES

The Ritchie and Fitz Sci-Fi Murder Mysteries starts with Murder on the Intergalactic Railway.

For Murdina Ritchie, acceptance at the Oymyakon Foreign Service Academy means one last chance at her dream of becoming a diplomat for the Union of Free Worlds. For Shackleton Fitz IV, it represents his last chance not to fail out of military service entirely.

Strange that fate should throw them together now, among the last group of students admitted after the start of the semester. They had once shared the strongest of friendships. But that all ended a long time ago.

But when an insufferable but politically important woman turns up murdered, the two agree to put their differences aside and work together to solve the case.

Because the murderer might strike again. But more importantly, solving a murder would just have to impress the dour colonel who clearly thinks neither of them belong at his academy.

Murder on the Intergalactic Railway, the first book in the Ritchie and Fitz Sci-Fi Murder Mysteries.

COMPLETE SERIES: THE TRAVELS OF SCOUT SHANNON

The complete six-book series THE TRAVELS OF SCOUT SHANNON begin with book one, Under Falling Skies.

Scout Shannon's whole family died the day the Space Farers dropped an asteroid on their domed city. Now she lives alone, out in the wild with only her dogs for company. She prefers it that way.

But Scout finds herself at a crossroads. One road leads back to a quiet life snug under the protective dome of a city. The other road leads to a life in the rebellion, a life of adventure and excitement but also danger. Dare she try to find the rebels hiding in the hills?

Then a chance encounter with a stranger from the other side of the galaxy threatens to derail what remains of Scout's life. The entire galaxy awaits her, if she survives the next four days.

"Under Falling Skies", a young adult science fiction novel, set on a remote planet with a distinctly Old West feel. For fans of gunslinging women and young girl assassins. And dogs.

Under Falling Skies, the first book in THE TRAVELS OF SCOUT SHANNON, available everywhere now.

SCI-FI SERIAL PODCAST!

Check out my new monthly podcast of serialized science fiction: THE TALES OF THE CHAI MAKHANI TRIO!

Elyot loathes the massive Commonwealth ships that hover menacingly over his home world of Adghal. He hates the Commonwealth enforcers who harass the populace even more. But with his mother missing and presumed dead, Elyot keeps his head down and strives to avoid notice. And he succeeds until the day two strangers enter his life...

New episodes of this sci-fi serial drop every 1st of the month.

Now streaming on Apple Podcasts, Google Podcasts, Spotify, Stitcher and more. Also available in eBook and print everywhere books or sold. For a complete episode listing, check out the page on my website.

ALSO FROM KATE MACLEOD

Love heists and capers? Then check out my new series, THE VIC HARPER CAPERS. The action starts with the novella THE THIRD POLE JOB.

Vic Harper and her gang retired wealthy from their life of thievery and heists. Whether in a luxury condo overlooking the river in Minneapolis or in a modernist mansion built into the side of a mountain in Colorado, life comes easy now.

Perhaps too easy.

When an old friend asks for a favor his niece, Vic and her mentor Chase Woodward leap at the chance to relieve a little of the boredom. But a quick bit of B&E in a wealthy suburb of Chicago leads to an even greater challenge.

The prize? Nothing much. Just the opportunity to level a playing field for their friend's niece.

But the heist? May prove to be their toughest ever. Because to get to the prize, they'll have to climb a mountain.

And not just any mountain. Their prize waits on the summit of Mount Everest.

THE THIRD POLE JOB, the first novella in the Vic Harper Caper series. For those who love capers, heists and other impossible missions.

Also from Ratatoskr Press, The Witches Three Cozy Mystery Series by Cate Martin, a mix of mystery and magic that begins with Book 1: Charm School.

Amanda Clarke thinks of herself as perfectly ordinary in every way. Just a small-town girl who serves breakfast all day in a little diner nestled next to the highway, nothing but dairy farms for miles around. She fits in there.

But then an old woman she never met dies, and Amanda was named in her will. Now Amanda packs a bag and heads to the big city, to Miss Zenobia Weekes' Charm School for Exceptional Young Ladies. And it's not in just any neighborhood. No, she finds herself on Summit Avenue in St. Paul, a street lined with gorgeous old houses, the former homes of lumber barons, railroad millionaires, even the writer F. Scott Fitzgerald. Why, Amanda can practically hear the jazz music still playing across the decades.

Scratch that. The music really, literally, still plays in the backyard of the charm school. Because the house stretches across time itself. Without a witch to protect this tear in the fabric of the world, anything can spill over. Like music.

Or like murder.

The complete series is out now, and it all starts with Charm School.

FREE EBOOK!

Like exclusive, free content?

To get two prequel short stories to THE RITCHIE AND FITZ SCI-FI MURDER MYSTERIES as well as a bonus prequel novelette to the completed six-book series THE TRAVELS OF SCOUT SHANNON, signup for my monthly newsletter at KateMacLeodWrites.com.

Thank you!

ABOUT THE AUTHOR

Photograph © 2016 Jonathan Conklin

Kate MacLeod has written stories which have appeared in Analog, Strange Horizons and Mythic Delirium, among other places. She is also the author of two young adult science fictions series: The Travels of Scout Shannon, and The Ritchie and Fitz Sci-Fi Murder Mysteries. She also contributes to a serialized science fiction podcast called The Tales of the Chai Makhani Trio. She currently lives in Minneapolis, Minnesota.

Find out more about the author and sign up for her newsletter at KateMacLeodWrites.com.

ALSO BY KATE MACLEOD

Novels

The Slums of the Solar System:

Mitwa

The Mars of Malcontents

The Whole World for Each

Books 1-3 Box Set

The Travels of Scout Shannon:

Under Falling Skies

In Quaking Hills

Among Treacherous Stars

Against Impassable Barriers

Over Freezing Altitudes

At Galactic Central

The Travels of Scout Shannon Books 1-3

The Travels of Scout Shannon Books 4-6

The Travels of Scout Shannon Books 1-6

The Ritchie and Fitz Sci-Fi Murder Mysteries:

Murder on the Intergalactic Railway

Murder in the Skies

Body in the Catacombs

Death on the Summit

An Undiplomatic Murder

A Lethal Betrayal

The Forgotten Planet

Raiding the Forgotten Derelict (Forthcoming September 2024)

Sci-Fi Novellas

The Intergenerational Tree

I Rise into a Daybreak

Caper Novellas

The Third Pole Job

The Twelve Days of Christmas Job

10-Story Collections

Tales of Blood and Ink

Tales of Old Gods and New

5-Story Collections

Tales from Heian-Kyo and Others

Tales from the Edges and Ends

Tales from Forgotten Days

Tales from Ancient and Future Times

<u>Tales from Across Space</u>